WHISPERS AMONG THE BLOSSOMS

A NOVEL

JACOB MCDOUGAL

MCDOUGAL PUBLISHING LLC

To my father, whose unwavering encouragement lit the path that led me to write this novel. Though you're no longer here, your belief in me echoes in every word on these pages.

To my mother, who planted the seeds of my imagination and nurtured the foundation of my creative spirit, shaping the storyteller I am today.

And to my beloved wife, Danelle, whose steadfast love and support have given me the freedom to chase dreams and wander through the worlds I create, always knowing I return to you. This journey would be impossible without you!

1

C HAPTER 1

At 11:30 p.m., a confidential informant contacted JB Phillips to report a body lying face down in an abandoned almond grove by Crows Landing Road, near the Tuolumne River. JB Phillips, an FBI Special Agent, made his way between the rows of trees, their withered white blossoms grazing his coat. Above the river, a dense fog hovered, its cold mist penetrating JB's bones as he crouched by the corpse. The sorrowful howling of a pack of dogs echoed through the valley, their cries mingling with the rustle of leaves, sending chills up JB's spine. He held his hands over his mouth, breathing warm air into his palms, and with each exhale, a white puff pierced the darkness.

JB held a flashlight in one hand and reached for a clump of dirt in the other. He patiently sifted the dirt through his fist, assessing the barren piece of land. Then, he shined the light toward the distant road, where car after car passed, unaware of the young girl's body lying in the dirt. He pivoted toward the river, shining light into the vast darkness. From where the body lay, it was three hundred yards in either direction. JB traced his fingers across the hardened claw marks in the ground, careful not to distress the trail of blood. He presumed the girl had tried to crawl toward safety during her last breaths. He shook his head, thinking about the futile expense of energy and the sheer fear and desperation she must have felt. His eyes stung as he gazed at the body, his throat constricting with a mix of sadness and anger as he dropped to both knees, the light fading toward the dead body.

JB made the call at 12:15 and within forty-five minutes the dark abandoned grove was filled with booming overhead lights. The crime scene was overrun with Stanislaus County Sheriff deputies and Modesto police homicide detectives. They marked the area with yellow tape and started to survey the crime scene for traces of evidence. The medical examiner determined a knife wound to the aortic artery was the cause of death, although several punctures to the right lung contributed. The forensics analysis and preliminary report suggested the young girl was executed at the scene of the crime. However, it would later be determined that her body was raped and beaten at a different location. Based on tracks and footprints at the scene, it was likely three individuals watched the young girl drown in her own pool of blood. The approximate time of death was estimated at seventy-two hours.

***

After a couple of hours of processing information at the scene, JB returned to his truck and made a call to his confidential informant. His hands clenched around the steering wheel; his knuckles bared white marks of a stress grieved body as he struggled to process the scene. The visceral image of the girl's blood-stained corpse seared in his memory.

He sat in his Toyota Tacoma, and took a moment to reflect, as he watched a swarm of lights flicker across the large twenty-acre lot adjacent to the river. He was distracted only by the thought of his wife. The two had argued as he pushed his way out the door earlier that morning. He couldn't deny the truth of her statement. The thrill of the job had become more important than his marriage or his son. Her words haunted him to his core. Hannah, his wife of fourteen years, hurled the statement in anger. He avoided the argument, as was typical, and continued to the truck in silence. One of the skills he learned in the military was to compartmentalize emotion and to be void of expression. It was a trait of a great soldier and undercover operator, but not an affectionate husband or father. He was caught between two worlds, each expecting his full and undivided attention.

As the forensics team and investigators continued to survey and process the crime scene, JB made his way to the intersection of Crows Landing Road and Olivero Street, a half mile away. He stopped at a red light, dazed from the events of the evening. The bloated image of the girl reminded him of the countless bodies he had handled during his time in the military. War had a way of revealing the reality of life and death, and for JB, it was a scar that cut deep. Suddenly, the intersection was intertwined with cars. The tires screeched and horns blared. An accident narrowly avoided in the nick of time. The chaos momentarily awakened JB from the malaise and memories he left overseas in a forgotten world.

Crows Landing Road was a thoroughfare on the South Side of Modesto, California. It stretched from the Tuolumne River and ran south through a neighborhood called the

Deep South Side or "Little Tijuana." The area was a collection of liquor stores, payday loan establishments, and low credit car lots. The American Dream a barren thought to immigrants, who generation after generation, toiled in the rich agriculture basin of the San Joaquin Valley. A proud community with a heritage built on the bonds of family and faith, now at odds with a culture rooted in drugs and street gangs.

JB turned his eyes from the near accident in the intersection to a crowd gathered at Marisol's Taco Truck, a local favorite of the neighborhood. It was parked in a large open lot. Across the way was an old tire shop and El Toro's Auto Sales. The street was lined with white and green flags that flickered in the wind, advertising zero percent financing for a ten-year-old car with over two hundred thousand miles. The area was marked with barred windows and gated yards. Graffiti adorned every imaginable space. The traffic was heavy for a surface street at 1:00 a.m. on a Friday night. The after-hour crowd brought hordes of young men and women who filled up their bellies after a night of drinking. And Marisol's was the place for cheap street tacos. It made for the perfect meeting location with a confidential informant.

While sitting in his truck, JB stared off into the distance, the low hum of voices in the parking lot blending into the background. The noise was distant, yet his mind kept drifting back to a time when life felt simpler, clearer. Fourteen years. It seemed like a lifetime ago when he first met Hannah. He could still picture the way she walked into his CrossFit class at the University of Oklahoma, her brown curls bouncing slightly as she laughed with her friends. She was chasing a New Year's resolution, but JB was already chasing something else entirely. From the moment she flashed that shy, sweet smile and said hello in her Southern drawl, he knew—somehow, someway—he was going to marry Hannah Davis.

He chuckled at the memory of his first attempt to ask her out. She turned him down so gently, so sweetly, that he almost didn't feel the sting of rejection. They spent the next few weeks moving awkwardly through class, their exchanges limited to shy glances and the occasional touch of her shoulder when he corrected her form. Her skin had been warm, and that light touch stayed with him long after the class was over.

It was one of her friends who finally gave JB the push he needed, telling him, "Hannah's not the type of girl to date a man who gives up that easily." That's all it took—a competitor like JB never could resist a challenge. He asked her out for coffee, and this time, she relented. Over the next six months, they became inseparable, like two halves of a whole he hadn't even realized he was missing.

It wasn't long before JB found himself weighing the post-graduate decisions. The thought of three more years in graduate school felt like a slow death—hours buried in books when the world outside was on fire. Iraq. Afghanistan. He couldn't shake the idea of joining the military, the pull to serve something greater than himself. His uncle, a Marine officer, had planted that seed long ago, and they'd had many long conversations about the life of a commissioned officer—what it meant, the honor and responsibility that came with it.

Now, two years after 9/11, JB felt like the country was at war, and so was he—a young, idealistic man, hell-bent on payback. The decision felt almost inevitable, except for one thing – Hannah. What would it mean for them? JB was unwilling to broach the subject, at least not until he'd made his decision. He couldn't stand the thought of seeing doubt or fear in her eyes, or worse, feeling like he was choosing the battlefield over her.

Weeks passed, and JB continued to mull over his choices. Hannah stayed busy planning her summer classes and day trips with friends. Finally, one quiet afternoon as they sat together—Hannah chatting about an upcoming trip to Dallas—he broke his silence. He mentioned his idea of joining the Marines, trying to keep his tone as casual as possible. The words hung in the air for a moment, heavy and unspoken between them.

They talked, though not deeply. Neither of them seemed ready to commit—JB to a future with her, or Hannah to the uncertainties that came with loving a man who could be called away at any moment. They danced around the edges of it, careful not to give voice to what they both feared most.

Six months into their relationship, JB made two decisions, the first one, he would join the Marines. The second, far more agonizing, was that he would leave for Officer Candidate School without proposing to Hannah. The weight of that decision pressed down on him, but he couldn't imagine asking her to wait—not for him, not for the war, not for the unknown.

At the end of the summer, he boarded a bus bound for Quantico, Virginia. As the city faded behind him, his thoughts drifted to Hannah, left behind with a thousand questions neither of them had dared to answer. Would they survive the time and distance? Only time would tell.

The FBI-issued cell phone in JB's front pocket vibrated, bringing his mind back to the rousing crowd at Marisol's Taco Truck. It was a text from his confidential informant, Emanuel "Manny" Velasquez. Three years prior, JB had received a tip through the FBI Hotline about Manny's uncle running drugs and guns out of their Modesto house.

Eventually, they raided the home and arrested Manny, his uncle, and four accomplices. Manny received a three-year sentence with the option for reduction with good behavior. However, it didn't take six months before he consulted with authorities about a plea deal and a plan to provide evidence to the state and serve as a confidential informant. At nineteen years of age, Manny knew the streets of the Deep South Side and the surrounding communities. He was small time in the drug and gun game, but he was knowledgeable of all the players and their sources.

***

Manny stood nervously in line at Marisol's, two people ahead of JB. He pretended to scroll through his cell phone, all the while watching the unattended parking lot fill with car after car. The air pulsed with the thumping bass of low riders, and the scent of sizzling meat wafted from the taco truck, drawing in the crowd. A late-night block party erupted around him, with locals circling their cars and blasting music from their trunks. Scantily clad club girls danced for the crowd, their movements mesmerizing.

As Manny waited, he scanned the parking lot, his gaze sweeping across the sea of faces. He searched for anyone connected to the West Side Familia, the notorious Norteño gang that ruled the streets of the Deep South Side. After a quick glance, he made his way to the front of the line and ordered his food.

While waiting for his order, Manny stood off to the side, observing the scene. His eyes darted back and forth, keeping a close watch on JB. He marveled at how the large man, with his strong athletic build, could blend into the crowd so seamlessly. The baseball hat and reading glasses made JB look nondescript, but Manny knew better. He had seen JB face down danger without flinching, his eyes piercing through the chaos.

Manny received his order and made his way to the rear of the taco truck, near a set of park benches. JB followed suit, sitting across the table from his confidential informant.

"This seat taken?" JB asked.

Manny surveyed the area, his heart racing with anxiety. He tapped his leg on the ground in time with his heartbeat, feeling like his lungs were suffocating under the weight of his nerves. He glanced around, ensuring no one was watching, before leaning in close to JB.

"Yo, homes, I don't know who did that girl like that," Manny said, pretending to eat a bite of his taco.

JB's eyes narrowed. "I need you to find out."

"Look, word on the street is chica was down with WSF." Manny's leg twitched faster.

"Manny, by God, get me a name or your ass is back to High Desert."

Manny's eyes shifted around the parking lot, searching for an escape. "It ain't that easy."

Manny felt the weight of his gaze as JB leaned across the table, his finger pointed accusingly at Manny's chest. "No, it is that easy," JB said, his eyes burning with intensity. "If she's connected to the WSF, someone gave the order. If no one gave the order, an active made a hit without authorization. The street will talk. Get me answers."

Manny's fingers drummed a staccato beat on the tabletop as he thought about the young girl in the vacant almond grove. The pressure of providing results, combined with the guilt of his past, began to suffocate him. He felt like he was drowning in his own secrets.

JB stood, his movements fluid and deliberate, and deposited his plate in a nearby trash can. Manny watched as he disappeared into the crowd, his tall frame fading like a ghost into the night. The sounds of the block party swirled around Manny, but he sat still, lost in his thoughts.

For thirty minutes, Manny sat at the table, trying to decide his next move. He knew a couple of names, but he wasn't willing to share them with JB, not yet. The weight of his secrets threatened to crush him, but he knew he had to keep them hidden, at least for now.

2

C HAPTER 2

After meeting with Manny, JB drove twenty miles south down Highway 99 to the town of Turlock, California. The time allowed his mind to wander to the teenage girl found in the abandoned almond grove. He imagined how her parents would take the news. He knew he would have to interview the family eventually, but for now, that responsibility rested with the detectives of the Modesto Police Department. He pulled into the driveway, exhausted from a long day and evening, and quietly shut the truck door. He tiptoed through the entryway when the old grandfather clock on the wall chimed 3:15 a.m., as if announcing an intruder had entered the home. He wondered what to expect from Hannah after their tense exchange earlier in the morning.

Four years ago, JB and Hannah had moved to Modesto, California, with the fragile hope of starting fresh. After years of drifting through deployments and long stretches apart, JB was finally transitioning from his military career to the FBI. Hannah had been the one to push for the move, seeing it as their last chance to reclaim the life they'd once dreamed of. She had imagined that Modesto could be the place where they'd build something solid, something lasting—a real home, rather than a series of temporary stops between his tours of duty.

But it wasn't that simple. The secrecy surrounding JB's military work had created a wall between them—thick, invisible, and impossible to scale. Even though he was home more often now, the habits of silence and distance had lingered. Hannah had never understood why he couldn't talk to her about what he did, where he had been, or why he sometimes woke up in the middle of the night, drenched in sweat, his eyes wide and unfocused. All she knew was that the man she married wasn't always the man who came home.

After sixteen years of deployments and a life lived in fragments, Hannah had finally begged JB to leave the Marines. She couldn't take it anymore—the long nights of waiting, the constant fear that the next knock on the door would shatter her world. She just wanted him home, to be a husband, a father, to rebuild what the years apart had worn thin.

Retirement had seemed like the answer. Modesto was supposed to be their fresh start, a place where they could put the past behind them. Leaving active duty and stepping into the FBI felt like a second chance—not just for JB's career but for their marriage. They had been so young when they married, convinced that love alone would be enough to weather any storm. But twenty years had a way of changing things. Dreams once vivid had blurred under the weight of distance, unspoken words, and the secrets JB never seemed willing to share.

Even now, Hannah still clung to the hope that they could build the life they had once imagined. But there was always something pulling JB away. He had stayed in the Reserves to secure his full retirement, a decision that kept one foot in the world he had sworn to leave behind. And though the deployments were fewer, the silences remained. The walls between them hadn't crumbled the way she had hoped. Instead, they had simply been rebuilt in different ways—new battles, new ghosts, the same aching distance.

Modesto was supposed to be where they found each other again. More often than not, it still felt like JB was just out of reach.

JB made his way to the kitchen and found a pot of coffee on the stove. In the adjoining room, Hannah lay asleep on the couch. He poured a cup of coffee and leaned against the refrigerator door, feeling the weight of his own emotional distance. He knew she deserved more than a part-time husband, who, even when present, was emotionally vacant. In his heart, he knew he had traded one set of professional secrets for another, and he regretted that she had to be a secondary priority in his life.

After a few minutes, he exhaled deeply and set the coffee on the counter. He noticed a stack of envelopes near the cup—routine bills and unwanted realtor cards. The last piece of mail caught his attention – a medical envelope from Northern California Fertility Specialists. It was a fertility clinic located two and a half hours away in the San Francisco Bay Area. He looked around the dark room, glanced at Hannah, and then opened the envelope. Inside was a pamphlet and a letter from her physician, Dr. Laura Kelly.

Her physician, he thought. When did she visit a fertility clinic? Why hadn't he known? The questions gnawed at him. Did he know she had an appointment and just not pay attention? His focus had been solely on his cases. He read the opening paragraph, a generic note of gratitude from the physician, and then moved to the second paragraph, which detailed ovarian cancer concerns and fertility issues. It mentioned elevated CA125 markers and the possibility of a tumor, requiring further lab work and a biopsy. Tumor? Lab results? Biopsy? His mouth went dry. The acid in his stomach surged. The thought of not being able to have children hadn't been on his radar, not with the timing of deployments and the adoption of his five-year-old nephew, Jared.

Jared's life had been shaped by chaos. His parents, both consumed by their addictions, were in and out of jail so often that Jared barely knew what stability meant. He had seen things no child should ever see—violence, drugs, exploitation—scars that were not visible but ran deep. Every time his parents disappeared into the system, Jared was left to fend for himself, sometimes with relatives, sometimes with no one at all. By the time Hannah took him in, the damage was done.

Hannah, a speech pathologist and teacher, had never expected to become a surrogate mother. But the moment she met Jared, something shifted inside her. He was lost, a boy adrift in a world that had failed him at every turn. She had always wanted children of her own, and when that dream began to fade, she poured all her energy into her students. Taking Jared in felt like a second chance, a way to fill the void that had been growing inside her for years. Determined to rescue him from the bleak reality of his past, she opened her home and heart to him, offering the stability and care he so desperately needed.

But that first year with Jared was anything but easy. Hannah's nurturing instincts were strong, but they couldn't erase the horrors Jared had witnessed—the nights he woke up screaming, the moments he would shut down completely, his eyes glazed over as he disappeared into some dark corner of his mind. She struggled to reach him, to break through the walls he had built around himself. Despite the challenges, Hannah refused to give up. Jared wasn't just a responsibility – he was her purpose. Without children of her own, this role filled her in a way she hadn't expected. Yet, the deeper she got into his world, the more she realized how far the damage had gone. Some days, it felt like she was fighting an invisible enemy, trying to reclaim the pieces of his lost childhood one by one.

JB slid the letter back into its envelope, hiding it beneath the stack of bills on the counter. His hands felt heavy as he reached for the bottle of Basil Hayden he kept hidden above the refrigerator; a place Hannah never looked. Basil Hayden was his bourbon of choice—smooth, familiar, comforting in a way nothing else was anymore. But on nights like this, it hardly mattered what he drank. He would have taken anything to dull the edges of his thoughts.

He poured a shot, downed it quickly, and then poured another. By the third, he stopped rushing—pouring himself a fuller glass, letting the liquid settle in his hand. He felt the burn slide down his throat, but the warmth didn't quite reach the cold knot tightening in his chest. With a sigh, he carried the glass into the family room, where Hannah lay curled up on the sofa, her breathing soft and even, lost in sleep.

JB sank into the recliner, bourbon in hand, and stared at her. She looked peaceful like this—so unlike the rest of the time, when the space between them felt like miles of unspoken words and unshed tears. He loved her. He knew that much. But why did it feel so distant, like an old photograph fading at the edges? What had happened to the connection they'd once had—the easy conversations, the shared laughter? Now, it was as if he had been standing on one side of a chasm, and she on the other, for years. How had he let it get this far?

He took another sip of his bourbon, his mind drifting back to the hundreds of conversations they'd had over the years. He wondered what he had missed, what had slipped through the cracks while he was away, distracted, disconnected, always one foot out the door. He had spent so many years surviving, pushing down every feeling that might slow him down. And now, he couldn't seem to turn it off. It wasn't just the military that had done this to him; it was everything after— the FBI, the cases, the secrets. How could he explain what it felt like to carry all that weight, all those lives, on his shoulders? How could he tell her what it was like to wake up every day and wonder if this was the day, he wouldn't make it home?

JB looked at Hannah again, still asleep, her face soft in the dim light of the room. He wanted to reach out, to touch her, to tell her everything— but the words sat heavy on his tongue, refusing to come. Instead, he took another drink, sinking further into the chair, lost in the swirling fog of his thoughts. Maybe tomorrow he would try. Or maybe tomorrow would be like today—another day where the distance grew, and the silence between them stretched on.

A few years before their move to California, they had dared to dream of starting a family. The excitement was appreciable back then, with Hannah enthusiastically buying pregnancy tests, each one a symbol of hope. But as months passed and hopes were dashed, the excitement faded, replaced by a quiet, growing tension. Hannah stopped taking the tests altogether, the weight of JB's unspoken disappointment too much to bear. He hadn't realized how deeply his reactions affected her—how every sigh, every glance, built a wall between them. Her silence on the matter only widened the gap, leaving a void neither of them knew how to bridge.

When they moved to California, they tried again, seeking fertility treatments that turned into two long, invasive years. JB couldn't forget the night Hannah first handed him the thick needle for her injections. He had stared at it, fear and hesitation written across his face, his hands shaking as he prepared to inject her. Hannah's quiet strength in handling the situation had both impressed and shamed him. It was a reminder of how far they had drifted—how she had taken on the burden of their infertility with a grace he couldn't muster.

It had been more than two years since Hannah stopped her infertility medication. As far as JB knew, it was a chapter they had closed—one that neither of them was willing to reopen. Yet here it was again, resurfacing in the form of a pamphlet and a letter from the physician, stirring up memories of failures and heartache he had tried to bury. He finished his bourbon in one last, deliberate gulp, letting the burn numb the ache inside him.

Leaning back in his chair, JB stared at the ceiling, his mind drifting through the past fourteen years of their marriage. How many decisions had he made without ever considering Hannah's feelings? The decision to reenlist—he hadn't even told her directly. She had found out through an offhand comment from a fellow military spouse, left to face another four years of loneliness without a choice in the matter.

Three years after reenlisting, JB was wounded in Afghanistan. His recovery had been long and grueling, but even then, he hadn't stayed. He went back—another decision made without Hannah's input. They had fought that night—the worst fight of their marriage, loud enough to draw the attention of neighbors. Hannah had demanded he choose between her and the military. And yet, even then, he hadn't listened.

He was tired. Tired of revisiting these painful memories, tired of feeling trapped in a role that demanded his emotional detachment for survival. But what could he do? The life he had built required him to shut down, to keep everything and everyone at a distance. The bourbon dulled the pain, and eventually, it lulled him into a restless sleep, filled with dreams of roads not taken and words left unsaid.

***

The next morning, JB was suddenly jolted awake to Jared's excited shout as the growing boy jumped into his lap.

"Awe, what's up, my little man?" JB managed a tired smile despite the grogginess. The effects of the long night—bourbon, stress, and minimal sleep—clung to him like a fog.

"Are we playing baseball this morning?" Jared asked.

"Yeah, man." JB rubbed his face, trying to shake off the exhaustion.

"Well, let's go already!"

From upstairs, JB heard Hannah's familiar, frustrated stomping. He didn't need to see her to know what was coming—every heavy step a reminder of her simmering discontent.

"Whoa, you gotta give me some time, buddy. It's only 7:30," JB said, stalling. "Tell you what—go out to the garage, grab all the gear, and put it in the car. Okay?"

Jared shot off like a rocket, leaving JB alone in the silence that followed. He knew what was coming next. They needed to discuss the fertility letter, the biopsy, and everything they'd been pushing aside. JB knew he couldn't ignore it any longer, but the weight of it all made him want to retreat. Hannah, however, was never one to wait. She entered the kitchen, her movements purposeful as she poured two cups of coffee. She handed one to JB, then fixed him with a look he couldn't avoid.

"Are we going to talk about yesterday?" Her voice was firm, leaving no room for evasion.

Caught off guard, JB hesitated.

"We have to talk about it," Hannah pressed. "I don't want to keep pretending everything is fine when it's not."

"What's the big deal?" JB asked, as he sipped his coffee.

"JB, it's a very big deal. This has been growing for a while, and it's not getting better. You left yesterday without a word."

The weight of her words hung between them. JB shifted uncomfortably. "I was going to be late for work."

"I know, but that's not the point. You're always meeting someone or dealing with a case. I'm talking about us."

"This is one of those times when work is crazy, and we just have to get through it like always."

"No, JB. This isn't normal. We've been like this for years."

"What do you want from me?" He couldn't keep the frustration out of his voice.

"I want you to be present when you're home. I want you to choose us—not be off somewhere else in your head."

"Okay. I get it."

"No, you don't get it. You just say you do. You always do this when we try to talk."

The anger flared in JB, a familiar response to feeling cornered. He dumped the coffee into the sink and set his cup on the counter, causing a clatter.

"Have you thought about joining the marriage ministry class like we discussed?" Hannah asked, her voice quieter now, but no less firm.

JB leaned against the counter, sighing deeply. He knew she was right. But admitting it felt like exposing a wound he had spent years covering up. "If that's what you want us to do, I'll do it. Sign us up."

"You realize you'll have to open up, right? Actually talk?"

"Yes. Whatever. Just sign us up." He glanced at the door, feeling the need to escape. "Can I take Jared to the ballpark now?"

Hannah shook her head, her disappointment evident. "It's the same thing you always do. Go ahead, JB. Go. It's what you do best."

Her words cut through him like shrapnel. He wanted to cry out—to tell her she was right, that he hated the distance between them, that he desperately wanted to change. But sixteen years of living among soldiers and conducting undercover operations had taught him to shut down, to lock away his emotions. And his own childhood, marred by stoicism and survival, left him unable to show vulnerability, even to the woman he loved.

Instead, JB quietly retreated to the garage, the echoes of their argument still ringing in his ears. The rest of the day passed in silence, with both of them avoiding each other, their unspoken grievances hanging heavily in the air like a storm waiting to break.

3

C HAPTER 3

Lilly Grace remained motionless, the bedside clock striking 7 a.m. as she drew the blankets up to her chin. The day's first light sneaked through the frost-laden window, casting the red maple tree's skeletal branches into silhouette against the morning clouds. The memory of her stepfather's touch haunted her, each image sharp with the sting of bourbon on his breath and the menace in his eyes. "I just want to touch something pure, something untouched," his voice from the summer whispered in her mind, a chilling reminder of her helplessness.

Lilly Grace's body stiffened at the sound of her stepfather's heavy footsteps thundering down the hallway. He was a formidable figure, his thick beard lending him an intimidating presence, sculpted by many years of strenuous work in concrete cutting. Nightly, he turned to bourbon and marijuana for comfort, yet Lilly Grace understood that these vices couldn't hide the scars of his poor choices.

As the knock sounded on her door, Lilly Grace's breath caught, her body tensing in apprehension. "Lilly, time to wake up," his voice filtered through, gruff and unyielding. She heard his footsteps recede down the hall, while the sound of bacon sizzling, and the robust scent of brewing coffee started to permeate the house.

The Harper family lived in a small, modest home in Lee's Summit, Missouri, situated on the wrong side of the tracks. Lilly Grace's stepbrother, Evan, was the favored son, blessed with natural size and athleticism. His father showered him with attention, and the girls at school admired him. In contrast, Jack, small for his age and awkward in his movements, found solace in his aptitude for math and science. His stepfather tolerated him but showed little affection.

As Lilly Grace stepped into the kitchen, she overheard her stepfather and Evan engrossed in animated talk about the upcoming high school football game. She lingered a few extra moments, savoring the fleeting tranquility before heading to the bathroom to prepare for her 15th birthday.

She had chosen her outfit the night before – a pair of jeans, a white top, a light brown sweater, and an old pair of boots that had seen better days.

In the bathroom, Lilly Grace took a quick, invigorating shower, then wrapped a towel around her chest. She applied eyeliner and mascara with practiced care, despite the commotion from her brothers fighting over who would use the bathroom next. The clamor from outside reminded her of the constant struggle for space in their crowded household, but today she was determined to find a moment of personal celebration amidst the chaos.

Jack rushed out, toothbrush in hand, and banged on the door. "Hey, I was going to go back in there!" he said.

Lilly Grace replied, "Brush your teeth in the kitchen."

As she opened the door, she narrowly escaped the mad rush of her brothers. The front door opened, and her stepfather entered the living room. Lilly Grace hesitated, towel wrapped around her chest, as he paused and glanced in her direction. He smiled, and she felt a shiver run down her spine. He continued into the kitchen, leaving her to wonder what the day would bring.

***

Lilly Grace trudged through the school day, her 15th birthday passing unnoticed by her classmates. She almost mentioned it to one of her teachers but hesitated, unsure of how to express her disappointment. Since the summer, when her stepfather first touched her, she had withdrawn from her friends and found solace in the anonymity of online spaces.

At 3:30 p.m., school buses queued along the curb, ready to transport student's home. Following a brief twenty-minute ride, Lilly Grace departed from the bus, exchanging a quick nod with a fellow classmate. Though her walk home spanned just a block, it seemed to stretch further with every step. Childhood birthdays had been occasions of festivity and celebration, a vivid contrast to the subdued and solemn atmosphere of the recent year. The delight and naivety of those times had faded, supplanted by a life eclipsed by the stark realities of her current circumstances.

Lilly Grace found it odd to see her stepfather's work truck in the driveway as she neared the house at 4:15 p.m. on a Tuesday. Meanwhile, Jack was in the front yard, casually throwing a football up into the air.

He paused when he saw Lilly Grace and, with a subdued tone, said, "I wouldn't go in there if I were you."

"Why, what's up?" she asked.

Jack did not say anything, he just lowered his head and walked down the street. Lilly Grace paused, and from the driveway she could hear the shouting voices of her parents. She cautiously walked toward the doorway. The voices grew louder. She realized there was no plan for a fifteenth birthday celebration.

Lilly Grace carefully entered the house and heard an argument coming from the master bedroom. Her mother burst out of the room, her hair disheveled and still wearing the same sweatpants from the morning. Lilly Grace stood near the front doorway, as her stepfather stomped down the hallway after his wife.

"We ain't through with this," he said, extending his hand towards her.

Lilly Grace watched her mother stop, as she stood near the kitchen sink, and turned toward her daughter. She could see the anger in her mother's eyes. Her stepfather entered the kitchen. He gripped his fists, and his body tightened.

"What are you going to do, hit me," Ava snorted. "Do it," she paused. "You're a fucking coward."

Her stepfather reached back and with an open palm, he slapped her across the face. The noise rang throughout the house. Ava held her hand to the side of her cheek bone as she stumbled around the kitchen. She looked up at her husband and the anger now turned to fear. With a wrathful tongue, he lashed out in a flurry of curse words. Ava spit in his direction. In a full rage, he punched her in the stomach. She doubled over and slid down the kitchen cabinet to the floor. He stood over his wife, panting and frothing from the mouth.

The trouble started a year earlier when Ava lost her job at the factory. For a middle-aged woman with three kids and no high school diploma, the options were bleak. The timing couldn't have been worse, and the repossession of her stepfather's pick-up truck was the final blow. As the financial strain mounted, so did the verbal and physical abuse.

To cope, Ava turned first to anti-depressant pills. When those lost potency, she sank deeper, gravitating towards cocaine and heroin. It was a slippery slope, and before long, her reliance on these substances became a dark fixture in her day. Lilly Grace had witnessed the consequences all too often. She had found her mother passed out in the bathroom on multiple occasions over the past year. Each time, Lilly Grace's heart sank as she wondered how her mother was managing to pay for the drugs with no job and no paycheck. She was certain her stepfather wasn't supplying the money.

The children knew their parents were struggling, but they never spoke about it. Lilly Grace kept silent, acutely aware that voicing their troubles would force them to take sides – an excruciating choice that she couldn't bear to make. The family's silence was a defense mechanism, a way to shield themselves from the painful reality that they were trapped in a cycle of addiction and abuse.

Lilly Grace stepped into the kitchen, as her stepfather towered over her mother. Ava looked up at her daughter standing in the doorway. Lilly Grace saw the shame in her mother's eyes.

"What are you doing?" Lilly Grace asked.

"If you know what's good for you, get out of here you little cunt."

Lilly Grace rushed over to her mother, knelt beside her on the kitchen floor, and brushed the hair off her face.

"You bitches' ain't worth it," he said, as he turned and left the kitchen.

He grabbed his truck keys from the armoire in the living room and left the house. Lilly Grace and Ava sat on the kitchen floor. They heard the pick-up truck and the squeal of the tires as he peeled down the street. After he left the house and Ava had a moment to gather herself from the altercation, she told Lilly Grace to go to her room. Upset at what she had just witnessed, Lilly Grace lay in her bed and listened to her mother cry, alone in her bedroom.

***

The hours passed and Lilly Grace heard nothing from her mother. Evan was spending the night at a teammate's house, and Jack was playing video games in his bedroom. It was near her bedtime when she decided to check on her mother.

Lilly Grace peeked into Jack's bedroom and told him that it was time to switch off the game and get ready for bed. She closed the door and stepped across the hallway where she stood outside the master bedroom door, her heart pounding. She knew it was locked, but she also knew about the master key hidden on top of the doorway frame. She grabbed the key and slipped it into the lock, the click of the door unlocking echoed in the dark hallway.

The room was pitch black; the curtains drawn tightly shut. A foul odor hit her immediately – stale cigarette smoke, dirty laundry, and the musty scent of mold. Her eyes slowly adjusted to the darkness, and she saw her mother lying face down on the bed, motionless.

A knot tightened in Lilly Grace's stomach as her gaze fell on the bedside table. A bowl pipe lay there, the edges still dusted with traces of cocaine. Panic surged through her. She hurried to her mother's side and gently tapped her on the back. There was no response. Lilly Grace leaned in closer, her breath catching in her throat as she checked for a pulse. Relief washed over her when she felt the faint rhythm of her mother's heartbeat. She was still breathing.

Lilly Grace listened, unsure what to do next. The sight of her mother in this state was becoming all too familiar, but it never got easier. She turned to the bedside table, her hands shaking as she cleaned up, wiping away any traces of the drugs. She carried the bowl pipe to the bathroom, dumping the remnants into the toilet and flushing it all away, trying to ease the evidence of her mother's addiction. She left her mother on the bed and returned to her room.

An hour passed, and there was still no sound from down the hall. The silence felt heavy, oppressive. Lilly Grace crept down the hallway and peeked into Jack's room. He was sound asleep, his small body curled up under the covers, blissfully unaware of the turmoil in the house.

It was getting late, and she decided to take a shower before bed. The hot water cascaded over her, soothing her tense muscles, washing away the grime of the day. She closed her eyes, letting the warmth envelop her, if only for a moment of peace. But as she turned off the water and wrung out her hair, reality came crashing back. She heard the familiar sound of her stepfather stumbling through the front door, his heavy footsteps thudding across the living room.

After five hours at the local bar, she could almost smell the alcohol seeping from his pores and could almost taste the bitterness that would be on his breath. Fear gnawed at her as she wondered what kind of mood he'd be in, especially after what she'd witnessed with her mother earlier that afternoon.

Lilly Grace wrapped a towel around her hair and secured a second one around her chest. She pressed her ear to the bathroom door, straining to hear his movements, hoping she could slip into her bedroom unnoticed. Slowly, she turned the doorknob, easing the door open just enough to peek outside.

Her heart lurched into her throat as he was standing there in the doorway, blocking her path. His eyes bore into hers, dark and predatory, like a wolf sizing up its prey. He didn't say a word, just stared at her with a look that sent a cold shiver down her spine. The way he looked at her, like she was something to be consumed, made her stomach turn.

Lilly Grace froze, clutching the towel tightly around her chest, every instinct screaming at her to run, but her feet were rooted to the spot. She could feel the danger in the air, thick and suffocating, as she braced herself for whatever was about to happen next.

"What's your mom been up to?" he asked.

Lilly Grace shook her head, and mumbled, "I don't know."

His finger brushed across the towel covering Lilly Grace's chest, a slow, deliberate motion that made her skin crawl. She flinched, instinctively taking a step back, her heart pounding in her ears. He chuckled softly, a cruel sound, and then waved her off dismissively, as if she were nothing more than an annoyance.

Without another word, he turned and staggered down the hallway, disappearing into his bedroom. Lilly Grace stood still for a moment; the air thick with the tension that had just passed between them. As soon as she heard his door close, she bolted to her own room, her hands trembling as she shut the door behind her. She leaned against it, trying to catch her breath, the reality of what had just happened sinking in like a heavy weight in her chest.

She lay in bed and stared at the ceiling as tears welled up in her eyes. A few minutes passed before she heard his footsteps rummaging throughout the house. He came down the hallway, and she heard his feet stop on the other side of the door. She gripped the sheets tightly and held her breath. The door opened and he stumbled through the room. He landed on the side of the bed where he gathered himself. He looked into Lilly Grace's eyes, and then he put his hand on top of the covers. Her body tightened as she felt the pressure of his hand on her stomach. He leaned toward her face. She could smell the cigarettes and bourbon on his breath.

"I'm sorry baby. I didn't mean to scare you earlier."

Lilly Grace held firm, no response.

"I understand if you're mad at me. And you have every right to be. I was wrong. In fact, I just talked to your mother, and everything is good between the two of us."

Lilly Grace knew he was lying because her mother had passed out in a drug-induced coma. She also knew that since he had come home, he had spent most of his time in the kitchen and not in the bedroom.

"Do you forgive me?" He slowly touched the blanket that was held close to Lilly Grace's chin. He lowered it and delicately touched her shoulder. "You've gotten so pretty."

He caressed the side of her face, moved his other hand from her stomach down to her thighs. The blankets were light so she could feel the palm of his hand and his fingers grip the inner part of her leg. Lilly Grace continued to lay motionless out of fear. He took the other hand and physically removed the blanket down to her knees. She lay in her underwear and a long white T-shirt that came down to her thighs. Lilly Grace was a petite girl with skinny legs and knobby knees. She had yet to discover her full female body. Her stepfather moved his hand up her inner thigh where he found the softness of her cotton panties. Lilly Grace quickly sat up in bed.

"What are you doing?" she asked.

He simply put his finger over her mouth. "Be quiet or I'll beat you like I did your mother. Do you hear me?"

He came in close to kiss her on the cheek. Lilly Grace slapped his face. He stared at her for a moment in disbelief. Then, in an instant, he returned the favor. She recoiled against the headboard and let out a sudden scream. He put his hand over her mouth, the calluses on his palm scratched her lips.

"If you scream out, I'm going to go into your brother's room and beat him. Do you understand me?"

Lilly Grace sat with her back to the headboard. She was still as the night and not sure what to do. She believed he would go into Jack's room. Jack was not his son, not by blood at least. He did not hold the same affinity for Jack as he did for Evan, his true blood son. And he was drunk enough that he may just do it. So, she lowered her body onto the bed. He stripped his pants down to his ankles, lowered her panties to her shins, and climbed on top of her. Lilly Grace felt him trying to enter but he was too soft. He rubbed himself against her pelvis. She felt him get harder and harder. Her body was too dry, so he spit on his hand and rubbed himself for a minute. With the saliva, he was finally able to enter Lilly Grace. The pain was unimaginable. He pounded through her tightness without regard to the gritting of her teeth and grimace on her mouth. Tears formed in the corner of her eyes. It only lasted a couple of minutes before he finished.

He finally backed off, sitting up on his knees and looking down at Lilly Grace with a sneer of contempt. "Skinny ass bitch, that wasn't even worth it," he muttered, his voice dripping with disdain.

He stood, pulled up his pants, and walked out of the room without a second glance. Lilly Grace lay there, paralyzed by a suffocating mix of shame and pain. She could feel the tears welling up, but she was too numb to cry. The sheets beneath her were stained, evidence of the horror she had just endured, but all she could do was stare at the ceiling, frozen and broken.

4

C HAPTER 4

Over the next few days, JB's calls grew increasingly frequent, heightening the pressure on Manny to produce results. The weight of his situation felt unbearable—he was haunted by the fear that the streets had already branded him a narc. How else could a nineteen-year-old Mexican American from the streets of Modesto walk free from County Jail after serving just six months of a three-year sentence for drug and gun charges? The possibility that he had been marked was a gnawing dread that he couldn't shake. It could have been paranoia, or perhaps the streets were indeed whispering his name.

Every night, Manny kept a vigilant eye on the street in front of his home, constantly scanning for any unfamiliar cars. He braced himself for the possibility that a hail of bullets might shatter his windows at any moment. The thought that someone might know he was working with the FBI haunted him, bringing Daniel Ortiz to mind. Daniel had turned state's evidence, betraying his crew. Word had spread quickly, and just weeks after his release, he was gunned down in front of his house. At his candlelight vigil, the WSF had defaced his photos with the word "rata." The message was unmistakable – loyalty was paramount.

Manny had never been a full-fledged member of the WSF but had been a loose associate, drawn in by the lure of easy money. It turned out that the money was anything but easy. Now, Manny was desperate to avoid a return to County Jail and even more terrified of ending up at High Desert. He was caught in a perilous situation – law enforcement was pressuring him to betray his neighbors and friends, but doing so would almost certainly mean his execution in jail. For a young man just trying to survive the streets of the Deep South Side, it was a dire predicament.

When Manny thought of the young girl in the abandoned almond grove, the first name that came to mind was Paco Ramirez. Paco was a 27-year-old native of Sinaloa,

Mexico, who spent his days on the front porch of a small 1950s-style bungalow at 1910 Spokane Avenue. It was a migrant neighborhood on the south side of Modesto, wedged between the Tuolumne River and Highway 99. Paco's home, like many in the area, was protected by a three-foot stone wall topped with wrought iron. The Deep South Side was a place where old, dilapidated modular trailers were repurposed as makeshift apartments, cramming thirty or forty people into each during the growing season. It was a community where the sidewalks and blacktop ended, and for many, it felt like a forgotten corner of Modesto.

Paco sat in a cheap wicker chair, where he rolled papers for his morning blunt. Mariachi music played from inside the house. Jade, wearing a black thong and white ribbed tank top, walked out of the front door. For a seven-teen year-old girl, she was physically mature. Her large round breasts and hardened nipples pointed through the ribbed tank top. Paco was focused on his papers when she sat on his lap. The papers rolled up and he lashed out at the young girl in frustration.

"Damn it chica," he said.

Jade wrapped her hands around the back of Paco's thick neck. She nestled her breasts into his tattoo covered face. It was the power that only a woman held over a man. Paco's body relaxed and he calmly started to reroll his papers.

Each morning, Manny passed by Paco's house en route to the corner market. Occasionally, if Paco felt sociable, they would share a friendly exchange. Today, Manny noticed the sound of Mariachi music emanating from four houses away. Despite its volume, nobody ventured to ask Paco to lower it. Manny observed him seated on the porch, Jade cradled in his arms.

"What's up, Mijo?" Paco said.

Manny stopped walking and faced the house near the gate of the stone entryway. "What's up Paco? What's the word on the street?"

Manny's uncle ran with Paco when they were boys, and he had seen him around the neighborhood and at his uncle's house. Paco tried to persuade Manny to join the WSF for years, but Manny always kept a healthy distance from officially joining the gang. Early on, Manny had a rough go in County Jail, but with his uncle and Paco's influence, he was able to pass through with little issues. He knew there would be a time when he would have to repay the favor.

Paco nudged Jade out of his lap and tapped her on the backside. He whispered, "Get me a forty." He preferred to drink a forty ounce of Negra Modelo with his morning blunt.

Manny stared at the deep curves of Jade's nearly naked body. It was covered in tattoos from her thighs all the way up the side of her body and neck. Based on her tattoos there was little doubt about her allegiance to Paco and the WSF.

Paco whistled and two more girls came out onto the porch. Victoria, a seventeen-year-old girl, and Tiffany, an eighteen-year-old, both troubled teens who bounced from one bad group home to another. They met Jade online and jumped at the opportunity to earn quick money and remove themselves from the binds of the foster system. As it turned out, they enjoyed the freedom of living with Paco, the lifestyle, and the money they earned from selling their bodies. They each came to a side of Paco, and he wrapped his arms around their waists.

"Mijo, you want a taste of one of these beauties?" Paco asked. Manny stood awkwardly on the other side of the stone wall; his eyes locked on the girls. "I won't even charge you."

"As much as I'd like to, I've got to get down to my mom's house, you know, help her out."

"Mijo, I know you; it'll only take a minute or two," Paco teased, enjoying the discomfort he was causing. "Especially with these girls. They know what they're doing."

Manny waved him off. As much as he was tempted, he knew better. There were no free gifts on the streets. Accepting would only lead to a debt, and he was already leveraged to the limit. "You gonna be at La Clandestina tonight?"

"Why? What's it to you where I'll be tonight?" Paco's tone stiffened.

"No reason, just askin'." Manny stumbled over his words, suddenly worried that Paco might sense something was off. "I just thought since I'm busy right now, maybe later, you know, I could take you up on that offer with one of them girls."

Paco stood up and walked to the edge of the porch. Though he wasn't tall, standing at 5'9", his thick, sturdy frame radiated a quiet threat. His tank top revealed a maze of tattoos covering his arms, shoulders, and neck, and a teardrop piercing adorned the outside of his left eye.

"Mijo, don't worry about where I'll be tonight – or any other night. You understand me?" Jade stepped onto the porch and handed Paco a forty. He took a long drink, wiped his mouth with the back of his hand, and said, "Now get along to your mama's house."

In the moment, Manny remembered the first time he witnessed Paco's true nature. It was at a high school house party where Paco was actively recruiting for the WSF. He had a few girls on his payroll, each taking turns luring boys to the back room with promises of alcohol, drugs, and sex. The boys, drawn by the allure of a wild night, were eager to join.

One freshman, however, refused to participate. As he stood in the living room, visibly shaking, Paco approached him with a friendly yet predatory demeanor. He draped an arm around the boy and asked if he wanted to join his friends for the night of his life. The boy stammered something incomprehensible in response. Paco's demeanor shifted sharply. His voice, once smooth, now dripped with malice as he repeated the question. The boy, overwhelmed by fear, took a hesitant step back, only to find his escape routes blocked by Paco's crew. The boy was trapped in terror.

Paco then accused him of thinking he was too good for his girls or possibly being gay. The boy tried to speak, but his fear rendered his words inaudible. Paco sneered and signaled his crew. They descended on the boy with brutal efficiency, beating him until he lay unconscious on the floor. The sounds of the altercation drew the other boys from the back room, and they were met with the horrifying sight of their friend battered and bloody.

Paco, surveying the scene with a cold gaze, addressed the other boys. "Do you want to join the WSF or end up like your friend?" The threat was clear, and the boys, paralyzed by fear, knew their fate hinged on their response. From that moment on, they were inducted into the WSF, bound by their terror and the harsh reality of Paco's power.

The memory shaken, Manny turned and walked away from the house, leaving Paco and Jade alone on the porch. Paco leaned back in his chair, took a long drag on the blunt, and exhaled slowly. He passed it to Jade, who took a long inhale.

"What's the latest on recruitment? We need some fresh cono," Paco said, his eyes narrowing slightly.

Jade exhaled and handed the blunt back to Paco. "I'm working on a few girls online, and I think I'm close to snatching this new one."

Paco raised an eyebrow. "Which one is this? The one from Minnesota or something?"

Jade corrected him, "It's Missouri, Papi, not Minnesota."

Paco waved his hand dismissively. "Whatever. Just get her hooked."

Jade's eyes gleamed with determination. "I almost got her, Papi. She's ripe for the picking."

***

Lilly Grace's world began to unravel after her stepfather's unwanted advances. Since the summer, he made regular visits to her room late at night. At first, it was when the two were alone. But eventually he became more brazen. Each time, Lilly Grace lay quiet, afraid of what he may do to her younger brother Jack. She became numb to his advances, withdrawing from school and friends, and seeking solace online. That's where she met Jade, a seasoned recruiter for Paco's prostitution ring. As the bottom bitch, a term given to the most loyal of Paco's crew, Jade's role was prospecting, discovery, and logistics for the prostitution business. Between Instagram, TikTok, SnapChat, and others, Jade had over a dozen accounts and profiles.

Lilly Grace's fingers trembled as she typed out her first heartfelt post, sharing her pain and struggles with her stepfather's abuse. She hesitated, then hit "share." The responses poured in, but one private message caught her attention: "You are not alone" from Jade. Lilly Grace's eyes welled up with tears; someone understood.

Over the next month, Jade and Lilly Grace exchanged messages, sharing stories and support. Jade's words were a balm to Lilly Grace's soul, filling the void left by her neglectful mother. Jade's messages were always timely, as if she knew exactly when Lilly Grace needed reassurance. Their online connection deepened, and Lilly Grace began to open up about her trauma.

Unbeknownst to Lilly Grace, Jade had mastered this approach, targeting vulnerable girls across multiple social media platforms. She sought out those hurting, seeking love and attention. Jade's true intentions remained hidden behind her empathetic messages. Her secure online membership site, showcasing girls' intimate content, had become a lucrative empire, eclipsing the WSF drug operations profits.

Paco's gravelly voice conveyed confidence as he outlined his vision to Jade. "We're gonna dominate the Valley, chica. Modesto, Stockton, Fresno – our clients are hungry for fresh talent." He leaned back, eyeing Jade with an air of superiority. "Our private sites go to the high-end clients, not like those street girls on Ninth Street or the motel rats. We're untouchable, Jade. Our clientele's too powerful."

Paco's words dripped with arrogance, but Jade sensed a hint of urgency beneath. He pushed her to expand their roster, to refine the girls' profiles, and to cater to the clients' escalating demands. Jade nodded, her mind racing with the weight of Paco's expectations. She knew the risks, but the lure of easy money and Paco's promises kept her invested.

Over the past year, the WSF prostitution network expanded rapidly, infiltrating Northern and Southern California, Oregon, and Nevada. Jade excelled at cultivating client relationships, tailoring services to high-profile events and travel schedules. When clients were away, Jade created and shared videos featuring girls, allowing clients to select their preferences remotely. This tactic kept clients engaged between trips.

Lilly Grace's narrative revealed a disturbing truth for what men craved, a 15-year-old virgin, innocent who was willing to fulfill any sexual desire. Lilly Grace embodied this coveted profile, naïve and vulnerable.

Paco leaned forward; his voice laced with impatience. "So, is she comin' or what, chica?"

"I've almost got her," Jade replied, her confidence unwavering.

Paco took a long drag on his blunt, exhaling slowly. "We need to seal this deal, Jade. What's it gonna take? Bus ticket, cash, or what?"

Jade's eyes narrowed, her mind racing with strategies. She had mastered manipulation under Paco's guidance, and Lilly Grace was her next target. Unbeknownst to Jade, Lilly Grace held the key to unraveling her deceit.

5

— · —

C HAPTER 5

The parking lot of the First Baptist Church of Turlock was alive with activity when Hannah and JB pulled in at 6:55 on Wednesday evening. Jared leaped from the minivan and dashed toward the church's entrance. Disregarding Hannah's plea to wait, Jared shouted, "Candy night at AWANA!" Hannah's smile broadened as she recalled the thrill of church events from her own childhood.

As she stepped out of the minivan, the evening air carried the sweet scent of blooming flowers and the sound of chatter. Hannah's thoughts turned to the Marriage Ministry class, hoping it would help bridge the growing distance between her and JB.

Inside the van, JB scrolled through his phone, his brow furrowed. A week had passed since the body's discovery, and with the DNA results still pending, the murder investigation appeared to have hit a roadblock, leaving the case shrouded in uncertainty. Hannah glanced at her watch, then peered through the passenger window at JB, her expression a mix of patience and concern.

"Come on, we'll be late," Hannah urged.

JB hesitated, his skepticism evident. "Why are we doing this again?"

"Seriously, JB? You're starting this now?"

JB stepped out of the van; his expression unyielding. "I just don't see the point. I don't know anyone in there, and you want me to bare all our problems?"

Hannah countered, "it's not about airing our problems. It's about sharing our struggles and working through them together. Besides, you do know people. The Millers are inside, and so are the Widman's."

"Who?"

"The Widman's! We met them at that potluck dinner a couple of weeks ago. Remember?"

"I don't recall meeting either of them." JB hesitated, stalling by tying his shoe on the minivan's bumper. "This just seems so unnatural."

"Unnatural is our stagnant marriage, JB. We're repeating the same patterns, expecting a different outcome. That's the definition of insanity."

JB finished tying his shoe, stood up straight and stared off at the church. "This seems forced, Hannah. Like we're pretending to be something we're not."

Hannah's grip on his arm tightened, her voice firm but desperate. "I'm already pretending, JB – pretending everything's fine when it's not. Let's go inside and confront our issues for once."

JB trailed behind Hannah; his reluctance evident as they crossed the parking lot. Upon entering the classroom, he scanned the room, taking in the sea of couples. His gaze swept across the tables, tallying the attendees. Twenty-eight couples, all between thirty and forty-five, filled the space. Every chair was taken, except for two.

Hannah spotted the last available seats near the front and swiftly claimed one, sitting beside the Widman's. JB hesitated, then occupied the remaining chair, his discomfort noticeable.

"Sneaking in failed," JB whispered with a hint of irony. "Widman proximity, that's a bonus."

The first half of the class devolved into a collective exercise in denial, with couples rationalizing why they didn't truly need marriage ministry. They cited desires for community with peers and mentorship from seasoned church members. JB slouched in his chair, silently longing for a glimmer of authenticity. He yearned for someone to shatter the façade, to confess their dead-beat spouse's infidelity with the pool guy. Or better yet, a wife tells the group that her husband couldn't get it up without a pornographic video. JB thought that would at least be honest.

JB's mind wandered to the disconnect between church personas and real-life secrets. He remembered his own transformation from a casual, holiday-only attendee to a regular churchgoer after retiring from the Marines. Now, he saw the hypocrisy up close.

Forty-five minutes of sappy tales finally gave way to the group leader's request to share the couple's personal marriage proposal story. Derek Widman, a polished bank executive, regaled the group with a cliched romance of roses, wine, and a sunset serenade atop a hill overlooking a picturesque valley. JB's eyes rolled in disgust, his mind screaming, "Please, spare me the contrived details."

As each couple tried to outdo the others with increasingly elaborate proposals, JB's turn finally arrived. His story, however, would shatter the sentimental façade.

JB's blunt response cut through the romantic haze, "I proposed over the phone."

The room fell silent, with a few wives exchanging uneasy glances. Derek Widman's jaw dropped, his eyes wide with disbelief, before his wife's subtle nudge beneath the table prompted him to snap his mouth shut.

The awkward stillness lingered until one wife broke the silence, her tone strewn with incredulity: "That's...it?"

Hannah, familiar with JB's deadpan delivery and reluctance to indulge in sentimentalities, stepped in to provide context, softening the abruptness of his statement. "We met at the University of Oklahoma, just after New Year's Eve, and things clicked. But our whirlwind romance was soon put to the test. JB left for Officer Candidate School, followed by TBS, and we barely had time to breathe, let alone make promises. Life was moving fast, and we were both swept up in our own worlds. When he returned that winter, we effortlessly fell back into our rhythm, but fate had other plans. His orders to deploy overseas tore us apart, adding another challenging chapter to our already strained relationship."

"Were you two still together when he deployed?" Angie asked, curiosity etched on her face.

Hannah's response was measured. "It's complicated. We weren't exactly apart, but we weren't fully together either. We were in limbo, I suppose."

JB shifted uncomfortably, sensing the group's scrutiny. As the women's gazes converged on him, he crossed his arms. The silence was evident, but eventually he spoke up.

"I didn't want to give her false hope when I was headed into a war zone. We loved each other, but we were both hesitant to commit. I had my reasons, she had hers. I couldn't ask her to wait, unsure if I'd return."

"So, when did it happen?" one of the wives asked.

"Six weeks of silence. No letters, no calls. Then, a 4:30 a.m. phone call from Afghanistan. I could hear the fear in his voice as he described his mission. Something inside me changed, I couldn't hold back, and I said, 'I love you. Come back safe.' I hadn't intended to reveal so much, but the emotion overwhelmed me."

All the women in unison, asked, "What did he say?"

Hannah gaze met JB's, a fleeting moment of understanding passing between them. She hesitated, aware that the truth might tarnish his image in the eyes of the group. With a subtle nod, she continued.

"He didn't declare his undying love or promise forever. He simply said, 'I know'...and then, 'Why don't we get married?'"

Silence enveloped the room, the women's expressions blending surprise with curiosity. JB's direct, unromantic proposal lingered in the atmosphere, sharply contrasting with the anticipated fairy-tale scenario.

Angie's voice was heavy with disdain, her words tinged with incredulity. "That's it?"

The room fell silent again, the women's faces reflecting their shock and disapproval. JB's proposal, devoid of romance and sentiment, seemed horrifying to them. They exchanged disbelieving glances, their eyes darting to Hannah with a mix of pity and confusion.

How could she settle for such an unemotional, seemingly uncaring partner? The unspoken questions served as callous judgements.

JB's voice cut through the criticism, his tone matter of fact. "Hold up, let me clarify. I was in a tent with ten other guys, all of us waiting to call our loved ones. I was already deployed, locked and loaded, before I left Oklahoma. I didn't propose then, but when Hannah said, 'I love you' over the phone...it hit me. I realized I'd made a mistake by not asking her before I left. So, in that moment, I just asked her to marry me."

His words lingered, a straightforward explanation that tempered the room's disapproval. The women's expressions softened slightly, their understanding of the circumstances evident.

Angie's suggestion was laced with a hint of sarcasm, her tone playful yet pointed. "How about 'I love you too'...and then wait until you got back home to propose? You know, a proper proposal, with some romance and emotion."

The women around the room nodded in agreement, their faces reflecting a collective "yes, that would have been better." JB's straightforward, practical approach was still hard for them to grasp.

Hannah however, smiled knowingly, her eyes locked on JB. "That's not how our story unfolded," she said softly. "And I wouldn't change a thing."

Hannah's words softened the room, and as quickly as the daggers had been drawn, they were sheathed, replaced by a flurry of comments about wedding sizes and guests lists. The group leader seized the opportunity to steer the conversation back on track, presenting the sixteen-week session calendar with a warm smile.

JB's eyes widened as he scanned the topics: Truth-Telling, Emotional Intimacy, Sexual Intimacy...his mind raced ahead to the potentially explosive discussions. If he thought this first class was challenging, he was in for a wild ride.

***

As the two-hour session ended, JB felt an overwhelming urge to escape the suffocating web of church connections and return to the familiarity of the streets. He quickened his pace, Hannah by his side, as they navigated the crowded church hallways. But their swift exit was thwarted by Angie Widman and her husband Derek, who flanked them like sentinels, their faces beaming with an unsettling intensity.

"Hey, JB, Hannah, wait up!" Angie called out, her voice dripping in a oversentimental sweetness. "We wanted to touch base with you both before you head out."

JB's anxiety spiked as the Widman's closed in, trapping them in a conversational corner. He exchanged a wary glance with Hannah, sensing a potentially awkward encounter brewing.

"Hi, Hannah!" Angie called out, her voice echoing caught up to Hannah and JB. Derek followed closely behind, his ten-year-old son, Yates, in step beside him. Yates outfit – khakis and a polo shirt – seemed eerily mirrored to his father's, giving off an air of miniature clone.

JB noticed Yates gaze fixed intently on him, his eyes wide with a mix of curiosity and weariness. JB offered a gentle smile, trying to put the boy at ease.

"Hey, Yates! What's up buddy?" JB asked, attempting to break the ice.

Yates response was a shy nod, his eyes darting to his father before returning to JB. Angie, meanwhile, continued her relentless pursuit of conversation.

JB playfully nudged Hannah, he whispered in amusement. "I swear, that kid is a miniature, Derek! Same serious face, same khakis...it's like he's already 40 years old!"

Hannah's eyes sparkled with amusement; her lips pressed together in a futile attempt to stifle her giggles. She nodded in agreement, her voice barely above a whisper. "I know, right? He's like a pint-sized version of his dad."

As they exchanged amused glances, Yates looked up at them, his expression unreadable. Angie and Derek, oblivious to the teasing, continued their approach, smiles plastered on their faces.

"I just want to say it was such a pleasure visiting with you tonight," Angie said. "We're so glad you're joining our little group!"

Derek Widman extended a firm hand, his smile wide and toothy. "And it was a pleasure to meet you, JB. Welcome to the family! The church family, that is!"

JB accepted the handshake, his grip firm, his smile polite. "Thank you, Derek."

Hannah echoed the sentiment, her voice warm. "Yes, thank you both. We're looking forward to getting to know everyone better."

Angie's eyes sparkled with enthusiasm. "We're hosting a church potluck in a few weeks, and we'd love for you and your family to join us! It'll be a wonderful opportunity to connect with the group."

Hannah hesitated, her expression polite but noncommittal. "Well, I don't know...we've got a lot of activities coming up. I'm not sure what our schedule will be."

Angie waved her hand dismissively, her smile unwavering. "That's okay, dear! You just let us know when you're free, and we'll make the time work. Our Sunday morning group is flexible, and I'm sure they'd all adore meeting you...and your boy, of course." Her gaze drifted to JB, her eyes lingering on him for a moment before returning to Hannah. The unspoken expectation awaited their commitment.

Derek's inquiry was laced with feigned interest, his eyes locked onto Hannah. "Yes, how old is he now? I'm wondering, does he know our boy Yates?"

Hannah eyes locked onto JB's, searching for an escape or a supportive cue. However, JB remained silent, his attention fixed on his shoes, offering no reprieve.

Hannah's words tumbled out in a rushed, awkward manner. "Oh, Jared's already in the car...and I don't know about the potluck...I'm sure we can find a time that'll work for all of us."

Derek's smile never wavered; his tone relentless. "Well, that's great! I'll tell the study group you're in for some time in the next couple of weeks. And we look forward to having you attend our Bible study on Sunday! You can meet everyone, and then we can sync our calendars to find the perfect day and time."

"Yes, it'll be wonderful! We'll get the kids together," Angie chimed in.

Hannah's polite smile began to falter, her eyes pleading for a rescue from the suffocating embrace of the Widman's' hospitality. Angie and Derek Widman strolled away, arm in arm, their son Yates in tow, exuding an air of precocious sophistication.

As soon as they were out of earshot, JB turned to Hannah. "What the hell was that?"

Hannah shrugged, equally perplexed. "I don't know."

"You just signed us up for a Bible study with Mr. and Mrs. Harvard?"

"I didn't say yes!"

JB countered, "She seems to think you did. And, honestly, you kind of did. You know the rules – no spontaneous commitments, especially with people like that."

"They're not that bad."

JB scoffed, "Oh really? Yates? Who names their son Yates? Have you ever met anyone with that name before?"

Hannah chuckled, "Well, now we have."

JB shook his head, "Don't worry, you'll come up with a reason why we can't join their Bible study group this Sunday. That's definitely not happening."

Hannah, still looking frazzled, got into the van, followed by JB. As they settled in, Jared asked from the backseat, "How did the conversation with the Widman's' go?"

"Oh, it went great, son. You're going to be best friends with a kid named Yates."

Hannah and JB exchanged a knowing glance, both thinking the same thing.

"Is he the kid in 5th grade who already looks like he's forty-five years old? I mean, who wears khakis to school in the 5th grade?

Hannah and JB burst out laughing, relieved to have escaped the Widman's' clutches.

JB chuckled, "That's the one! Yates, the miniature version of his old man."

Hannah added, "And don't forget the polo shirt – he's a true fashion icon."

Jared giggled, "Yeah, I've seen him. He looks like he's going to a job interview."

The three shared a hearty laugh, bonding over their collective amusement of the Widman's' eccentricities. As they pulled into their driveway, the warmth of their laughter-filled escape began to fade. JB's work phone pierced the air, a harsh reminder of his grim reality. He glanced at the screen, his heart sinking.

"Manny," he muttered, his tone suddenly serious.

Hannah's expression turned concerned. "What is it?"

JB's eyes scanned the brief message: "1 am tonight at La Clandestina Nightclub – I'll text you when it's time to come inside."

His gut tightened, anticipation and dread swirling together. The horrors he faced daily came flooding back, eclipsing the fleeting joy of their laughter.

"Work," JB said curtly, his mind already shifting gears.

Hannah's understanding nod acknowledged the unspoken truth – their respite was over. JB's duties as a special agent beckoned, drawing him back into the darkness.

6

— • —

CHAPTER 6

JB drummed his fingers on the steering wheel, his eyes fixed on the clock as it struck half-past midnight. The parking lot of La Clandestina Night Club was bustling with revelers, while the neighboring Riverwood Inn and Standard Inn motels catered to those seeking cheap encounters. This stretch of South 9th Street renowned for its illicit activity, infamous for its prostitution and drug trade.

JB was well-versed in the local underworld. Without hard evidence, he was certain that Paco, the head of the WSF prostitution ring, ran his operations separately from the happenings inside La Clandestina. Paco took a share from the pimps in the Deep South Side, overseeing their activities with a vigilant eye.

Waiting for Manny's signal, JB's mind wandered through the tangled web of graft and exploitation surrounding him. The neon signs of La Clandestina cast a garish light, luring those seeking indulgence and decadence. His phone lay silent, its screen a constant reminder of the impending meeting. JB remained alert, scanning the crowded lot for any sign of Manny or the members of Paco's outfit.

At 1:15 in the morning, JB's phone buzzed, shattering the silence. The message from Manny was succinct: "Inside now." JB quickly typed a reassuring text to Hannah: "Mission go!"

The coded message, a vestige of their time in the military, carried profound significance. Hannah's heart used to beat faster with every news report from the Middle East, each potentially signaling JB's engagement in perilous operations. To alleviate her concerns, JB began sending updates before and after missions. Over time, these updates became succinct messages: "Mission Go" indicated the commencement, and "Home Safe" confirmed his safe return.

Tonight, as JB prepared to enter La Clandestina, this familiar routine offered a sense of comfort. He checked his wires, ensuring the audio transmission was secure, and took a deep breath before stepping out of the Tacoma. Blending into a line of partygoers, he pushed open the creaky door and was immediately enveloped by a thick cloud of smoke. The interior of La Clandestina Night Club was a cramped, rectangular space, pulsating with energy and packed to the brim. The air was a pungent mix of sweat, cheap perfume, and stale beer.

His trained eyes scanned the room, instincts on high alert. To his right, a mariachi band performed on a makeshift stage, their lively tunes contrasting with the underlying tension. On the opposite side, a small room overflowed with patrons, their faces obscured by darkness and smoke. JB's gaze swept the area, identifying potential threats and exits. He spotted a possible rear door, partially hidden by a beaded curtain. His experience in high-risk environments, like the Tijuana raid, honed his ability to read the room. As he navigated through the crowd, the temperature shifted from the chilly outside air to the swelting interior which made breathing difficult. JB's focus remained sharp; his senses heightened.

Manny awaited him near the bar, a familiar face in the sea of strangers. The two exchanged a brief, firm embrace, a silent acknowledgement of the mission ahead.

Manny's subtle nod directed JB's attention to a stout, imposing figure on a barstool, his presence commanding attention. Beside him, a young woman exuded sensual confidence, her dark hair, mini skirt, and revealing top accentuated her curves. Her tattoos added an edgy allure, though JB remained unmoved by her provocative demeanor. The woman's body language screamed seduction, her movements deliberate and enticing. Her companion, oblivious to JB's scrutiny, remained engrossed in conversation with the bartender, his focus elsewhere. JB's trained eyes absorbed every detail, his mind processing the dynamics at play. The woman's sexual charisma seemed calculated, a tool to manipulate those around her. He wondered if she was a player in Paco's operation or merely a patron seeking thrills.

Manny's whispered identification of Paco on the barstool sent a surge of focus through JB. He watched as Manny expertly navigated the crowd, inserting himself beside Jade, the tattooed woman. A sharp knock on the bar announced Manny's presence.

JB positioned himself behind Manny, attempting to discreetly lean in and eavesdrop on Paco's conversation. However, the mariachi band's lively music and the din of patrons' chatter thwarted his efforts, rendering Paco's words indistinguishable. JB's eyes locked onto Paco, studying his demeanor, searching for tells or signs of nervousness. Paco's expression remained inscrutable, his attention fixed on the bartender, as he continued speaking in hushed tones.

The bartender's inquiry went unanswered, as Manny remained transfixed by Jade. The bartender moved on, leaving Manny unnoticed.

JB discreetly nodded at Manny, redirecting his attention to Paco, seated to their right. Manny acknowledged the cue, recognizing the need to engage. JB skillfully created a diversion, circling to the opposite end of the bar to order a beer. His actions drew Paco's attention, prompting him to turn away from his conversation.

Paco's gaze locked onto Manny, a mixture of curiosity and caution etched on his face. Manny seized the moment, beginning to make his way toward Paco, his movements deliberate and calculated.

Paco's warm greeting, "¿Qué onda, mijo? ¿Cómo estás?" was met with Manny's brief response, "I'm good, Paco. Good."

Manny's gaze swept the area, searching for JB, but he had seamlessly blended into the crowd.. Manny refocused on Paco. "I'm sorry about earlier today. I was headed to my mom's house and needed to get goin'. You know what I'm sayin'?"

Paco's expression softened.. "No worries, Mijo." The understanding tone implied a deeper connection, a bond between them.

Manny's awkward silence stretched, his eyes shifting between Paco and Jade, as he struggled to find words to sustain the conversation. The weight of Paco's reputation, forged through whispers of ruthless cunning and intuitive suspicion, weighed heavy.

Just as Manny's discomfort seemed insurmountable, JB's timely intervention broke the tension. With a deliberate bump, JB sent Manny stumbling against the bar, creating a diversion.

"Manny is that you?" cut through the din of the crowded bar, intentionally loud enough to capture Paco's and Jade's attention. His convincing portrayal of a slightly inebriated patron added a layer of authenticity to the encounter.

Manny, too, was taken aback by JB's impressive performance, his raised eyebrows betraying a flicker of admiration for his partner's skillful acting. Paco's gaze narrowed, his eyes darting between JB and Manny, as he assessed the situation, Jade's interest was piqued, her gaze lingering on JB with a mix of curiosity and contempt.

"It's been a long time," Manny said. The two men clasped hands, sharing a brief embrace.

JB's gaze shifted from Paco to Jade, monitoring their reactions. Paco's expression remained inscrutable, while Jade's eyes narrowed.

"Manny, what's it been, a year or so?" JB asked, feigning casualness.

"Yeah."

JB's strategic approach emphasized authenticity, opting for an unscripted conversation to maintain realism. He had previously briefed Manny on this tactic, ensuring a seamless collaboration. "Let's keep it natural," JB had advised. "No scripted lines or rehearsed responses. Just react genuinely, and I'll steer the conversation."

Manny recalled JB's reassuring words: "If we're ever in a tight spot, trust me to lead the way. Answer truthfully if I ask you something, and I'll guide you through."

With this understanding, Manny felt secure, knowing JB would expertly navigate any challenging situation. He was primed to follow JB's cues, agreeing with his statements and adapting to the unfolding conversation.

"You still slogging those carpets?" JB asked.

"No man, I'm workin' at Home Depot now."

"Cool, man," JB replied. "Can I get you a beer? Are these your friends? Can I get them one as well?" he asked, offering his hand to Paco.

Paco regarded him with a skeptical look and declined JB's offer for a handshake.

"Manny, Quien es?" Paco asked.

Manny turned his attention to Paco. "He's good. We worked together at Carpet Supply."

JB caught the bartender's attention, ordering three more beers, and positioned himself between Manny and Paco. With beers in hand, JB handed one to Manny. However, his offer to Jade and Paco was met with swift rejection, as they promptly pushed the beers back toward him.

"I said I didn't' want one," Paco asserted.

"My bad. I'll drink it if you don't want it," JB responded.

JB placed his hand on Manny's shoulder as he asked, "So, how do you guys know each other?"

"We live on the same street and my cousins went to high school with him."

JB, undeterred, offered his hand again, his deep voice accompanying the gesture of introduction, "JB."

Paco's glaze locked onto JB's outstretched hand, eyes narrowing as if searching for hidden intentions. The seconds ticked by, heavy with unspoken tension. JB's hand remained steady, his expression open and friendly. Finally, Paco's hand emerged from his pocket, his movements deliberate. His handshake was firm, but brief, as if testing JB's strength without yielding too much. JB's grip was equally firm, his smile unwavering.

In that fleeting moment, the two men sized each other up, their handshake a silent negotiation of power and trust. Manny watched, his eyes darting between them, sensing the fragile balance of their encounter.

"Is this your girlfriend?" JB asked.

"What's it to you?" Paco said.

JB raised his hands, palms up, "Easy, I'm just checking. You know it's getting late around here."

"That seems to be your problem, amigo," Paco said, drawing a clear boundary, his eyes glinting with a mix of warning and challenge.

JB swiftly shifted his attention to Manny, asking, "What's up Manny, you got any hookups with some ladies tonight?" The question seemed innocuous, but Manny sensed an underlying motive, as if JB aimed to redirect the conversation, or perhaps exploit a potential weakness.

Manny's response would either placate or provoke, as the dynamics between the trio continued to simmer, fueled by unspoken tensions and untested alliances.

JB's gaze turned toward Jade, his question seeping with a flirtatious intent, "What about you? You got any girlfriends in here tonight?" But Jade's response was icy, her words slicing through the air, "You may be a friend of Manny's, but you ain't no friend of mine."

JB's smile faltered, his eyes widening in mock innocence, "Wow, no hard feelings." He glanced around the bar, his tone casual, "I'm just lookin' 'round and it seems like it's all dudes in here. I'm just seeing if there are any other options. You know?"

His attention snapped back to Manny, his voice taking on a conspiratorial tone, "You know any girls who might be willing to entertain. You know what I mean?" The implication hung heavy, his words seeping with suggestion.

Manny's discomfort grew, sensing JB's true intentions.

Jade's hostility and Paco's watchful gaze created a volatile mix, as JB's probing continued to test the boundaries of their tolerance. The air thickened, anticipation building, as Manny's response would either defuse or ignite the simmering tensions. Manny's gaze darted to Paco, seeking guidance or reassurance, but his friend's expression remained cold and unamused.

JB seized upon Manny's hesitation. With a fluid motion, JB extracted his wallet, flaunting a thick wad of cash. He riffled through the twenty-dollar bills, the crisp paper rustling, as he announced, "I'm willing to pay."

The unspoken offer lingered, dripping with entitlement. Paco's eyes narrowed, his jaw clenched, as he regarded JB with a mixture of disdain and wariness. Jade's glaze flashed with anger, her lips compressing into a thin line.

Manny shifted uncomfortably, sensing the escalating tension. JB's brazen move had altered the dynamics, testing the trio's resolve and loyalty. The silence stretched, punctuated only by the soft hum of the bar, as the group weighed their response to JB's provocative offer.

Paco's stoic demeanor remained unwavering, his eyes boring into JB with a warning. "Mijo, you need to tell your friend to get the hell out of my bar."

Jade and Paco synchronized their movements, turning away from the pair, their bodies language screaming disinterest and dismissal. The subtle yet potent gesture left JB isolated, his advanced rebuffed. Undeterred, JB's smile twisted, his voice taking on a sinister tone, "If my money's no good, that's fine. I'll find something in here tonight. Hell, I probably won't even have to pay for it."

The air thickened, the atmosphere in the bar growing increasingly charged. Manny's discomfort intensified, trapped between his loyalty to Paco and his association with JB. Jade and Paco's deliberate exclusion heightened the tension, daring JB to make his next move. The silence pulsed, a ticking time bomb waiting to unleash its fury.

JB's brief embrace with Manny served as a calculated distraction, allowing him to slip away unnoticed toward the bathroom. He lingered, biding his time, before reemerging to surveil Paco and Jade from the shadows. For thirty minutes, JB observed their interactions, his eyes scrutinizing every gesture, every whispered conversation. He absorbed the dynamics between them, searching for vulnerabilities or clues.

Satisfied with his reconnaissance, JB decided to retreat, vanishing into the night as stealthy as he appeared. His departure went unnoticed, leaving Paco and Jade oblivious to the scrutiny they had faced.

An hour later, Paco and Jade departed La Clandestina, their exit marking the end of a tense encounter. Unbeknownst to them, JB's interest had only just begun, his observations fueling a hidden agenda, waiting to unfold in the shadows.

***

The soft glow of the living room lights enveloped Jade and Paco. Jade settled into the sofa, a blanket over her lap, her fingers deftly rolling two blunts with practiced ease. The sweet aroma of marijuana wafted through the air, mingling with the promise of relaxation.

Paco emerged from the kitchen, a bottle of Mezcal cradled in his hand, its amber liquid glowing like liquid gold. He sank onto the sofa beside Jade, accepting the blunt she offered. The first puff filled his lungs, and he exhaled slowly, letting the tension melt away. Jade reclined, her eyes scanning the messages on her phone, her thumbs scrolling with a gentle rhythm. The soft hum of the night, the haze of smoke, and the warmth of the moment wrapped around them, a tranquil shield from the world outside.

In this peaceful sanctuary, they found solace, their bond strengthened by the unspoken understanding of the evening's events. The silence between them was comfortable, a testament to the trust and familiarity they shared. As they indulged in the Mezcal and marijuana, their minds unwound, letting go of the night's lingering tensions.

"Chica, I don't know how you keep track of all those personalities of yours," Paco teased.

"All these personalities keep you satisfied."

As Paco retreated to the bedroom, Jade remained, her eyes aglow in the dim light, her fingers dancing across the screen. Her nocturnal routine began, connecting with girls worldwide, seeking out those who shared tales of pain and abuse. With empathy and understanding, Jade responded, sharing her own experiences, offering solace and validation. Her messages whispered hope and resilience, reminding each girl that she was not alone in her struggles.

In this virtual sanctuary, Jade wove a tapestry of support and connection, her multiple personalities blending into a singular purpose: to heal, to comfort, and to empower. As the night wore on, her digital footprint traversed the globe, leaving a trail of compassion and solidarity.

In the shadows, Jade's true essence emerged, her empathetic words and shared experiences, mere bait to lure vulnerable souls into her web of deceit.

***

Jade's drug-induced slumber was shattered by the insistent beep of her phone. Groggily, she sat up, rubbing the haze from her eyes. The message from Lilly Grace flashed on the screen, "What happened? You, ok?"

With a calculating swiftness, Jade revitalized herself, inhaling a bump of cocaine to shake off the lethargy. Her focus sharpened; she knew the prostitution business demanded constant availability. This message from Lilly Grace was an opportunity to reel in a potential client.

Jade swiftly primped, camouflaging the telltale signs of her late-night escapades. A quick nasal pinch, a dap of concealer under her eyes, and she transformed, ready to present a captivating façade.

Her thumbs danced across the phone's keyboard, crafting a response designed to ensnare Lilly Grace. The words flowed, laced with empathy and concern, "Hey baby! Yeah, I'm good. Just had a long night. You'll never guess what this guy offered me?"

Jade's message was a velvet trap, soft and inviting, carefully set to capture Lilly Grace's trust. The game had begun, and Jade was poised to manipulate the outcome, her fingers hovering over the keyboard, awaiting the next move.

Her eyes sparkled with excitement as she continued to type, "He paid me $500." Weeks of patience had led to this breakthrough. She leaned forward, her phone clutched tightly, awaiting Lilly Grace's response.

The message pinged back and forth:

"How? Fow what?"

"A rando guy on the internet paid me $500 for a photo of my feet lol!"

"What!"

"Yes, some weirdo on IG Venmo'd me $500 for photos of my feet."

The conversation flowed, Jade expertly guiding it:

"That's it?" Lilly Grace asked.

"Yeah, that's it."

Jade's subtle nod to herself, a mental checkmark. She had Lilly Grace hooked, intrigued by the easy money. The seed was planted, and Jade was ready to nurture it, leading Lilly Grace down a path of temptation and exploitation. The $500 mention was merely bait, a taste of lucrative possibilities. Jade's fingers flew across the keyboard once again, crafting the next message, poised to reel Lilly Grace in further.

"What'd you get $100 for each toe lol?"

Jade's eyes gleamed with triumph, knowing she had Lilly Grace precisely where she wanted her.

Jade's response was casual, yet calculated, "Lol, no. He saw a photo of me touching my breast and wanted to see more. I told him $500, and I'll send you a photo. And he did it."

"And you sent it?"

"Heck yeah! It's $500 for a photo."

The bait was set, and Jade waited patiently for Lilly Grace's response. The vulnerable teenager took the lure.

"I'm not as pretty as you. I don't have breasts, at least not like yours. No guy would ever want to see mine."

Jade's mental nod confirmed her assessment – Lilly Grace was hooked. The younger girl's insecurity and admiration created the perfect opening. Jade's next message would be the gentle tug on the line, reeling Lilly Grace deeper into the dangerous waters of exploitation.

Lilly Grace's painful secrets poured out, a heartbreaking litany of shame and abuse. Jade listened attentively, her responses carefully crafted to foster trust and validation. The hour-long conversation sealed their bond, Lilly Grace vulnerable and exposed.

Jade's moment of triumph arrived. She extended the invitation, "Want to FaceTime?"

The response was immediate, Lilly Grace eager to deepen their connection. Jade's phone buzzed, the video request flashing on the screen. With calculated excitement, Jade accepted the call. The screen flickered to life, revealing Lilly Grace's hesitant smile. Jade's warm, encouraging gaze met hers, a reassuring presence.

In this intimate, virtual space, Jade's manipulation would reach its crescendo. Lilly Grace, fragile and trusting, was primed for exploitation. Jade's mask of empathy and friendship concealed her true intentions, as she prepared to exploit Lilly Grace's vulnerabilities for her own sinister purposes. The FaceTime connection solidified their bond, paving the way for Jade's next move.

Jade's provocative attire was carefully chosen to tantalize Lilly Grace's curiosity. The black thong panties and white tank top showcased her tattoos and nipple rings, teasing Lilly Grace's innocence.

Lilly Grace's gaze lingered, drawn to the nipple rings peeking through the fabric. Jade's knowing smile acknowledged the fascination, her eyes sparkling with a mix of mischief and seduction.

"Like them?" Jade asked, her voice husky, as she leaned in with her chest thrust forward, accentuating the nipple rings.

Lilly Grace's cheeks flushed, her eyes darting away, then back, unable to resist the allure. Jade's playful laughter put her at ease, encouraging Lilly Grace to embrace her curiosity.

"They're beautiful," Lilly Grace said softly.

Jade's triumphant smile hinted at the control she wielded. She had Lilly Grace entranced, primed for further manipulation. The virtual connection hummed with tension, as Jade gentle caresses and soft moans created an intoxicating atmosphere, drawing Lilly Grace deeper.

"Does it hurt?" Lilly Grace asked.

"At first, yeah...but now, it's pure pleasure."

As Jade continued to fondle her breasts, the touch grew more sensual. Lilly Grace's eyes remained fixed, her cheeks full flush.

"I wish you were here, so you could feel them," Jade purred, her eyes locked on Lilly Graces.

Lilly Grace's innocence teetered on the brink, as Jade's provocative words and actions beckoned her toward a forbidden realm.

Lilly Grace's voice trembled, "I...I don't know."

"Don't worry."

Lilly Grace did not respond. Jade knew it was a delicate matter, and she had to be careful with how far she pushed the conversation. Lilly Grace had to be ready, and the moment had to be right for her to strike.

"When a guy sucks on them, it feels so amazing."

"What? Really?"

"Yes."

Jade leaned down and pulled her breast up to her mouth and sucked on her nipple. Her large voluptuous breast filled her face. Lilly Grace's eyes were wide open. She touched her face as she started to feel flush and hot. There were feelings that she was feeling down her body that she had never felt before. Jade and Lilly Grace had become so close over the past month with their conversations, sharing intimate details of their lives. They shared things with each other that Lilly Grace would never dare share with anyone else. Who could she tell about her stepfather? If she told her mother, she would not believe her and probably wouldn't care. She could not tell her little brother, and Evan wouldn't believe her anyways. Lilly Grace lived in fear and had no one except Jade to confide in her innermost thoughts.

"Let me see your breast," Jade asked.

"What?"

"Yes, I showed you mine, now you show me yours."

"I don't really have breasts. At least not like those."

"Yes, you do. I bet they're beautiful. Let me see."

Lilly Grace hesitated. Then, sitting on the bed in her room, the same bed that her stepfather had sexually abused her in, she slowly raised her long T-shirt up and over her head. She raised the phone to reveal her half naked body.

Lilly Grace was petite with very little curves. She held the phone with one hand and with the other hand she cupped her small breast in the palm of her hand, imitating Jade's movements. As she cupped her small breast, Jade lay back on the sofa and put her hand in her panties. Lilly Grace was confused. She felt warm all over her body. She started to pulsate as she felt a rush of blood throughout her pelvic area.

"What are you doing?" asked Lilly Grace.

"You are so beautiful. I'm just enjoying being with you and it feels so good."

"But I've never."

Lilly Grace lost her words at the sight of Jade slowly sliding her panties down her thighs. The sight alone caught Lilly Grace's breath. She lost all words as her brain was unable to comprehend the unfamiliar emotions. Over the next thirty minutes, they explored each other's bodies and Lilly Grace felt something she never had before. And it was satisfying.

As the days passed, Jade's grip on Lilly Grace tightened, their virtual encounters growing more intimate and frequent. Unbeknownst to Lilly Grace, she was ensnared in a web of manipulation, Jade's influence insidiously seeping into her psyche.

Their daily messenger video chats became a ritual, with Jade expertly guiding the conversations, probing deeper into Lilly Grace's desires and fears. The younger girl, entranced by Jade's charisma and validation, willingly surrendered her secrets and insecurities. Jade's calculated seduction continued, her words and actions weaving a spell of trust and dependence. Lilly Grace, enthralled by the attention and connection, remained oblivious to the danger lurking beneath the surface.

The serpent's fangs, indeed, had taken hold, injecting a potent venom of manipulation and control. Lilly Grace, now deeply enthralled, was poised to surrender her innocence, unaware of the devastating consequences that awaited her.

7

—◆—

CHAPTER 7

JB's eyes flew open as the alarm clock's blare cut through the darkness, its insistent ring shattering the early morning calm. Next to him, Hannah shifted, her sleepy mutterings revealing her aversion to the 5:45 a.m. wake-up call. Usually, JB would savor a few more moments of slumber, but the night's occurrences at La Clandestina lingered in his mind, robbing him of the comfort of additional sleep.

Paco Ramirez's enigmatic aura and Jade's compelling confidence lingered in his thoughts, forming an elusive puzzle that resisted resolution. JB's mind whirred, analyzing Paco's deliberate composure and Jade's steadfast certainty. Fragments of their conversation danced in his memory, igniting his curiosity and fortifying his resolve.

Determined, JB threw back the covers, ignoring Hannah's drowsy complaints. He proceeded through his morning routine with deliberate vigor, spurred on by the previous night's mysteries. Refreshed by the cool morning breeze, JB began his run. The moon's silver light illuminated his route, creating elongated shadows that moved rhythmically with each step. His breath kept time with his pace, a steady 6:55 per mile, reflecting his commitment to staying fit.

Returning home, sweat-drenched and energized, JB seamlessly transitioned into his AMWRAP workout. The intense 20-minute session pushed him to his limits, his muscles responding eagerly to the challenge. Each movement was fueled by his need to channel the restless energy from the night before into something productive.

Refreshed and revitalized, JB showered and poured himself a steaming cup of coffee. Thoughtfully, he prepared an extra cup for Hannah, placing it in the microwave for her to enjoy when she arose. With his morning routine complete, JB was ready to tackle the day ahead. His mind, now clear and focused, returned to the intriguing events of the previous night – Paco Ramirez and Jade's mystique lingering, refusing to be dismissed.

JB stepped out of his Toyota Tacoma, the crisp morning air greeting him as he began his purposeful stride across the empty parking lot. His mind was already immersed in the task ahead, fueled by a sense of determination. As he approached the office entrance, his thoughts raced with possibilities. He was driven to uncover the truth about Paco Ramirez, Jade, and their potential connection to the young girl's tragic demise in the abandoned almond grove.

JB's focus narrowed on the court records and FBI database, seeking clues about Paco's criminal past, gang affiliations, and associations. The memory of Paco's distinctive tattoos – the dot by his right eye and cursive script on his neck – lingered, potentially holding significance. With Manny's testimony as a foundation, JB aimed to validate Paco's ties to the WSF. He was resolute in his pursuit of justice, driven by the haunting image of the girl and the unsettling encounter with Paco.

As he entered the office, JB's eyes locked onto his computer, his fingers poised to dive into the digital realm, seeking answers and connections. The hunt for truth had begun.

***

JB rubbed his eyes, frustration mounting from the elusive search results. He had scoured countless records, court documents, and databases, yet Paco Ramirez and Jade remained ghosts, shrouded in mystery. As he pondered his next move, from down the hallway he heard a familiar voice break the silence, "Hey, JB! How's the case going?"

Andy Warnall, the Chief Agent in Charge, was not only JB's superior but one of his best friends. Their wives attended church together and often studied the bible together. Andy was a career federal agent who had served in the FBI for nearly twenty years. During that time, the Warnall's had moved across the United States. It was a shared experience that created an instant bond between the wives.

Warnall grabbed a cup of coffee and strolled up to JB's cubicle. In a joyful tone, he said, "You look like crap."

"Thanks, appreciate it!"

"No, seriously. You look like crap."

"I didn't sleep much this weekend. This case with the girl found near the river is eating me up. I've got a CI that says he thinks he knows who is behind it, or at the very least has a contact that would know." JB paused, he rubbed his eyes and stretched his arms over his head. He had the attention of his friend and supervisor.

"And?"

"We met last night at a dive bar on 9th street. He introduced me to a man and a girl that he said are involved in prostitution and other gang related activities."

"What happened? You get anything out of it?"

"He's hard core for sure. He's tatted up and seems to be connected to the Norteño crew. Based on where the CI says he lives, I would say it's the WSF set. The girl with him couldn't have been more than twenty-one."

"What was she like?"

"I can imagine her being connected to a prostitution ring. There was an emptiness in her eyes."

"What? Do you think she could be the killer?"

"I'm not saying that. Of all the criminals I've ever come across, rarely do I find someone that doesn't have some good somewhere in their heart. When I looked into her eyes, they were dark, and almost, like, soulless eyes."

"What do you want to do?"

"We need to set up a net around the south side. We need to start street interviews and target the local truck stops. We've got to see whether any dots connect to these two outside of what the CI says."

"Is the CI reliable?"

"Yeah, he's solid. He grew up in the neighborhood and he knows everyone. He said his uncle used to run with this guy and he vouches that he is connected to the WSF."

"What information do we have on the WSF? I thought they were low-level set compared to some others?"

"The CI is hearing people talk. He says things have been changing and they're considering making a move."

"Who is leading that crew now?"

"The crew used to be led by a guy named Ricardo Avina. He was killed in Pelican Bay a few years ago. He's got a son that's in his mid-20's. The word on the street is he's the one calling the shots."

"Do we need to bring him in for discovery?"

"Yeah, maybe, but while I want to catch whoever killed this girl, I also want to know if there is something larger happening with this crew. If so, then I don't want to scare them underground. The DNA test is more than likely going to tell us who raped the girl.

That'll be significant because we can see if he is connected at all to WSF. Let's do the normal screenings and street interviews and see if we can connect a few dots."

"It sounds like this is going to take some time."

"Don't they all?"

"Tell me what you need, and we'll get it done."

"Sounds good."

Warnall started to walk away, but after a few steps, he turned around with a big grin on his face. "Oh yeah, one more thing, I hear you're going to be starting a new bible study group on Sunday mornings."

"I'm not starting anything. If Hannah wants to go, she is more than welcome to attend."

"And I suppose you and that banker are going to become golf partners at the Country Club?"

JB took the pencil that was in his hand and threw it towards Warnall's head. He swiftly ducked and turned away laughing.

"I'm going to kick your ass. Better yet, I'm going to tell Hannah to invite Stephanie so you guys can come and join us."

Andy just waved his hand goodbye. JB could hear his laughter all the way down the hall. He returned to the computer screen and continued to scroll through the database. He didn't know it yet, but in a few days the DNA results would come back with intriguing results.

8

—·—

C HAPTER 8

Paco's phone buzzed with an incoming call from Eric Avina, his cousin and WSF leader. Eric's voice was low and urgent, cutting through the night air with a sense of gravity. He instructed Paco to meet him at their usual spot by the Tuolumne River, nestled between John Thurman Baseball Field and Dryden Golf Course. The proposal from Pelican Bay leaders to expand their operation throughout the Central Valley required immediate discussion, along with logistics and a crucial introduction to cartel figures.

For six years, Eric and Paco had used this secluded location to avoid law enforcement scrutiny. The arrest of Eric's cousin, a casualty of a wiretap, had bred a deep-seated paranoia. To avoid tracking, they left their cell phones at home, and Eric used a coded designation for their meeting spot to ensure Paco's understanding.

As the sun dipped below the horizon, casting a warm orange glow over the valley, Eric and Paco arrived at the designated spot. They leaned against the hood of Eric's car, the distant neighborhood lights beginning to flicker to life and punctuating the evening's calm. Eric produced a blunt from behind his ear, lit it with a practiced flick of his lighter, and handed it to Paco.

The night settled around them as they took a moment to savor the brief respite, their conversation taking on a more urgent tone as they delved into the details of the impending expansion and the steps required to solidify their plans.

"We're getting attention from above. This opportunity doesn't come often. You feel me?" Eric said.

Paco inhaled deeply, passing the blunt back to Eric. "What's the timeline? What's expected of us?"

"All I know is Eduardo Hernandez, a leader from Fresno, is bringing someone from down south. Word is this guy's a major player in Mexico."

"Hernandez? You've dealt with this guy before?" Paco asked.

"He's the extortionist who rolls through the valley, bleeding us dry."

"Can we trust him?"

"I don't trust no one." His stare drifted toward the horizon, deep in thought, Eric changed the subject. "How can a place so beautiful be so fucked up?"

Paco chuckled, smoke escaping his lip. "What the fuck do you mean?"

Eric's eyes never left the sunset, where the sun dipped below the edge of the western slopes of the valley. The beauty of the fiery glow seemed almost surreal against the harsh reality of life. He took a deep drag from the blunt, the smoke swirling around him as if to mask the turmoil within.

"Think about it, man," Eric said. "What was this place like a hundred years ago? Fifty years ago? Now, we've got trailer parks filled with struggling families, homeless people shittin' on our sidewalks...and us, turnin' these kids into soldiers before they're even ten years old."

Paco, observing Eric with a mix of concern and irritation, passed the blunt back. "You're high as fuck."

Eric took another hit, exhaled slowly, his voice filled with conviction. "No, man, it's not just the weed talkin'. Look at this view – it's beautiful. And we're here destroying something that's fuckin' amazing. It's like we're tearing down something so beautiful. It feels like we're fightin' against something that was here long before us, something that was perfect in its own way."

Paco shrugged, trying to refocus the conversation. "It's not about beauty and whether we're destroying it or not. It's about survival. We're at war. That ten-year-old will die either way. At least with us, he'll have a choice, a chance to fight to get what's his."

"Sometimes, I look at these kids, and it just eats me up. I can't stand the thought of seeing them lying in the streets, bleeding out, and knowing I had a hand in it."

Paco placed a hand on Eric's shoulder. "You're just seein' yourself in these kids. It's fuckin' with your head, homes. There is no what could've been or what should be. There is only what it is and that's it."

Eric took another long drag. "I hate seein' them lyin' in the streets, bleeding out and shit. I ain't up for that shit no more."

"That's why you need to turn him into a soldier, so he's a lion and not a lamb. Trust me, the street's gunna come for him one way or the other. At least with us, he's got a fightin' chance. ¿Comprendes?"

As they stood there, the weight of Paco's words seemed to settle over Eric. He knew Paco was right about the immediate threats, but his thoughts kept drifting back to the streets.

Paco continued. "This goes beyond drugs, guns, and prostitution. Our community relies on us, our family, and this shipment. Think about the lives we've touched – people with food on the table, kids in college, thanks to our efforts. You need to see the bigger picture. If we don't step up, someone else will, and we'll be answering to them. We gotta protect our turf, our people."

The two men shared a firm handshake, a silent agreement that marked the shift from personal to business. Their focus now turned to the logistics of the upcoming meeting with Eduardo Hernandez. In just two weeks, Eduardo would introduce them to the Ghost, a formidable cartel leader from Mexico, a move that would elevate their crew's status significantly. Only select leaders from Bakersfield, Fresno, Modesto, and Stockton were to receive invitations, underscoring the exclusivity and importance of the event.

As they leaned against the car, Eric and Paco delved into the details of the impending gathering. They discussed streamlining their supply chains, optimizing product distribution, and reinforcing security protocols to ensure the operation ran smoothly. Each point was scrutinized with meticulous attention, their plans aimed at solidifying their influence and avoiding any potential pitfalls.

The conversation was marked by a blend of urgency and careful calculation, both men aware that the success of their forthcoming ventures hinged on their ability to execute these plans with precision. Yet, for Eric, the night's quiet and the fading light only deepened his sense of unease, the weight of his choices pressing heavily on him as he grappled with his place in a world that seemed to offer nothing but struggle.

***

On Friday at 4:30 p.m., Eric Avina watched as Tony Baird escorted the final customer from the Baird Tractor Supply Company's parking lot. Situated along the Tuolumne River, just off Highway 99, the Baird Tractor Supply Company offered an ideal setting for the rendezvous with Eduardo Hernandez and the Ghost.

Tony, a childhood friend of Eric's father, Ricardo Avina, had remained loyal despite their diverging paths. While Ricardo's football career was cut short by injury, Tony pursued higher education at UC Davis and established a successful business. The contrast between their lives was stark, yet their friendship endured, bridging the gap between businessman and gang affiliate.

Ricardo Avina's descent into the criminal underworld, founding the West Side Familia (WSF) gang, had cast a long shadow over Eric's upbringing. Ricardo's ambition to expand WSF was driven by his desire to provide for his son, recruiting young Latinos, forging alliances, and establishing connections with cartels. However, in 2002, Ricardo was indicted on multiple felony counts, including conspiracy, murder, assault, and narcotics distribution, receiving a fifteen-year sentence at Pelican Bay State Prison.

With Ricardo's imprisonment, Eric's childhood was largely shaped by Lola Martinez, his mother. Ricardo's street life kept them apart, and Eric's emotional detachment at his father's sentencing reflected their strained relationship. The WSF struggled, losing ground to rival Sureño and MS13 crews during Ricardo's absence.

Tony Baird, honoring a promise made to Ricardo, became a surrogate father figure to Eric, offering him a deeper bond than he had ever known with his biological father. Despite this, the pull of the streets and Ricardo's legacy eventually drew Eric back. Ricardo's influence, though physically absent, grew in strength, as he secured the trust and loyalty of Nuestra Familia cartel members at Pelican Bay.

As the WSF regained its footing, Eric was positioned for leadership, a role that Tony faced with mixed feelings. Balancing loyalty to Ricardo with his responsibility to protect Eric, Tony chose to guide him, allowing Eric to carve his own path while ensuring his safety—an obligation he had struggled to fulfill with Ricardo.

The black Mercedes with dark tinted windows arrived, carrying Eduardo and the Ghost. Paco and Eric exchanged a glance, sensing the gravity of the meeting.

To cut through the tension, Paco calmly asked Eric a question. "How'd your pops meet Eduardo?"

Eric nervously shifted his weight from one leg to the other. "They met in prison. He's connected with the crew at Pelican Bay. This other guy, nobody knows his real identity. The story is that he handles all the cartel logistics out of Mexico. So, if he doesn't like what we got here the drugs ain't comin'."

Eduardo Hernandez, an imposing 48-year-old man from Fresno, California, emerged from the rear seat. He stood tall, with a strong frame and a distinctive thick black mustache. His black suit was sleek, sans a tie. A second man exited the opposite rear door, noticeably shorter at around 5'8" with a stocky build, also dressed in a black suit. The duo surveyed the yard before ascending the staircase towards Eric and Paco.

"Good afternoon, gentlemen," Eduardo said as he embraced Eric at the top of the stairs. "Mijo, it's been many years since we've last seen each other."

"Yes, I remember my pops speaking highly of you." Eric took a step back and turned toward the doorway of the office building. Even as a child, he never trusted Eduardo and the story he shared about what really happened to his father. "Why don't we go inside?"

Normally the desktop was full of invoices and contract paperwork. However, on this day, Tony had ensured the room was spotless.

"Gentlemen, you may be wondering who our guest is with me today. He doesn't need a name because it's not important. Let's just say he will be driving the conversation. And gentlemen, make no mistake about it, he is on authority from the highest."

Eric and Paco nodded in agreement.

In a thick Mexican accent, the Ghost said, "The word on the street is that the WSF is the crew we want to help build our pipeline and distribution. But you are not ready yet to handle what we can offer. That's why I am here now. You will be in the next 9 months."

The Ghost had a rolled-up paper map. He pulled it out of cylindrical tube and rolled it across the table. It was a detailed map of Mexico and the West Coast.

"As I was saying, to make this happen, we're going to need to provide you all with people who can connect from one location to another. We'll call it supply chain gaps or bottlenecks. Due to the advance of our colleagues and the skill of law enforcement agencies, we need to rebuild our pipeline. That means we must put new people in different roles and replace some leadership roles throughout the chain."

Paco glanced at Eric. He wanted to say something, but he bit his lip.

"For example, our crew can get shipments through the border. We've got that covered, and our Southern California affiliates are ready for distribution. What we need is unification and leadership to help us get through Bakersfield and up through Stockton. That's where Eduardo and you come into play."

Eric looked down at the map and noticed a few different points of interest. The first was the border crossing at Calexico. From there, the highlighted marker went to Riverside, California, then up through Bakersfield, Fresno, and Modesto. Outside of Fresno, twenty miles in the country, was a small, highlighted circle.

"You said people in new roles and leadership changes?" Paco asked. "How does that impact us?"

"Who are you again?" the Ghost asked.

Paco stood a little taller and firmer in his stance. He was growing weary of Eduardo and the Ghost. "I handle recruitment and membership retention."

"Good mijo. My job is to assess whether the local affiliates can handle the size of distribution we're bringing north. Do you have the right people? Do you have storage facilities? Do you have the security to enforce? And most importantly, are you protected by the local law enforcement."

"What do you mean? Do we pay off the police or something?" Eric asked.

"Yes mijo. I've been crossing the Calexico border crossing for years. I've rarely had a car even get inspected through that crossing. The dogs don't even come out on my cars. Do you think I'm just lucky Mijo? No. I pay the right people to look the other way. Do you have people looking the other way?"

Paco looked at Eric, who kept his eyes down on the desktop. The two realized that their local gang was not capable of handling a shipment of this magnitude. Up to this point, they had grown their own marijuana and had small amounts distributed through Fresno.

"So, what are we talking about in terms of the size of this shipment?" Eric said.

Eduardo stepped forward.

"We're going to do a couple of test runs to see how our supply chains are working and to make sure we can keep the heat off at each of the distribution sites. After we're confident that we can get through, drop, and get to the next point of contact, we'll then start running through the major shipments. We're talking shipping, 500 lbs. of cocaine, $2,000,000 in cash, over a hundred different firearms, 50,000 M30 fentanyl pills and tablets, 100 lbs. of meth, 40 lbs. of fentanyl powder, and 250 lbs. of processed marijuana."

"What's our cut on these numbers?" Paco asked.

"That's to be determined," Eduard said.

"What's your storage capability like right now?" the Ghost asked.

"Not enough to capture this much weight," Eric said.

Up to this point, the WSF was utilizing the Baird Tractor Supply shipping containers for storage. And they had a small rental house on the south side where they kept a stash in a closet. But these numbers needed not only storage but also a security strategy.

"We can help with identifying the proper storage and finding the right security," Eduardo said. "But that's going to cost you, and it'll come out of your cut."

"What's your liability?" the Ghost asked.

Again, Paco and Eric looked at each other with confused looks. They were just two young guys running drugs on the streets and pimping out prostitution. This was leading them down a path of no return. They knew they were in a big-league conversation with heavy hitters. And they didn't exactly know how to respond.

The Ghost followed up. "You know, liabilities? What are your weak points where you can either get scrapped by a rival or law enforcement?"

"The sets in Modesto keep to their neighborhoods for the most part. We haven't had too many times when we've had major issues. Mostly our issues extend to small beefs here and there and don't really involve large business-related issues."

"How have you handled members leaving?" Eduardo asked.

Paco started to speak, but the Ghost simply put his finger up.

"Do you track the members for the past five years who have been arrested? Where did they do their time? How long did they do their time? Who did they do their time with? I want to know who you're sleeping with at night. I want to know who in your crew is not producing. I want to account for every piece of product that goes out the door and every dollar that comes back in the door. We're talking about businessmen here, not some street thugs running drugs or some chulo out here corriendo con putas."

The Ghost rolled up the map and put it back in the cylindrical tube.

"And gentlemen, most of all, I want to know if we have any ratas in this crew."

"Eric, we're going to need you to put these lists together and get a report back to me before next month. Time is critical because we can't get started on this until we know exactly who we're partnering with on the supply chain," Eduardo said.

And with that, the men shook hands and Eduardo, and the Ghost left the Baird Tractor Supply yard. Paco and Eric stayed in the office to debrief the meeting. Eric's head was spinning with the amount of work that was involved with cataloguing the crew numbers, the history and connection points of each member, past and present. Did he even have access to this information, and if not, how could he go about getting it? Paco, on the other hand, was fuming at the disrespect he detected from Eduardo and the Ghost.

"I don't like this, Eric. They're coming in here and telling us how to run our business. It won't be long before they decide to take over our crew. Hell, if they don't like what they're seeing they'll just decide to replace us all together."

"Stop worrying about what ifs. We've always said we wanted to expand and now they're giving us that opportunity. Let's just take one step at a time. Let's divide the list and get to work. You get me a list of every name that's been associated with us, past and present. I'll get to work on the background checks, and I'll look into our storage capacity options. We need to button this thing up quick."

"How you gunna get background checks?"

"I got that covered," Eric said.

Eric and Paco spent the next hour sifting through names and poring over rosters of WSF members from the past decade. The list was long and detailed, but as they reviewed it, they began to grasp the extent of their disorganization. The lack of a cohesive record left them vulnerable and unsure about the reliability of their own crew.

Frustrated by the complexity of their situation, Eric's thoughts turned to a trusted ally who might be able to help. There was one person who had consistently provided valuable court-related documents in the past, someone who had connections and access to legal records that could be crucial in this moment of uncertainty. But the question lingered – would she be willing to assist them now, given the precarious nature of their situation? And more importantly, the precarious nature of their relationship.

Eric glanced at Paco, who was absorbed in a particular section of the roster, and said, "I think I know someone who might be able to help us get a clearer picture. But we need to see if she'll answer. It's a gamble, but it's our best shot."

"You think she'll cooperate? After everything that's gone down?"

Eric sighed, pulling out his phone. "She's been reliable before, but we'll see. It's worth a try."

He dialed the number, his fingers drumming anxiously on the table as the phone rang. Each ring seemed to stretch into eternity, a reminder of the gravity of their situation and the slim margin for error they faced.

9

—·—

CHAPTER 9

Lilly Grace froze in the hallway, her heart hammering. A man stood just feet away—out of place, too at ease. Every instinct screamed danger. She forced a breath, willing herself to stay steady as the past pressed in, heavy and unrelenting.

The man's eyes met hers briefly, but he offered no recognition. With a gruff mutter about needing to finish up, he shuffled past her, moving toward the master bedroom. Lilly Grace's hands shook as she tightened her grip on her backpack, desperate to avoid any confrontation. She quickly retreated toward her room, her mind racing with the unsettling encounter.

The house, once a haven from the outside world, now felt cold and alien. As Lilly Grace closed her bedroom door behind her, she leaned against it, trying to steady her breath. The muffled sounds of the man's footsteps gradually faded, but the sense of intrusion remained. She opened the door slightly, peaking into the hallway. In the distance, she saw her mother stumbling off the bed, struggling to put on her pants. Her mother's legs gave way, and she collapsed to the floor, clearly incapacitated.

Out of nowhere, the strange man placed his hand on the door, pushing inward toward Lilly Grace. She did her best to push against him, but he was too strong. The sight of his imposing figure and the menacing air he carried filled her with dread.

"Hey, pretty girl, how you are doing?" he asked.

Lilly Grace's gaze pierced through him; her eyes empty, unresponsive. She was unable to muster a reply, even if she wanted to.

"Have a good day at school?" he continued, looking around her bedroom.

Lilly Grace's mind raced. Why did he care about day or her well-being? He was a stranger, an intruder in her home. Her thoughts sprinted through possible explanations for his presence, each scenario more unsettling than the last.

He released his palm from the door, and Lilly Grace managed to close it and retreated into her bedroom, locking the door behind her. His chuckle echoed as he headed towards the kitchen.

She dropped her backpack by her desk and sat down, her eyes fixed on her iPhone. Anticipation fluttered in her chest as she checked for messages from Jade. Thoughts of Jade consumed her every waking moment – her captivating presence, the way she made Lilly Grace feel seen and valued. With Jade, Lilly Grace felt beautiful, respected, and heard. She was the sole confidante in Lilly Grace's troubled life, privy to secrets hidden from the world – her mother's drug addiction and the unspeakable abuse inflicted by her stepfather.

Lilly Grace's heart sank when she saw no messages from Jade. She quickly sent a text, seeking a conversation. Suddenly, a knock on the door made her jump. She concealed her iPhone and replied, "Yeah."

Leaning back in her chair, she watched as the stranger entered with key in hand, closing the door behind him. He meandered around her room, scrutinizing photos on her dresser and nightstand. Finally, he sat on her bed, his hand spreading across her blanket. Lilly Grace's mind perplexed, wondering what he was thinking. Her mother's presence in the house should have deterred him, yet he seemed brazen. His actions sent a shiver down her spine.

"So, you ever been with an older man?" he paused, his gaze lingering on her.

Lilly Grace shook her head, the man's question causing her to stiffen with apprehension.

"You might like it if you tried it," he said. Lilly Grace's horror deepened as he leaned forward. "Your mama said I could get a two for one today."

She was paralyzed, unable to respond to his vile suggestion. He rose, his movements deliberate and approached her. His touch sent shivers down her spine as he caressed her shoulders, then ran his fingers through her hair. Lilly Grace's body tensed, recoiling from his unwanted touch.

She winced at the smell of his hot breath as he whispered in her ear, "I can't wait to smell you." Lilly Grace's stomach churned with nausea, repulsed by his depraved words.

Tears pricked at the corners of her eyes, but she refused to give him satisfaction. Before she could react, he clenched a fistful of hair, yanking her face close to his. His grip was painful, his eyes menacing.

"Don't even think about telling anyone," The stranger said. "And don't ever think about saying no to me. When I want you, you'll say yes. Do you understand?"

Lilly Grace's heart racing, she nodded, desperate to escape his grasp.

Agony shot through her scalp as he yanked her hair, silencing her. He pulled harder, his voice angry. "Do you understand me, you little cunt?"

Tears streaming down her face, Lilly Grace managed a trembling "Yes, yes, I understand."

He released his grip, and she collapsed onto her chair, gasping in relief. Without a word, he turned and left the room. Lilly Grace scrambled to her bed and hid under the covers, seeking refuge. She curled into a ball, her body shaking, and eventually succumbed to exhausted sleep.

***

Lilly Grace stirred awake to her phone's gentle glow, indicating a new message. The clock read 8:30, she had slept for three hours. With a mix of excitement and trepidation, she opened the message from Jade.

"Hey girl, what's up? I can't wait to talk. You'll never guess what happened to me."

Lilly Grace's fingers flew across the keyboard. "OMG, you'll never believe what happened to me. Can you video chat?"

Minutes passed, and then her phone rang, signaling a video chat request from Jade. Lilly Grace's heart swelled with joy. She accepted, and Jade's radiant smile filled the screen. Jade wore a fitted flannel shirt and jeans, her hair pulled back in a sleek ponytail. Lilly Grace admired Jade's curves, feeling a pang of envy.

"Are you okay? Did he hurt you again?" Jade asked.

Lilly Grace's words tumbled out in a rush. "No, it was someone else. I came home to Mom with some stranger. He...he came into my room afterward, saying he could get a 'two for one' deal.

"What? That's disgusting! What did he do?"

"He pulled my hair, threatening me. Said he could have me whenever he wanted."

"Oh, Lilly Grace, I'm so sorry. You don't deserve this. What are you going to do?"

"I don't know. It's all so overwhelming. But let's talk about something else. What's your news?"

"No, Lilly Grace, this isn't okay," Jade said firmly. "You deserve better than dealing with your mom's issues, your stepfather's abuse, and now strangers threatening you. You need help, a safe escape."

"It's fine, he was probably harmless."

Jade urged. "Why don't you leave? Get out of there?"

"Where would I go?"

Sensing her moment to strike, Jade offered a lifeline. "Come to California, stay with me."

Lilly Grace hesitated. "How would I even get there

"I don't know. You could take a bus or something."

"No. I couldn't leave my little brother."

"He'll be fine. You gotta think about yourself. You can't keep finding yourself in these situations. One time it's going to get bad. You know what I mean? Real bad."

"Forget about it. This just seems so crazy. I don't want to talk about this right now. Tell me about that weirdo guy. The guy who wanted money for your feet."

"Yeah, it was weird, like a hundred dollars for my feet. And then five hundred for my boobs."

"Did he message you back?"

"Yeah."

"For what?"

"He wanted me to make a video for him."

"A video of what?"

"He wanted me to masturbate on video and send it to him."

"And you did?"

"Yeah, why not? He's not touching me or anything. All I got to do is have a little fun and then send it off. Easiest $1,000 I've ever earned."

"I guess."

"Why don't you send me a video of you doing it and I'll send it to him so you can get some money?"

"I don't know."

"Look, it's easy. Plus, maybe you can make some money and get a bus ticket so you can get out of there and get to Cali. Besides, I would love to go to the beach with you and hang out. It would be so much fun."

"I don't know."

"Yes, you do. Let's make a video right now and I'll send it off to the guy. It'll be the easiest $1,000 bucks you'll ever make. And next week you can be on your way to Cali."

Lilly Grace's longing for Jade's acceptance clouded her judgement, leading her to discard her doubts. Initially, she recoiled at sharing intimate content, but soon, she succumbed to the thrill, lost in the moment. Unbeknownst to her, the promise of payment was a deception. Jade would transfer $1,000 from a fictitious account within twenty-four hours, paving the way for Lilly Grace's departure. Weeks later, Lilly Grace would board a Greyhound bus bound for Modesto, California, entwined in Jade's web.

10

— · —

C HAPTER 10

The valley, once shrouded in darkness, slowly awakened, bathed in the warm, golden light. In the predawn stillness, JB found solace in the Central Valley's serene landscape, the familiar stillness washing over him like a long-lost hymn.

He set off on his usual route, winding along the aqueduct channels that crisscrossed the valley like veins of the land. His feet beat a steady rhythm along Upper Lateral Three, pulling him eastward from Turlock to Denair. The channel eventually merged with the Turlock Main, guiding him southward. As he pressed on, the morning air thick with the scent of damp earth, JB's mind drifted. Paco's crew, the girl in the abandoned almond grove, the waiting DNA results—all of it churned restlessly in his thoughts.

But none of it weighed as heavily as Hannah. She was like a stone in his chest, each step tightening the knot of worry within him. The distance between them had stretched into a yawning chasm, silent and unspoken, as vast as the Central Valley itself.

He looped back toward Turlock, legs burning, but his mind couldn't quiet. The hours spent pounding the dirt offered little in the way of answers. He hit Upper Lateral Four and ran westward through Turlock's heart, where familiar streets failed to bring comfort. Golden State Boulevard was his last leg, a straight shot home, but even the six-mile stretch felt endless.

By the time JB arrived home at 7:00, he felt just as lost as when he'd set out. Inside, Hannah was a flurry of motion in the kitchen, hands busy crafting pie crusts for the church dinner she'd volunteered to host. She'd invited their Marriage Ministry table group, despite JB's protests, and included the Widman's—an invitation that had reignited a long-simmering tension between them.

Hannah, it seemed, was forever extending olive branches while JB clung stubbornly to the grievances of the past. She longed for family, for the comfort of Oklahoma holidays spent with her parents, but that was a dream lost to distance and expense. JB knew she missed them deeply. During his deployments, her parents had been her rock. Now, left to face these challenges alone, she felt their absence more keenly than ever. And JB, despite his best efforts, was no replacement.

JB conceded to hosting the church group, hoping to lift Hannah's spirits. He was eager to showcase his new smoker by preparing a mouth-watering turkey. Secretly, he sought to impress Hannah's father, a grilling expert, and prove his skills. Their shared experiences in Naval Intelligence, and the Marines, had forged a bond between them, allowing JB to connect with his father-in-law on a deeper level.

With time ticking away, JB rushed through his shower and hurried to the kitchen. He knew the smoked turkey required seven hours of preparation, and he aimed to have dinner ready by 3 o'clock in the afternoon. The clock was ticking.

JB stepped into the kitchen, Hannah looked up, her face lighting up with a mischievous grin. Flour dusted her apron, and the scent of butter and sugar filled the air. "Did you get lost out there?" she teased, pausing from kneading dough to swipe a streak of flour across her cheek. "I thought I'd have to send out a search party."

JB smirked, grateful for the levity, even if only for a moment. "Maybe I was avoiding KP duty," he shot back, stealing a quick kiss as he reached for the coffee pot. Their shared laughter felt like a rare reprieve, a brief window into what their relationship had once been—light, teasing, and uncomplicated.

But the moment was fragile, like a bubble waiting to pop. As JB turned to grab a mug, his eyes fell on the stack of pie crusts she'd already finished. The church dinner. The Widman's. The tension slid back in like a shadow across the room.

"I still don't get why you invited them," JB muttered. The lightness between them evaporated as quickly as it had appeared.

"JB, we've talked about this. They're part of the group," she replied, though the warmth in her tone was gone. She turned away, focusing on the task in front of her, as if that would soften the blow of his words. "It's important to me that we try."

JB sighed, leaning heavily against the counter. "I just... I don't see why we have to invite them; we don't really like them."

"Because it's what we're supposed to do," she said quietly, the playfulness completely erased now, replaced by something far more resigned. She glanced over her shoulder, her eyes meeting his, and in that instant, the weight of everything they weren't saying pressed down on both of them.

"What's the arrival time for everyone?" JB asked.

"Three o'clock," Hannah replied, not looking up from the dough she was rolling out. "I told them we'd serve dinner around four."

As Hannah worked, JB sneaked up behind her, dipping a finger into the pie batter on the counter. She swatted his hand with a playful grin. JB chuckled, dodging around the sink like a mischievous child.

"Perfect timing," he said with a smirk. "The turkey should be ready by then."

"How's it looking?" Hannah asked, nodding toward the smoker outside and pretending the tension was gone.

"It looks great. Why?" JB replied, trying to sound casual, though a hint of pride seeped into his voice.

"No reason," she said, her eyes sparkling with amusement.

"Really?" JB feigned offense, puffing out his chest. "You doubt my culinary skills?"

"No, I think you've got this."

JB grinned, pulling out a bottle of sweet tea from the fridge. "I'll prove it, too. I'll make sure your dad knows who the real grill master is this year."
Hannah playfully rolled her eyes. "Just make sure the ham's ready, in case."

Catching the mischievous glint in her eye, JB pretended to be offended, and a playful chase ensued around the kitchen counter. They ended near the refrigerator, where JB caught her and pulled her into a kiss. It was light, teasing at first, but the kiss lingered longer than intended.

"Ooh, really?" Jared's voice broke the moment as he walked in, raising an eyebrow at them.

JB, ever the joker, prolonged the kiss a second longer, savoring the connection. Hannah laughed softly, pulling away and returning to her pie crusts. JB ruffled Jared's hair as the boy darted past.

"Headed to the schoolyard!" Jared called over his shoulder, dashing out of the house.

"We're just letting him run off without checking now?" he asked, his tone suddenly more serious, the lightness momentarily gone.

Hannah looked up, still focused on her baking. "It's fine," she reassured him, wiping flour off her hands. "I talked to Jennie. She's down the street with a few of the boys. They'll keep an eye on him."

JB nodded but couldn't quite shake the sudden unease. He reached for a celery stick, munching absently.

Hannah glanced at him, her expression unreadable, before JB shifted the conversation. "So, please tell me we're not going to talk about the marriage book at the dinner table tonight."

Hannah paused, confused. "What?"

"You know, I get enough of the Marriage Ministry on Wednesdays. I don't need a second-round tonight."

"What are you talking about?"

"Nothing," JB sighed. "I just don't want Derek and Angie judging me all night like usual. It's like they get a kick out of it."

"Are you serious right now?"

JB recognized the warning signs but stumbled over his attempt to keep things light. "Why are you getting upset?" he asked.

"You really don't get it, do you? You're always so quick to brush off what I'm saying. You make jokes, but you never actually listen."

"I'm not brushing anything off—"

"It sounds like it," Hannah cut in, her voice laced with frustration.

For a moment, the room held its breath. The warmth from earlier now seemed distant, replaced by the weight of words left unsaid. JB took a step toward her, wanting to close the space between them, but hesitated, unsure how to bridge the growing divide.

Hannah turned back to her work, the tension thick between them, as if the very air had changed in the span of a few short minutes.

Hannah's movements became deliberate and slow. She shoved the casserole dish toward the counter, the ceramic scraping against the tile. She untied her apron, the fabric rustling as she laid it beside the dish.

"You want to know why I'm upset?" Hannah's eyes locked onto JB's. "I'm upset because, after three classes, you haven't shared a genuine concern about our relationship or family," Hannah said.

"What are you talking about? I shared details about our relationship on that first night."

"Oh, yes, 'our love story'". She mimicked with air quotes. "You barely shared anything, and I had to intervene to save you from appearing completely insensitive."

JB was stunned by the rapid escalation. One moment, they were lost in a tender kiss; the next, they were locked in a heated confrontation. The shift was jarring, leaving him reeling.

"Why are you getting so upset?" JB asked.

"I'm not upset, I'm tired," Hannah corrected. "Tired of you going through the motions. You're present, but emotionally absent. It's like our entire relationship – you're there, but not really."

"You asked me to join the class, and I did. You didn't specify how much I should participate."

"I shouldn't have to spell it out. You should want to engage, to share our struggles, and work through them with others who understand. Your indifference is suffocating me."

"Really, you think that's what those people are doing in that class?" JB asked.

"Yes, I do," Hannah replied.

"Oh, you're so naïve!"

Hannah's eyes narrowed. "What?"

"You don't see it, do you? That Brooks lady is only interested in recruiting you for her direct sales scheme, she's not genuinely supporting our marriage."

Hannah's expression fell. "What are you talking about?"

"Are you kidding me? That Brooks lady flaunts her company's water bottler and her husband's logo-emblazoned polo shirts. They aren't share nothing meaningful. It's all superficial."

"You're something else, JB."

"And the Allens? They're only here because Pastor begged them to join. He was desperate for numbers."

Hannah's eyes widened, taken aback by JB's vitriol.

"Don't even get me started on the Widman's," JB continued. "He's angling to lead the next class, padding his resume with Rotary President, Chamber of Commerce President, and Marriage Ministry leader. It's all about appearances, not genuine faith or compassion."

Hannah's face fell, her eyes filled with a mix of sadness and alarm. "Do you hear yourself, JB? When did you become so jaded? So cynical? You're tearing apart people's motives, questioning their faith...What's happened to you?"

"You think I'm jaded, Hannah? You think I'm cynical? I'm just seeing the world for what it is. I'm witnessing the darkest depths of humanity every day." He paused, collecting his thoughts. "I don't share it with you because I don't want to shatter your innocence. I don't want to break your heart." His eyes clouded, memories flooding back. "I spend my nights chasing gang members, arresting them, only to see them replaced by more. I spend my days pretending to be a vulnerable child online, luring predators into a trap. But it's not just numbers, Hannah. It's faces. It's lives." His voice trembled. "Three weeks ago, I found a sixteen-year-old girl's body in an abandoned almond grove. Raped, stabbed, and left to drown in her own pool of blood. They watched her suffer, Hannah. They watched her die." JB's eyes locked onto Hannah's; his gaze intense. "This is my reality, Hannah. This is what I see. And you wonder why I'm jaded? Why I question people's motives?"

Tears streamed down Hannah's face as JB's raw emotions unfolded before her. His pain and anger hung in the air like a heavy mist.

"It haunts me," JB confessed. "That's why I don't open up to strangers. They haven't earned the right to hear my truth."

"They may not have, but I certainly have, JB. I'm your wife, your partner. I've earned the right to share your burdens."

The FBI issued cell phone buzzed, shattering the tense silence. JB's gaze fell upon the screen, his expression grim. "Meet at HQ in 30 minutes." He drew a deep sigh knowing what it meant.

Hannah's eyes widened. "What? What's it says?"

JB hesitated, knowing he was going to have leave Hannah in this fragile state. "They want me at the office in thirty minutes?"

"For what?

"I'm assuming there is a DNA match, and they know who raped the little girl."

"So, you're going to go out today? It can't wait until tomorrow?"

"Do you hear yourself?"

"Will you be back in time for dinner this afternoon?"

"Yes, it shouldn't take long to get everyone organized and put this guy on the ground."

JB's deception tasted bitter, but he justified it as necessary evasion. He couldn't bear to exacerbate the tension, not after unveiling the darkness he confronted daily. Letting Hannah believe he'd return for dinner seemed a harmless fib, a temporary reprieve from the truth. JB craved the adrenaline rush of the impending raid, a welcome escape from the stifling superficiality of their church group. The prospect of confronting gang members, though perilous, felt more authentic than navigating the shallow relationships with the Brooks, Allens, and Widman's.

As he headed out, JB's dual worlds collided: the gritty reality of his work and the polished façade of his personal life. The lie lingered, a testament to the emotional distance growing between him and Hannah.

11

— • —

C HAPTER 11

November 14th brought a serene silence to Lee's Summit, Missouri, as a winter weather advisory cast a peaceful spell over the town. Lilly Grace settled into her living room couch, entranced by the gentle snowflakes dancing outside her window. The frozen grass transformed before her eyes, gradually surrendering to a blanket of white.

As the snowfall intensified, Lilly Grace's thoughts drifted to the impending holiday chaos. The traditional family gathering loomed, an exhausting ritual of divided loyalties. This year felt particularly daunting, following a maelstrom of challenges that left her wondering how things could worsen. Her parents' frayed nerves would likely reach a breaking point.

Dreading the Saturday afternoon family gathering, especially with her stepfather, Lilly Grace feigned illness. Her parents, their holiday spirits dampened, agreed without objection.

The morning unfolded with detachment, each family member going through the motions. Jack's frantic cries echoed from the bedroom, where Evan wreaked havoc. Meanwhile, her stepfather and mother navigated the house like strangers, avoiding eye contact and conversation. The tension was palpable, contrasting starkly with the typical holiday joy. The phrase 'two ships passing in the night' echoed in her mind, poignantly describing her parents' estrangement.

Lilly Grace longed for the chaos to subside, craving a moment of solitude. Just then, Jack and Evan tore through the living room, their energetic shrieks filling the air. The two brothers burst through the front door, Jack clinging to the advantage as Evan's feet flew out from under him on the icy walkway.

As the commotion outside subsided, Lilly Grace's stepfather waited impatiently in the minivan, engine running. Ava, lingering behind, entered the living room and settled beside Lilly Grace on the couch. For a fleeting instant, they sat together in silence, a brief respite from the turmoil.

"Are you sure you won't come with us?" she asked.

"No."

"Is everything all, right?"

Lilly Grace shrugged. "Everything is fine. I'm just not feeling well, and I don't want to be around everyone."

"Your Grandma is going to miss you."

"She's not really my grandmother. She's his mother, and honestly, I never liked her anyways."

"Lilly, that's not true. She cares about you deeply."

"Mom, you can go now. I'm not going to change my mind."

"Lilly, you've been acting very strangely lately. Is everything okay?"

"Everything's fine."

Ava's eyes narrowed. "No, really. You've been off. Where did the happy-carefree little girl who was the life of this house go? I haven't seen her lately."

Lilly Grace averted her gaze from her mother's intense scrutiny. "I'm still here, just not feeling my best."

"It's not only about today, honey. You've seemed distant for quite some time."

"And how would you notice? You're perpetually secluded in your room, hardly conscious. Now, all of a sudden, you're the caring mother. Spare me. You've been missing for the past year."

"Lilly?" Ava said.

"Honestly, Mom, you and Dad barely speak unless you're fighting. We don't want to be around that toxic environment. And what's with the strange men constantly coming and going? It's embarrassing."

"Lilly, what are you talking about?"

"Don't play dumb, Mom. I heard you offer that guy a 'two for one' deal the other day. He had the nerve to repeat it to me, thinking it was some kind of sick joke." Lilly Grace's words stung Ava, her gaze dropped, eyes fixed on the floor, unaware that her daughter had the nerve to confront her addiction troubles. "You thought I was oblivious? I know about the others too. Your drug habits don't pay for themselves. Unemployed and unmotivated, unless you count selling yourself as a job."

Ava's face contorted in shock and shame, her hand instinctively flying to Lilly Grace's face, delivering a stinging slap. Lilly Grace's head recoiled, her palm cradling her cheek. She turned to face her mother, her voice eerily calm, "Did that make you feel better."

Without another word, Lilly Grace rose from the couch and walked away, disappearing into her bedroom, leaving Ava shattered and silent.

***

Two hours passed since the house emptied, yet Lilly Grace remained quite in bed, consumed by anger and disgust. Her mind reeled with the thought of her mother's obliviousness to her stepfather's abuse. She wondered if her mother ever detected the scent of sex on his skin as he left her room and rejoined her mother.

Lilly Grace's thoughts swirled with questions. How could her mother be so blind to the truth? Was she truly naïve, or did she choose to ignore the signs? A chilling realization dawned on her that maybe her mother knew everything and simply didn't care. Maybe her addiction to antidepressants and heroin had rendered her powerless, trapping her in a cycle of silence. The thought sent a shiver down Lilly Grace's spine. Her mother's dependence had created a toxic dynamic, where speaking out seemed impossible. It was easier to feign ignorance, to pretend the abuse wasn't happening. Lilly Grace felt a deep sense of betrayal, her heart heavy with the weight of her mother's complicity.

Lilly Grace's body betrayed her, sweating and trembling as memories of her stepfather's abuse flooded her mind. The images and sounds haunted her, refusing to be silenced. She screamed until her throat ached, but the anguish persisted.

Consumed by rage, Lilly Grace lashed out at the reminders of her tormentor. She tore down curtains, ripped posters off the wall, and sought a hammer in the garage. Finding a sledgehammer instead, she wielded it with a mix of fury and desperation. With each crushing blow to her bed, she targeted the depths of her pain. The bed, a haunting reminder of her violation, remained intact – for now. Lilly Grace's hesitation was a fleeting moment of restraint, a promise of further destruction to come.

With every strike of the hefty sledgehammer, the dresser gave way. Glancing upward, she gathered her strength and swung the sledgehammer at the ceiling fan, dislodging it from its mount and leaving it dangling by the electrical wires. Taking a deep breath, she harnessed her remaining energy, directing it towards the bed, the ultimate emblem of her suffering. The sledgehammer descended, shattering the headboard and collapsing the front legs, tipping the bed sideways onto the floor.

Exhaustion overwhelmed her, and Lilly Grace collapsed, her body convulsing from the intense exertion. As she lay amidst the devastation, she surveyed the room. Furniture lay shattered, walls punctured, doors crushed. The ceiling fan dangled precariously from a single wire. Each blow had been a cathartic release, a rebellion against her stepfather's violations. Now, amidst the ruins, Lilly Grace felt drained, her screams silenced by emotional exhaustion.

As reality set in, she contemplated the consequences. Her mother and stepfather would discover the destruction, and she'd face the impossible task of explaining her actions. The daunting prospect of revealing the truth loomed before her. Would anyone believe her? Fear and uncertainty gripped her, as she wondered if she'd ever find the courage to expose the secrets hidden behind the shattered remnants of her bedroom.

Lilly Grace rose from the floor, her determination driving her to uncover the truth. She crossed the hall to her mother's room, expecting chaos, but instead found a tidy space. The folded laundry, vacuumed carpet, and streaming sunlight created an eerie sense of normalcy.

Her search began. She scoured the end table, dresser drawers, and bathroom cabinets, hunting for evidence of her mother's addiction. Ibuprofen, acetaminophen, and Pepto Bismol lined the shelves, but then, hidden behind them, a prescription bottle emerged. Zoloft, a medication for depression and anxiety, stared back at her.

A reckless impulse seized Lilly Grace. She popped three pills into her mouth, washing them down with sink water. Gazing into the mirror, she confronted the turmoil within. The prescription bottle seemed to weigh heavier, its significance daunting.

A haunting thought crept into her mind; one she'd never considered before. The bottle's power both fascinated and terrified her. With a sense of desperation, Lilly Grace grabbed a handful of Zoloft and swallowed them, the water rushing down her throat like a toxic escape.

Lilly Grace stumbled back into her ravaged room, the destruction a haunting reflection of her inner turmoil. As she gazed upon the shattered furniture and bed, a creeping sense of dread seized her. Her heart racing, palms slick with sweat, and spine dripping with perspiration, Lilly Grace felt her world unraveling. The room began to spin, a maddening vortex threatening to consume her.

Desperate for comfort, she collapsed onto the broken bed, reaching for a tattered teddy bear. Clutching it tightly, she curled up, her fragile form trembling. As the darkness closed in, Lilly Grace's consciousness slipped away, her world fading to black. The silence was oppressive, punctuated only by the soft whisper of her labored breathing.

12

— · —

C HAPTER 12

JB arrived at the FBI office in Stanislaus County right on time, his punctuality a hallmark of his professionalism. As he stepped into the briefing room, his sharp eyes immediately found Special Agent Warnall, deep in conversation with the Stanislaus County Sheriff. Warnall's eyes flicked up, meeting JB's. With a brief nod, he ended his conversation and made his way over.

The room hummed with activity, agents murmuring amongst themselves, the shuffle of papers underscoring the seriousness of what was to come. JB's chest tightened with a familiar sense of urgency. Something was off.

Warnall stopped a few feet in front of him, and JB cut straight to the point. "What's the deal?"

"We got a match on the DNA."

JB's pulse quickened. "And?"

"It belongs to Hector Valdez. Twenty-two. From Modesto. Recently released three months ago from County. Did two years for stolen vehicle possession, drugs, intent to sell, and a prior warrant violation."

JB's jaw tightened. His mind raced ahead, piecing together the implications. Another piece of the puzzle had just fallen into place—one that brought them closer to something ugly lurking just beneath the surface.

"What's his address?"

"1821 Fort Worth Street, Modesto."

JB's eyes narrowed as the name clicked in his mind. "That's WSF territory?"

"Affirmative," Warnall said with a nod. "We got the match late last night. I wanted you in first thing to assemble a team. We need to assess his associations and review tactical responses for recovery."

"Do we know for certain he's at this address?"

Warnall's eyes flicked around the room before refocusing on JB. "We've got assets on the ground, tracking him. Once we get confirmation, we move. But we need to be ready if things go south."

"Are all agencies in position for deployment?" JB's voice was sharp, focused.

"Affirmative," Warnall replied. "They'll be here by 1400. SWAT's leading, with backup from StanCo, MPD, and DEA."

"DEA?"

"Valdez's past drug charges flagged them. Plus," Warnall lowered his voice, "we've got a secondary target."

"Secondary target?"

Warnall continued, "Aerial surveillance picked up four large units north of the property. Could be growing operations."

"If Valdez catches wind of this, he'll disappear. We can't let him slip."

As they moved to finalize preparations, JB pulled out his phone, firing off quick updates to key team leaders. But amid the tactical chaos, his thoughts strayed for a moment to Hannah. Guilt twisted in his gut, but he buried it. There would be time for apologies later – at least, he hoped there would be.

With a hint of regret, JB typed a text to Hannah: "Hey love. Unexpected meeting should wrap up by 3:00. Hoping to be home by 3:30 for dinner. Fingers crossed."

He sent the message, acknowledging the uncertainty of his schedule, while holding onto the hope for an evening with Hannah.

Warnall noticed JB's distraction. "Everything okay?"

JB sighed. "Hannah's cooking dinner for our Marriage Ministry group. I'm already on thin ice."

Warnall chuckled. "Perfect timing for this op, my friend."

"If I miss this dinner, Hannah might never forgive me. My rap sheet's already long enough."

"Let's hope our assets don't spot Valdez until tomorrow."

JB's desperation grew. "For my sake, I hope so. Otherwise, you might as well bury me in the next op."

Just then, Warnall's phone rang, and he swiftly exited the room, leaving JB to his anxious thoughts.

***

It was 2:00 sharp, the briefing room buzzed with the Special Investigators Unit. All eyes fixed on the large projection screen displaying Hector Valdez's mugshot, accompanied by his extensive arrest record and active warrant. Below, a tri-view layout showcased the residence of 1821 Forth Worth Street: a frontal view, rear elevation, and aerial photography highlighting potential entry points.

Special Agent in Charge Warnall stepped up to the podium, commanding attention. "Ladies and gentlemen, today's operation targets Hector Valdez, a high-priority suspect. Our objective is to apprehend Valdez and dismantle an adjacent growing operation.

Warnall's voice was solemn, his eyes scanning the room. "We have a suspect in the brutal murder of a 16-year-old girl from Ceres, California. Her body was found between the Tuolumne River and Crows Landing Road. DNA evidence conclusively identifies Hector Valdez, released from County Jail just three months ago, as our prime suspect."

The projection screen behind Warnall displayed the suspect's information and residence. "Valdez is believed to be hiding at 1821 Forth Worth Avenue in Modesto. Our operation will unfold in two phases: surveillance and arrest."

Warnall emphasized the critical unknowns. "We need confirmation of Valdez's presence and whether he's alone or with others. Are they potential threats or hostages? This intel will dictate our tactical operation."

He acknowledged the assembled team. "We have a unified force in this room, comprising our Special Investigators Unit, FBI, DEA, ICE, and Modesto Police Department, and Stanislaus County Sheriff."

With a nod, Warnall relinquished the podium to JB, who stood at the rear of the room, surveying the unit leaders with a discerning eye. JB's tenure in the Valley had fostered familiarity and respect among the joint task force operatives. His reputation preceded him as a seasoned tactical operator, adapt at decisive action in high-pressure situations. This distinction was a testament to his military background as a special operator.

JB navigated the crowd with a deliberate, unhurried pace, exuding the calm confidence of a battle-tested veteran. His presence commanded attention, earned through experience in live fire combat. As he approached the podium, the room fell silent, anticipating his strategic outline for the operation.

JB adjusted the microphone, his voice clear and authoritative. "Thank you, Agent Warnall. I'd like to acknowledge our Violent Crimes Unit and Street Gang Units for their invaluable contributions. Intelligence suggests Mr. Valdez may be affiliated with a Norteño street gang, specifically the West Side Familia of South Modesto. While Valdez is a suspect in the rape, his involvement in the murder remains uncertain. It's crucial we apprehend him intact to uncover the events of October 31, 2018."

JB nodded to the administrative lead, who swiftly replaced Valdez's image with aerial views of the staging areas and residence. The room's atmosphere shifted as the operators focus intensified. The aerial imagery captivated the room, heightening senses and underscoring the operations' gravity. JB sense the collective tension, a palpable acknowledgment of the mission's complexity and stakes.

JB continued, "As shown, our staging area is located west of Henshaw Elementary, providing stealth access via Hatch Road and the aqueduct channel on Alpine Avenue. This will be our final checkpoint for weapon checks, last-minute target analysis, and critical communications before initiating the operation."

He pointed to the aerial image. "The go-point is the residence's entrance at Glenn Avenue and Forth Worth. The target residence, a 698 square-foot, two-bedroom, one-bath home, is situated three houses west of the intersection. Note the single-entry points at the front and rear."

JB highlighted key features. "Due to the home's layout, the front door likely offers a direct line of sight to the rear door. The rear shed may be an occupancy shed, indicating potential additional occupants. Be prepared for a potentially crowded residence." He emphasized operational caution. "Exercise extreme vigilance in weapon handling and protocols. The residence is obstructed by a large tree and surrounded by shrubbery, including the rear fence line, posing potential concealment risks."

Special Agent in Charge Warnall returned to the podium, his expression serious. "Gentleman, I'd like to add a crucial update. We've identified a secondary target, the residence to the north, visible in the aerial photos. It appears to have at least four large units, indicative of potential illegal drug operations." He paused for emphasis, "We're actively working to secure a search warrant for this premise, to be executed concurrently with our primary operation. This secondary target presents an opportunity to disrupt potential criminal activity and dismantle a larger network."

Warnall's gaze swept the room, ensuring everyone understood the expanded scope. "Let's capitalize on this intelligence and maximize our impact."

JB returned to the microphone, "Gentleman, this operation presents multiple threats, demanding our utmost focus. Considering the subject's criminal history, the severity of the crime, and the secondary target, our objective is to secure a comprehensive perimeter around both residences. My preference is to execute a surprise breach of the primary residence and secondary target simultaneously, maximizing tactical advantage. We still lack critical information on potential co-inhabitants at both locations. As Agent Warnall mentioned, the surveillance phase will provide crucial threat assessments for both targets, informing our operational decisions."

The room fell silent, operators absorbing the briefing, their minds racing with the accelerated timeline. Typically, surveillance phases unfolded over weeks or months, meticulously gathering intel on patterns and behaviors. However, the DNA results had injected a sense of urgency, fueled by the community's outrage and fear. The heinous crime had left a young girl's life taken, and the public demanded swift justice. The agency's rapid progression through the surveillance and arrest phases reflected this pressing need for closure. Operators understood the gravity of the situation, their focus intensifying as they prepared to bring Valdez to justice.

DEA Special Agent, Thomas Shelter sat in the front row, abruptly he raised his hand, his voice inquiring, "Do we have definitive confirmation that Valdez is still in the city, or is the Fort Worth residence simply his last known address?" He sought clarification, "Has there been any recent surveillance or intel suggesting he's still local, or is this operation based on outdated information?"

Another DEA Special Agent, Tony Cardena, chimed in, seeking further clarification. "Regarding the secondary target, are the occupants' known criminals or is this merely a suspicion-based operation? Crucially, are there juveniles or young children present at either residence?"

Agent Cardena pressed for details, "Do we have intel on the individuals potentially involved in illegal activities, or is this a precautionary measure based on the proximity to the primary target?"

JB addressed the concerns, "Excellent questions. Currently, we lack confirmation of the primary target's presence at the residence. Our covert surveillance assets are gathering intel, identifying breach points, and monitoring the secondary target."

He outlined the operational framework, explaining that this room would serve as the Tactical Operations Center (TOC), staffed by himself and Criminal Incident Response Group personnel. Field agents would communicate with the TOC via radio and cell phone. Meanwhile, the FBI command post, managed by SAC Warnall and agents, would be established on a separate floor.

JB detailed the surveillance plan, assigning color designations to the target house. White for the front, Green for the left side, Red for the right, and Black for the rear. He described the team assignments, explaining that Team One would approach from Butte Ave, flowing south on Fort Worth. Team Two would hold at Glenn Avenue for a back-alley approach, while Team Three would maintain a fixed position at the Glenn Avenue and Forth Worth intersection. Team Four would utilize an armored approach with tactical foot support.

"On command," JB concluded, "we'll execute the warrant with a surprise attack." He paused, inviting further questions from the room.

The room was silent, anticipation hanging in the air as everyone awaited crucial intel from the surveillance team. JB's gaze drifted to the clock, 2:45. His mind wandered to Hannah, wondering how she'd responded to his previous text. He discreetly checked his personal phone, revealing four missed calls from Hannah, no voicemails. A knot formed in his stomach. He couldn't' leave, not now, with the operation urgency escalating.

JB hesitated, weighing his options. A call would only ignite another argument. He opted for a text, typing a brief message: "won't' make it for dinner. Will explain later." He slipped the phone back into his pocket, rejoining Warnall and the team as they finalized preparations for the impending raid on Hector Valdez.

JB's focus returned to the mission, but the tension with Hannah lingered, a nagging concern in the back of his mind.

13

CHAPTER 13

At 4 o'clock, the surveillance team remained vigilant, but Hector Valdez was nowhere in sight at 1821 Fort Worth Avenue. A rusted-out van, strategically positioned at the corner of Fort Worth and Glenn Avenue, served as a static lookout post. From this discreet vantage, the team had a clear view of the residence's entrance and any potential exits. Meanwhile, a second group kept watch from the north, stationed at the corner of Butte Avenue and Fort Worth, expanding their coverage. The agents sat tight, their gaze unwavering, every twitch in the shadows potentially signaling Valdez's return.

The afternoon sun hung low, casting long shadows across the quiet streets. Despite the stillness, the neighborhood simmered with an underlying tension—the kind you feel before something breaks. The surveillance teams, though hidden, were coiled like springs, ready to snap into action. Every second counted, and they knew that once Valdez reappeared, they'd need to move fast.

Several blocks away, JB sat behind the wheel of his Toyota Tacoma, parked along the railroad tracks on 8th Street. The distant hum of traffic faded into the background as he stared at his phone. He had sent a quick message to Manny, requesting an urgent meeting at Jessica's Taqueria—a well-known spot along Modesto's famed "taco truck row." As JB waited, his thoughts drifted to Hannah. The impending confrontation loomed like a dark cloud on the horizon. She deserved better, he knew that. The job had consumed him—again—and the space between them only seemed to widen with each passing day.

A knock on his window snapped him back to the present. Manny had arrived. JB rolled down the window and handed over a manila envelope. Manny took it without a word, tearing it open to reveal a photo of Hector Valdez. His eyes locked onto the image, taking in every detail, his brow furrowing with intensity.

"What's this supposed to be?" Manny asked. His gaze lingered on the photo, his expression unreadable. JB awaited his response, knowing that Manny's connections on the street could prove invaluable in tracking down Valdez.

"I was hoping you could tell me," JB replied.

"Homes, why you got my house lighted up on this last page?" He tapped the red mark on the aerial view, his tone laced with a mix of curiosity and wariness.

JB leaned in closer. "You know that's Hector Valdez. Don't play with me," JB said. "We believe Valdez might be hiding in plain sight. His connection to the WSF territory, specifically this area, suggests he might be seeking refuge among familiar faces."

Manny's gaze lingered on the highlighted area, his mind racing with connections. "You think he's hiding with someone I know?"

JB nodded. "A Norteño gang member, with priors for drugs and car theft, pulls up with a residence inside WSF territory. You telling me he's not connected with Paco?"

"I don't know what he's got cookin' with that asshole. Why don't you go ask Paco? Or better yet, if you know who he is and where he lives, why don't you go arrest him Mr. FBI?"

JB felt his jaw tighten, a familiar heat rising in his chest, but he kept his composure. He knew better than to rise to Manny's bait, especially now when the stakes were this high.

"Don't play stupid with me Manny. You know everybody in the Deep South Side. I know it and you know it. So, are you still looking me straight in the eye and trying to tell me you've never heard of this guy?

"Man, I don't know every scum bag that lives in our hood."

"Why don't you do me a favor Manny, take a look at that last page." He watched Manny sift through to the last page in the envelope. "Pull it out. Give it a good long look."

Manny pulled the page all the way out of the envelope sleeve. He stared intently at the image of the sixteen-year-old girl. Her decomposed and rigor mortis body lay stiffened with ruptured blisters from the fluid build-up in the internal organs. Her frail petite body is now nearly twice its size due to the bloating. Manny put his hand over his mouth as if he could smell the foul odor of her decomposed body through the photo. He put the photo back in the envelope and handed it through the window to JB.

"What do you want me to say homes?"

"I want information on who would do something like that to a young girl. Her life is over and the people that did this might get away with it if good people don't come forward and give us information to apprehend these perpetrators."

"Up to this point you've asked me for information on gang connections and small-time kids who were slinging dope in the hood. What you're asking me now is putting a target on my back."

"Choices have consequences Manny."

"Homes, they got people watching me come and go from my house. I can feel it. I can feel them watching me."

"You're paranoid Manny."

"Somebody came and asked my mom's if I lived at the house. And it wasn't some white dude in a suit. You catch my drift."

Manny pivoted his feet in the ground. He cautiously looked around the small parking lot.

"Manny, do you know Hector Valdez? Do you know if he's still living at 1821 Fort Worth?"

Manny banged his hand against the window ledge of J.B.'s door. "Fuckin' 'eh homes! You ain't listenin' to me. I keep tellin' you what's up. They gonna put me in the ground right along with this little girl if I keep tellin' you what's up on these streets."

"Do you know Hector Valdez?"

Manny's words spilled out in a frantic torrent, his hands gesturing emphatically. "Hector Valdez? That pendejo's a wannabe, thought he was above the game. Got busted for his own arrogance."

JB's eyes locked in on Manny's, processing the information. "So, you're saying Paco Ramirez might know something about the girl's involvement in prostitution?"

Manny nodded vigorously. "Paco's the one who runs that shit. If she was in the life, he'd know."

"And Eric Avina? What's his connection?

Manny's expression turned grave. "Nothin' moves in this hood without Avina's approval. If Valdez was involved in a gang-related incident, Avina's got his fingers in it."

JB's grip on his notebook tightened, the leads unfolding like a dark web. Paco Ramirez, Eric Avina, and Hector Valdez – each name a thread in the intricate tapestry of corruption and violence. He knew that unraveling this web would lead him deeper into the heart of darkness.

"I don't know where Valdez is, okay?" Manny said. "I'm not his fuckin' babysitter."

"Find out. I need to know if he's still in the neighborhood."

Manny scoffed, crossing his arms. "Homes, you're really pushing me against it. I'm tryin' to stay under the radar."

"You're already on the radar, Manny. Cooperate, and I might give you some breathing room."

Manny's eyes flashed with anger, his fists clenching at his sides, but he knew he was cornered. "Fine, shit," he spat, his voice sank with frustration. "I'll ask around, okay? But you gotta leave me the fuck alone."

JB didn't flinch. "You call me the minute you've got details. Don't even think about disappearing, Manny. I will find you."

For a moment, the two men stared each other down, the silence heavy with unspoken threats. JB held Manny's gaze for a beat longer before turning away, pulling the truck into gear. Gravel crunched under the tires as he drove off, leaving Manny standing there, seething with pent-up anger. But beneath that fury was something else—an awareness of just how fragile his situation had become. The thread holding his freedom felt dangerously thin, and with each passing second, it frayed just a little more.

As JB disappeared down the street, Manny let out a frustrated breath, his mind already racing through names and places. He hated being boxed in like this, but he knew one thing for sure—JB wasn't bluffing.

***

The Phillips home buzzed with activity as guests began to arrive. First through the door were Derek and Angie Widman, their cheerful greetings filling the space. Close behind, Yates Widman strode in, sporting a polo layered with a sweater and tan khaki pants. His slightly stiff entrance earned a quiet chuckle from Hannah and Jared, who exchanged a glance, sharing the unspoken amusement.

Soon after, Jonathan and Melanie Brooks made their entrance, their three-year-old daughter clinging to Melanie's leg while their five-year-old son darted into the room. Hannah couldn't help but notice Jonathan's branded polo and Melanie's water bottle, both emblazoned with their direct sales logo. She still felt a pang of skepticism, but had to grudgingly admit JB had been right about the Brooks.

The Allens arrived next, their ten-year-old son and twelve-year-old daughter in tow. Hannah greeted them warmly, but her mind was elsewhere—flitting between the guests and the kitchen, wondering if the turkey had turned out all right after the rushed preparation.

The dining room table gleamed under soft candlelight, the floral arrangements, charger plates, and fine China adding an air of elegance. Jared took pride in helping his mother set the scene, carrying in the smoked turkey with a smile and a comment about finishing the job in JB's absence. His words struck a bittersweet chord in Hannah, a reminder of the void JB's work often left behind.

As the guests settled into their seats, Hannah couldn't shake her lingering worry that the turkey might be dry. Hosting had felt more challenging than usual, balancing the demands of the day, the food, and the guests, all while JB remained conspicuously absent.

Steve Allen, with his calm demeanor and deep voice, led the grace. His polished words reflected his role as a deacon, and Hannah silently acknowledged the pastor's wisdom in recommending the Allen family for the marriage ministry class. As the plates began circulating, the low hum of polite conversation filled the room. There was warmth in the air, but it was tempered by a faint strain—an undercurrent that Hannah couldn't quite place.

Carrie Allen leaned into Hannah and said, "Hannah, I'm sorry JB wasn't able to join us for dinner tonight."

"It's okay, he got called in on a case today and it's pretty important."

Eavesdropping on the conversation, Angie Widman interjected, "It must be so hard to have him always gone for work. I couldn't imagine having a husband leave as often as he does with such irregular hours."

Hannah observed the pretentious tone of voice of Angie Widman. There were reasons her friend circle was limited. But as usual, Hannah Davis responded with class.

"We're sort of used to it after twelve years in the military."

"Yes, but you have to do all this work by yourself, and he isn't around to help. I don't know how you do it," Angie continued.

As dinner progressed, Hannah tried to maintain a cheerful demeanor. She engaged in small talk with the guests, her smile a practiced mask over her true feelings. Angie Widman chatted animatedly about their recent family trip, and Hannah made an effort to show genuine interest, nodding and responding with enthusiasm. Yet, every laugh, every lighthearted comment seemed to amplify the emptiness she felt in JB's absence.

When Jonathan Brooks shared a funny anecdote about their kids' antics, Hannah forced a laugh, but her mind was elsewhere. The description of the little girl found in the abandoned almond grove haunted her thoughts, mixing with her frustration over JB's choice of work over family. Each story and joke felt like a reminder of the reality JB faced daily—one she was struggling to comprehend and accept.

As Steve Allen led the conversation into a discussion about community and support, Hannah tried to focus on the positive aspects. She interjected with observations about how grateful she was for the support of friends and community. But even as she spoke, her words felt hollow, a mere reflection of her desire to bridge the growing chasm between her and JB.

Jared, ever the supportive son, helped keep the conversation flowing. He excitedly recounted his day, his enthusiasm a stark contrast to Hannah's internal struggle. She leaned into him, feeling both pride and sadness. In the midst of the social interaction, she struggled to keep her own emotions at bay, offering smiles and polite laughter, even as her heart ached.

After the guests left, Hannah found herself alone in the quiet of her home. The house, now echoing with the whispers of the night, felt both comforting and isolating. She retreated to her bedroom, closing the door behind her. The weight of the day's events and her ongoing frustration with JB's absences pressed heavily on her shoulders.

Sitting on the edge of her bed, Hannah picked up her Bible again, the pages worn from frequent use. She opened it to a passage she had read earlier, but the words seemed distant, failing to provide the solace she had hoped for. She prayed once more, her voice trembling as she spoke. She prayed for strength to understand JB's world, for the little girl and her family, and for peace within her own heart.

The room was dimly lit, the only sound the soft rustle of pages and her quiet, halting prayers. Tears began to fall, her pleas for peace mingling with her tears of frustration. The chasm between her and JB seemed as wide as ever, and the more she tried to bridge it, the more elusive the connection felt.

Eventually, exhausted from the emotional turmoil, Hannah set the Bible aside and lay down, staring at the ceiling. The peace she had sought throughout the day remained just out of reach, leaving her with the harsh reality of her loneliness and the ongoing strain of JB's career on their relationship. As she drifted into a fitful sleep, her mind continued to churn with unanswered questions and a deep, aching desire for resolution.

***

JB and Warnall were in the TOC with a few of the Stanislaus County Sheriff's officers when he received a text from Manny. The text read, "You owe me, call for details."

JB tapped Warnall on the shoulder, "We got something. Hold on." He dialed Manny with eager anticipation. "Manny, what's the word?"

"Valdez's not at Fort Worth."

"Where's he at?"

"He's a mile away stowed up in a trashed-out RV on Olivero Street."

"Olivero? Olivero? Why does that sound familiar?"

"Olivero's a dump homes. The entire street should be bulldozed. Hell, I don't even walk down that piece of shit street. It's nothing but a bunch of migrants living twenty deep in the back of trailers and shit."

"Why do I vaguely remember that street?"

"Cause man, we met there a few weeks back when we ate Marisol's. That's on the corner of Olivero and Crows Landing Road."

"Is it a home or a back yard? What's it looks like where he's staying?"

"It's a home on the street side but behind the home is another building that houses like fifty people. He ain't in either of those. From what I hear, he's stored up in the back of the lot in a rundown RV. It's a bad place, homes. He's gotta be in a bad way if he's stickin' it out in that POS."

"Manny, I owe you big time. We'll catch up down the line."

"Like I said homes, you owe me big time for this one. I'm thinkin' a little vacation or something."

"Yeah, yeah, we'll see what happens."

Warnall was listening intently to JB's call. As soon as JB ended the call with Manny, Warnall already had a team headed toward Olivero Street to get eyes on Valdez. JB immediately sent an alert to all personnel involved with the Tactical Operation Command to return to the TOC for briefing. JB instructed administrative staff to provide an aerial view of Olivero Street. The section of Olivero Street was known for junk yards, makeshift greenery houses, and multi-family residences. On first impression, JB clearly understood why this section of Modesto was referred to as "Little Tijuana". As he scanned an aerial view on Google Maps, he realized the recovery site of the girl in the vacant lot was less than one mile away. He tried to prevent his mind from wondering if the young girl was raped in this dilapidated RV in the back lot of the residence. He wondered what a little girl was doing with a man like Hector Valdez. But then the reality of life on the streets in a neighborhood like the Deep South Side was different than any experience he could have imagined as a child.

JB was amazed at the news report and how they depicted a sixteen-year-old girl found murdered in a dirt lot in South Modesto. The indications were a mother and father grieving the loss of their little girl. The candlelight vigils at the scene of the crime painted the picture of a beloved girl whose life was suddenly taken. A life that was full of promise that would never be fulfilled. In contrast to the reports, when JB entered the home to interview the mother of the girl, he found a thirty-one-year-old woman who wore the eyes of a life that saw more than any person should ever see. The marks on her arms provided evidence of an addiction problem. The house was dark and dirty with three and five-year-olds screaming at their mother. The first words out of her mouth when JB introduced himself was, "I already spoke to the cops about that little bitch. What do you want?" A life full of promise he thought. Yes, a life full of promise that was taken away the moment she breathed her first breath of air. Did the news reports tell that story?

By now, the TOC was full of agents from the FBI, DEA, and Stanislaus County Sheriff's Office. The room was buzzing with excitement as word spread of the positive ID on Hector Valdez. The operation was a go pending final logistics and operation status update. At 7:30 in the evening, Hector Valdez would be sitting in a basement office at the Stanislaus County Courthouse. And sitting across the table from him would be JB Phillips.

14

—•—

C HAPTER 14

It was Wednesday evening, 6 p.m. when JB dialed Hannah's number, leaving a voicemail: "Hey, Hannah, it's me. I'm sorry, but I'll be working late tonight. We've got a breakthrough in the case, and I need to see it through." Hannah listened. She'd heard this excuse before – a lead, an interrogation, a case demanding his attention. It was always something. For the fourth time in six weeks, JB wouldn't be joining her at their Marriage Ministry class. Hannah felt a familiar sting of disappointment and frustration. She'd attend alone, again. Results drove JB's world, but Hannah craved connection, commitment, and shared priorities. She deleted the voicemail, her heart heavy with silent sorrow.

With renewed determination, Hannah strode across the parking lot, her chin held high. The weight of others' judgement, once a burden, now felt insignificant. She had reached a turning point, a moment of liberation. As she entered the room, familiar faces turned her away, their eyes filled with a mix of curiosity and sympathy. But Hannah no longer felt the sting of their unspoken criticism. She stood tall, her confidence radiating from within.

For the first time in a long time, Hannah Phillips was unapologetically herself, unfazed by the opinions of others. Her marriage, her struggles, and her triumphs were hers alone. She refused to be defined by the whispers of others. With a quiet strength, Hannah was ready to face the evening's discussion, her heart filled with a newfound sense of self-assurance and independence.

Hannah's footsteps echoed in the hallway as she walked away from Room 105A, Jared's enthusiastic chatter fading into the distance. She smiled, grateful for his friendships at church. As she passed other couples, their warmth and togetherness seemed to accentuate her solitude. Hannah's pace slowed, her heart with longing. She felt like an outsider, observing the intimate connections of others.

Approaching her classroom, Hannah hesitated, tempted to turn back and escape the discomfort. But then, a gentle touch on her shoulder arrested her retreat.

Mrs. Adams' kind face and warm smile offered a sense of comfort. "Hi, Hannah, how are you tonight?" she asked, her voice soft and genuine.

Hannah's defenses weakened, and she felt a lump form in her throat. Maybe, just maybe, she didn't have to face this alone.

"Hi, Mrs. Adams," Hannah replied, forcing a smile.

"Is everything okay, sweetie?" she asked.

Hannah wrapped her arms tightly around her stomach, as though trying to hold herself together. She shifted her weight, her gaze dropping, as she fought to control her emotions. The facade of bravado was slipping, like a dam on the verge of bursting.

Barb placed a reassuring hand on Hannah's shoulder. "Hey, come here," she said, guiding Hannah into a warm embrace. "Is JB at work tonight?"

The kindness and compassion in Barb's gesture proved too much for Hannah. Tears began to flow, and she surrendered to the emotional release, letting Barb hold her as she cried.

The subtle distinction in Barb's wording wasn't lost on Hannah. "Again" would have implied a recurring pattern, a hint of criticism. But Barb's thoughtful phrasing, "tonight", acknowledged the situation without judgement.

Hannah's gaze met Barb's, her eyes welling up with tears. She nodded. "Yes, he's working...tonight."

Barb's expression conveyed understanding and empathy. She didn't push for details, simply offered a supportive presence. Hannah felt a sense of gratitude toward this kind-hearted woman, who seemed to understand the unspoken struggles.

In that moment, Hannah's defenses crumbled, and she deepened her hug with Barb. Tears flowed freely, a mix of sadness, frustration, and relief. Barb held her tightly, a silent guardian of Hannah's emotions.

Hannah's gaze drifted into the distance, lost in thought. The unspoken question lingered, why hadn't she said "again"? The truth stung – JB's absence had become a pattern.

The curious glances from the ladies at her table shuttered her heart. Whispers of marital issues, divorce, and speculation swirled around her. Hannah's defenses, honed from years of military life, began to crumble.

Barb's gentle voice interrupted her thoughts. "Hannah, I could use some quiet time tonight. Would it be okay with you if we skipped tonight's class and went to the chapel to talk?"

More tears welled up, and Hannah's voice caught in her throat. She nodded silently, overwhelmed by the kindness and understanding in Barb's offer. Together, they slipped out of the classroom, seeking the serenity of the chapel. The soft glow of candles and the peaceful atmosphere enveloped them, a refuge from the turmoil within. In this sacred space, Hannah's tears flowed freely, and Barb listened with a compassionate heart, offering a haven for her emotions.

Barb's eyes sparkled, and a gentle smile spread across her face. "Oh, honey, love is about perseverance and redemption. My Chuck and I have been married for over 40 years, but our journey together began long before that and don't think it hasn't been without its ups and downs."

Hannah leaned in, intrigued. "I can't imagine Mr. Adams any other way than the kind, gentle soul he is today."

Barb chuckled. "Well, let's just say he had a rebellious streak back in the day. My father, a stern man, didn't approve of Chuck's wild ways. He thought Chuck wasn't good enough for me."

"No way! Really."

Barb nodded, a faraway look in her eyes. "Yes, really. But Chuck proved himself, and my father eventually saw the good in him. It's a testament to the power of love and faith."

As Barb shared her story, Hannah felt a sense of connection, realizing that even the most seemingly perfect relationships have their challenges and triumphs.

Barb continued. "Yes. One night he came to talk to my father. You know, back in those days boys still had to ask permission to do those kinds of traditional things. Well, they had a conversation in my father's office, and my father told Chuck that he would not give him his blessing because my father would not allow his daughter to be courted by a man who was unequally yoked."

"He did not!

Barb chuckled. "He sure did."

"What did Mr. Adam's say?"

"He hadn't gone to church a day in his life. There wasn't much he could say in return."

"How old were the two of you when this conversation happened?"

"We were just about to graduate high school."

"What happened after that?"

"Chuck joined the Army after high school. I went off to college. And I didn't see or hear from him for the next four years."

"So now I'm dying to know. How did you get back together?"

"After college I returned to Turlock and lived with my parents again. Back in those days a young lady didn't live alone, unmarried. One day, I was at the grocery store and this tall handsome man walked up behind me and whispered, *you're the prettiest thing I've seen in four years.*"

"Smooth Mr. Adams. Smooth. I knew he had game."

"Yes, that game is what my father was trying to protect me from I suppose. By this time, we had transitioned from the 1950's and into the early 1960's. The world was changing rapidly, and the old traditions and culture started to fade. I wasn't 18 anymore so I didn't exactly ask permission this time around. I think Chuck was more determined to prove my father wrong and win his approval than he was worried about winning my affection. I was certainly shocked when he started to attend church with me on Sunday mornings. Well anyways, it must have worked because 18 months later we were engaged."

"That was a quick courtship."

"Oh honey, I was in love with him ever since we were five years old. I don't call that a quick courtship. And we were married right here in this chapel."

The two ladies looked around the old chapel. Hannah held her palms to her cheeks getting lost in the story.

"Barb, what a fairytale."

"Hannah, you see us today some fifty years later. All the scars have scabbed over, and the decades smoothed them out. Those early years were a real struggle. Chuck's been sober for the past forty-five years. It was a hard adjustment for him coming back from Korea and integrating into the real world. Especially a world that was changing so quickly."

Barb paused for a moment. She stared at the ceiling. Hannah noticed the tears forming on the edges of her eyes. She reached down and touched her hand.

"It's been a long time since I've talked about this. And to tell you the truth, I didn't realize I would be so emotional."

Barb patted the corner of her eyes, and then continued. "By this point we were married for five years, and Chuck was bouncing around from one job to another. It didn't seem like he could stay employed for more than six months. I had stopped working because that's what new wives did back in those days. I was almost 28 years old. Most of my girlfriends were on to their second and third children by this point. And Chuck and I still didn't have any children."

Hannah squeezed Barb's hand tightly. She wiped away the tears from her cheeks, and said, "But I see you with your kids and all your grandchildren every week?"

"It's a story that hasn't been shared in a long time. Mainly because after all these years it just doesn't seem relevant anymore. Our children are all adopted. All our grandchildren are blessings from those adoptions. And frankly, our kids are our life, and it doesn't matter if they came from my womb or through an adoption agency. Those three kids were chosen by God, and he chose us to give them a good home."

By now, the tears fell uncontrollably down Hannah's face. She rubbed her red cheeks, embarrassed by the emotion.

"And Chuck, when we learned that I was unable to have kids, he is the one who told me that God would provide. And not only did God provide, but through the ordeal, God helped Chuck realize that he needed the Bible more than the whiskey. It's one thing to show up to church every week and listen to the pastor. It's an entirely different experience when you immerse yourself in the community of church, read the Bible and pray daily. You must talk to God. When you start laying your problems at his feet, he will move mountains and earth for you."

There was a long pause as the ladies held on to the moment.

"Hannah, are you just walking in and out of these doors weekly or are you truly trusting God and laying your problems at His feet? I mean in real honest and tearful conversations."

Hannah let go of Barb's hand and shifted back in the pew. It was a gut punch. A sweet and sincere knockout blow. It was set up with grace and sensitivity. It was the type of punch that does the most damage. The one you don't see coming. Hannah didn't know whether to be angry or relieved. She never realized those two emotions could hold the same space at the same time.

"I don't know Barb," Hannah paused to carefully choose her next words.

"Hannah, you've been coming to my church for nearly three years. Since you and JB moved to California. I see the two of you come and go. You're the last ones in and the first ones out. Your life isn't any of my business, but from what I can see, it's not anyone else's business either. And that is a dangerous and lonely place to be. When I see you, I see myself nearly fifty years ago. I see a woman who cries herself to sleep every night. I see a woman who loves a man so deeply that she's willing to hold on so tightly. I see a woman who is broken and in need of a lifeline. I can't sit here and tell you that life turns out just the way we want it to. All our stories are different. But what I can say is when you give it to God, and not just a piece of it, but all of it to God, you'll be amazed at how your story ends up."

"You're right. A lot is going on right now and I do need to give it to God. And yes, with JB's workload I've had to go it alone a lot more lately. But his work goes in cycles, and this, like all the other times, will come to an end. And we'll get back to spending more time together."

"I didn't invite you in here to press you on your personal business. In fact, I don't think I joined the two of us together. I think God put me at your table in this class. My healing journey of grace happened so many decades ago. I've forgotten just how powerful and amazing God is and how he cared so much for me during those turbulent times early in our marriage. I didn't ask for my challenges and obstacles when I found myself unable to have children and with a husband who I love but he was unable to figure out his own demons."

Barb paused again and Hannah sensed she was studying her reaction. She continued, "May I give you a scripture to read and pray upon this week?" Hannah was amazed at how Barb would always ask a question knowing the other person would never say no. Hannah just nodded in agreement.

"A scripture that carried me through some very dark days, was 2 Corinthians 12:10. It reads 'That is why, for Christ's sake, I delight in weaknesses, in insults, in hardships, in persecutions, in difficulties. For where I am weak, then I am strong."

The two ladies embraced. Hannah felt comforted knowing someone she admired shared a similar past to her own. Suddenly, she didn't feel so alone.

"Now Hannah Phillips, would you do this old lady a favor and escort me back to my husband?"

As the two ladies walked through the halls of First Baptist Church, Barb continued to share stories of perseverance. And little did Hannah Phillips know, in the not-too-distant future, she would have her own story of obstacles to overcome.

15

CHAPTER 15

Eric's thoughts were a whirlwind as he considered the Ghost's request. He required access to arrest records to uncover potential infiltrators within the WSF. While Paco and he possessed member records, forging a link with the Stanislaus County Sheriff's Office was essential. A name came to mind – Anita Lopez, an old friend from his youth. Despite their complex history, Eric was hopeful that their shared past might pave the way for assistance.

Memories of numerous nights spent pushing the limits of adolescent desire flooded back, their bond an intricate weave of affection, desire, and teenage defiance. Their parting was less than idyllic, yet Eric remained optimistic that any bitterness on Anita's part had not fully set in.

Choosing a subtle method to avoid leaving a digital footprint, Eric had a local youth deliver a message to Anita, sweetened with a $100 note, inviting her to Cardenas Market. The note hinted at additional payment should she agree to meet at 6 p.m.

Eric's iconic 1962 Chevy Impala, painted in distinctive corona cream, was parked outside Cardenas. The car was a well-known emblem of Eric's presence in the Deep South Side, garnering both attention and respect. As the time neared, Eric's anticipation intensified. Would Anita show up, ready to delve into their complex history and offer her help? The Impala's engine purred quietly, reflecting Eric's patience and strategic risk-taking.

Promptly, Anita emerged from the Cardenas entrance. Her features, marked by a hint of wariness, fixed on the Impala. Eric watched, appreciating her form as she made her way to the vehicle surveying her surroundings.

"What is this shit?" Anita asked as she threw the $100 bill through the window and onto the on the passenger seat.

Memories of his time with Anita flooded back, colored by both nostalgia and regret. It had been a year after Anita had given birth to her first son when he'd reconnected with her. She was nineteen, overwhelmed by the demands of new motherhood and the absence of her boyfriend, who was serving time in County Jail.

Eric had found himself drawn back into her life, not just out of lingering affection but also a genuine concern for her well-being. Their visits had been filled with a mix of old familiarity and new responsibilities. He remembered the way she had introduced him to her baby, the way her eyes had lit up when he played with the little boy. It was a brief respite for Anita from the daily grind of poverty and single parenthood.

But the moment her boyfriend returned from jail; everything had shifted. Eric's visits had abruptly ceased. He could still recall the tension in Anita's voice when she had mentioned her boyfriend's return, a subtle indication that their relationship had resumed despite its turbulent history. Within months, Anita was pregnant again, and her boyfriend was back behind bars. Eric's departure had only deepened her sense of abandonment.

Now, as he stared at Anita through the Impala window, he saw traces of the young woman he had known, but time had weathered her. The challenges she faced had etched lines of worry and fatigue on her face, replacing the youthful idealism they once shared. The weight of their unresolved history hung between them, a reminder of the choices and consequences that had shaped their lives.

Eric reached into his pocket and pulled out a stack of bills. He counted a thousand dollars out and placed them on the passenger seat. "Get in. Let's talk."

"You think I need your money?"

"Listen, give me a few minutes. Besides, if you do what I ask, they'll be a lot more than a thousand dollars in it for you."

"So, you want me to do something illegal for you?"

Eric shrugged his shoulders and patted the seat once again. "Please, just get in the car."

Anita poked her head above the car and looked around the parking lot of Las Cardenas Market. It had been quite a few years since she had been a hood rat girl chasing gang bangers in the Deep South Side. It felt like a lifetime ago and the last thing she wanted was to feel like she was back on the streets, and worse, indebted to Eric Avina. She looked back down at the seat and the thousand dollars. The eighteen dollars an hour she was making at the Sheriff's Office wasn't paying all her bills. Feeding her three kids and the expense of youth sports was draining her bank account. The temptation of wondering how much more was going to be offered was too much to pass up.

"I ain't doing no illegal shit for you," she said as she relented and got into the car. "You got that?"

Eric reached his arm across the back of the seat and leaned in toward Anita. "Calm down, alright."

"Calm down? It's been six years since you even came around my house or even took the time to talk to me. And you have the nerve to send a little gang banging boy to my house with a hundred-dollar bill. What is that kid, eleven years old? You training 'em up that young these days? Shit, tell me to calm down."

Eric's hand moved from the back of the seat to the top of her shoulder blade. He gently caressed the top of her back. Anita flinched at the subtle pressure of his hand. Eric rubbed with a little more pressure. He could feel the tension in her back ease and her body fell into the seat.

"I was wrong for not calling or talking to you since, you know. But life's gotten busy and complicated for all of us."

"Complicated? That's what you're calling it?"

"How are the kids doing?"

Eric knew she wasn't ready to hear what he wanted her to do. It was going to take some time for her to forgive their history.

"They're fine. What's it to you?"

"How's David doing?"

"He's fine."

"I know he's fine. But how is he doing?"

"Why do you suddenly care? You stopped caring when you stopped coming around."

"I heard he was playing soccer. How's it going?"

Anita's tough exterior started to melt away as she looked into the eyes of the man who she had loved ever since she was a little girl on Imperial Avenue. Her body relaxed, and so did her armor.

"It's good. He's actually pretty good. He's fast, you know. He can handle the ball really good. He practices in the yard all day."

"That's good. I'm glad he's doing well. And the other two? How are they?"

The two spent the next ten minutes talking about kids, family, and generally catching up on the last six years. As much as Eric was interested in Anita's family, he knew it was time to ask her for the favor.

"I'm glad to hear everyone's doing good." Eric paused for a moment, as he tried to think of a way to ask what he knew was a question that would not be well received.

"What? What is it?" Anita asked.

"How would you like to make a few thousand bucks?"

"I knew it. What you want me to do?"

"We're working on something big. It could bring us all a nice payday. You know what I mean. But we need some help to get it off. I'm hearing we may have a rat in our crew. I want to make sure everyone that's ridin' with the WSF is legit. You know what I mean?"

"How's that involve me?"

"Cause girl, you work at the County Jail, and I need a list of all our crew who's been arrested."

"I don't know who all's in your crew."

"I'll get you the list, you just need to cross reference it for me."

"What'd you want me to do, look up these assholes one by one?"

"I don't know how you can do it. Look at the list and let me know what you think is the best way to do it."

"How many names we talkin' about?"

"I don't know, about a hundred, hundred and fifty?"

"Shit, that's a lot. Don't you think somebody's going to notice me looking up that many people?"

"I just need to know if they've been arrested. Look, I can go through the list and narrow it down."

"The list will be narrowed down significantly depending on whether they're juveniles or adults. All the juvenile cases will be sealed and I'm not sure I can even access that information."

Eric reviewed the list with Anita and marked all the names of those who were juveniles. Out of the one-hundred and twenty-eight names, the juvenile numbers accounted for eighty-four.

"If I'm goin' put my ass on the line like this, I need a bigger cut than a few thousand dollars. You understand me?"

"Yeah, you do this for me, and I'll make it right for sure, you know?"

Anita agreed to focus on the other forty-two names. It wouldn't be long before a couple of familiar names would make the short list of potential rats.

16

Three weeks had passed since Valdez's arrest, and Hannah's resentment grew as JB became consumed by the case of the missing girl and the possible ties to the WSF and a man named Paco Ramirez. JB's frustration was evident when he told her how little the interrogations had yielded. Hector Valdez, hardened by the code of the street, refused to spill any details that might implicate the WSF. JB had explained that Hector would rather face life in prison than betray the code, knowing the alternative would be a swift death at Pelican Bay or High Desert – if he even survived the journey from County Jail.

Hannah watched helplessly as JB spent every waking hour buried in case files, pouring over a web of relationships that spanned a decade. His obsession with the case was consuming, overshadowing everything else in their lives. At night, he would come home, his mind still trapped in the labyrinth of gang affiliations and criminal histories. Hannah felt like a ghost in her own home, eclipsed by Hector Valdez, Paco Ramirez, and the WSF. JB seemed to know more about these men and their deadly secrets than he did about her upcoming medical appointments.

Hannah had scarcely seen JB since the raid on Hector's house. He hadn't been to church or the marriage ministry class, and he was only home for a few hours on Thanksgiving. It was a hurried dinner before he disappeared back to the office, engrossed in the case. She'd thought about telling him about the oncology appointment but decided against it. Part of her wanted to respect the pressure he was under at work, and another part convinced her that it wasn't important. But mostly, it was anger and resentment that kept her silent – how could he be so oblivious? After all, she'd told herself, it was nothing. There was no need to worry about the results.

Yet now, sitting alone in the sterile, quiet medical office, waiting for the physician to arrive, Hannah couldn't shake the gnawing doubt. Maybe she should have told JB after all.

Hannah observed the gynecology assistant intently, seeking any sign in her behavior that might reveal something about the lab results. However, the assistant maintained a professional demeanor, giving away nothing that could soothe Hannah's anxiety. Hannah had reassured herself that the issue was minor, possibly just a polyp or cyst. The thought of cancer hadn't even crossed her mind. But as she waited for the doctor, an overwhelming sense of dread engulfed her. Time seemed to crawl, each minute feeling like an eternity. Her hands became damp with sweat, and her stomach twisted into a tight knot.

The assistant and Hannah had shared a bond for three years, the kind that stems from a deep relationship. If all was well, she would have spoken up, wouldn't she? If it weren't cancer, she would have alleviated Hannah's concerns. As these thoughts swirled in Hannah's head, she confronted the possibility of cancer for the first time.

A sharp knock on the door startled Hannah out of her reverie. Dr. Garcia came in, sharing a quick, comforting hug before taking a seat behind the desk. She then opened Hannah's medical file, her expression blending professionalism with concern.

"Hannah," Dr. Garcia began, "what I'm about to share may come as a shock. I know you're not prepared for this, but the lab work came back with an elevated tumor marker."

Hannah nodded, barely comprehending the weight of the results.

Dr. Garcia continued, "The good news is that we caught this fairly early, and it's very treatable."

Hannah's gaze drifted past Dr. Garcia; her eyes unfocused as they settled on the window. At first, she couldn't find the words. When they finally formed in her mind, her mouth refused to cooperate. It took all her effort to force out the question that gripped her heart. "Dr. Garcia, did we catch this in time? Am I going to live?"

Dr. Garcia leaned forward, her tone reassuring. "Oh yes, as I said, we caught this early, and you don't need to worry about long-term effects on your health. I'm confident we won't even need to consider chemotherapy or radiation."

Hannah latched onto the phrases: very early, no long-term side effects, no chemo or radiation. Relief began to surface, but then another fear crept in, almost too terrifying to voice. She barely managed to whisper, "What does this mean for my ability to have children."

Dr. Garcia looked down, placing both hands on the desk before scooting forward and leaning in toward Hannah. "Hannah, given that we caught this early and considering your overall health, there are options that could still allow you to conceive."

Hannah shook her head, confusion and fear tightening in her chest. "I'm sorry, I just…I'm not understanding what all this means. I have a tumor, but do we know if it's benign? What if it's just a benign tumor?"

Dr. Garcia's expression softened with sympathy. "I'm sorry, Hannah, but based on your blood work, your CA 125 levels are very elevated."

"CA one twenty – what?"

Dr. Garcia paused for a moment. "CA 125 is a cancer antigen we find in the blood. It's a test that measures the amount of this protein in your system."

Hannah's mind raced. "But on our consultation call, you told me this was probably nothing more than a cyst or a polyp. That's what you said on the phone. What changed?"

Dr. Garcia sighed; her voice measured. "Yes, in most cases, it is just a cyst, polyp, or a benign tumor. I didn't want to alarm you with a scenario that usually doesn't happen. But in your case, I believe it's a cancerous tumor in your ovary. We'll need to run more tests to see if it's spread and whether we can keep the other ovary. I just want you to be prepared for what's next."

Hannah felt like the ground was slipping away beneath her. "I'm sorry, I'm not prepared, and I – I, don't understand. You told me on the phone that it was probably nothing more than a cyst or polyp. And just a minute ago, you said I was otherwise healthy and could conceive. Now you're telling me we need more tests to see if you can even keep my other ovary, or if the cancer has spread?"

"I understand this is overwhelming," Dr. Garcia said gently. "I'd like to send your results to our oncology review board for further evaluation. Are you okay with that?"

"Yes, of course," Hannah replied.

As the minute ticked by, Hannah's agitation grew. She stared at Dr. Garcia with a mix of frustration and disbelief. "You've been my gynecologist for three years. If I hadn't gone to a fertility specialist in the Bay Area who then referred me to an oncologist, you would never have found this. Why didn't you catch it earlier?"

Dr. Garcia's expression softened, acknowledging Hannah's distress. "I understand your frustration. I'm glad you sought a second opinion. The reality is, I only see you once a year, and these cancers can grow quickly. That's why it's crucial we send your records to the oncology review board immediately and schedule the next appointment without delay."

"How many women have you misdiagnosed over the years?" Hannah's voice cracked as she spoke, her arms folded tightly, tears streaming down her face. "How many times?"

Dr. Garcia looked pained. "Hannah, I'm deeply sorry. There's nothing I can say to make this easier right now. I'll have Lorrie come in to schedule your next appointment. Is that okay?"

Hannah nodded numbly, processing the gravity of her diagnosis. Just a month ago, she had been hopeful about seeing a highly recommended fertility specialist. Now, only weeks later, she faced the possibility of losing her most intimate parts.

***

Hannah lay in the quiet of the dim room, her thoughts besieged by a deluge of concerns and trepidations. The silence of the home seemed to magnify her unease, with every groan of the floorboards and remote noise from the street echoing her solitude. The heaviness of her fertility struggles, exacerbated by the added strain of JB's regular departures, seemed like an insurmountable load.

Curled up with a pillow between her legs for slight comfort, she was haunted by the fear of an uncertain future. The thought of possibly never conceiving, a dream dearly held by her and JB, weighed heavily on her. Cancer, a preexisting worry, compounded her anxiety. She grappled with the distressing questions: What if the treatments were ineffective? What if the cancer had advanced, presenting an even more serious threat?

The apprehension about JB's response and their shared future was becoming overwhelming. Their union had been strained by infertility issues and his taxing career. The prospect of further difficulties appeared to only widen the gap in their relationship.

In the darkness, tears quietly traced down her cheeks as Hannah held onto the hope of better times. Facing these challenges alone seemed overwhelming, yet she strived to muster some inner fortitude. The prayer from earlier that day had given her a momentary solace, now delicate and tenuous, eclipsed by the trepidation of what lay ahead.

Sleep finally arrived, yet it was an uneasy rest, peppered with disjointed dreams and the constant murmur of her worries. For a short while, her consciousness escaped the day's distress, but the doubts and concerns would surely resurface at dawn.

17

— · —

C HAPTER 17

The cream-colored Impala, gleaming under the harsh midday sun, was parked conspicuously at the corner of Hatch Road and Church Lane. Manny had tipped JB off that Eric could be found at Jose's Mexican Restaurant every Wednesday for lunch – one of the few predictable aspects of his schedule. Despite the interrogation of Hector Valdez yielding little information, it was clear Hector was willing to stay silent, adhering to the street code. JB knew that all cues pointed toward Paco Ramirez and Eric Avina, but he lacked the evidence to implicate either in the murder.

JB pulled into the east side of the parking lot, making a few slow circuits to survey the area. He knew Eric was unlikely to engage in anything suspicious in a public place. After parking next to the Impala, JB admired the classic car, appreciating the care and passion evident in its restoration.

He opened the door to Jose's and found the restaurant empty. Stepping back outside, he double-checked the address. The strip mall was small, housing only four businesses: a tax specialist, a Stop 'N' Save Grocery Mart, and two less identifiable establishments in between. Returning to the restaurant, JB peered inside. A waitress stood behind the counter, and a Mexican couple, who did not match Eric's description, occupied a booth near the front. In the farthest booth, near the back, sat a solitary man. JB scanned the room before walking through the restaurant, and without permission, he slid into the booth across from Eric Avina.

"¿En qué te puedo 'ayudar'?" Eric asked.

JB leaned slightly forward. "Por favor, hable en inglés.," he replied, his tone firm.

Eric leaned back, his hands resting on the table. JB's eyes flickered to the imprint of Eric's gun pressing against his hip under his shirt. The two men scrutinized each other, each assessing the other's demeanor.

"What, are you a cop?" Eric asked.

"I'm a special agent with the FBI. I thought it was time we had a conversation."

"And why would the FBI want to meet with me?"

JB's eyes narrowed. "I was considering spending more time in the Deep South Side, and I thought I'd pay my respects to the man who runs this part of town."

The waitress approached the table, offering JB a menu. Eric waved her off. "Es J.B. Phillips del FBI y no puede comer en ningún lado de esta ciudad. The waitress looked puzzled, unsure if it was a joke. Eric told her to leave them alone as they had business to discuss.

"Stopping me from eating anywhere in town? That's not very welcoming," JB said.

Eric leaned back further, his posture casual. "We're not friends," he replied flatly.

"No, I suppose we're not," JB agreed.

"I'm a very busy man," Eric said. "I'm sure you didn't come all this way just to say hello."

"Why did you do it?"

"Do what?"

"Why did you have that girl executed?"

"Executed? What girl are you talking about?"

"There aren't exactly many girls in the Deep South Side who've been raped, had their throats slit, and drowned in their own blood," JB said, leaning in slightly.

"Ah, yes. I heard about that poor niña blanca," Eric replied, his expression remained cool.

"Did you know the coroner ruled the cause of death as asphyxia due to blood aspiration in the respiratory tract?"

"I wasn't aware of the details, but I'm sure you're about to enlighten me."

"Did you also know she was stabbed in her right lung?" JB pressed.

"No. I didn't know that."

"The ironic thing is, she was stabbed multiple times. The coroner counted a total of fourteen wounds," JB said.

"Is that so?" Eric responded, his tone nonchalant.

"Yes, and fourteen is a number closely tied to the Norteño, is it not?"

"I've seen it graffitied all over this neighborhood. Thanks for the cultural lesson."

"It's everywhere around here," JB continued. "From what I know, you're the man who's familiar with the significance of fourteen. If a girl was executed in this manner in your neighborhood, you'd be the one to authorize it."

"Mr. FBI, you're making a lot of assumptions for someone in law enforcement," Eric said coolly.

"It's like solving a puzzle. You start with the edges, work your way around, and then piece together in the middle. I'm betting you're the key piece in this puzzle."

"I wasn't much into puzzles as a kid. But I did play that game where you smack the thing when it pops up. You know, the one with the little hammer. What's that called?"

JB studied Eric, noting the calm that radiated from the young man—a serenity that felt both deliberate and dangerous. Eric's eyes held a confidence beyond his years, like someone who'd seen enough of life's brutality to embrace it without flinching. JB wondered how long that confidence would last, and where the real meaning behind Eric's words would lead.

"Yeah, that's right," Eric continued, his voice disturbingly casual. "It was Whack-A-Mole. You ever play it as a kid?"

JB leaned in closer, lowering his voice to a razor-sharp whisper. "I'm looking forward to the day I put you behind bars. You might not have slit that girl's throat yourself, but we both know you gave the order. Your boys might fear you, but loyalty's a weak currency. All it'll take is one small-time punk, desperate not to rot in prison, and he'll sell your ass out. Who do you think that kid's gonna be, huh?"

Eric's smile didn't falter, but a flicker of something—resentment or maybe recognition—passed behind his eyes. He leaned back in his seat, his fingers tapping rhythmically on the table, as if the world's chaos were nothing more than background noise to him.

"I see what you're doing. You think you've got me pinned in some corner, waiting to make a move. But let me tell you something." His voice dropped, a mix of dark acceptance and a strange calm. "You do what you gotta do. 'Cause what I know? This life—" He spread his hands out, his voice growing softer, almost philosophical. "—this life owes me nothing. We come into this world with nothing, and that's how we leave it. What happens in between? It ain't mine to control. It's just borrowed, and someday we gotta pay it back. Whether we're saints or sinners, doesn't make much difference in the end, does it?"

JB clenched his jaw. Eric's words danced on the knife's edge between remorse and cold indifference—an admission of guilt wrapped in fatalistic surrender. Was this just another game for him? Or was there a man beneath the surface, struggling between the dual forces that threatened to consume him?

"So that's how you sleep at night?" JB asked, a thin smile creeping across his face. "By pretending none of it matters. All this blood on your hands, and you just shrug it off like you've got some higher understanding? You think acting like a philosopher makes you any less guilty?"

Eric chuckled softly, shaking his head. "You think I'm playing philosopher? Nah, man, I ain't that deep. I just don't buy into all that good and evil crap you're pushing. There's no angels or devils in this world. Just people trying to survive in the mess they were handed. Some of us make it look good, others... not so much. But don't get it twisted; we all pay the same price in the end."

"You're wrong," JB said. "You may think you've got everything figured out, but deep down, you're just a scared kid pretending not to care. You can talk about fate and borrowed time all you want, but you're running out of time, Eric. And when that final payday comes, you'll have to decide what kind of man you really are. The one who hides behind excuses, or the one who faces the consequences of his choices."

Eric stared at JB for a moment, his gaze unreadable, the faintest hint of something—fear? regret? —surfacing and then disappearing just as quickly.

He shrugged, a thin smile tugging at his lips. "I guess we'll see."

JB stood abruptly, slamming his fist on the table, the sound reverberating through the small restaurant. He stormed out without another word, his mind racing with frustration and fury. He needed to take Eric down, not just because of the crimes, but because Eric's surrender to fatalism and his denial of accountability infuriated JB on a level far beyond the badge.

Outside in the parking lot, JB drew a deep breath, forcing himself to focus. He walked over to Eric's pristine 1962 Chevy Impala and pulled out his business card. Without hesitation, he slid it under the windshield wiper.

The chess game between JB and Eric was far from over. That night, the stakes would escalate as Eric prepared to make his next move.

18

— • —

C HAPTER 18

Three weeks after Lilly Grace nearly died of an overdose, she found herself on a Greyhound bus headed for Modesto, California. It was an exhausting forty-six-hour trip. The longest vacation she had ever gone on had been a weekend in St. Louis for a baseball game with her family. The bus ride provided an opportunity for her to see the Colorado Rockies, the Utah salt flats, the Las Vegas skyline, and the fertile fields and almond trees of the Central Valley. More importantly, it gave her time to think about her stepfather, the fact that her mother was barely sober most days, and the connection she had developed with Jade.

In one of their recent video chats, Jade shared details about a recent trip to the beach. She painted a picture of beautiful sand beaches, clear cool ocean water, and a group of friends that spent the evening telling stories around a fire pit. For a girl from the Midwest, it seemed like something that only happened in the movies. Unfortunately, the stories had all been fabricated by Jade to create a sense of belonging for Lilly Grace and to tap into an innocent mind's desire to form positive connections.

The anticipation of meeting Jade, and experiencing the California lifestyle, held her captive throughout the grueling trip. Lilly Grace hoped more than anything for the opportunity to see the Pacific Ocean. Jade had promised to take her to Monterey and up Highway One to Santa Cruz. The two talked often about experiencing a new life together. A life far away from the abuse of her stepfather. A life without the negativity of her drug addicted mother. Lilly Grace already missed her brothers, but she knew they were safer with her gone. Sadly, she would soon realize the Jade she had met online and communicated with for the past three months was a mirage. The reality was that she was the devil incarnate waiting for her next victim.

The bus pulled off Highway 99 and after a couple of turns, headed up I street toward downtown Modesto. Lilly Grace was in awe of the number of homeless people and their tents strung along the highway. Almost every exit and off ramp had hordes of tents, bicycles, and trash strewn along the roadside, each making its own type of encampment or community. Once in the heart of downtown Modesto, she was mortified by the panhandlers on every street corner. In Lee's Summit, there were a few homeless people or panhandlers, but they were usually confined to the downtown area.

The bus stopped prematurely at the entrance to the depot parking lot. The passengers looked at each other and wondered why they were not continuing to their full stop. Lilly Grace stood up in her seat and saw a man and a woman standing in front of the bus. They appeared to be arguing over something, but their voices were inaudible. She overheard a few of the passengers near the front of the bus ask the driver what was happening.

He responded, "They ain't arguing over anything." The passengers seemed confused. He continued, "They're high as kites on meth and they're arguing with ghosts. We call them yackers." Lilly Grace slid down in her seat and clutched her bag to her chest. "They're all over town yelling at the air and yacking about this and that. They make no sense at all. They're like walking zombies."

After a couple of blasts of the horn, the couple made their way out of the entrance of the bus depot driveway. The bus started forward again and after a few seconds came to a stop at the Modesto Greyhound Depot.

"Alright passengers, you made it to Modesto, California. This is the end of the line for this bus. You can go inside and look on the board for connecting buses. If this is your last stop, welcome to Modesto. It's the land of water, wealth, contentment, and health."

Lilly Grace's first impression of Modesto, California was a dirty city overrun with homelessness and poverty. She wondered who held the wealth. And how could anyone be content in this town. She stepped off the bus and wandered aimlessly toward the depot building. She glanced from right to left and over her shoulders for any sign of Jade. The noise of the downtown traffic and the near dozen idling buses cut through her fear. Another yacker stood next to a trash can yelling into thin air. It was hard to make out what he was saying, but it had something to do with a sofa that was stolen. Lilly Grace observed that he was very angry at whoever took his sofa. She saw an older Mexican gentleman standing near the doorway to the bus depot. His elderly face held an innocent gaze. The wrinkles around his eyes and the slouch in his posture made her feel comfortable that he was no threat. It was the first sign of security she had since leaving home. He was a short man, standing near Lilly Grace's height of 5'5". He wore a low brimmed cowboy hat with boots. He had a small suite case at his feet. When she approached, he took a couple steps away. Lilly Grace mustered a light hello, but he just stared at her. She asked him if he was from here, and he again, just stared at her blankly. She said, "My name is Lilly Grace."

He finally spoke, "No hable englis." He picked up his suitcase and walked away.

For the first time since leaving home forty-eight hours earlier, Lilly Grace thought that she might have made a mistake in leaving home. She grabbed her bag and moved toward a park bench underneath a grove of trees between 9th street and the depot parking lot. The clock on the downtown tower read 1:30 p.m. It was two hours past the time that Jade had said she would arrive.

Finally, a few minutes later, a red 1962 Pontiac Catalina with gold rims rolled into the south entrance to the depot. All the bystanders turned their eyes to the car as it slowly rolled through the parking lot blaring mariachi music. The car pulled along-side the curb in front of Lilly Grace. The windows were darkened, and it was difficult to see who was inside. Finally, the window rolled down slightly, and smoke billowed out from the darkened interior of the car. Then Jade popped her head out of the passenger window.

"Hola chica!"

Lilly Grace, confused and overwhelmed by the timing and the environment, sat frozen on the park bench.

"Lilly Grace, my girl!" Jade hollered again.

Jade jumped out of the car and ran toward Lilly Grace. A familiar face gave her a sense of comfort. The two embraced. Jade grabbed Lilly Grace's bag and threw it in the back seat of the car. Lilly Grace stood paralyzed. Jade used two hands to push Lilly Grace toward the open car door. Lilly Grace put her hand on top of the car, and before she entered, she looked around the parking lot to see if anyone noticed the mistake she was about to make. Jade grabbed her by the elbow and ushered into the car.

"Let's get out of here chica."

Lilly Grace noticed a Hispanic man driving the Catalina. Jade didn't introduce him, and she was too nervous to inquire. Instead, she sat in the back seat and tapped her foot on the floorboard.

The Catalina travelled south through an industrial area of downtown Modesto. Lilly Grace sat in the backseat eyes wide open to the surging traffic. To her left and right were semi-trucks coming and going from the freeway. There were metal buildings and factories on either side of the road. She hadn't seen a decent patch of grass since she left the bus depot. The car turned right on B Street and crossed a set of railroad tracks. The pavement turned to dirt and dust as they crossed out of the industrial area and headed toward the Tuolumne River plain. The radio now pumped out hardcore rap music, but it was hard for Lilly Grace to make out the words. Jade reached over the seat and handed her a blunt.

"You look like you could use a hit," Jade said.

"What is this?"

"It's weed girl."

Lilly Grace put the blunt in her hand but was unsure as to how to smoke it. She pushed it back toward Jade. "I don't think so."

"C'mon. It's been a long trip for you. It'll help you relax a bit."

Lilly Grace relented and accepted the blunt. "How do I do it?"

"Like this." Jade took it back and savored a long deep inhale, holding her breath for a few moments. Finally, she let out a long smooth billow of smoke. With a cough at the end, she handed it back to Lilly Grace. She laughed, "Just like that." The two chuckled as Lilly Grace tried to perfect her technique.

Lilly Grace kept her eyes on the man driving the Catalina. Their eyes met a few different times in the rear-view mirror. And each time, she quickly diverted her eyes. Her instincts told her that she should fear this man. As the car made a left turn on 7th Street, Lilly Grace's mouth started to taste funny. The acid in her stomach started to rise in her throat. Her cheeks started to drown in saliva as she tried to prevent the acid from coming into her mouth. The air around her head started to spin.

"Look at the tiger on the bridge," Lilly Grace chuckled.

"What?" Jade asked.

"The tiger on the bridge." Lilly Grace continued as she pointed at the entrance to the 7th Street Bridge.

"It's a lion. Not a tiger," Paco corrected.

"Whatever. Tiger, lion, same thing. Why are they there?"

"The lion represents the light of the world," Paco continued, his tone reverent. "It's also the great destroyer of darkness. The lion statue has been around nearly a hundred years. They say the lions protect the gates of this city. Some say, that at night, when there is no moon, the lions come to life and give a mighty roar."

His eyes sparkled with a mix of pride and mystery as he recounted the tale. "It's more than just a piece of art; it's a symbol of the city's strength and resilience. At night, when the streets are empty and the shadows grow long, the locals believe the lions keep watch, ensuring that no harm comes to those who live here."

The story held a certain enchantment, a blend of folklore and local pride. It was as if the lion statues, towering over the city gates, were not merely ornamental but carried the weight of the city's guardianship.

Lilly Grace listened, captivated by the myth and the way it seemed to intertwine with the city's identity. The grandeur of the tale stood in stark contrast to the harsh reality she had encountered so far. She found herself momentarily lost in the fantasy of the roaring lions, hoping that the protection they symbolized might extend to her own uncertain journey in Modesto.

The bridge covered the vast flood plain of the Tuolumne River, which held very little water as it waited for the impending melting snowpack of the Sierra Nevada Mountains. On the edge of the riverbank was a myriad of walkways and bicycle trails. On the south side of the bridge, across the river, was a Pepsi Distribution Center and a large run-down Mobile Home Park, likely multi-family units. The railroad track ran parallel with the bridge and the entire expanse of the bridge was covered in a variety of graffiti tags with the letters JBF.

"Who is JBF?" Lilly Grace asked.

The question went unanswered as the car veered off 7th Street and turned right onto Crows Landing Road. For one mile, on both sides of the road, auto wrecker yards, auto mechanic shops and low-end car lots lined the desolate landscape. After crossing Highway 99, the right side of the road was an abandoned almond grove that stretched all the way to the riverbank.

"Welcome to the Deep South Side," Jade said.

"What?"

"Our hood," Paco replied.

Lilly Grace had crossed not just half the United States but also into an entirely different realm. The vibrant images of California she had envisioned dissolved into the harsh reality of a city marred by poverty and despair. The stark contrast between the hopeful dream she had chased and the unsettling truth before her left her feeling lost and vulnerable. For the first time, the gravity of her hasty decision weighed heavily on her shoulders. As she looked around at the sprawling encampments and the bustling yet unwelcoming city, Lilly Grace would have given anything to rewind time, to return to the familiarity of her old life, and to undo the choices that had led her to this daunting and disheartening new world.

19

CHAPTER 19

Warnall sat behind his desk and intently peered through files on the computer when JB entered his office. While staring at the computer screen, he motioned for JB to sit down. Warnall was known as a task driven agent, which is why he had advanced through the ranks of the FBI quickly. He was meticulous with case details and a stickler for following protocol. He admired JB's ability to thrive in the field and operate undercover. He knew JB brought value to the team that they had been missing in the Central Valley ranks. The two made a dynamic duo given the capacity and blend of their unique skillsets.

While waiting for Warnall to look up from the computer, JB started sifting through files on the desk. He wasn't looking for anything, he knew it aggravated Warnall when his files got moved out of place. It was one of the few things that could get a reaction out of his focused supervisor, and JB enjoyed drawing the ire of his friend and boss. After a few minutes, Warnall closed the computer files and looked up at JB.

"Tell me what's going on with the case. Where are we at?" asked Warnall.

"Valdez is a dead end. I don't think we're going to get anything from him at this point. We're running his background and conducting a relationship analysis with patterns and anything that might lead him to Paco Ramirez or Eric Avina."

"Anything pop on that? Any connections?"

"Not really, I mean they run in the same circles but there is nothing that is concrete to this point."

"What do you want to do next? Where do we go from here?"

"I met with Eric Avina, and -"

Warnall interrupted JB, "you did what?"

JB noticed the concern on Warnall's face. It was something he would never have approved of in advance. But JB learned in the military years ago that it was better to ask for forgiveness rather than permission. Plus, in the field, he knew sometimes you had to get your hands dirty to get results.

"The CI told me where he likes to hang out and I met him there to pay a visit."

"Why did you think this was a good idea?"

"The leads with Valdez aren't turning anything up for us and I wanted him to know that we are watching him."

"What happened to not wanting to spook him?"

"That was then, this is now. If he knows we're on to him and what he's got going on than he may be more willing to make a mistake."

"Yes, or he may be more willing to pull up stakes and shut it all down."

"No, I don't think so. From what the CI says there is something big happening and he's not willing to let it go because of a little heat."

"What did he say?"

"Nothing. As you would expect he proclaimed his innocence and that he is a law-abiding citizen."

"Yeah, we know that's not the case."

"Well, I would like to request full surveillance on Ramirez and Avina. They're leading this in the streets, but I want to know who is pulling the trigger. Because I can tell you it isn't these two."

"You got it, I'll request the warrants. Go make it happen."

JB started to get up and walk away when Warnall waved for him to sit back down. JB noticed a subtle change in Warnall's demeanor.

"How are you doing?" asked Warnall.

"I'm doing fine. Why?"

"No, I mean how are you really doing?"

"I'm fine."

"Look, I'm dedicated to my job and I'm usually the first one in and the last one out. These last few weeks I've noticed that you are basically living in the office. I know you're a dog with a bone and that you think you're close to locking in on these two. But the reality is we have an entire team of agents out there doing their jobs so you can do yours."

"I know and it's all coming together."

"Yes, it's all coming together here. But how is it coming together at home? You can't be here as much as you have been and be at home at the same time. Something's gotta give."

JB felt blindsided by the depth of the question. Over the past three years, the two had become as close as a superior and subordinate could get. It reminded JB of his relationships in the Marines. There was an honest give and take regardless of rank. This was different. This hit different than other times. Perhaps it was the guilt JB felt. Or it was the directness with which Warnall hit his target.

"Did Stephanie set you up for this?" JB asked.

"Stephanie doesn't have anything to do with this."

JB studied his supervisor. He wondered why he was suddenly so concerned. And had Hannah told Stephanie? How did this game of phone tag close its circle to Warnall?

"Look, you and I have a good relationship. I hope it's good enough that I can tell you what I'm observing. It's not my place to worry about another man's wife, but I'm telling you something isn't right. I've seen Hannah at church these past few weeks and I've noticed a change. If you don't find out what's going on, or at least be more present to understand what's going on, then you're going to crash and burn at home. And let me tell you, the agents that crash and burn at home are the ones who ultimately crash and burn at work. And with the number of hours, you're putting into this case, and the focus you're putting on this case, let's just say I've seen it before in agents like you."

JB looked at Warnall in disbelief. For the first time in their relationship, he felt caught off guard. He felt disrespected. He wanted to lash out and tell Warnall he didn't know how it felt to be an operator in the field because he desk jockeyed his way up the ranks. He had never put real time out in the field. JB had spent ten years in Afghanistan and the Helmand Province as a Marine Forces Special Operations Command (MARSOC). He had participated in a variety of special operation task forces in multiple international locations during his tenure. He was decorated and respected in the ranks. Now, as a Special Agent with the FBI, he was seen as just another agent. He felt an erosion of respect for his qualifications and experience as an operator. He never thought it would be Warnall, of all people, to question his ability to perform.

"You don't have to worry about me. Okay? We're doing fine and I've got it covered. I'll take care of it." He was fuming as he left the office and walked down the hall.

"Tell Hannah I said hello," Warnall said.

JB waved his hand over his head. "Yeah, yeah."

JB walked back to his office and tried to go through files and identify any relations from the WSF members. For every face he encountered, his mind went back to Warnall. He questioned how his friend could question the sanctity of his marriage? After an hour, he realized he wasn't going to get much work done after that conversation. He left the building and walked out to his Toyota Tacoma. He drove back toward Turlock but wasn't ready to go home yet. He needed time to digest Warnall's words. He parked his truck at the edge of an aqua duct on the north side of town. There was something he found peaceful in the water streaming down the canal. In the distance were fields, and beyond that, the crest line of the Sierra Nevada Mountains. It was the place he could always go to to find peace and solace. He analyzed his relationship with Warnall and the conversations they shared during their men's bible study. JB had entrusted Warnall with details of his marriage with Hannah. He wasn't ready for Warnall to take that information and confront him with so much conviction. Deep down, he knew Warnall was right. He knew he was in the red and needed a break. Warnall had seen agents flame out the same way JB had witnessed operators flame out in the field. He thought he was different than the others. He thought he would always be able to recognize the signs. But he couldn't recognize this time, and he had certainly missed the signs with Hannah. He cursed himself for lacking the ability to focus on his marriage. He couldn't understand what was preventing him from giving his wife the attention she deserved. After an hour alone, he decided it was time to head home and spend the evening with his bride.

***

JB stopped by a flower shop and purchased lilies, a favorite of Hannah's. As he continued home, he replayed the conversation with Warnall. After some self-reflection, he knew he was right and had to prioritize Hannah and Jared. He knew he needed to be more present and focused on home. He was ready to make the commitment and focus his energy where it was needed most.

The house was dark when he arrived. He walked into the kitchen and noticed the dirty dishes in the sink. That was rare because Hannah never liked to end the day with a dirty house. He put the flowers in a vase and placed them in the center of the dining room table. He walked around the house and opened all the blinds to let the fading light flow through the open space. He opened the back door to air out the odor from the overflowing trash can and dirty dishes. He walked upstairs and found Jared's room empty. He figured he was probably at a friend's house, which is where he was spending more and more of his free time after school. The upstairs laundry room was full of dirty clothes piled up on the floor. The master bedroom door was closed and there was no sound coming from inside the room. He quietly opened the door and found Hannah asleep in the bed. The room was a disaster with dirty clothes and wet towels on the floor. Hannah Phillips ran a tidy ship, and this was not normal. He was confused. He opened the blinds and opened the bedroom window to allow for natural air. Hannah stirred and turned her body to face away from the window and the light. JB sat on the side of the bed and placed his hand on her hip.

"Hannah, Hannah baby, it's time to wake up." She just mumbled and put the pillow over the top of her head. "Baby, its 4:30 p.m. in the afternoon. It's time to get up."

"Leave me alone."

"I'm not going to leave you alone. I came home early today to spend time with you and Jared."

"I'm tired. I just want to sleep."

"I know I haven't been home much these past couple of weeks, but I think we need to talk about what's going on."

Hannah started to wake up, but she refused to take the pillow off her head.

"I don't want to talk right now."

"I know you don't want to talk right now. But it's important."

"Why? Why now? Why is it important now?"

JB lay on the bed with his body braced up against Hannah's. He reached his hand under the pillow and stroked her hair away from her forehead.

"Listen, I know what's going on with the fertility specialists. I saw the letter in the kitchen a few weeks ago."

Hannah took the pillow off her head and turned around to face JB.

"You saw the envelope? So, you've known about what is going on all this time and you haven't said anything?"

JB put his hand up to defend himself against Hannah's growing anger.

"You didn't tell me about the fertility specialist in the Bay Area, nor did you show me the envelope. So, I didn't think it was my place to bring it up to you. I figured you would talk about it when you wanted to talk."

Hannah got up from the bed and walked around the bedroom.

"We haven't talked about a lot of things in the past few weeks. There's a lot going on in this house. You probably didn't know that Jared comes home every day and tells me about this group of kids that's been bullying him at school. Or the fact that he's failing two classes. Now you supposedly found the time to care. You've missed four marriage classes in the past six weeks. God knows what you've missed during that time."

"Hannah, I know you are upset."

"Upset? You think I'm upset? That's the word you want to use. I'm beyond upset. Upset is I overcooked the chicken for dinner. Upset is I didn't get a raise at work. I'm beyond upset. Our marriage is hanging on by a thread and I don't know what to do to save it. I don't know what to do to wake you up, so you see that it is failing too. I've prayed. I've prayed a lot for us. I'm so upset because I don't feel like God is answering my prayers. And I'm trying to be patient. I am, but I just don't know what to do to try and get you to care as much as I do."

"Whoa."

"You know what, forget about it."

Hannah left the bedroom and headed downstairs. JB quickly followed in pursuit.

"Hannah, this isn't over. You hear me?"

Hannah circled the kitchen and stood near the sink staring directly at JB.

"I'm not perfect, okay. I know I've got a long way to go. But you know what, you're not perfect either."

"Perfect? That's the scale you're working with huh?"

"I'm saying that I know I have to change. But you could change a little too."

"Okay, so now it's my fault. I'm the one who has to change a little so you can change a lot? You have the audacity to look me in the eye and tell me that I need to change too. Really? You want to stick with that one?"

"I'm saying we both need to change."

"What do you think I've been trying to do for the past six weeks when I've been attending the marriage ministry class? What do you think we've been talking about in those classes? Do you think it's a wives club or something? We're literally talking about what we need to do to change our behaviors and attitudes for the sake of our marriages. But you wouldn't know that because you don't show up. Just like you don't show up for Jared's practices or games." Hannah hesitated for a moment, then she put the biggest dagger in J.B.'s heart. "And just like you didn't show up for my oncology appointment when they told me I have cancer."

Hannah broke down in tears, and continued, "You weren't there when they told me that I'd have to remove my ovary. And if everything works out, I'll be able to keep my other one. And maybe, if everything goes well, I'll have a shot at conceiving a child one day. A child mind- you, that I haven't been able to conceive in the fourteen years that we've been married."

The tears flowed from Hannah's eyes. Her body shook as she spoke out loud the feelings she had kept inside ever since the diagnosis. JB walked around the kitchen island and put his hands on Hannah's hips.

She hit him in the chest and continued, "No. No."

He pulled her in close to him and held her tightly. "It's okay. I'm here now. It's okay."

"I'm not going to have a baby. I know it. I can feel it in my bones. I'm not going to be able to give you a baby."

Hannah sobbed deeply.

"Hannah Davis Phillips, I married you because you are my best friend. I married you because you saw something in me that I never saw in myself."

JB took a step back and gently extended his arms. He held her shoulders squarely and stroked the hair out of her face. He continued, "When I married you, I said until death do us part. I didn't say until we had a baby or didn't have a baby. I love you. I love you more than anything else in this world. I can promise you one thing, we will find our way through this and I'm going to be with you each step of the way."

"Why is God not allowing me to give you the greatest blessing a wife can give her husband? Why is God doing this to us?"

"Baby, I don't know why this is happening, I truly don't. But I know God tests us with trials and tribulations to see how we react. Do we give it to him, or do we try and face these things on our own? Because I can tell you for sure, if it weren't for God, I don't think we would've survived these last few years."

"I don't see God in my life right now. I go to church faithfully, I pray nightly, and I just don't see or hear him in anything that is happening in my life."

"It's not about us. He'll reveal himself to us when it's his time. Not our time."

"When did you become so wise?"

"You may not have thought it all these years, but I've learned a thing or two from you Hannah Phillips."

***

Hannah spent the next hour showering and cleaning up the upstairs bedrooms and bathrooms. JB took that time to barbecue chicken breasts, toss a Cesar salad, and pop a bottle of pinot noir. He made a phone call to the neighbor and asked if they would keep Jared a couple of extra hours. It was important that they finished their conversation earlier in the evening.

Hannah came downstairs in a pair of old jeans, a light sweater, and her hair pulled up in a bun. It was a look that reminded JB of when they first met, and she had finished a workout at the gym. He always thought she was so beautiful when she didn't try. He set the plates and repositioned the flowers at the center of the table. Hannah kissed him on the cheek. He pulled out a chair for her to sit. He pushed her in and poured a glass of wine. He put salad on her plate along with the chicken breast. He then sat down at the head of the table.

"You sure are trying pretty hard, aren't you JB Phillips?"

Hannah took a sip of her wine and gave JB a wink.

"Let's just say I'm trying to take a first step."

He raised his glass in a toast, and continued, "Here's to first steps, and to relying on God to carrying us through."

They took a few minutes to enjoy the meal JB had prepared. But it was time to address the elephant in the room. After a pause, JB continued, "So, the gynecologists said your markers were elevated and the next step is to an oncology review board. Is that right?"

"Yes, that's what I was told was the next step. But I gotta tell you I don't feel very good about Dr. Garcia and about how all of this was handled. I don't have confidence that they know what they're doing."

"So, what do you want to do? Do you want to get a second opinion?"

"I do, but I don't know where to go."

"What about the fertility specialist? They were the ones to find out about all of this. What if we contact them and they give us someone to go to for a second opinion?"

"I suppose we could start with them. I don't know what to do." Hannah paused for a moment, "what if they have to remove everything and I can't have a child. What would you think of me then?"

JB put his glass of wine on the table. He walked around to the side of her chair, leaned in and pulled her arm in close so he could wrap her up. He stroked her hair and gently kissed her forehead as he caressed her back and rocked back and forth, ever so slightly.

20

— · —

CHAPTER 20

On the couch, snuggled up to Paco Ramirez, were Victoria and Tiffany. Lilly Grace stood in the corner of the living room, trying to avoid their death stares. Paco leaned forward, his fingers deftly rolling a blunt on the coffee table with the precision of someone who had done this a thousand times before. Each cut of the marijuana was deliberate, almost meditative, as if this small ritual brought him a rare moment of peace in a chaotic world. His normally cold and distant eyes softened ever so slightly as he concentrated.

The girls leaned back and began scrolling their cell phones, but their interaction wasn't as casual as it appeared. Victoria's hand briefly brushed Tiffany's knee, a subtle reassurance, a reminder that they were in this together. There was something unspoken between them, a bond that ran deeper than their scant clothing or flirtatious demeanor. For a moment, Victoria's smile faded as she stared blankly at her screen, a flicker of something vulnerable crossing her face before she masked it again.

Lilly Grace couldn't help but stare at the two girls. Their outfits, barely covering their bodies, left little to the imagination – shorts that clung to their hips and tops that showcased the fullness of their round, well-developed breasts. It wasn't just the clothes that unsettled her; it was the way they seemed to hang on Paco as if seeking his approval or protection. The casual intimacy between the three made Lilly Grace wonder about the dynamics of their relationship. Were they all involved with each other? The thought was confusing, unsettling, and not at all what she expected to find when she arrived in California.

After a few minutes, Victoria got up and walked to the kitchen. Each step deliberate, accompanied by an extra shake of the hip. She pulled a Modelo Negra from the refrigerator, then gave Lilly Grace a side-eyed look as she returned to the couch. Handing Paco the beer, she smirked, "You still owe me for the last one."

Paco's lips curled into a half-smile as he took the bottle, "Put it on my tab, chica."

The banter was light, but there was an underlying tension, as if both knew there was a debt between them that went beyond a simple beer.

Lilly Grace felt more isolated than ever. The air in the room was thick with unspoken words, leaving her paralyzed in the corner, trying to blend into the shadows. From the rear of the house, she could hear Jade's voice, low and urgent, as she spoke on the phone. The conversation was tense, conducted in rapid Spanish that Lilly Grace couldn't quite follow, but the tone made her uneasy.

Jade suddenly appeared from the hallway, still on her phone, cutting through the living room like a ghost, her presence barely acknowledged by the others. She didn't even glance at Lilly Grace as she passed by and entered the kitchen. Lilly Grace strained to catch a few words of the conversation, but they were lost in the low murmur of the television and the sound of Victoria and Tiffany giggling over something on their phones.

A moment later, Jade re-emerged, her face set in a tense mask as she walked back down the hall toward the rear bedroom. The others in the room remained indifferent, lost in their own worlds, leaving Lilly Grace feeling more scared and alone than she had ever been.

Paco lit the blunt, the flame briefly illuminating his focused expression before he leaned back on the couch, passing it to the girls. Victoria and Tiffany took turns inhaling, their movements languid, as if the smoke that began to fill the room was a familiar, comforting haze. The smell quickly invaded Lilly Grace's senses, turning her already queasy stomach from the car ride into a churning pit of nausea. She felt trapped, the heavy air suffocating her, and the sharp, judgmental glances from Victoria and Tiffany only added to her discomfort.

Lilly Grace shifted awkwardly, trying to decide her next move. The thought of interrupting Jade, who was still on the phone, made her hesitant, but staying in the room with Paco and the girls was unbearable. Their indifference toward her had turned into disdain, and she knew that if she didn't lie down soon, she might vomit all over Paco's carpet – something that would surely not go over well.

Summoning her courage, she walked toward the hallway, each step feeling more uncertain. The voices from the living room faded slightly as she moved closer to Jade's door. After a moment of indecision, she gently tapped on it a few times before pushing it open.

Jade was still on the phone, her tone now clipped, as if the conversation had taken a more serious tone. She glanced at Lilly Grace as she entered, her expression unreadable.

"Hey girl, what's up?" Jade asked, not pausing the conversation with the person on the other end.

"Do you mind if I lay down?" Lilly Grace's voice was small, almost apologetic.

"Yeah, sure. Whatever." Jade brushed off a pile of clothes from the bed and tossed them onto a chair by the dresser, not really paying attention to Lilly Grace's discomfort. As Lilly Grace moved toward the bed, she noticed the starkness of the room. There were no decorations, no photos on the dresser, no personal touches that might reflect a teenage girl's life. It was just a bed and a dresser – bare, impersonal, as if the room itself was an afterthought.

Lilly Grace lay down on her side, curling up as she watched Jade from the corner of her eye. Jade's conversation grew more intense, her voice low, rapid stream of Spanish that Lilly Grace couldn't understand. She felt a pang of isolation, as if the language barrier was just one more thing that set her apart from everyone else here.

After a few minutes, Jade abruptly ended the call and left the room without a word, her presence vanishing as quickly as it had appeared. The silence that followed was deafening. Lilly Grace stared at the blank wall in front of her, feeling like she had come all this way only to become invisible, a ghost in a house full of strangers.

***

Two hours later, Lilly Grace awoke to the pounding bass of rap music reverberating through the thin walls. The sound was so intense it felt like the house itself was shaking. Footsteps thudded up and down the narrow hallway, voices mingling with laughter and the occasional shout. It was clear that a party had erupted while she slept, and the chaos outside her door only worsened the pounding in her head and the churning in her stomach. She grimaced, silently vowing never to touch marijuana again.

Suddenly, the bedroom door flew open, and a man and young girl stumbled inside, their giggles spilling into the room. They froze when they saw Lilly Grace on the bed. "Oh, sorry!" the girl slurred, clearly drunk, before they both staggered out, their laughter trailing behind them as they disappeared into the next bedroom down the hall. Lilly Grace lay still, listening as their muffled voices turned to strained moans and groans through the paper-thin walls. It didn't last long; soon she heard them leave, their footsteps fading back into the noise of the living room.

The last thing Lilly Grace wanted was to face the crowd of strangers on the other side of the door. The thought of Paco Ramirez and his intense, unreadable eyes made her stomach twist with fear. But she knew she needed to find Jade. This wasn't what she had been promised. Jade had painted a very different picture over the phone. Lilly Grace wanted to tell her that she had made a mistake, that she wanted to go home, to leave this nightmare behind.

Taking a deep breath, she pushed open the bedroom door. The heavy, pungent smell of marijuana hit her immediately, stinging her eyes and making her cough. The hallway was thick with hazy smoke, and as Lilly Grace moved toward the living room, she could see that the house was packed. Teenagers and young adults crowded the rooms, some draped across the furniture, others huddled in corners with bottles in hand. A few people looked older, mid-twenties maybe, but to Lilly Grace, they might as well have been ancient.

As she walked through the room, she felt every pair of eyes turn toward her, the young, blonde girl who didn't belong. Her pale skin and light hair stood out starkly among the crowd of darker complexions and black hair, making her feel more out of place than ever. In the kitchen, a group of teenagers gathered around a man holding a glass pipe. He ignited something inside it, the water in the glass bowl at the bottom bubbling furiously. The smell of burning chemicals wafted through the air, mixing with the ever-present marijuana.

Lilly Grace scanned the room desperately for Jade but saw no sign of her. Panic began to creep in, tightening in her chest. She didn't belong here. She needed to get out, to find Jade and tell her she was leaving.

Finally, she spotted her in the backyard. A large group gathered around a rectangular table, and at the head sat Paco Ramirez, his square shoulders and thick frame making him easy to recognize even in the dim light. Jade was perched on his lap, a forty Modelo in her hand. The sight of her friend so comfortably entwined with Paco sent a jolt of fear through Lilly Grace. This wasn't the Jade she thought she knew.

Their eyes met across the distance. Jade raised her hand, motioning for Lilly Grace to join them at the table. But her legs felt like lead, and she remained rooted to the porch steps, unable to move. She watched as Jade sighed, then pushed herself off Paco's lap and sauntered over to where Lilly Grace stood, her expression once of mild annoyance mixed with concern.

"Hey, what's wrong?" Jade asked as she reached her.

Lilly Grace opened her mouth to speak, but the words caught in her throat. The noise from the party seemed to fade into the background as the reality of her situation crashed down on her. She was in over her head, and she didn't know how to get out. Jade escorted her from the porch to the table where the men were playing dominoes.

"Hola chicos, presentarles a mi nueva chica, Lilly Grace." Jade's voice cut through the din of the backyard gathering. A few of the men at the table nodded in acknowledgment, but most of the women and girls in the yard greeted Lilly Grace with cold, assessing stares.

Jade resumed her place on Paco's lap, her hand casually draped over his shoulder. Lilly Grace stood awkwardly behind them, watching as the men played dominoes with a focused intensity. Paco leaned in close to Jade and whispered, "Necesito enganchar a esta chica antes de que corra a casa con mami." His voice was low, but Lilly Grace could sense the urgency in his words, even if she couldn't understand them. Jade responded by stroking his face, her expression calm and reassuring. "Todo bajo control," she murmured back.

Jade tilted her head back and called out, "Hey girl, you need something to drink?"

"No, I'm fine." Lilly Grace replied.

"No, really, we threw this party for you," Jade insisted.

"I'm okay. Really."

"Look, I'm going to have my friend make you one of my favorite drinks. I promise you'll love it." Jade whistled to a girl standing near the back door. The girl's head snapped up immediately, and she responded with a quick nod.

"Traeme un trago con un chorrito, sabes a lo que me refiero?" Jade's voice carried a note of authority that made Lilly Grace uneasy. She watched the exchange, feeling a knot tighten in her stomach. The snickers and side glances from the people around the table only heightened her sense of being the butt of some inside joke. The girl quickly turned and went inside the house.

Lilly Grace kept telling herself she was being paranoid. Jade wouldn't do anything to harm her – she was her friend; someone she had trusted for months. But the doubt gnawed at her, growing with each passing second.

A few minutes later, the girl returned with a red cup and handed it to Jade, who then passed it back to Lilly Grace. She hesitated, lifting the cup to her nose and cautiously sniffing the contents.

"What is it?" she asked.

"You'll love it. It's vodka with watermelon infusion," Jade replied.

Lilly Grace took a tentative sip, the strong taste of vodka immediately burning her throat. The watermelon aroma was pleasant, but it did little to mask the alcohol's potency. She forced down another sip, feeling the liquid churn in her already queasy stomach. Jade watched her closely, her gaze unwavering, as the others around the table began to chat, "Chug, chug, chug!"

With the pressure mounting, Lilly Grace took a deep breath and swallowed a large gulp. The yard seemed to spin slightly as the alcohol hit her system. She tried to finish the drink in one go, but the taste and her uneasy stomach made it difficult. After a few more attempts, she finally emptied the cup, earning a cheer from the crowd.

In that moment, the tension she had been feeling seemed to melt away, replaced by a hazy sense of belonging. Jade snapped her fingers, and another drink was promptly placed in Lilly Grace's hand. This time, she drank it more quickly, the alcohol dulling her anxieties. By the time she started on her third drink, the crowd had shifted their focus back to the dominoes game, the men shouting and laughing as the game grew more heated.

One of the men suddenly slammed a domino onto the table causing a loud crash, making Lilly Grace jump. The other players erupted in laughter, passing money to the winner with grins on their faces. Lilly Grace's vision started to blur as she watched the man count his earnings.

Jade stood up and grabbed Lilly Grace's hand, pulling her toward the back door. "Let me introduce you to a few people," she said, leading her through the kitchen. The teenage girl who had brought Lilly Grace's drink was busy mixing more drinks when Jade tapped her on the shoulder.

"Conoce a Lilly Grace, mi nueva chica," Jade said with a smirk.

The girl glanced at Lilly Grace with a knowing look that sent a shiver down her spine. "La chica tiene que estar haciendo lo que quieras en treinta minutos," the girl replied..

"Perfecto," Jade responded, her tone cold. "Déjame encargarme de que haga las rondas."

Lilly Grace watched the exchange, feeling a growing sense of dread. There was something about the way the girl looked at her, a mixture of sympathy and resignation, that made Lilly Grace's skin crawl. She could feel her body growing limp, her fingers tingling with numbness. The sounds of the party – the music, the laughter, the clinking of glasses – blurred into a distant hum as her legs began to give out beneath her.

"What did you guys just say?" Lilly Grace asked, her voice shaky as she struggled to comprehend the conversation.

"Nothing, Mija. I was just telling her you're new to town, from the Midwest." Jade's voice was smooth, her smile reassuring as she patted Lilly Grace on the back and gently guided her out of the kitchen.

"Oh. Okay," Lilly Grace mumbled, still trying to shake off the unease gnawing at her.

They made their way through the living room, greeting various people as they went. By now, Lilly Grace's legs felt like they were no longer part of her body. She attempted to clench and unclench her fists, but her fingers were numb, unresponsive. It was as if her body was slipping away from her, inch by inch.

Jade eventually led her to a couch where an older man was seated, flanked by a couple of girls. He was in his early thirties, tall and lean, with tattoos creeping up his neck and covering his knuckles. The sight of him made Lilly Grace's heart race with a mix of fear and confusion.

Jade leaned in and spoke to him in a low voice, her words sharp and businesslike. "¿Quieres ser el primero con esta nueva chica?"

The man glanced up at Lilly Grace before replying, "¿Qué me va a costar, jefa?"

"Ella es nueva, es virgen."

The man raised an eyebrow, his tone skeptical. "Eso no siempre es bueno, ¿sabes a lo que me refiero?"

Jade shrugged casually. "¿No lo quieres? Se lo suelto a otro."

The man turned his attention to the girl on his left, then back to Jade. "¿Consigo a las dos chicas?"

The man reached into his pocket and pulled out a thick wad of cash, flashing it briefly before stuffing it back. "¿Cuánto?"

"Desde la primera vez, los dos son un regalo." Jade replied.

"Sin juegos. ¿Cuánto?"

"Quinientos."

"¿Quinientos? ¡Eso es un robo!"

Jade's mile didn't falter. "Es lo que es, ¿lo quieres o no?"

The man hesitated, his eyes switching between the girl on his left and Lilly Grace, who clung to Jade's arm, her fear growing with every passing second. She could feel the man's gaze roving over her, scrutinizing every inch of her as if she were a piece of meat.

Lilly Grace' mind was spinning, her thoughts disjointed and sluggish. She knew they were talking about her, but the words were slipping through the haze clouding her mind. The possibility of what they were discussing – sex for money – had never even entered her consciousness. The idea of going into a bedroom with a strange man was utterly foreign, horrifying.

But the Rohypnol, the tranquilizing drug that Jade had secretly slipped into Lilly Grace's drink, was already beginning to take effect. Her body was betraying her, sinking deeper into a fog where fear and reason could no longer reach her. She leaned heavily on Jade, her vision blurring as the room around her started to tilt and sway. The man's voice, Jade's laughter, the noise of the party – it all blended into a distant an echo as Lilly Grace felt herself fading away.

Lilly Grace leaned into Jade's ear, and asked, "What is happening?"

Her words were nothing more than a slur. The pulse of her heart was noticeably faster, and her legs were barely able to hold her upright. The man looked up at Jade, and with disgust, got up from the couch.

"Chica, tú eres un demonio." He paused, the thought simmering in his mind before adding, "Seguro que quiero ser el primero en probar a esa perra blanca. La vamos a tratar bien." With a smirk, he pulled five hundred dollars from his pocket and handed it to Jade who began counting the bills without hesitation.

Lilly Grace felt a wave of panic as he grabbed her arm, dragging her toward the back bedroom. Her heart raced, her thoughts a tangled mess. She looked back at Jade, desperate for help, but saw only the cold, detached focus on the money.

"No. Get your hands off me!" she cried, trying to pull away, but his grip was ironclad.

"Jade! No! Jade, what's happening? Please!" Lilly Grace's voice cracked as she struggled, but Jade's only response was a fleeting glance before turning away, leaving Lilly Grace to her fate. Ther room felt distant, the party sounds fading into an eerie silence as she was forced down the hallway.

Inside the bedroom, her strength waned. The world around her blurred as she was shoved onto the bed. Everything felt wrong – disconnected. Her body refused to respond, weighed down by an invisible force as the girl began removing her clothes. Lilly Grace's mind screamed to fight back, to stop this, but she was trapped within her own body, powerless.

She caught a glimpse of the man as he approached, his shirt now unbuttoned, revealing a tapestry of tattoos. The cold air hit her skin as the last of her clothes were stripped away. She felt his rough hands on her, the sensation scraping against her numb skin. The last image burned into her mind was the girl kissing him, as her world slipped into darkness.

21

CHAPTER 21

Manny pinched the living room blinds, his eyes scanning the front yard with practiced precision. The house was engulfed in darkness, not a single light to give away his presence. He had spent most of the night stationed near the window, every nerve on edge, waiting for something – anything – that seemed out of place.

A dark blue Honda Accord caught his attention, rolling slowly down the street. Manny's breath hitched as he recognized it; this was the third time that evening it had passed his house. Each time, it had made the same right turn at the stop sign, disappearing around the corner.

As the car once again turned right at the stop sign, Manny began to pace, his footsteps muted on the carpet. It was 10 p.m., when he finally texted JB, "The third day in a row," attaching a blurry photo of the car. The darkness outside obscured the license plate, but the silhouette was unmistakable.

Earlier that week, he had told JB about the car that seemed to tail him after work. It had been parked across from his job pulling out as soon as he drove by, shadowing him for miles. And then at Graceda Market, he was sure he was being followed through the isles by a couple of men. But when he voiced his fears, JB dismissed them, chalking it up to paranoia. But Manny's instincts, honed by years on the streets, screamed otherwise. He was certain they knew he was the rat.

By 2:30 in the morning, exhaustion finally overcame him. He slumped onto the love seat, eyes heavy, but sleep brought no comfort. Five nights in a row, he'd kept vigil, lying awake until the early hours, only to wake drenched in sweat a few hours later. His appetite was gone, and the little food he managed to eat sat like lead in his stomach. His body, pushed to the limits by his demanding job, was beginning to falter.

***

The next day, after an exhausting eight-hour shift of stocking shelves, Manny pulled into an Arco AM/PM. He needed something to take the edge off, and a twelve-pack of beer with a pack of sweet swishers seemed like the answer. Parking behind the gas station, he walked around the side of the front entrance, his eyes scanning the street and parking lot for anything that might be off. The paranoia from the past week was eating him, and he wasn't about to let his guard down now.

Once inside, he made a beeline for the cooler, every nerve on high alert. He kept his gaze low but his awareness sharp, noting each customer's behavior, searching for anything out of the ordinary – a glance that lingered too long or eyes that shifted away too quickly. His instincts were in overdrive, survival guiding his every move.

At the counter, his hands trembled as he fumbled with the bills, feeling more like a strung-out addict than the confidant man he once was. He grabbed his change and exited swiftly, his eyes sweeping the lot as he hugged the building's exterior. For a moment, he allowed himself to relax, rounding the corner to the rear of the building, then he saw it. The dark blue Honda Accord was parked right next to his car.

A chill ran down his spine. He knew it without a doubt – it was the same car that had been cruising his street night after night. Panic surged as his hand instinctively reached for his .45 tucked into his waistband – only to find it wasn't there. He patted his side frantically, then cursed under his breath as he remembered he'd left it in the car. The gun, a gift from his cousin after he confessed his fears about being an FBI informant, was his lifeline. But now, with the enemy right in front of him, he was defenseless.

Manny's heart pounded as he realized that everything he had feared over the past week was coming to a head. But instead of terror, a strange calm washed over him. He straightened up, lifting his chest and chin high, determined to face whatever was coming. The dark-tinted window of the Accord rolled down halfway, and Manny stared into the abyss, waiting for whatever came next.

"¿Qué pasó, homie?"

Manny's heart skipped a beat as he recognized the voice form the car. It was Gustavo Perez Medina, or GP as he was known on the streets, an enforcer with a fearsome reputation on the Deep South Side. From a young age, GP had been by the side of Eric Avina, a bond forged in high school and solidified through countless battles on the streets. Manny, a few years younger, had always known of GP, a legend in his own right, known for his iron fists and cold-blooded loyalty to the WSF gang. Years in and out of Juvenile Hall, followed by a stint in County Jail for assault and battery with a weapon, had only added to GP's notoriety.

"What's it to you?" Manny shot back, trying to keep his voice steady.

"We hear you've been talkin' bout our business," Gustavo Perez Medina said.

Manny leaned forward, "You heard wrong."

Manny placed the twelve-pack of beer on the trunk of his car, his mind racing. He caught a glimpse inside his car, spotting the .45 resting between the driver's seat and the center console. For a brief, reckless moment, he considered lunging for it, imagining the feel of cold steel in his hand and the power it would give him. But then he saw it – a young man in the backseat, AR-15 trained right on him. One wrong move, and he'd be dead before he hit the ground.

He forced himself to stay calm, to think. Maybe he could talk his way out of this.

"Who told you I've been sayin' anything to anybody?"

"I've got sources sayin' you the one that got Hector locked up. They say you've been talkin' with the FBI. They say I should take you out so you can't say no more."

Manny's muscles tightened, his body going rigid as he squared up to the car window.

"¡Órale, ese!"

"Your time will come, pinche cabrón. The clock is on."

The window rolled up, and the dark blue Honda Accord pulled away from the gas station, leaving Manny standing alone in the lot. He grabbed the twelve-pack off the trunk and slid into his car, but his hands were shaking so badly he could barely get the key into the ignition. When he tried to push in the clutch, his leg trembled uncontrollably.

Overcome with desperation, he gripped the .45 tightly in both hands, tears brimming in his eyes. In a surge of frustration, he struck the steering wheel with his hand. He attempted to reach JB, but to no avail. As the voicemail sounded, Manny unleashed his fears, disclosing everything to JB – the encounter with GP, the gas station incident, and the looming threat over his life. He implored JB to extract him, to arrange protective custody before time ran out.

22

— • —

C HAPTER 22

The next morning, Lilly Grace felt the pressure of a warm, naked body pressed against her in the double bed. Her eyes fluttered open, struggling to adjust from the enveloping darkness to the soft, muted light of the room. A throbbing pain pulsed at the side of her head with every beat of her heart. As she became more awake, she noticed Jade lying beside her own naked body. Panic surged through her.

Where am I? Why am I naked? Why is Jade naked? What happened last night? The questions swirled in her foggy mind, each one more confusing than the last. The one thing she knew for sure was that she wanted to be anywhere but here.

Silently, she eased herself over Jade's body and slipped out bed. Her bare feet were cold against the floor as she tiptoed toward the bedroom door, her heart racing. Peeking into the hallway, she saw that the house was eerily quiet. The living room, visible from where she stood, was a chaotic mess of discarded beer cans and bottles. The remnants of the previous night's revelry were strewn about the tables and counters.

The last thing she remembered was playing dominoes in the backyard, surrounded by a jumble of unfamiliar faces and laughter. The faces blurred together, and now, her memory was a void. She needed to get out, to return to some semblance of normalcy.

She made her way to the bathroom and turned on the shower. Steam began to fill the room, enveloping her with warmth. She looked at her reflection in the mirror, a stranger's face staring back at her. Her disheveled hair and pale skin seemed foreign, as if they belonged to someone else.

After a hasty shower, Lilly Grace returned to the bedroom, her mind in thought. Jade stirred as she approached, pulling a sheet to cover her naked body. With a sleepy gaze, Jade popped herself up on one elbow and looked at Lilly Grace with a wry smile.

"¿Qué pasa, chica?" Jade's voice was groggy.

"What?" Lilly Grace asked, struggling to make sense of the situation.

"What's up? How you feeling?" Jade's eyes were soft, but her words felt distant.

"My head hurts really bad, and my stomach feels nauseous."

"Lo siento."

"Why are you talking to me in Spanish? You know I don't understand you."

"I'm trying to teach you, so you'll start to understand me."

"What does lo siento mean?"

"I'm sorry."

"Why are you sorry?"

"I'm sorry because your head hurts. Did you have fun last night?"

"I can't remember much. I recall the party starting, people everywhere, and then the backyard with you and Paco playing dominoes. You introduced me to some people, but after that, everything's a blur."

Jade sat up in bed, stretching her arms above her head. Lilly Grace couldn't help but notice the curves of her body and the roundness of her breasts. Jade had shown her these curves online but seeing them in person felt different – more intimate, more real. The fact that they had slept together naked added another layer of complexity to Lilly Grace's already tangled emotions.

Jade walked across the room to the dresser and pulled out a pair of boy's style boxer briefs before throwing on a t-shirt. Lilly Grace shifted to the spot Jade had just vacated and sat on the edge of the bed, trying to make sense of her thoughts.

"Is that all you remember from last night?" Jade asked.

"Yeah, why?"

"No te rayes, no pasa nada."

"Again, in English, please."

"I said don't stress, it's nothing."

Lilly Grace's thoughts drifted to her arrival in Modesto, California. From the moment she got there, she had felt an overwhelming urge to return home. It wasn't that she was excited about going back, especially not to see her mother or stepfather, but she missed her brothers. She realized that Jade and Paco were not where she wanted to be either.

"Jade, I'm glad I came out here and met up with you. But I think it's best if I book a return ticket home."

Jade's eyes widened, a flash of anger crossing her face. "You want to go back to that piece-of-shit asshole who was abusing you?"

Lilly Grace flinched at her harsh words. "Well, no, I don't want to go back to him."

"Then stay here," Jade insisted, her tone softening. "Look, I get it – missing your family. I'd miss mi Hermanos too. But you need to give them some time. And you need to give yourself some time."

"I know, but I miss my brothers, and I feel like I need to talk things through with my mom."

"Look, I understand missing your family. But sometimes a change of scenery can help clear your mind. Let's not make any rash decisions. How about we take a day to ourselves? We can go to the beach, have a bit of fun. Think of it as a girl's trip."

"I don't know."

"Chica, no puedes venir hasta California y no ver la playa, ¿o qué?"

"Again, in English, please."

"I said, you can't come all the way to California and not see the beach."

"All right," Lilly Grace sighed. "I'll go to the beach, but then I want to get a bus ticket home."

"Okay, okay," Jade said, smiling. "We'll handle that later. For now, let me go wake the girls up. We'll head to the beach today and clear our heads."

***

It was late in the afternoon when the girls arrived in Santa Cruz, California, a quaint beach town along the northern coast. Known for its nostalgic boardwalk with roller coasters and games, Santa Cruz was also famous for its darker side – abduction and crime. Lilly Grace marveled at the lush green mountains that hugged the coastline, their peaks shrouded in distant fog that obscured the ocean miles offshore. It was breathtaking.

Santa Cruz was a familiar haunt for Paco and Jade, a place they frequented with the girls, and the hometown of Jade. Tonight, like other nights before, it was not about enjoying the sun, sand or carefree fun. They grabbed a quick bite to eat, and by 7 p.m., they were at the Red Nightclub, a local bar nestled in the heart of the town. Jade had arranged for the girls to stay at a house a few blocks away, convenient for both the night's activities and Lilly Grace's initiation into their world.

The Red Nightclub was a dive bar with a storied history, a place favored by locals rather than tourists. When they arrived, the bar was nearly empty, allowing the girls to mingle with a handful of regulars. Jade, familiar with the bartender and a couple of the locals from the Norteño family, felt right at home. For Lilly Grace, however, it was a far cry from her comfort zone. Jade noticed her unease and brought her a cocktail to help ease the nerves – a Red Bull and Vodka with more Red Bull than Vodka.

As Lilly Grace sipped the drink, she raised her glass to Jade, trying to mask her discomfort. The first hour passed with the girls playing darts and making small talk with a few random guys. The music in the bar was loud and throbbing, a background hum that made conversation difficult. Lilly Grace clung to Jade and spoke little to anyone else.

By 11 p.m., the bar was packed, and the space had transformed into a lively, crowded venue. The energy was high, and the noise made it hard to focus. Lilly Grace seemed more anxious with every passing minute. Jade decided it was time to escalate the night.

A couple of local Nortenos approached the dartboard where Lilly Grace, Tiffany, and Veronica were playing. Their presence provided a welcome distraction. Jade seized the opportunity to head back to the bar. She ordered another Red Bull and vodka, subtly mixing in a vial of Gamma Hydroxybutyric acid. The liquid dissolved easily, and the drink was ready for Lilly Grace, designed to keep her fully conscious but under the influence.

Jade carried the drink back to Lilly Grace, a casual smile on her face as she offered it. "Here's another round for you," she said, her voice light and friendly.

Lilly Grace took the drink, oblivious to the hidden danger it held. She took a sip, her nerves beginning to dull as the night continued its descent into chaos.

"Girls, come over here," Jade called out, her voice cutting through the noise of the Red Nightclub.

The three girls gathered around the bar, drawing the attention of the crowd. At this point, they had become the main attraction, and the bar was alive with cheers and shouts. Tequila shots lined the bar, accompanied by chasers. Lilly Grace's chaser was a potent mix of Red Bull and Vodka, spiked with GHB – a date rape drug.

Jade held her shot glass high and shouted, "¡A la verga las scrapas!" She downed the shot in one swift motion, then chugged the chaser drink. "¡Vámonos, viejas, por la escotilla!"

Lilly Grace, feeling the weight of the night's events, leaned towards Tiffany and whispered, "What did she say?"

Tiffany leaned back and whispered, "Fuck them Suréños and finish this drink."

Reluctantly, Lilly Grace and the other girls downed their shots and chugged their chasers. The men around them erupted in cheers and high-fives. Lilly Grace's stomach churned with the excessive amount of alcohol. The drink Jade had mixed for her pushed her past her limits.

Jade noticed Lilly Grace's hesitation. He expression hardened, and with a cold, commanding tone, she shouted, "¡Vete a la verga, putita! ¡Bebe esta pinche bebida ahora!"

Lilly Grace stared at Jade, her heart pounding in her chest. The warmth and kindness she had come to associate with Jade were gone, replaced by a fierce, menacing demeanor. The girl she thought she knew had vanished, leaving behind a cold, threatening presence. For the first time, Lilly Grace felt a sharp pang of fear.

She looked to Veronica and Tiffany for support, but their gazes were steely and unyielding. The realization hit her with brutal clarity, she was isolated, surrounded by people who were not her friends but captors. The room seemed to close in on her, the loud music and raucous laughter becoming a blur of chaotic noise.

Jade's voice cut through her paralysis, sharp and demanding, "¡Bébelo ahora, pinche!"

Lilly Grace's hands trembled as she held the vodka in her right hand and the chaser in the left. The fear made the world move in slow motion. With a deep breath, she forced herself to down the shot and chug the chaser. The alcohol burned her throat, and the room spun as she fought to keep her composure.

"Chingado sí," Jade yelled over the din of the bar. "Se llevan un pedazo de esta pinche en una hora."

The harsh words pierced through Lilly Grace's haze, and her stomach lurched violently. Panic surged as she stumbled towards the bathroom, her vision blurring with fear and the effects of the alcohol. She barely made it to the bathroom before the contents of her stomach erupted. The cold, grimy tiles of the bathroom floor felt like a brutal reality check as she knelt, her breath coming in ragged gasps.

Tiffany watched Lilly Grace retreat with a mix of curiosity and detachment. She turned to Jade, her voice hesitant, "Should I go check on her?"

Jade's eyes were cold and unyielding as she replied, "That little bitch is going to find out tonight why she was brought here. She'll understand her fucking role in this crew."

The words were delivered with a chilling finality. Lilly Grace's heart pounded as she tried to steady her breathing, her mind racing with fear and confusion. She had hoped for a distraction, a reprieve, but the reality of her situation was sinking in with every passing second.

For the next thirty minutes, Lilly Grace remained in the bathroom, clutching the toilet as she vomited repeatedly. The contents of her stomach, a mix of everything she had consumed throughout the day and night, overflowed into the grimy bathroom floor. The relentless spinning of the room made it difficult to focus, and a numbing sensation spread along her spine. Beads of sweat formed on her forehead, trickling down her face.

Desperate for relief, she staggered to the sink, rinsing her mouth with cold water. She splashed her face, hoping the shock of the cold would bring some clarity. A tingling sensation spread through her fingers and down through her legs, an unsettling energy that she couldn't quite place. Her body felt like it was vibrating with a strange, almost alien force.

Despite the chaos inside her, a new, unnerving urge began to well up. It was as if an intense, pulsating energy had been awakened in her blood, flowing erratically through her veins. This sensation left her feeling disoriented, yet oddly compelled.

After a few minutes, Lilly Grace managed to pull herself together and exited the bathroom. She felt a strange, fleeting sense of relief as she walked back to the bar. The room still felt surreal, a dizzying blend of lights and sounds. She approached the bar where the girls and a half dozen men were gathered.

"Can I have another drink?" Lilly Grace asked, her voice wavering slightly.

Veronica, with an unforgiving look, handed her a red solo cup filled to the brim with another mix of Red Bull, vodka, and more GHB. Lilly Grace took the cup, its contents sloshing slightly as she raised it to her lips. She sipped the drink, trying to steady herself, as Jade raised her hand to command attention from the small crowd. The noise of the bar seemed to fade as Lilly Grace focus narrowed, feeling the potent mix beginning to take hold once more.

"Vamos a llevar esta peda a la casa," Jade announced.

They finished their drinks and filed out of the Red Nightclub, a mixed group of Jade, her three girls, and seven men. The men ranged from college students to construction workers in their mid-thirties. Lilly Grace could feel the effects of the GHB coursing through her veins, heightening every sensation and dulling her judgment. As she walked up the street, her gaze wandered to the night sky, lost in the mesmerizing expanse of stars. The cool night air brushed against her face, offering a fleeting, refreshing respite from the chaos inside.

One of the college-aged men sidled up next to her. His hand slid onto her backside, and he squeezed it firmly, pulling her closer. The strength of his grip caught her off guard, but there was an odd, unsettling pleasure in the pressure. She felt the warmth of his body pressing against hers and instinctively wrapped her arms around his neck. Their lips met in a heated kiss.

He paused, then positioned his hands around her backside, lifting her off the ground. Her legs wrapped around his waist. The pulsating rhythm of his body and the pressure of his thrusts created a disorienting blend of sensations. As she adjusted to the rhythm of his movements, she felt his buddy approach from behind. The second man began to kiss her neck, and Lilly Grace turned her head, still elevated, to meet his lips with hers.

"Pendejo, you don't get taste the merchandise unless you pay. ¿Entiendes?" Jade's voice was cold and commanding.

The guy reluctantly let Lilly Grace slide down from his body, gently setting her feet on the ground. "Yeah, sure. How much do we gotta pay?"

"What's he talking about?" Lilly Grace asked, her voice slurred and confused.

"Este es tu compa de la noche buena. A hundred bucks each and you guys can do whatever you want. But you gotta do it at the house."

The men exchanged surprised glances at the surprisingly low price.

"What about the other two girls? They good to go to?" of the men asked.

"No, gillpollas! The only girl for sale is this one."

For sale? Lilly Grace's mind was foggy with confusion, but she felt an unsettling calm. The group made their way into the house, where music thumped, and drinks were immediately served. Victoria and Tiffany began to perform, slowly disrobing and teasing the men with kisses. Lilly Grace, petite and out of place among the more voluptuous women, watched the display, trying to mimic their provocative movements. She found an odd pleasure in the way her body responded and how the men's eyes followed her.

An older man approached Jade, "So when do we get to take this bitch to the back?"

"You give me the money and she is all yours."

Each man handed over a hundred dollars to Jade. One of the college kids asked, "So what? Do we take turns?"

"No. That's not how this is going to go. I want you all to go back there and treat this bitch right. You've got one hour for a hundred dollars. I don't care where you stick her, just make it rough and hard."

By this time, Lilly Grace was struggling to stay upright. Her breathing was rapid, and her legs were weak. One of the men picked her up, her nearly naked body limp in his arms, and carried her to the back room. The other six men followed.

Unlike the previous night, Lilly Grace was fully conscious of each encounter. The men took their turns, and occasionally, two or three at a time. Her body was overwhelmed by the harsh and relentless treatment. When the hour was finally over, she lay on the bed, her body aching and bruised, her mind drifting in and out of consciousness. The last man to leave was the college-aged boy who she had first kissed. As he looked back at her, his eyes were filled with a fleeting glimpse of shame and remorse, before he turned and left the room.

A few minutes later, Jade entered and sat on the edge of the bed beside Lilly Grace. "Mi putita, ¿te gustó eso?" Jade's fingers traced Lilly Grace's face, watching her struggle to focus. "Soy dueña de ti, sabes, pequeña perra. After your family and friends see the videos of what you did these last two nights, you'll never want to go back home." She leaned in close, her breath hot against Lilly Grace's ear. "Ain't no man going to want to marry you after he sees what you've done. If you think about leaving or going home, we'll make sure we put these videos on every social media platform available for all to see. And that little brother of yours – if you think what you've done is bad, wait until we get a hold of him. Eres una puta natural por cómo te comiste esas pollas. Lo harás muy bien para nuestro equipo, pequeña perra."

Lilly Grace lay there, unable to move or comprehend the full extent of Jade's threats. Her body was spent, and her mind was numb. She tried to cry out for help, but no sound emerged. The weight of Jade's words settled heavy on her, and she was left alone in the dim room, overwhelmed by fear and uncertainty about what her family and friends would think of her once they saw what had happened.

23

C HAPTER 23

Hannah's appointment was set for 9 a.m., on Monday morning at the Stanford Women's Cancer Center in Palo Alto, California, a picturesque suburb in the San Francisco Bay Area. The recommendation came from the fertility specialist at the Northern California Fertility Clinic. Given her prior conversation with her gynecologist, and her diminishing faith in that doctor, the two-hour drive felt worthwhile for the peace of mind that came with knowing she was seeking the best care possible. The early morning commute extended the journey by an additional hour and a half. Despite the time and distance, Hannah was content, seeking it as an opportunity to spend quality time with JB, without Jared, reminiscent of their pre-adoption days.

Initially, their conversation was marked by awkward silences, punctuated by JB's occasional outbursts at the erratic drivers. By the time they reached the Altamont Pass, JB had settled into a steady rhythm, and their conversation began to flow more naturally.

The Stanford Women's Cancer Center, nestled on the north side of the Stanford University campus, was surrounded by the lush greenery of Palo Alto. The drive through the city was stunning. Hannah marveled at the tree-lined streets and the stately homes. As they passed through the charming downtown area, she pointed out various shops and restaurants, subtly hinting at her intention to make this more than just a clinical appointment. In her mind, it was a day date – like they used to make to Dallas – a chance to savor their time together despite the somber reason for their visit.

Hannah chuckled as JB refused to hand over the keys to the valet. Instead, he parked the minivan, now with over two-hundred thousand miles and showing its age, in a spot farthest from the entrance. JB wasn't comfortable letting a stranger handle it, especially with the pleasant Bay Area weather providing a refreshing breeze for his short walk back to the entrance.

As they left the Central Valley and entered the world of Palo Alto's affluence, everything felt new and unfamiliar to JB – the luxury cars, the upscale shops, the pristine streets. Hannah squeezed his hand as they approached the clinic entrance. The casual ease of their drive was replaced by the heavy reality of their situation. JB squeezed her hand back and placed a gentle kiss on her forehead, a small gesture of support amidst the looming uncertainty.

Entering the reception area, they joined a few other patients in the waiting room. Women of various ages and backgrounds filled the space, a stark reminder of cancer's indiscriminate nature. Hannah was struck by the realization that cancer didn't discriminate – it touched lives regardless of age, ethnicity, or financial status. It was a formidable foe, but she was resolute in her determination to fight it with every ounce of strength she had.

Lost in thought about what the future might hold, Hannah barely noticed the nurse calling her name.

"Hannah Phillips," the nurse announced again.

JB gently tapped Hannah on the shoulder, together they followed the nurse through a doorway into a patient room. The room was familiar, reminiscent of any other examination room they'd visited in Turlock or Modesto. Hannah sat on the edge of the bed, her nerves on edge, while JB settled into a small chair in the corner of the room. They waited in silence until the door opened, and Dr. Lorenzo Balke walked in.

"Good morning, Mrs. Phillips. I'm Dr. Lorenzo Balke, a gynecologic oncologist with Stanford Healthcare. My role is to ensure that you feel supported and confident in the care you receive as we navigate this healthcare journey together."

Dr. Balke gently took Hannah's hands in his, his demeanor calm and reassuring. He then turned to JB and introduced himself.

"Now, I'm sure you must have all kinds of questions," Dr. Balke said with compassionate smile. "I'm quite confident you've become an expert on ovarian cancer since your diagnosis." Hannah wanted to laugh at the truth of his words but couldn't muster the strength to smile. Dr. Balke continued. "And I'm sure you've spent countless hours researching my background and reading reviews. True?"

"Well, maybe a little," Hannah admitted.

Dr. Balke proceeded to outline his credentials with Hannah and JB, demonstrating his extensive experience in gynecologic oncology. Both were impressed by his accomplishments and the quality of research his team had accumulated. Dr. Balke's confidence and clarity offered a sense of reassurance.

He then asked if they had any questions before discussing the next steps. Hannah shook her head, feeling a mix of respect and trust in his directness and professionalism. Dr. Balke turned toward the large screen on the wall and pointed to a scanned image.

"As you can see on the screen," he began, "the biopsy results and ultrasound imaging indicate with high confidence that you have ovarian cancer. What we need to determine is whether it is confined to one ovary or if it has spread to the other ovary or other parts of the body."

Hannah's heart raced. "How will we know if it has spread?"

"It is my recommendation that we proceed with a surgical procedure called an exploratory laparotomy."

"A lapa what?" JB asked.

"A laparotomy," Dr. Balke explained. "It's a surgical procedure where we make an abdominal incision to examine the organs within the pelvis and abdomen. We can take samples of tissue and fluids from the ovaries, fallopian tubes, neighboring lymph nodes, and other areas to test for cancer."

"What happens if we find cancer in those other areas?" Hannah asked.

"Our team will review the samples in real time during the surgery. If we find evidence of cancer, we will have the option to remove as much of the cancerous tissue as possible."

"Wait a minute," JB interrupted. "Are you saying that this surgery could involve removing an ovary?"

"Yes, if tissue samples show cancer, we would have the option to remove the cancerous tissue, which may include an ovary. Depending on the spread, we might also need to remove other affected areas."

"I'm confused," JB said. "Do you think the cancer has spread?"

"It's not entirely clear," Dr. Balke replied. "However, given what we've seen on your images and blood markers, there is a likelihood that we need to be prepared for that possibility. You both need to decide how you'd like us to proceed once we're in the operating room."

"So, we need to make the decision now about removing other body parts?" JB asked.

"Yes, we are at a critical juncture," Dr. Balke confirmed. "With the aggressiveness of this cancer, we need to act quickly."

"But what about biopsies of those other parts if you think the cancer has spread?" Hannah asked.

"That's an option, but not preferred," Dr. Balke said. "With this type of cancer, biopsies can cause the cancerous tissue to spread. It's more effective to remove the tissue entirely."

"Have we even considered chemotherapy or radiation?" JB asked. "Why are we moving directly to surgery?"

"That's a good question," Dr. Balke acknowledge. "In more advanced cases, we might consider chemotherapy before surgery. However, in Hannah's case, the likelihood of needing chemotherapy before the exploratory laparotomy is low."

Overwhelmed by the information and the gravity of the situation, Dr. Balke left the room to give Hannah and JB time to discuss their options. As soon as the door closed behind him, Hannah's composure shattered. She collapsed into JB's shoulder, tears streaming down her face.

"They're going to remove all of me, JB." She cried, her voice breaking.

"It's okay, Hannah," JB said softly, trying to offer comfort.

"No, it's not," she sobbed. "You don't understand. We're never going to be able to have a child."

"You don't know that, Hannah," JB reassured her. "He said if he only removes one ovary, we still have a chance of getting pregnant."

"That's not going to happen. He's going to go in there and remove it all," Hannah declared.

"You don't know that."

"I know it. I can feel it in my bones."

Hannah broke down, leaned over, and put her face in her hands. JB felt helpless as he tried to console her, holding her close and stroking her hair. After a moment, Hannah gathered her resolve. She told JB that she trusted Dr. Balke and wanted to proceed with the surgery, even if it meant the aggressive removal of all cancerous tissue. Dr. Balke returned to the room, and Hannah gave him permission to proceed with the surgery, determining to fight the cancer with everything she had.

As Dr. Balke left the room, Hannah lay there, feeling the weight of the news settle heavily on her chest. The darkness of the moment seemed to match the overwhelming sense of loss she felt. JB, seated next to her, continued to hold her hand and gently stroke her cheek, trying to comfort her despite his own distress. Hannah's thoughts were tangled mess of emotions – grief for the potential loss of her ovaries, anxiety about her future, and a profound sense of isolation despite JB's presence.

***

Hours later, as the hospital's nighttime quite enveloped them, Hannah drifted into a restless sleep. JB, exhausted and worried, settled into the small couch near the window, his mind running through the day's events. The steady beep of the heart monitor and the soft rustle of the IV drip provided a monotonous backdrop to his fitful slumber.

The sudden ring of JB's phone shattered the quiet. Startled, he fumbled to answer it, his heart racing with anticipation of bad news. The name on the screen confirmed his fears – it was Warnall.

"Hello?" JB answered, trying to mask his anxiety and keep his voice low not to wake Hannah.

"JB, it's Warnall," came the grim voice on the other end. "I'm sorry to call you so late, but there's been a development."

"What's going on?"

"It's about your CI."

JB interrupted. "What happened?"

"I'm afraid," Warnall continued, his voice hesitating. "He's been killed."

The words hit JB like a punch to the gut. His mind raced to process the information, the weight of it crashing over him. Manny had been a crucial part of the investigation, the linchpin that connected many of the dots in their case.

"What? How? When?"

"It happened tonight. We've got preliminary reports, but it looks like it was a targeted hit. Someone wanted to silence him and send a message."

JB's grip tightened on the phone. "This changes everything. What do we know about the circumstances? Did he leave any messages or clues?"

"Not much yet. We're still gathering details, but his death looks like a calculated move. We need to act fast. The suspects in our case might be making their next move, and we need to anticipate it."

JB felt a surge of frustration and determination. "We can't let this derail everything we've worked for. I need to get on top of this immediately."

"I agree, but first you need to be with Hannah and make sure she is supported. We can handle this for now. We'll talk when you get back into town."

The call ended, leaving JB with a knot of dread in his stomach. He looked back at Hannah, still deeply asleep, and felt the weight of his dual responsibilities pressing heavily on him. As he thought about the events of the night, he knew that his duty to the case and to Manny's memory now demanded his attention.

24

— • —

CHAPTER 24

Based on an eyewitness account, a dark blue Honda Accord had slowly pulled up to the front of Manny's neighbor's house. The car lights were turned off as it rolled to a stop. It stayed parked for a few minutes before three men jumped out of the car and sprinted across the lawn toward Manny's house. One of the men then peeled off and ran toward the rear of the home. The other two pressed hard, charging toward the front porch and kicking through the front door. The neighbor said the driver of the Honda rolled the car forward and parked in front of Manny's house. It was at that moment that the witness heard multiple gun shots. The report said the eyewitness hit the floor before he crawled to the phone and dialed 911. He said he observed three men rush out of the house and jump in the car before it quickly tore off down the street. It was a few minutes before the eyewitness came out of his house to see what had happened next door. When he did, he noticed Manny's house was ablaze. A fire burned inside the living room. The curtains next to the front windows were on fire and the roof started to catch fire too. The eyewitness, who was still on the line with the 911 operator, said he feared the neighbors were dead and the house was on fire. It was at that moment that the house blew up and knocked the eyewitness to the ground.

Based on the forensic analysis of the scene, after they killed Manny, his grandmother and nephew, they turned the gas stove on and lit the house on fire. It was a few minutes before the fire caught the gas fumes and exploded. The autopsy and review of the crime scene showed Manny, and his nephew were killed in the hallway. Based on how their bodies were recovered, it seemed Manny tried to protect his nephew as he ran towards the living room when the men entered the house. The young boy was shot three times in the back and once in the back of the head. The detective's assumed Manny was held at gunpoint while one of the men went into the bedroom and executed the grandmother while she lay in bed. After she was executed, they returned to the hallway where a gun was placed to the side of Manny's head. Manny executed at close distance with a point-blank shot to his temple. At that point, they lit the house on fire and rushed out before they left the scene of the murder.

***

JB's thoughts were consumed by Manny as he wandered aimlessly through the hospitals halls. The initial report – how the suspects executed Manny, then burned his body and house – left JB numb with regret. Just hours earlier, Manny had sent texts and voicemails, now rendered hauntingly final. The pain was familiar, one he'd faced may times as a Marine. Whether driving through South Modesto or sitting outside a barracks in Fallujah, the observation was the same: young men drawn to loyalty, seeking acceptance, often fleeing desperation. The only difference was the uniform. On either side of the world, the line between good and evil blurred. JB believed it was his duty to show the men under his command where that line was, ensuring they came home to see another sunrise. But with Manny, he'd failed. And that failure cut him to the core.

A nurse at the huck station, clearly annoyed by his pacing, asked if he could take his walk outside instead of up and down the hallways. JB was relieved to escape the hospital's confines, to breathe the cold, damp air of the Bay Area fog. The parking lot lights shimmered through the mist, offering a peaceful moment to reflect. But his mind replayed Manny's desperate voicemails and texts on a loop. Manny had always been high-strung, prone to seeing threats where there were none. Each time, JB had talked him down, reassuring him it was all in his head. This time, though, it wasn't paranoia, it was real. And the result was tragic. Manny had been JB's responsibility, and he had let him down.

After hours of wandering through the parking lots, JB quietly entered Hannah's hospital room, making his way to the sofa sleeper by the window. He lay down, pulling a light blanket over his shoulder, and glanced at Hannah. She was sound asleep, her breathing steady. JB matched his own breaths to hers, a small attempt to find some calm. Exhaustion weighed on him, his eyelids heavy, but a nurse's quiet knock broke the stillness as she entered to check Hannah's vitals. The slight interruption sent a surge of adrenaline through him, shattering any hope of rest. When the nurse left, he tried to sync his breathing with Hannah again, but the brief calm was lost. Another nurse entered soon after, and JB sat up, staring out the window, his thoughts restless.

He opened his phone, scrolling through emails from Warnall, who was keeping him updated on Manny's case. Time slipped by unnoticed until the parking lot lights flickered off as dawn crept over the Bay Area foothills. The dense fog gradually lightened, revealing the lush green mountains on the western side of the Bay – a stark contrast to the Central Valley.

Hannah stirred in bed, her body tensing with each painful movement. JB stood and moved to her side, gently placing a hand on her shoulder and kissing her forehead. The morning dragged on with doctor rounds and discharge paperwork, but by noon, Hannah was cleared to leave. The two-hour drive over the mountains back to the Central Valley was quiet, Hannah subdued by pain medications. JB's mind oscillated between Manny and Hannah – her fear of not being able to conceive, and the raw emotions that had yet to surface. He dreaded how she would cope once the post-surgery haze lifted. Meanwhile, thoughts of Manny's case consumed him - Eric Avina, Paco Ramirez, the entire WSF crew in Modesto. The brazenness of their attack, the message they sent – it all haunted him. He knew he couldn't have saved the little girl in the almond grove, but he could have saved Manny. And for that, he vowed retribution, determined to see justice served.

Back home, JB made sure Hannah was settled comfortably in the bedroom before heading to the pharmacy for her medication. He prepared a simple bowl of soup, knowing her stomach couldn't handle much. By six o'clock, he kissed her forehead and told her he'd be at the office for a few hours. Hannah didn't know about Manny – JB hadn't mentioned his name. That was a boundary he wasn't ready to cross.

Warnall informed JB that an all-points bulletin had been issued for the dark blue Honda Accord, with an arrest warrant out for Gustavo Perez Medina. The Modesto Police, Stanislaus County Sheriff's, and the FBI were all focused on finding the man responsible for the cartel-style hit on Manny.

***

JB arrived at Warnall's office just after 7 p.m., finding his friend and supervisor buried in weekly logs and reports – a routine JB despised. He'd never intended to be desk-bound, preferring the adrenaline of the field, where he could jump fences and chase down bad guys. It's what he loved about the Marines and Special Forces.

As Warnall continued to shift through paperwork, JB cut in, "All right, give me the scoop on everything we know so far."

Warnall closed his laptop, looking up with a slight smile. "Good to see you too. How's Hannah doing?"

"She's fine," JB brushed off the sentiment. "So what do we have so far?"

"JB, take a breath. I know Manny was your CI, and you feel responsible, but this isn't on you. He knew the risks. It was his lifestyle that led him to this point, not us, and certainly not you."

"That's bullshit, and you know it," JB shot back. "We put him in a situation where he didn't feel like he had a choice. He asked for help, and I didn't give it to him. I have to live with that, but it doesn't absolve me of responsibility for his death."

Warnall leaned back, folding his arms across his chest. "I think you need a break. You're too close to this."

"No, don't pull this crap."

"Look, with everything going on – Hannah's cancer, the surgery, Manny being your CI – it's too much."

"I'm fine. We need to move, and we need to move now."

"Move on what? Our CI is dead, and we don't have a confirmed location for Medina. So where do you suggest we start?"

"Let's go after Eric Avina."

"And charge him with what?"

"Murder. At the very least, conspiracy to commit murder."

"Do you hear yourself? There's no connection to Avina in any of this. The wiretaps haven't linked him to the case. He's clean."

"Then bring him in for questioning. Make him sweat."

"He'll lawyer up and stay silent. We'll have to release him in hours."

"So what? We bring him in, he doesn't talk, and they let him go. But every kid in that hood is going to be wondering what he might have said. We can use it to stir things up, make them nervous. Right now, they think they're untouchable."

Warnall ran his hands through his hair, considering the implications. Finally, he leaned forward, arms on the desk. "Okay. Go through tactical SIU channels, get a team together, and bring him in for questioning."

JB pounded his fist on the desk and stood up to leave before Warnall could change his mind. At the door, he turned back. "We're going to tighten the noose on this crew. Eventually, they'll slip."

By the afternoon, the Special Investigators Unit gathered in the conference room. Eric Avina wasn't the type to run or hide; he was easy to find. The challenge was ensuring the team had the right support to handle any surprises during the apprehension. The SIU team, gathered around the table, was engaged and ready. JB took the podium, highlighting Avina's residence on the screen, along with his photo. They discussed the tactical plan, addressing concerns about community safety, street-level activity, and possible on-site threats. It was a solid plan, and the team was prepared. By the next morning, JB would be face-to-face with Eric Avina once again.

25

— · —

CHAPTER 25

Eric Avina had been detained in the basement of Stanislaus County Jail for three hours when JB eventually arrived. In that period, over four special agents took turns in the interrogation room, each employing various strategies to break his resolve. The initial agent, from the Street Gang Task Force Unit, tried to connect with Avina by recounting tales of life in gang-afflicted neighborhoods. He sought to establish a connection, to make Avina let down his guard. However, all attempts were futile – Avina remained silent, speaking only to ask for his lawyer.

The second and third agents adopted a more straightforward method, presenting the case's facts and explaining how Avina's actions had implicated him. Nevertheless, Avina stayed silent, consistently responding only with a request to speak to his attorney.

Upon reaching the holding area, JB halted outside the room, observing Avina through the two-way mirror. The man sat stoically, his face giving nothing away. The Special Agent in Charge, Warnall, stepped into the room with a clipboard and presented it to JB to sign.

"So far, he's been in custody for three hours and hasn't spoken a word to any of the agents," Warnall said. "I don't think he's going to say anything to anybody. And that includes you."

"He doesn't need to say anything to me," JB replied, signing the clipboard. "The fact that he's in custody already sends a message on the streets. I'm just going to remind him of that."

Warnall gave a slight nod. "Alright, let's see what you've got."

JB stepped into the interrogation room, the door clicking shut behind him. The air was thick with tension, the kind that comes from a battle of wills. Avina didn't look up, but JB could see the flicker of recognition in his eyes. This was a man who understood the game, who knew that sometimes silence spoke louder than words.

JB pulled out a chair and sat down across from Avina, letting the silence hang between them. He didn't need to ask questions or press for answers. He was here to plant a seed, to let Avina know that his time in custody wouldn't go unnoticed on the streets. JB placed a thick folder on the table. He stared at Eric for a solid two minutes. Neither man broke eye contact.

Finally, JB interjected, "I told you this day would come. You didn't believe me, huh?"

Eric's steeled-eyed glaze remained unbroken.

"What, no call for your lawyer?" JB taunted. "You've been briefed, right? Let me set the stage for you. Three months ago, a young girl was raped and murdered, her body dumped in an almond grove near Crows Landing Road and the river. Hector Valdez is singing like a bird, and we believe you and your partner are behind it. Conspiracy to commit murder."

Eric's eyes blinked at the mention of Hector Valdez.

"Last night, Emanuel Velasquez, his grandmother, and nephew were murdered. Your buddy Gustavo Perez Mendia made that hit. You know him, don't you?"

JB stood up, rifling through the papers in the folder, before settling against the wall.

"At the restaurant, you had plenty to say. What happened to that tough guy?"

Eric shifted in his seat, sweat beading on his forehead. JB knew he was getting close.

"Hector and his buddies rapped that girl, got high on fentanyl, then decided to kill her. They panicked and slit her throat. She was on your payroll, so they called Paco Ramirez. You and Medina put out a hit on Manny to send a message. Medina went full cartel and executed him, then torched his house. But you made a mistake – Medina's not going down for you."

JB placed a photo on the table. "Your old man was a rat, wasn't he? That's why they killed him in prison. How's it feel knowing the streets are whispering if you're a chip off the old block?"

Eric's rage bubbled over. "El pendejo, te voy a matar."

JB leaned back. "Is that a threat against a federal agent?"

"You think you're big, with me chained up? You've got nothing on me. I'll be out of here in forty-eight hours."

JB leaned in. "Word on the street is you've lost control. The cartel's running your hood. Your dad built this crew, and now you're losing it all."

"You don't know anything about my father. Or what he built."

"I know your mother tried to keep you from this life. What would she think of you now?"

"You don't know anything about my life!" Eric spat. "You want to talk success? In my hood, success is survival. No fathers, no mothers – just survival. You didn't grow up wondering if the car rolling up on you would open fire. You were probably off stealing liquor from your daddy's liquor cabinet."

"So, when did survival turn into building this empire?"

"Empire?" Eric laughed bitterly. "This isn't about an empire. It's about surviving in a world where no one gives a damn about us."

"I'm giving you a chance, right now, to do the right thing."

Eric shook his head. "The police don't give out chances. You've got nothing on me. Charge me or release me. We both know you have nothing."

"This won't end well for you, Eric. You know that, right?"

"It's the modern-day story of the Mexican American. A real Sleepy Lagoon."

"Let's see how your crew reacts when they start wondering if you're a rat."

"Pendejo," Eric muttered.

JB left the room, meeting Warnall outside. They held Eric for forty-six hours before releasing him back to the streets.

26

— · —

C HAPTER 26

The day following Christmas marked two weeks since Lilly Grace's return from Santa Cruz. In that time, she rarely had a moment of clarity. Jade kept her on a relentless rotation of alcohol, marijuana, and crystal meth, and her days and nights had blurred into a haze of men who paid for her services.

In the late afternoon, Lilly Grace was roused by the sounds of a fierce argument coming from the kitchen—Paco and Jade, their voices elevated, their words charged with anger. Lying in bed, she felt a mix of confusion and disorientation, cringing with each outburst of Paco's rage. Memories of her home, her mother and stepfather, felt like a far-off dream.

She stumbled to the mirror, staring at the dark bags under her eyes, her face a map of exhaustion. Her head pounded with each pulse, and she pressed her temples, desperate to make the pain stop. It didn't. Her gaze shifted to the side of the bed, where a clear zip lock bag of rock candy lay – Jade's stash from the night before. Her hands twitched as she debated taking a piece, fear of Jade's wrath holding her back. But the need won out. She quickly snatched a couple of pieces, feeling a rush of energy as the drug took hold.

Jade's footsteps echoed down the hallway, accompanied by Paco's angry voice. Lilly Grace glanced at the bag again, then decided to take another piece. Before she knew it, the bag was empty, and her body tingled as if her soul were drifting away. A fleeting thought crossed her mind – what would Jade do? But it vanished as the pressure in her head faded.

The bedroom door flew open as Jade charged in, with Veronica and Tiffany trailing behind her. Paco shouted something in Spanish before he dashed through the living room and out the front door.

Jade circled the room before heading to the end table, where she held up the empty bag of rock candy. She grabbed Lilly Grace's wrist and felt for a pulse – her heartbeat raced. "Pinche perra."

She slapped Lilly Grace's cheeks, attempting to awaken her. Lilly Grace's eyes flickered open and closed, her stare drifting without focus.

"Veronica, get in here now!" Jade ordered.

Veronica rushed in, glanced at Lilly Grace, and asked, "What's up with this chick? Is she dying?"

Jade stood and pointed at Lilly Grace. "Get this bitch ready to hit the road. We're leaving for Reno tonight. And make sure she doesn't take any more drugs unless she gets them from me. I want her cleaned up and ready to produce tonight."

Veronica pulled Lilly Grace's pants off while Tiffany wrestled her shirt over her head. They heaved her limp body across the hallway to the bathroom. Veronica turned on the shower, and they dumped Lilly Grace over the edge of the bathtub. Water cascaded over her head, washing away the black mascara that streamed down her face. Tiffany squeezed shampoo onto her scalp and began scrubbing.

By the time Lilly Grace came to, she would find herself in a roadside motel near downtown Reno, Nevada.

***

Lilly Grace awoke to the dull hum of tires on wet pavement, her body heavy and sluggish from the long, drug-induced sleep. The car rolled to a stop, jarring her slightly as she blinked groggily, trying to make sense of her surroundings. Outside, the world was a blurred mix of rain and snow, the cold seeping into the car, leaving the windows fogged and the air damp.

She squinted through the condensation, her heart sinking as she recognized the dim neon sign of a rundown roadside motel on the outskirts of Reno, Nevada. The sickly yellow glow from the motel's sign barely cut through the gloom, casting eerie shadows on the cracked asphalt. The whole place felt like it was forgotten by the world, a perfect setting for something sinister.

In the front seat, Jade scrolled through her phone, her face expressionless, as if this were just another mundane stop on a long journey. Next to Lilly Grace, Veronica and Tiffany chatted casually about casinos and gambling. Everything felt surreal, like she was caught in a nightmare she couldn't wake up from.

She spotted Paco Ramirez in the motel office through the foggy windshield, his face lit by the flickering fluorescent lights inside. When he emerged, he moved quickly, his eyes hard as he handed a key to Jade and barked orders in rapid Spanish. Lilly Grace only caught fragments – something about the Peppermill, the nightclub, and the rooms. Her mind struggled to keep up, the reality of what was happening suffocating her like the thick air in the car.

"Alright, girls, you heard him. Let's get inside and get dressed for the club," Jade said.

The trunk popped open. Jade was first out, grabbing her bag and disappearing into the dark, the motel door swinging open briefly before closing behind her. Veronica and Tiffany followed without hesitation, their heels clicking on the wet pavement, leaving Lilly Grace alone in the back seat, frozen in place.

She wanted to move, to escape, but her body refused to cooperate. Her limbs felt leaden, her thoughts a tangled mess of fear of confusion. The urge to cry out for help was smothered by the knowledge that no one would hear, no would care, in this desolate place.

Paco's gaze cut through the darkness as he turned to look at her, his eyes narrowing with irritation. "Get out of the fucking car," he snarled.

The command jolted her, sending a shiver of dread through her veins. With trembling hands, she fumbled with the door handle, the cold metal biting into her skin as she finally forced herself to obey, the weight of her reality crashing down. She stumbled out of the car, her body swaying unsteadily as she retrieved her bag from the trunk. The cold air bit at her skin, the dampness from the lingering snow settling into her bones. As she closed the heavy trunk, she watched Paco's car peel out of the parking lot, the taillights fading into the distance like a bad omen.

She shuffled toward the motel room, her feet dragging as if the very ground was pulling her back. The motel stood in stark contrast to the twinkling lights of downtown Reno, which glimmered in the distance like a cruel reminder of a world she was no longer a part of. Inside the room, the low lighting cast long shadows, adding to the sense of suffocation that had been tightening around her since she woke up.

Jade was already inside, her voice low and businesslike as she spoke on the phone, likely setting up the night's rendezvous. The conversation was fluid, her tone shifting from flirtatious to commanding as she discussed the details of a party at the club inside the Peppermill. It was one call after another, her voice a constant murmur in the background as if she was the conductor of a dark orchestra.

In the small bathroom, Veronica and Tiffany were busy with their makeup, transforming themselves into the seductive images expected of them. The clatter of brushes and the chatter of their conversation filled the air, but it all felt distant to Lilly Grace, as if she were observing from underwater.

Her body gave out before she could make it any further, collapsing onto the bed. The worn-out mattress creaked under her weight, but she barely noticed, her consciousness slipping in and out like the flicker of a dying candle. The room spun around her, the excitement of the other girls a cruel contrast to the dread gnawing on her insides.

The drapes were drawn open, revealing the Reno skyline. The sight was almost mocking in its beauty, a sharp reminder of life continuing just beyond her reach. Veronica and Tiffany, dressed in tight miniskirts and tank tops, their stilettos clicking against the floor, were a blur of motion as they prepared for the night ahead.

Jade, still glued to her phone, sat across the room at the small desk, her voice growing sharper as she lined up customers with the precision of someone who had done this a thousand times before.

Veronica perched on the edge of the bed; her expression twisted with annoyance as she tapped Lilly Grace's leg. "Is sleeping beauty joining us?" she asked.

Jade paused her conversation, lowering the phone just enough to bark, "You two, get her dressed and put some makeup on her. She needs to be ready to go in ten minutes."

Tiffany sighed, digging through Lilly Grace's bag until she found a set of clothes. She laid them out next to Lilly Grace, her movements brisk and indifferent. Veronica, always the less patient of the two, snapped, "Let's go, get showered quickly."

Lilly Grace struggled to focus, the world spinning around her as she mumbled, "What time is it?"

"Midnight," Tiffany replied.

The fear creeping into her words. "Where am I?" Lilly Grace's voice wavered.

Veronica rolled her eyes, cutting Tiffany off. "We're in Reno. Now let's get going – we've got to meet Paco at the club."

"What club? Where am I?" Lilly Grace repeated.

Veronica's patience snapped. "What am I, your mother? Hurry the fuck up, let's go."

"My head hurst. I can't feel my legs," Lilly Grace whimpered, the disorientation and nausea overwhelming her.

"Bitch, let's fucking go!" Veronica said.

"I'm serious, I can't feel my legs, and my head hurst. I feel nauseous," Lilly Grace repeated, the desperation in her voice growing.

Veronica threw her hands up in frustration. "Jade, what do you want me to do with this bitch? She won't move."

Jade lowered the phone again, her eyes narrowing as she snapped, "Just get her in the shower and wake her ass up. We've got five minutes before we must leave. Let's fucking go."

Veronica and Tiffany exchanged glances, both clearly irritated. Neither wanted to babysit Lilly Grace for the night; they were here to make money, not to deal with dead weight. But there was no choice – Paco's orders were absolute, and they knew better than to defy him.

"What do we do? I don't want to carry this bitch all night," Veronica said.

"She needs a hit or a bump – something to get her going," Tiffany replied.

"You got anything?" Veronica asked, glancing nervously toward the door.

"No."

"Great. Let's just drag her to the shower like earlier. We'll figure it out from there."

With a resigned sigh, Veronica and Tiffany each grabbed one of Lilly Grace's arms, dragging her toward the bathroom. Lilly Grace screamed, her legs kicking out in desperation, but her resistance only fueled their determination. The struggle was chaotic, her body writhing as they tried to contain her flailing limbs.

Suddenly, Jade stormed into the bathroom, her patience worn thin. "We don't have time for this shit. Go get the kit from my bag. A hit will get her moving."

Veroncia left the bathroom and rummaged through Jade's bag, while Lilly Grace, tears streaming down her face, begged, "No. No. I don't want anymore. I feel like I'm going to throw up."

"This will help you feel better," Jade said with icy indifference.

"No, I need to throw up. Now!" Lilly Grace's voice was desperate as she crawled toward the toilet, her body convulsing as she vomited violently. The sound echoed off the tile walls, filling the small space with the acrid stench. Tiffany turned away, covering her nose with her hand, while Veronica grimaced, disgust etched into her features.

Jade's patience snapped. "We don't have time for this fuckin' shit. Give me the bag. Hold this fucin' bitch down."

Jade seized Lilly Grace by the back of her head, yanking her down onto the cold tile floor. Lilly Grace's weak attempts to resist were futile against Jade's strength.

"No! No!" Lilly Grace cried.

"Bitch, take this shit now and get in the shower," Jade growled.

"No!" Lilly Grace's protest was cut short as Jade's foot connected with her ribs, sending a sharp pain radiating through her body. Jade didn't want to hit her face – she knew the damage would be bad for business – but the kicks were enough to subdue her.

"Grab her arms," Jade ordered, and Veronica and Tiffany quickly obeyed, flipping Lilly Grace onto her stomach. The cold tile pressed her cheek as she struggled beneath their grip, panic flooding her senses.

Jade left the room briefly, returning with a needle in one hand and a spoon in the other. Lilly Grace's eyes widened in horror as she watched Jade prepare the mixture, her hands trembling as she screamed, her voice hoarse and desperate.

Jade worked with cold efficiency, mixing the meth with water in the spoon. She held the syringe up, flicking it to release a small stream of liquid into the air, then tied a tourniquet around Lilly Grace's upper arm. Lilly Grace's screams echoed in the small bathroom as the needle pierced her skin, the sight of blood seeping into the barrel only intensifying her terror.

Jade loosened the tourniquet and pressed the plunger down, injecting the drug into Lilly Grace's vein. "There, now get this bitch cleaned up. We've got five minutes."

Lilly Grace's screams subsided into weak whimpers as the drug began to take effect. Veronica and Tiffany quickly stripped her down, the room spinning around her as they forced her into the shower. The cold water hit her skin like needles, but her body no longer had the strength to resist. Within minutes, Lilly Grace was out of the shower, her movements sluggish as they dressed her in the tight clothes laid out for her. Her mind was a haze, her body moving on autopilot as the drug took hold. The world outside was just a blur of neon lights and darkness as they prepared her for a long night at the club, the last shreds of her resistance slipping away into the abyss.

27

C HAPTER 27

It was the first Tuesday of the New Year, and Hannah lay curled up in bed. The early morning hours stretched on as she remained motionless, a pillow tucked between her legs, its softness offering a fleeting comfort to her aching body and soul. The rhythmic sound of rain drumming against the windowsill filled the room. With each droplet that fell, the crushing realization that she would never bear her own children settled deeper into her bones. It was pain that cut to her core, pulling her into a dark abyss.

JB, ever the caretaker, took over the morning routine in silence. He made Jared's lunch, packed his school bag, and ensured everything was for the day ahead. Their neighbor had stepped in to help, taking Jared in the afternoons until JB could return from work. In those quiet moments with his son, JB found a semblance of peace – something new for both of them – a connection that helped dull the sharp edges of his own grief and the guilt her carried over Manny's death.

Hannah, however, was trapped in her own thoughts, unable to escape the spiral of sadness that had taken hold. She thought of Claire Burgess, a woman from their marriage ministry class. Claire had once stood before the group, all five foot four of her, sharing her story of infertility with tears streaming down her face. It was the first time Hannah had heard someone else speak of the same heartache she had feared. At the time, Hannah still held onto hope, unaware of the storm that was brewing inside her own body.

Now, following the surgery that had stripped her hopes, Claire's story echoed in her mind with a newfound, harsh clarity. There would be no miracle child, no elated instance of presenting a positive pregnancy test to JB. Those dreams had vanished, snatched away by the merciless twists of fate. The basic capacity to conceive, once assumed as a given, was now an impossibility. The grief was overwhelming, and with it came an outpouring of tears, as Hannah pressed her face into her pillow, mourning for what could never be.

***

At work, JB gazed at the phone, feeling the gravity of the impending conversation. He had contacted Barb Adams earlier that day, unsure of his words but convinced that she was the one who could offer assistance.

When Barb answered, her voice was warm and familiar. "Hello?"

"Mrs. Adams, this is JB Phillips, Hannah's husband."

"Oh, yes, JB. How are you doing? How is Hannah?"

JB hesitated, the words catching in his throat. "Well, that's why I'm calling. I could use your help."

"What's wrong?" Barb asked.

"Nothing's wrong...I mean, I don't know what's wrong. She just hasn't been herself since the surgery."

"What do you mean?"

"She hasn't gotten out of bed for three days. She barely eats, and she just seems so...lost."

Barb sighed, understanding the depth of his worry. "She's been through an awful lot, JB. A cancer diagnosis is hard enough, but everything else on top of it...it's more than anyone should have to deal with in this life."

"I don't know what to say to her. I was hoping you might be willing to talk with her."

"I'd be happy to visit with her, JB. I'll bring some soup this afternoon and see if I can help."

"Thank you, Mrs. Adams."

"My pleasure, JB. But how are you going? This can't be easy on you either."

JB forced a smile that Barb couldn't see. "I'm fine. Just focusing on work and trying to keep things running smoothly at home."

"Well, if you need anything – anything at all – don't hesitate to ask. Chuck and I are here for you both."

"Thank you, ma'am."

"I'll stop by later today."

"Thank you, Mrs. Adams."

As JB hung up the phone, he felt a mix of relief and apprehension. He hoped that Barb's visit would be the first step in pulling Hannah out of the darkness that had swallowed her.

***

Later that day, Barb Adams arrived at Hannah's house with a loaf of bread and a pot of tomato basil soup. She knocked on the door, but there was no response. After waiting a moment on the porch, she decided to try the door, easing it open and stepping inside.

"Hannah?" Barb called out gently, her voice echoing in the quiet house. When no answer came, she moved through the living room, noting the stillness that hung in the air. The kitchen, though messy, showed no signs of recent activity. She sighed, placing the food on the counter before heading upstairs.

As JB had described, Hannah lay on her side in the bedroom, a pillow clutched between her legs, her eyes fixated on the rain-spattered window. Barb approached cautiously, her heart aching at the sight of her friend so consumed by grief.

"Hannah, dear," she called softly, but there was no response, not even a recognition. Barb sat on the edge of the bed, placing a gentle hand on the small of Hannah's back.

"Hannah how are you feeling?" she asked again.

Hannah remained motionless, her gaze still locked on the world outside, as if she were somewhere far beyond the walls of this room. The void in her expression worried Barb. She had seen this kind of emptiness before in her years of ministry – women who had faced unimaginable pain and retreated deep within themselves. Each one had to find their own way out, in their own time.

Barb hesitated for only a moment before she circled around to the other side of the bed. She kicked off her shoes and lay down beside Hannah, not saying another word. The silence stretched on, the minutes slipping away as the rain drummed softly against the window.

Eventually, Barb felt a slight pressure on her shoulder – Hannah's hand, tentative, but there. She blinked awake, rolling over to face her friend.

"Well, hello there," Barb said gently, sitting up with Hannah. "How are you feeling?"

Hannah's eyes were clearer now, though red-rimmed and tired. "What are you doing here?" she asked.

"JB called and asked if I'd check on you. He's really worried," Barb replied, studying Hannah's face for any sign of how she was truly feeling.

Hannah's lips twisted into a bitter smile. "He's so worried he hasn't been here hardly at all since the surgery."

"Hannah, you know he cares deeply about you. This is hard for him too, even if he doesn't always show it the way you need him to."

"Caring and compassionate? That's not JB. Not unless it's about his job," Hannah said.

Barb reached out, taking Hannah's hand in hers. "Let's not worry about this right now. I'm here for you. How are you doing? When I got here, you were just staring out the window. You didn't even acknowledge me."

Hannah's eyes filled with tears, and she wiped them away with the sleeve of her sweatshirt. "I'm scared Barb. I'm scared that they didn't get all the cancer out. It feels like it's still inside me, waiting for the right moment to come back. And there's nothing I can do to stop it."

Barb squeezed Hannah's hand, her voice steady and calm. "Why did you go to Stanford for the surgery?"

"Because it's one of the best places for surgical oncology," Hannah replied, a hint of doubt in her voice.

"And your surgeon?"

"He's one of the best," Hannah continued.

Barb pressed gently. "And you trusted him, didn't you?"

"Yes," Hannah whispered.

"And who else do you trust?" Barb asked, her eyes locking with Hannah's, searching for the faith she knew was buried beneath the fear.

Hannah sniffled, "I don't know."

"Hannah, you are a child of God, a woman of deep faith. When it comes to matters like this, whom do you trust and put your faith in above all else?"

"I know. I k now," she said as the tears flowed freely.

"So, trust that the Lord placed that surgeon in your life to help you, to cleanse you of this cancer," Barb said, her voice firm yet compassionate.

"But what if he didn't get it all?" Hannah asked.

"Then we'll face that together when the time comes. For now, we must have faith. Remember, Matthew 17: 'If you have faith as small as a mustard seed, you can say to this mountain, 'Move from here to there,' and it will move. Nothing will be impossible for you."

Hannah chuckled through her tears. "Mustard seed...that's about as much faith as I can muster right now."

Barb smiled and wrapped her arms around her friend, holding her close as Hannah's body shook with sobs.

"Oh, sweet girl," Barb whispered as she stroked Hannah's hair.

"I'll never have a child of my own, Barb," Hannah cried, her voice filled with grief that cut to the bone. "I'll never see my daughter's eyes looking back at me, never feel her tiny body against mine. What does it mean that God took that away from me? What did I do to deserve this?"

Barb held Hannah tighter, her own tears threatening to spill over. "Hannah, God doesn't work that way. We don't always understand His plans, but that doesn't mean He's abandoned you. We must trust in His wisdom, even when it's hard."

"What's my purpose now, Barb? If I can't have a child, what's left for me?" Hannah's voice cracked.

Barb paused, holding back her own emotions. "Your purpose is still unfolding, Hannah. There's so much more to your story than this moment. JB loves you, and together, you'll find your way through this. But for now, we take it one day at a time, and we trust in the Lord to guide us."

"I don't know if I can," Hannah whispered, her voice small and broken.

"You can," Barb replied firmly, stroking her friend's hair. "And until you find your strength again, I'll be here with you, every step of the way."

The room fell silent once more, but this time, the silence was filled with the comfort of shared pain, and the beginnings of healing.

28

C HAPTER 28

The trip through Reno, Nevada, had stretched on for several weeks, and now, as January drew to a close, Lilly Grace found herself in Fresno, California, staring at a grimy dumpster tucked away in a downtown back alley. The distant, snow-capped Sierra Nevada Mountains near Reno seemed like a distant memory. Fresno, the agricultural heart of the San Joaquin Valley, was a regular pit stop on Paco and Jade's endless road trips. Here, the Norteño connections provided them with the resources they needed – fuel, supplies, and a safe haven after two weeks on the road. Paco had a rule: never stay in one place too long, a rule he enforced with ironclad resolve.

Lilly Grace slumped in a battered lounge chair; her gaze vacant as she stared out the cracked window of a downtown motel room. In the alley, two homeless men argued, their voices rising and falling like the meaningless hum of static. For the past two weeks, Lilly Grace had spiraled deeper into the abyss of methamphetamine and OxyContin addiction, the drugs blurring the edges of her reality. What had been a lucrative New Year's Even run for Paco and Jade had been nothing short of a nightmare for Lilly Grace. Night after night, she was forced to work, her body nothing more than a tool for a procession of nameless, faceless John's. The drugs dulled the pain, numbing her to the endless cycle of abuse, but the toll they took was evident in every hollow inch of her being.

As the days bled into nights, Lilly Grace found herself pleading with Jade for more – more injections, more pills, anything to keep the agony at bay. Jade ensured that Lilly Grace never experienced a moment of sobriety, keeping her constantly high on a potential cocktail of despair. Now, as she sat in that dingy motel room, her eyes fixed on the world outside, Lilly Grace felt the weight of her existence pressing down on her, a burden too heavy to bear.

As Lilly Grace sat slumped in the chair, a sudden, piercing pain shot through her pelvic region. She winced, instinctively slipping a hand into her panties. When she pulled her fingers back, they were slick with blood. Panic surged through her – Jade and the other girls were gone for the afternoon, and thankfully, Paco was nowhere to be seen. Doubling over in the chair, she groaned as the throbbing pain intensified, sharp and relentless. Desperation took hold, and she began to scour the dingy motel room for any remnants of drugs.

She tore through Tiffany and Veronica's bags, her hands shaking, but all she found was a Ziploc bag of hash and a few rolled blunts. The thought of lighting one up crossed her mind, but she knew the pain was far beyond what marijuana could soothe. She needed something stronger, something that would obliterate the agony. Stumbling into the bathroom, she spotted a bag Jade had stashed beneath the sink. With trembling hands, she opened it to find two bottles – one filled with Oxycontin, the other with meth laced with fentanyl. Without hesitation, she poured three pills into her palm, tossed them into her mouth, and bent over the sink, frantically drinking water from her cupped hands.

Minutes passed in a blur. Lilly Grace dragged herself back to the chair, sinking into it as she gazed out the motel window. Her eyes locked on the brick wall across the alley, its surface a patchwork of faded orange and brown, smeared with streaks of gray where the owner had tried to scrub away graffiti tags. The dumpsters were overflowing with trash, and a foul-smelling liquid seeped from the base of the wall, pooling into a rancid puddle. Time seemed to stretch as Lilly Grace's vision blurred, her focus drifting between the squalid alley and the two homeless men loitering nearby. The daylight dimmed, and the sky grew ominously dark, a low rumble of thunder vibrating above the motel's ceiling.

One of the homeless men shuffled down the alley, disappearing from Lilly Grace's sight. The other – a tall, gaunt figure with long, unkempt brown hair – began to approach her window. As he drew closer, she could see the deep lines etched into his weathered face, the weary gray in his beard. He wore a tattered trench coat, and a beanie pulled low to shield himself from the elements. At first, she thought he was muttering to himself, but then she realized he was gesturing toward her. He motioned for her to come outside, his movements growing more insistent with each passing moment.

Confusion clouded her drug-addled mind. She glanced around the room, then back at the man outside. Why would he want her to come out into the alley? He waved at her again, more urgently this time, his gestures becoming increasingly frantic as she remained unresponsive. Each time he walked away, he returned, his frustration mounting as Lilly

Grace continued to stare blankly, paralyzed by a mix of pain, fear, and the numbing effects of the drugs.

Lilly Grace didn't feel any fear as the man approached; there was something gentle in his eyes, a softness that drew her in. Finally, compelled by an unexplainable force, she decided to open the door and see what he wanted. Standing in the doorway, she saw his lips moving, but no sound reached her ears. Frustration welled up within her as she strained to understand his words. The sky darkened, and heavy raindrops began to pelt the pavement, each one echoing like a warning. The man, undeterred by the storm, began to walk away, motioning for her to follow.

Lilly Grace hesitated, glancing down the alley toward the main street of downtown Fresno. The homeless man continued down the alley, disappearing into the growing shadows. A deafening roar of thunder reverberated through the narrow passage, shaking her to her core. Yet, she felt a pull, an invisible thread leading her to follow. She stepped out into the alley, her heart pounding as the storm intensified. The man was a block away, waving her onward, his silhouette fading into the gloom.

Just as she was about to turn the corner and leave the safety of the alley, a blinding bolt of lightning split the sky. It was as if time slowed, and she watched in horror as the lightning descended from the heavens, striking her directly. The sensation was surreal; she saw herself from above, as if her soul had been momentarily lifted from her body. Her veins glowed beneath her skin, branching out like the wild limbs of a tree. She hovered there, watching as her lifeless body crumpled to the ground, her skin turning an ashen white.

In that moment, she realized the man had been no ordinary vagrant. His presence, the storm, the lighting – it all carried a weight of divine significance. The thunder was not just a warning, but a call, and the lightning was more than a strike; it was a celestial sign. She had been unable to respond, her soul too lost in the darkness of addiction and despair.

Suddenly, she felt a tapping on her face, drawing her back to the present. She awoke in the motel room, the dim light from the table lamp revealing Jade's concerned expression as she examined Lilly Grace's eyes. It took a moment to orient herself, but when she glanced back out toward the alley, the sky was clear, a serene blue, and the pavement was completely dry. There was no sign of the storm, nor the mysterious man who had tried to lead her out of the darkness.

Tiffany and Veronica frantically paced the room, rifling through their bags. Their frustration boiled over, and they hurled accusations at each other before turning their anger toward Lilly Grace. Still reeling from her surreal experience in the alley, Lilly Grace was barely aware of her surroundings. Jade shook her roughly, trying to snap her out of her daze.

"Chica, what the hell is wrong with you?" Jade demanded, her voice sharp.

Lilly Grace, still in shock, struggled to process what she had just encountered. The effects of the fentanyl and methamphetamine coursing through her veins made her feel like she was trapped in quicksand. Everything around her moved in slow motion, and it was a struggle just to breathe. She could see Tiffany and Veronica arguing intensely, though the room was eerily silent to her dulled senses.

Jade stormed into the bathroom, searching through her bag under the sink. From the other room, she shouted, "You stupid bitch, what did you do? What did you take out of this bag?"

Returning to the room, Jade stood in front of Lilly Grace, her eyes blazing with anger. "What did you take out of this bag? ¡Perra estúpida! ¿Te estás queriendo matar?"

"Yeah, the dumb bitch is trying to kill herself," Veronica chimed in.

"She's fuckin' dyin' isn't she?" Tiffany asked. "What are we gonna do?"

All three women paced nervously, unsure of what to do. The idea of taking Lilly Grace to the hospital was quickly dismissed – they couldn't risk getting law enforcement involved.

"Call Paco, he'll know what to do," Veronica urged.

Jade pulled out her phone and dialed Paco's number.

"What's up?" Paco answered.

"I think that bitch OD'd in our room," Jade blurted out.

"What the fuck? What are you talking about?"

"She's sitting in this chair and can't fuckin' move. She can barely keep her eyes open."

"Is she breathing?" he asked.

"Barely. She's all pale and clammy and shit."

"All right, calm the fuck down. Go to my bag in the closet. In the side pocket is some Narcan. Shoot her up with 2 milligrams of that shit. It should wake her ass up."

Jade rushed to the closet, pulled out the Narcan vial along with a tourniquet, syringe, and needle. She tossed the tourniquet to Veronica. "Tie off her arm," she ordered.

Jade mixed the Narcan with the saline solution and approached Lilly Grace, tapping her veins to find a good spot. She injected the first dose and waited, but Lilly Grace remained unresponsive.

"She' still not responding, Paco. What now?" Jade asked.

"Hit her again. Just keep shooting her up until she wakes the fuck up. If she dies, she dies. We'll get rid of her sorry ass. I'm about done with this whiny bitch anyway"

Jade prepared another dose, repeating the process. Tiffany and Veronica watched anxiously, holding their breath. Finally, after what felt like an eternity, Lilly Grace gasped for air and collapsed to the floor. Jade quickly rolled her onto her side, relieved but still shaken.

"Did she wake up?" Paco asked.

"Yeah, she's awake. It worked," Jade replied.

She hung up the phone and tossed it onto the bed. The room fell into a tense silence as the reality of what had just happened began to sink in.

Lilly Grace lay on the floor, her body trembling as the effects of the Narcan slowly pulled her back from the brink. Her eyes fluttered, struggling to focus, and she tried to speak, but her words were muffled by the choking and retching that wracked her body. Jade knelt beside her, roughly patting and rubbing her back, trying to help her expel whatever was blocking her airway. After several agonizing minutes, Lilly Grace's breathing began to stabilize, and the others could finally make out what she was trying to say.

"The old man?" Lilly Grace rasped, her voice barely above a whisper.

"The who?" Jade asked.

"The old man in the alley. Is he okay?"

Jade exchanged confused glances with Tiffany and Veronica. "What are you talkin' about? What old man?"

"In the alley," Lilly Grace insisted, her eyes wide with desperation. "When you got me out of the alley, did you see the old man?"

The girls looked at each other, their expressions growing more perplexed. They had no idea what Lilly Grace was referring to.

"There was an old man in the alley," Lilly Grace continued. "A homeless man. There were two of them. They argued, then one left, and the other one came toward the window, trying to talk to me. I went outside to follow him, but a storm came, and I was struck by lightning."

Jade shook her head, pointing to the window. "I don't know what the hell you're talking about. It hasn't rained here in a week. Look at that pavement – it's dry as a bone. There wasn't no storm."

"And there probably wasn't' any old man either," Veronica added, rolling her eyes. "You're probably just hallucinating from all that fentanyl."

"No," Lilly Grace insisted, her voice pleading. "There was an old man."

She slowly sat up, her eyes scanning the room before turning to the window. The pavement outside was indeed dry, and there was no sign of any recent rain or storm. No trace of the lightning bolt she was so certain of had struck her. It was as if the entire experience had vanished into thin air.

Later that evening, the other girls prepared to leave for a house party on the south side of Fresno. Jade and Paco had a heated argument over whether Lilly Grace should join them. Jade, in a rare moment of compassion, argued that pushing Lilly Grace too hard would render her useless, convincing Paco to let her have the night off.

Lilly Grace spent the evening sitting by the window, her mind racing. The alley was empty, devoid of any sign of the homeless man or the storm she remembered so vividly. She couldn't shake the feeling that what she had experienced was more than just a drug-induced hallucination. She had felt the storm, seen the lightning, and heard the man's whispered pleas as he tried to communicate with her. But now, as she stared out at the quiet, dry pavement, she wondered if it had all been a figment of her imagination – a desperate mind grasping for some form of salvation amid her torment.

Yet, deep down, Lilly Grace couldn't shake the feeling that the old man had been real. Perhaps he wasn't just a homeless man but something more – an angelic figure sent to rescue her, only for her to be too lost to respond. And the lightning? Could it have been a divine intervention, a warning, or a sign of the battle raging within her soul? The questions gnawing at her, leaving her uncertain of what was real and what was not, as she sat alone, waiting for the answers that might never come.

29

— · —

C HAPTER 29

Hannah's heart felt heavy as she readied herself to rejoin the marriage ministry group at the First Baptist Church of Turlock. More than a month had passed since her previous attendance – prior to her surgery and the subsequent lengthy recovery. Numerous group members had visited, bringing meals and offering comforting words, yet she had remained isolated, shunning any interaction. Now, after such an extended absence, Hannah recognized the necessity of going back. She longed for their companionship, their connections, and above all, the solace provided by their shared faith.

Over the past two weeks, one conversation in particular kept echoing in her mind – Barb Adams' words had struck a deep chord within her. Hannah had spent those days lying in bed, wrestling with her faith and questioning her trust in God. She had spent years reading the Bible, attending small group studies, and investing hours in marriage counseling. Yet now, all that she believed was being tested. The word that lingered in her thoughts the most was "mustard seed." She wondered if her faith, once so strong, had shriveled into something barren and poisonous, devoid of the love and fulfillment that came with motherhood. And if so, she couldn't help but ask why God had allowed her to be stricken in such a way.

As she pulled into the church parking lot, something felt different. The pavement was still damp from a late afternoon sprinkle, the streetlights cast a warm, yellow glow, and a thin veil of fog hovered over the church's steeple. The last time she had walked through these doors, her faith had been unwavering. Now, for the first time, she felt a deep uncertainty.

The ladies met in a small, private room behind the chapel, located in the upstairs wing of the church. As Hannah stepped through the door, she immediately noticed Barb Adams at the back of the room, deep in conversation with an elderly woman who had recently lost her husband of fifty years. Barb had always been the one people turned to in their time of need. She was a beacon of warmth and compassion, and as Hannah watched her, she couldn't help but notice the gentleness that radiated from Barb. The way she touched the elderly woman's hand, the soothing tone of her voice – it was clear that Barb was using her God-given gifts to comfort and heal.

As Hannah scanned the room, she caught eyes of a few of the women, but they quickly averted their gazes, pretending to be engrossed in other conversations or busying themselves with something else. She understood their discomfort; the news of her surgery and subsequent infertility had spread through the church like wildfire. It was the kind of story that sparked hushed conversations and sympathetic glances, but not many knew how to address it directly. She didn't blame them – she herself wouldn't have known what to say if she were in their shoes.

Suddenly, she heard her name called across the room. It was Angie Wideman, the church's unofficial queen of gossip. Hannah braced herself, unsure of what kind of welcome she would receive, but she knew that tonight, she had to face whatever was coming. It was time to confront her doubts, her pain, and perhaps, in doing so, find a way to restore the faith that had once been her anchor.

"Hannah, I'm so glad you were able to make it out tonight." Angie's voice was bright, almost too bright, as she gave Hannah a quick side hug. The forced cheerfulness in her tone wasn't lost on Hannah, and she responded with a polite, if somewhat strained, half-smile. But despite the lack of genuine warmth, Hannah had to admit that Angie was at least good at breaking the ice. Her enthusiastic greeting seemed to signal to the others that it was safe to approach, and one by one, the women began to come forward, offering hugs and expressing their happiness that Hannah was back.

For a few moments, the room buzzed with quiet chatter as the women took turns reconnecting with Hannah, sharing kind words and small updates on their lives. The warmth of their welcome, though perhaps awkward and hesitant at first, began to chip away at the wall of isolation Hannah had built around herself. She found herself beginning to relax, even if just a little.

Once everyone had had a chance to say their hellos, Barb Adams gently called the group to order. The room quieted as she led them in their customary expressions of gratitude, a practice that always helped to center their minds and spirits. The women shared moments from their week – small victories, answered prayers, unexpected blessings. Hannah listened quietly, drawing comfort from the ritual, even as her own heart remained heavy with unspoken burdens.

When it came time for the spiritual reading, Barb's voice was steady and soothing as she led them through the passage for the week. The familiar words washed over Hannah, reminding her of the many times she had found solace in these very scriptures. Yet tonight, they seemed to touch her in a different way, resonating with the doubts and questions she had been wrestling with for weeks.

As they concluded the reading, Barb asked the group to share their prayer requests, a practice that always brought the women closer together. One by one, they spoke, each request revealing a glimpse into the struggles and hopes that lay beneath the surface of their lives. When it was Hannah's turn, she hesitated, unsure how to put her thoughts into words. She felt the weight of their expectant gazes, and for a moment, she considered holding back, offering something vague and safe. But then, she realized that this was exactly why she had come – to confront her fears and doubts, and to lean on the faith of these women when her own felt so fragile.

Finally, she spoke, her voice quiet but clear. "I would appreciate prayers for strength and understanding. I've been struggling a lot lately...questioning my faith, questioning God's plan for me. It's been hard to find peace, and I'm not sure what the path forward looks like. But I know I need to find my way back to trust to belief...belief in Him, in myself, in everything." She paused, her eyes searching the faces of the women around the room. "So, I guess what I'm asking for is...faith. That God will help me find it again."

The room was silent for a moment, the weight of Hannah's words hanging in the air. Then, Barb reached out and placed a hand on Hannah's arm, her touch warm and reassuring. "We're here for you, Hannah. And we'll be praying for you every step of the way. God's love is still with you, even in the doubts. Especially in the doubts."

The others murmured their agreement, and Hannah felt a small, but significant shift in her heart. It wasn't an answer, but it was a start – a first step back toward the faith she so desperately needed to reclaim.

***

As the last of the women filtered out of the room, Barb caught Hannah's eye and motioned for her to stay back. Hannah's curiosity piqued as she approached Barb, who seemed uncharacteristically hesitant

"Hannah, do you have a few minutes? There's something I wanted to discuss with you. It may not be the right time, but it's time-sensitive, and I wanted to gauge your interest."

"Sure, Barb. What's going on?"

"Here, take a seat for a minute," Barb suggested, gesturing to a nearby chair.

Hannah sat down, studying Barb's demeanor. There was a seriousness in her tone that made Hannah wonder what this could be about.

"First, let me say that I understand it was literally only two weeks ago that we had our first conversation in your bed. And I have to say, you've come a long way since that day. I'm grateful that you've allowed me to visit with you during that time and share your heart with me. I don't take that lightly. I'm so very proud of you."

"Barb, what is it? Is everything okay with you and Mr. Adams?"

"Oh, heavens, yes. Everything is fine with us."

"Well, what is it? You're kind of scaring me."

"Oh no, that is not what I'm trying to do at all. My hesitation is that I'm just not sure this is the right time to bring this up to you. I've been praying nonstop the last few days," Barb confessed.

"Okay, just go ahead and tell me. I'm okay, I promise."

"Hear me out, okay, then you can share your thoughts with me. Alright?"

"Sure, just go ahead."

"Do you know Mrs. Amanda Perry?" Barb asked.

"I don't know her really. I know her from church. Why?"

"Well, Mrs. Perry is on the board at Faith Hope, a child welfare agency for Stanislaus County."

"Okay?"

"A case was brought to her attention a couple of weeks ago, and she shared some of the details with me. I'm not sure how you would feel about this, but I thought of you," Barb said.

"For what?" Hannah asked.

"There are two girls, siblings, who came through the system. In fact, over the past two years, they've been in and out of the foster system. The agency is looking for a qualified family to assist these two young girls as a foster family. It's only a temporary situation until they can go through a process in the system to find an adoptive family."

"Why me? Why did you think of me?"

"I know you've got a lot going on with recovery from surgery. But based on what I can tell, you are recovering and healing well. And, when it comes to a woman who has so much love in her heart and a willingness to share that love with children, I couldn't think of anyone else but you," Barb said softly.

"I don't get it. Don't you have to be qualified to be a foster parent? Plus, I've got so much going on at home already," Hannah countered, feeling overwhelmed by the sudden proposal.

"I know. I know. We do need to pray about this and make sure it is the right time for you and your family," Barb acknowledged.

Hannah noticed Barb's use of the word "we" and found herself intrigued by the idea, despite all the reasons not to be.

"What would I have to do? How long would this be for?"

"You wouldn't have to do anything other than be yourself. The agency is looking for a family to house these two young girls and provide a positive environment for them while they go through the system and the process for adoption," Barb explained.

"How long does it take?" Hannah asked.

"Six months, and possibly up to eighteen months?"

"What would I do with girls for a year and a half?"

"I doubt it would take that long," Barb said reassuringly.

Hannah leaned back in her chair, trying to process the conversation. She was healed from surgery, and her doctor had cleared her to resume normal activities. But what would Jared or JB say? How would Jared react to two girls suddenly living in their house? For all the reasons not to do it, the idea still held a strange appeal.

"Barb, I don't understand why you think this is a good time for me to even consider something like this. I mean, JB and I aren't exactly on the best of terms right now. And I'm not sure if bringing two girls into the house is the best thing for Jared. What would he think?"

"Hannah, I'm not asking you to say yes tonight. I would request that you take some time to think about it. Think about what a great resource you could be for these two girls. Their past foster experiences have not been the best. I think you and JB could really be a good thing for these two," Barb urged.

"I don't know, it seems like we're dealing with a lot of heavy issues already, and now you're asking me to add more stress and problems onto my plate. It can't be easy taking in girls who are part of the foster system. I mean, they've probably got all kinds of problems and issues," Hannah reasoned.

"Hannah, you are a teacher at heart. You are a giver, and God has given you this gift. I'm not saying it's going to be easy. What in this world worth doing is easy? I'm saying that I think you would be perfect to give these two girls a proper home that is full of love. It's something they've never seen in their entire lives," Barb said, her voice full of conviction.

"I don't know, Barb," Hannah replied.

"I know it's scary, and it's a big idea I've thrown at you. Just take a couple of days to think about it. I'm confident that once you meet these two girls, you'll just fall in love with them," Barb encouraged.

"Barb, why do I think you've already decided that I'm going to say yes?" Hannah asked, a small smile playing on her lips.

"I would never suppose anything of such. Besides, God tells us what we need to do; we just need to be silent and listen for His nudging," Barb said with a gentle smile.

They shared a lighthearted moment, joking about the strangeness of God's timing. As they continued to talk about Hannah's recovery, the thought of the two girls lingered in Hannah's mind. The idea of providing a home for them, despite the challenges in might bring, began to take root in her heart.

30

Eric was alone in the softly lit office; the rattle of the ceiling fan was the sole disruption of silence. His fingers tapped rhythmically on the desk, eyes darting to the door at each groan from the aged structure. The impending meeting's gravity bore down on him, constricting his breath as he awaited.

The arrival of a black sedan broke the night's stillness, its occupants stepping out into the streetlight's faded halo. Their silhouettes striking against the backlight, climbed the narrow staircase, their footfalls echoing through the empty structure.

Rising, Eric swiped his hands across his cotton clad pants and swung the door open. "Coffee?" he proposed.

"No, thanks," Eduardo replied smoothly, while the other man, known only as the Ghost, moved past Eric without a word.

The Ghost began his silent inspection of the office, methodically checking under piles of paperwork, running his hand beneath the tables, and studying the light fixtures with a narrowed gaze. Eric felt a chill run down his spine as he watched, the man's silence more unnerving than any words could have been.

Unable to stand the tension any longer. "You think they bugged the office?" Eric finally asked.

The Ghost paused, eyes narrowing as he glanced at Eric, but he didn't respond. Instead, he continued his search, his attention now on the electrical outlets.

Eduardo stepped beside Eric, placing a reassuring hand on his shoulder. "Mijo, relax. It's standard procedure. He knows what he's doing."

Eric nodded, but the knot in his stomach only tightened.

After what felt like an eternity, the Ghost pulled out a large map of the Tulare and San Joaquin Valley. The map was marked with red and yellow highlights, each point a silent threat.

Eduardo began, "Eric, if you look at the red trail mark down near Tulare – "

"First," the Ghost interrupted, his voice low and commanding, "tell me how our visit with the Feds went."

Eric blinked, caught off guard by the sudden question. He glanced at Eduardo, searching for reassurance, but found none. The room seemed to close in on him as he tried to gauge how much fear he should be feeling.

"It was no big deal," Eric stammered. "They don't have anything on me."

The Ghost's eyes locked onto his, unblinking. "These transactions are worth millions of dollars. Everything is a big deal. What did they say?"

Eric swallowed hard, his mouth dry. "Nothing. They tried to pin a few things on me that happened over the last few months."

"It is my understanding," the Ghost continued, his voice devoid of emotion, "that until recently, you had never been detained by authorities. Is that correct?"

"Yes, that's correct."

"Therefore, you have no understanding of how they operate. So, let's try this again. How many authorities visited you?"

Eric's pulse raced. "Four."

"What types of questions did the first authority ask?"

"He didn't really ask any questions," Eric began, his voice shaking slightly. "He just talked about our hood and how he grew up in a similar hood down south. He told me if I cooperated, it would reflect better for me at trial."

The Ghost's eyes squinted further. "Good. What about the second?"

"He stated the facts of three different cases. He laid out how I was connected to each case. He showed me mug shots and photos of a dead girl's body."

"The third?"

"He focused on one particular case – "

"Which case?"

"I don't know."

The Ghost leaned in. "Which case?"

Eric flinched. "He talked about a confidential informant that was murdered in our neighborhood."

"That's it?"

"He questioned my knowledge of the informant. My knowledge of the person who was arrested for the murder."

"What is your relationship to Hector Valdez?"

"He's a member of our crew," Eric answered, but the words felt flimsy even to him.

"You don't think I know that?" The Ghost leaned closer, his voice dropping to a near-growl. "What is your relationship to Hector Valdez?"

Eric felt the floor tilt beneath him, his knees silently weakening. "We went to grade school together and high school together."

The Ghost's hands slammed down on the table, the sudden noise making Eric jump. "What is your relationship with the man, Hector Valdez? Is there anything that can tie you to him and the murder of this girl?"

Eric's shoulders slumped, the fight draining out of him. "No. No. Look, he's a low-level member of our crew that's known to get drunk and high. The homies that run with him are just as crazy. But I had nothing to do with that girl."

"Did he call you for help?"

Eric's throat tightened. "Yes, he called me, and I told him to just take care of it."

"You told him to take care of it. Is that what you said?"

"Yes, something like that."

The Ghost's lips curled into a cold smile. "So, if I'm an authority, what I just heard was you gave approval to put a hit on this girl. Your man, a member of your crew, contacted you via phone and you gave the order to murder this girl."

"That's not what I'm saying at all," Eric said, shaking his head frantically.

The Ghost raised both of his arms, a mock surrender. "Okay. Here's the deal. I'm in charge now. Nothing happens without my approval. ¿Comprende?"

Eric opened his mouth to respond, but the Ghost's hand shot up, silencing him. "We will take care of Hector Valdez and his homeboys in-house. Just like we took care of the authority's CI. And we'll take care of Medina and his boys in-house."

Eric knew the Ghost saw the weakness in his eyes, knew that the mantle of leadership had just slipped from his grasp. From this point forward, the valley was the Ghost's territory.

"Don't worry about Valdez, Medina, or any other pendejo testifying in court. We'll make sure that never happens. You need to get your crew in order. You understand me?"

"Yes, I understand," Eric said, nodding his head.

"Good," the Ghost said, his tone softening just a fraction. "Now, Eduardo, please continue."

Eduardo stepped forward, pointing to the map and describing the logistics of the shipments. "In two weeks, we'll bring one of the largest shipments up from Mexico. The test shipments made it across the border and up through Riverside County without any delays or issues. A few small shipments continued up Highway 99, over the Tehachapi's, and down into Bakersfield. All logistics worked smoothly. The Ghost made sure the storage area outside Bakersfield was locked down with security in place. The next phase was transportation through the Central Valley from Fresno to Modesto, and up through Stockton and Sacramento. Ultimately, it'll go up to the far Northern Sacramento Valley and into Redding."

Eric listened, the words barely registering as his mind churned with everything that had just transpired. The Ghost had taken control, and Eric was no longer the leader of the WSF. He was a soldier, nothing more.

"What are we talking about on loads for these first shipments?" Eric asked, his voice hollow.

"The test shipments are approximately 1,000 pounds of meth; 9 kilos of fentanyl powder and 330,000 fentanyl pills; 25 kilos of cocaine; and 15 kilos of heroin. We'll have a shipment of guns for support and upwards of $500K in cash," Eduardo replied.

The Ghost added, "And Mijo, know that this is a test run. Once we're sure security is in place and distribution points are set, we'll increase supply month over month."

"Eric, I've known you for a long time, Mijo. I knew your father back in the day," Eduardo said in a soft tone. "We're here because we believe in you and your crew. You're like family to us, Mijo. But we must be certain that you've got your crew locked down. We can't have any distractions like what happened with that little girl."

Eric squared his shoulders, trying to summon the confidence that had been drained from him. "Look, I've got the crew locked in, okay? There's nothing to worry about as far as that goes. We've made progress on detailing our membership and identifying any rats."

Eduardo nodded, a small smile on his lips. "That's good, Mijo. As I said, you are like family to us. Your father's name carries a great deal of weight up on high. But we can't have any more issues. If the Ghost gives you an order, you follow it without questions. Understood?"

Eric nodded, feeling more like a puppet than a leader. "Understood."

31

C HAPTER 31

JB sat in his office, surrounded by mug shots and rap sheets scattered across his desk. The list of names associated with the WSF was daunting – over one hundred and forty in total. Most were low-level street kids arrested for drug possession, loitering, tagging, or vandalism. JB's eyes scanned the pages, noting the core thirty members of the crew, with a handful having done time in County Jail or returning from the state penitentiary. To his surprise, two names were notably absent from the list: Eric Avina and Paco Ramirez. Neither had shown up in any legal system records.

His FBI-issued cell phone buzzed, interrupting his thoughts. An unknown number from the 209-area code flashed on the screen. The text was short and to the point: "Manny said to call you if I needed help." JB's heart skipped a beat at the sight of Manny's name. He had never mentioned to JB that he'd told anyone about his role as a confidential informant or that he gave his phone number to anyone else. JB stared at the message, reading it over and over, unease creeping into his gut.

He quickly ran the number through the FBI database, and a hit came back on Dominique Velasquez. Dominique was a twenty-four-year-old from Ceres, a small town on the edge of the Deep South Side of Modesto. JB pulled up his record: Dominique had done five years from age eighteen to twenty-three, with a few trips to juvenile hall in his teens. His arrest record was littered with charges – drug and firearm possession, and attempted burglary. The notes flagged him as a Norteño affiliate, with six of the ten criteria for gang affiliation, which included a dragon tattoo with G14 in its body, gang attire, Norteño symbols, and identification by a reliable source. He'd been released from High Desert nine months ago and was listed as residing at 914 Pleasant Avenue, a notorious spot on the Southwest side of Ceres – a place where bodies were often found, and even local law enforcement treaded lightly.

JB's mind raced. Manny had never mentioned a cousin, nor had he confided his informant role to anyone, as far as JB knew. Trusting the message was risky; it could easily be a setup to lure him into a vulnerable position for a hit. If they were to meet, it would have to be in a public place, with backup on site, preferably with a scoped rifle. JB texted back: "How do you know Manny?"

Minutes ticked by before a response came: "He was mi primo." JB digested the reply, his mind weighing the possibilities. The screen showed typing again, and JB waited, tension coiling in his chest.

Finally, Dominique's next message appeared: "I've got info you're going to want to hear."

JB hesitated, memories of Manny's desperate plea for help flashing through his mind – the call that had ultimately cost Manny his life. If his cousin was reaching out now, it had to be serious. But the brazen nature of Manny's murder made JB wary. He had to act fast, but cautiously.

He offered to meet in Ceres, but Dominique was quick to decline, insisting on meeting out of town, ten miles south, along Golden State Boulevard. JB thought carefully about the location. It had to be open, public, and with a clear line of sight for long-range support. And most importantly, it needed to be a place where the presence of WSF members would be easily noticeable.

***

At the corner of Taylor Road, near the northern edge of Turlock, the aqueduct ran silently along the landscape. A dirt road intersected Taylor and North Quincy, tracing the aqueduct's entire expanse. Two hundred yards away stood a small farmhouse with outbuildings. JB had stationed a sniper atop one of the two-story buildings, providing overwatch, and positioned cars strategically for quick access. Now, he sat in his Toyota Tacoma by the aqueduct, waiting.

A metallic green 1974 Monte Carlo approached slowly from the west, its engine a low growl. JB recognized the make and model – it had to be Dominique Velasquez. He stepped out of the Tacoma, moving to the rear of the vehicle, keeping himself shielded. The Monte Carlo pulled onto the dirt road, stopping on the opposite side of the intersection. A man exited, scanning the area. After a tense moment, Dominique began walking across North Quincy toward the Toyota Tacoma.

Dominique wasn't an imposing figure – thin, about five-eleven, with tattoos covering his arms, neck, and creeping onto his face. As he reached the front of the Tacoma, JB called out, "That's far enough. Turn around and put your hands on your head."

"What the fuck is this," Dominique snapped.

"Do as I say. Hands on your head, turn around."

Dominique complied, grumbling under his breath. JB stepped out from behind the Tacoma, his gun drawn, eyes scanning the road for any signs of backup. Nothing. His spotter atop the outbuildings gave the all-clear. JB moved in, kicking Dominique's ankles apart. Dominique didn't resist; he knew the drill. JB patted him down, starting at the waistband, moving down to the ankles. No weapons.

"So, this is how you treat someone who's trying to help you?" Dominique sneered.

"I don't know who you are," JB shot back. "Turn around."

Dominique turned, stepping toward the front of the Tacoma. JB noted his fidgeting – was it nerves or something else?

"Why did you text me?" JB asked.

"Bro, I text you because your sorry ass let my cousin get killed."

The accusation hit JB like a punch to the gut. No one had said it out loud before, but it was something he'd told himself repeatedly. The words stung, cutting deeper than he'd expected.

"What information do you have?" JB pressed, trying to regain control of the conversation.

"Before I give you anything, you gotta help me."

"Help you? From what I can tell, you're tied up with WSF, and it was your crew that put the hit on your cousin, not me." JB's tone hardened. "Your boys did this, not me."

"No, man. He asked you for help, and you didn't do shit. You left him to get executed in his own house. He called me when he couldn't reach you."

"What did he tell you?" JB demanded.

"Everything. How he was working with you to get his sentence reduced. He was panicking, saying the crew was coming for him. He said cars were following him, weird shit was happening." Dominique's eyes blazed with the accusation.

"Now he is dead. What do you have for me?" JB asked, trying to push past the guilt gnawing at him.

"You're a cold piece of shit, you know that?" Dominique spat.

"I'm a busy man," JB retorted, his patience wearing thin. "I don't have time to listen to you blame me for your cousin's choices. He lived and died by those choices."

"Fine, fine," Dominique said. "Look, I got out two years ago. Since then, I've been trying to get my shit together. I've got a two-year old and another on the way. It's hard, man. Coming out of prison, you got nothing. No job, no help. I'm out here every day, tryin' to find work. How am I supposed to support my family like this?"

"I don't have much time for your sob story," JB interrupted. "I'm here to solve a murder. Can you help me or not?"

"Yeah, I can help," Dominique admitted. "I'm still connected. There are people in our hood that ain't from our hood. Shit's getting' out of hand. And I know who killed Manny. I know the piece of shit that put a bullet in his head and burned his body. If you don't take care of him, I will."

"The driver of the Honda Accord was Gustavo Perez Medina. We haven't been able to locate him since the murder."

"You won't," Dominique said, his voice low. "But I know where he is. And I know the other three who were with him."

"Who gave Medina the green light?" JB asked.

"Eric Avina," Dominique replied. "But this goes way higher than him. We've got homies up from Mexico. I've never seen these dudes before. Something big is going down."

"Can you help us locate Medina and the others?" JB pressed. "Will you testify?"

"What are you gonna do for me?" Dominique asked. "I can't be getting killed out here while I wait for you to figure out what to do."

"If you give me solid evidence, with written testimony and a court appearance on Medina, I'll get you and your family protected," JB promised.

"You get us protected now, and I'll get you what you need," Dominique countered. "I've seen how this works, and your track record ain't that good homie."

JB nodded. "Go home and pack up your family. I'll send you a text with the location where you'll be safe. Okay?"

"You get us safe, and I'll get you what you need," Dominique agreed.

"What I need is for this entire house of cards to come crashing down," JB said, his voice cold. "I want Avina, Ramirez, and Medina. I want them all behind bars for life."

The men shared a tense embrace before walking in opposite directions. As soon as Dominique was out of sight, JB called Warnall, informing him of the breakthrough and the potential lead. They needed to secure protection for Dominique and his family immediately. The wheels were already in motion.

***

Dominique returned to his house in Ceres, the weight of the day's events pressing heavily on his shoulders. As he entered through the front door, his eyes darted around the living room, searching for his girlfriend and little boy. "Mija?" he called out, but there was no response. He made his way to the kitchen, where he spotted his two-year-old son playing in a sandbox in the backyard. Relief flooded through him, but it was short-lived.

Dominique rushed outside, scooped up his son, and hurried back into the house. As they reached the steps, he saw his girlfriend, six months pregnant, standing in the kitchen, chatting on the phone. Her carefree demeanor contrasted sharply with the panic coursing through him. He motioned for her to hang up, rocking their little boy in his arms, his movements urgent.

She frowned at his agitation, covering the phone's mouthpiece. "What's going on, Dom?"

"We're getting out of here, Mija," he whispered, his voice strained. "Hang up the phone."

"What are you talking about?" She turned back to the phone, dismissing his urgency. "Mom, I gotta go. Dom just got home, and I need to see what he's up to. I'll call you later, okay?"

"Babe, please," Dominique urged. "Hang up. Now."

Finally, she hung up. Dominique grabbed her hand and pulled her through the house to the back bedroom, his grip firm. He set their little boy down on the bed and began frantically searching through the closet. Clothes were tossed to the floor in his haste until he found a suitcase buried at the back. He dumped its contents and thrust it into her hands.

"What the hell are you doing, Dom?" she demanded.

"We've got to go, and we've got to pack. We have to do it now."

"Dom, you're scaring me. Just tell me what's happening."

"They came for Manny, and they're coming for me next. And when they hit me, they're going to hit you too."

Her eyes widened in disbelief. "Who's coming for you? What are you talking about?"

"The crew killed Manny, and they're going to kill me too."

"Why?" Matha said, fear starting to rise through her voice. "You're not involved with the FBI."

"This isn't normal hood shit," Dominique said. "This is bigger. This is coming from up high, and they're using cartel guys to run things now."

"I thought Eric and Paco were running the crew?"

"They ain't runnin' shit anymore. They just don't know it yet."

"Where are we supposed to go?"

"I don't know yet," Dominique admitted. "I'm waiting for a text from the FBI guy Manny was working with. He said he'd get us somewhere safe."

She shot him a doubtful look. "Didn't he promise the same thing to Manny? And look how that turned out."

"I trust this guy, Mija. I looked into his eyes, and I trust him," Dominique said as he paced the floor. "I don't know what happened to Manny, but we don't have any other choice. I've got to trust him. Now, please, just pack the damn bag."

Dominique's girlfriend hesitated for a moment, then began stuffing clothes into the suitcase, her movements stiff with fear. Dominique, meanwhile, headed to the bathroom. Under the sink, he lifted a loose floorboard, revealing a hidden stash. He grabbed a couple stacks of hundred-dollar bills, his hands shaking. Back in the bedroom, he reached into the nightstand, pulling out a .45 and a Ziplock bag filled with marijuana. He knew it was only a matter of time before they linked his name to Manny's death.

Returning to the bedroom, Dominique's heart pounded in his chest as he shoved the money into the suitcase and tucked the gun behind the back of his waistband. His girlfriend looked at him, fear etched across her face, but she said nothing. They both knew the gravity of the situation.

"We need to go. Now," Dominique said.

She nodded, clutching their little boy. As they hurried out of the house, Dominique couldn't shake the feeling that time was running out. Every second counted, and with every step they took, the walls of their old life crumbled behind them.

32

— · —

C HAPTER 32

It was a quiet Friday morning, and the First Baptist Church of Turlock's parking lot was nearly empty, save for five scattered vehicles. As Hannah stepped onto the church campus, the stillness felt surreal. The usual hum of activity was absent, and the echoes of her footsteps bounced off the brick walls, amplifying the silence. Normally, by the time she dropped Jared off, the choir would already be four songs deep in worship. But today, there was only silence.

Barb Adams had assured her that this was merely an exploratory conversation, a chance to learn more about the fostering process. But to Hannah, it felt less like a discussion and more like she was walking into an ambush – one set by a cunning predator.

The Pastor's executive assistant greeted Hannah warmly at the door, offering coffee or water. Hannah politely declined, her nerves making the thought of consuming anything unappealing. The assistant guided her down the quiet hallway to a large conference room. Upon entering, Hannah was met with the expectant faces of Barb Adams, Amanda Davies from the Faith Home Christian Adoption Agency, and Pastor Wilkins.

After exchanging pleasantries, the atmosphere quickly shifted as Barb took charge, cutting straight to the point. "We all know why we're here today and the opportunity at hand. There are two young girls for whom we are seeking temporary housing. Mrs. Davies, could you share more details about the girls and their situation?"

Amand Davies nodded, reaching into her briefcase and pulling out four manilla file folders. Hannah took one and opened it, revealing the photos of two young girls. The first was a headshot of Abigale Furtado, a seven-year-old with solemn brown eyes. The second was her younger sister, Sariah Furtado, five years old, with a similar look of guarded innocence. Both girls had long brown hair and a beauty that tugged at Hannah's heart. Yet, what drew her in most was their eyes – especially Sariah's. There was an innocence in them, tinged with the numbness of a child who had seen too much. Abigale's eyes, on the other hand, held a weariness far beyond her years, her smile forced as if she already understood too much of the world's harsh realities.

"As you can see, these are sisters Abigale and Sariah Furtado," Amanda began. "They've been in the foster system for the past two years. Their father's whereabouts have been unknown since Abigale was two years old. Their mother, unfortunately, has spent much of the last three years in and out of County Jail on prostitution and drug charges. Currently, they're housed in a group home with several other foster children. Their mother was recently arrested again, and her court case is coming up in a few weeks. Our goal is to find a positive environment for these girls as they await, they're outcome."

"What does it mean to be a foster parent?" she asked.

Amanda smiled gently. "That's a great question, Hannah. The first step would be an interview with you and your husband followed by a walkthrough of your home. Thankfully, you come highly recommended by both Mrs. Adams and Pastor Wilkins, so pending a background check, interview, and home visit, you and your husband could be qualified as foster parents for the Furtado sisters."

Hannah nodded. "I understand the process. But what I don't understand is what I'm supposed to do with these girls. How long will they be in my care? What if they don't like our house? I just don't know about any of this."

"We understand that you have a lot of questions, which is why we're here today. If the girls were to come into your care, your primary role would be to provide them with a safe and loving environment. They would continue attending school just like any other child. As far as the timeline is concerned, the shortest period they could be in your care would be the remainder of the school year – so around five months. The longest could be up to eighteen months, as we work to find them a long-term adoptive family."

Pastor Wilkins, who had been quietly listening, took a long sip of his coffee. He was a man of stature within the community, having served as the pastor of First Baptist for twenty-six years. He knew nearly every member of the congregation by name, having presided over countless births, baptisms, and funerals. When he spoke, people listened, regardless of the occasion. Now, he ran his fingers through his gray beard, a thoughtful look on his face.

"As far as the girls not liking your home, Mrs. Phillips, I don't see how that would be possible," he said, his tone kind but firm. "Consider where they've been living – correct me if I'm wrong, Mrs. Davies, but they're currently in a group home with about twenty-five other children, right? I'd imagine that your home would be a welcome reprieve for them."

Hannah hesitated, feeling the weight of his words, but she couldn't shake her concerns. "But I haven't even talked to JB about this yet. I don't know how he's going to respond."

The truth was, she and JB hadn't spent much time talking about anything meaningful in recent weeks. Their only significant moment together had been the day of her surgery. But ever since Manny's death, JB had become increasingly distant, consumed by the case against the WSF. Deep down, she worried that they wouldn't even make it through the interview phase – assuming JB would even agree to attend an interview.

"Aren't there any other families you could consider for these girls?" Hannah asked.

Barb's expression softened. "We're overwhelmed with the number of children needing quality homes. The support just isn't there to meet the demand. These girls need a loving and stable environment, and Pastor Wilkins and I both believe you would be an excellent candidate to provide that."

Hannah's thoughts were a whirlwind of objections as she sought an escape. "You mentioned the mother's court case. If she goes to jail, what happens to the girls? And what if she gets out? Won't they just go back to her?"

Amanda leaned forward. "Our agency is recommending that the girls be permanently removed from their mother's care. Given the nature of her repeated offenses, her refusal to seek help, and the general neglect of the girls, we believe the court will grant us the ability to move forward with adoption."

"What about Jared?"

"What about him?" Barb asked.

"How will he handle having these girls in our home? What if he gets attached and then they have to leave? Is that fair to him?"

"That's a valid concern," Amanda replied, nodding. "We would include him in the interview process, with your permission. This would give us an opportunity to meet him and explain the situation. You would have the chance to discuss fostering with him and gauge his feelings on the matter."

As Amanda spoke, Pastor Wilkins quietly stood, walked to the credenza, and poured himself another cup of coffee. Hannah could feel his gaze on her as he listened, and she knew he was about to say something to which she'd have little to respond. He returned to the table and sat beside her, placing a gentle hand on her arm. The gesture felt like a lifeline, yet also like a trap.

"Hannah," he began, his voice soft but commanding, "when you look at these photos, I believe you see what your heart already knows – that you and your family could be a source of healing for these girls. You've mentioned reasons why you think this might not work – yourself, Jared, JB. But there's one question you haven't asked." He paused, letting the weight of his words settle over the room. "Have you asked yourself if God has placed you in this moment, with the trials you've recently faced, so that you and these girls can help each other heal?"

Hannah looked into his eyes, unable to speak. She saw the truth in his words, but the enormity of the situation left her paralyzed. She hadn't prayed for this opportunity; it had come to her through Barb, unbidden and unexpected. And now, she felt utterly unprepared.

The Pastor gave her arm a reassuring squeeze before continuing. "I suggest you pray on this, Hannah. Ask God how He can use you, and how He can use these girls, to bring about healing in your lives. And when we come for the home interview, I'd like to have a conversation with JB as well. I have a feeling these girls might be able to help him more than he'll ever know. Would that be, okay?"

Hannah, still unable to find her voice, simply nodded. The conversation continued for another thirty minutes, with Mrs. Davies explaining the legal process in detail. But Hannah's thoughts remained fixed on the photos before her, on the soulful brown eyes of the young girls who seemed to be pleading for a chance. Despite her fears, a connection had formed, and she couldn't help but feel a pull toward these children. She knew, deep down, that meeting them in person would change everything.

33

— • —

CHAPTER 33

Anita opened the front door and was greeted by the sight of a young girl standing awkwardly on the porch. The girl's small frame seemed out of place against the backdrop of Anita's neatly kept home. In her hands was a small square envelope. Anita's heart skipped a beat, a flutter of anxiety crossed her mind. Was Eric, okay?

"Are you Anita?" the girl asked.

"Yes, I am," Anita replied.

The girl's eyes darted around nervously as she handed over the envelope. "A man told me to give this letter to you and only you."

Without waiting for a response, the girl turned and sprinted back down the steps, her sneakers thudding against the lawn as she hurried back to her house. Anita closed the door behind her and turned her attention to the envelope, her hands trembling slightly. The handwriting on the envelope was unmistakably Eric's.

Anita carefully opened it and pulled out a note, which read:

Anita, if you remember where we used to go when we were teenagers, meet me there tonight at 10 pm. Eric.

The words pulled her back to Riverdale Park, a small sanctuary on the edge of the Tuolumne River. It was a place where she and Eric sought refuge from their chaotic lives as teenagers. Riverdale Park had been their escape, a quiet spot away from the harsh realities of the neighborhood. It was there they first shared their dreams of leaving the Deep South Side behind, where they had their first kiss, and where they had spent countless nights talking about their hopes and fears.

Anita's mind replayed those nights. She remembered walking down the block to Eric's house, the drive down Hatch Road, and the sense of freedom they felt as they followed the river westward. Her father's frequent stints in County Jail and her mother's descent into addiction had left a void in her life, one that Eric had helped to fill, even if only for a few hours under the stars.

Riverdale Park was nestled in a quaint neighborhood of a few hundred homes, shielded from the hustle of West Modesto by the river, and just far enough west from the Deep South Side to feel like a different world. It was a place where everyone knew their neighbors, and security was found in the familiarity of the community.

***

The letter had stirred a whirlwind of emotions – anticipation, worry, and a touch of nostalgia.

As she parked and stepped onto the familiar grounds of Riverdale Park, the cool night air and the soft rustling of leaves brought a flood of memories. The swings creaked in the distance, and the river's gentle murmur seemed to whisper secrets of their past. The envelope had ignited a connection to a time when life seemed simpler, even if only in memory. As she waited, she couldn't shake the feeling that this meeting was more than just a nostalgic reunion; it felt more like a turning point, an intersection of past and present that could change everything.

Over the past month, Anita had diligently compiled a list of over a hundred names of current and former WSF members with records in the County Jail system. This resource had proven invaluable to Eric and the Ghost, aiding in their preparation for distribution channels and security measures. The recent arrest of Hector Valdez and Manny's death had intensified their urgency. It was crucial to stay ahead of law enforcement and ensure their shipments could navigate the valley without facing internal and external threats. Sometimes, the internal risk assessments were even more critical than the external.

Riverdale Park was nearly dark except for a single light illuminating the small parking lot. The cream-colored Impala slowly pulled into the parking lot. Anita's heart pounded as she took sight of Eric's car. The last time she and Eric had been here was nearly nine years ago, just before her son was born. She stood at the park entrance, trying to mask her nerves.

Eric, leaning over the bench seat of the Impala, opened the passenger door for her. For a moment, Anita felt like she was eighteen again, sneaking off to the park with Eric. She slid into the passenger seat, and Eric looked at her with a mixture of curiosity and concern.

"What's up?" Eric asked.

"It's getting hot, E. Are you sure you want to keep going with these guys?" Anita's voice was tense, betraying her anxiety. As much as she wanted Eric to walk away, she knew it wasn't in his nature.

"What do you mean?"

Her body tightened. "I'm hearing that people are talkin'."

"Who's talkin'?"

"I don't know." Anita turned her head away from Eric, staring out the passenger window. She fought back tears. "I've known you since we were little. We've shared so much – good and bad. And I'm telling you, it feels like you need to walk away."

"Walk away? What are you talkin' about?"

Anita placed her hand on Eric's. "A friend of mine who works in the community services unit told me they're coming for you."

"They've always been comin' for me."

"This is different. You've crossed a line. They didn't care much before 'cause you were confined to your own territory. They let you exist as long as you policed your own and kept things quiet. But now, with the people you're involved with, you've crossed their boundaries. That's what my friend's tellin' me."

"What else they sayin'?"

"They're putting pressure on Hector, and he might crack. And those other two guys who run with him – I wouldn't trust them."

"We're handlin' those issues. You know what I mean?"

"But there's more. They're workin' with another informant, and they're building a case to take you down."

"We took care of Manny. Who else they workin' with?"

"I don't know exactly. My friend says they're walking around extremely confident right now and that you need to lay low for a while."

"Lay low? Are you kiddin' me? We've got a major shipment comin' up from Mexico in the next couple of weeks. There's no layin' low. I need names, specifics. I'll make a call and deal with Hector and his crew. His ass should've been taken care of a long time ago. I need to know the name of their second informant."

"Yeah, yeah, I'll try to get it to you. But you need to be careful."

Anita found herself inching closer to Eric, butterflies forming in her stomach. She yearned to relive a night from years ago in this familiar car and this familiar park. Time had moved on, but her heart still ached for Eric Avina.

"How is everything else? How's David?" Eric asked.

"David's fine."

"Maybe I'll come see one of his games. When's he playin' next?"

"I don't know. You don't have to do that."

"No, I mean it. I'll check out one of his games."

"Okay, whatever."

Anita laughed softly, unsure if Eric was serious. Over the years, he had made similar remarks, never following through. Yet something in his tone made her wonder if this time might be different. She had never told Eric that David was his son. Maybe she didn't need to because the moment Eric saw the baby he had already known.

34

— · —

C HAPTER 34

Paco Ramirez leaned back in his wicker chair, savoring the fresh morning air as he rolled his blunt and sipped from a bottle of Mezcal. The sun was just beginning to rise over the neighborhood rooftops, casting a warm glow over the quiet street. He took a moment to reflect on the recent trip, considering the profitability, the connections made, and how best to capitalize on the next opportunity. Yet, this morning, his thoughts were also consumed by Jade and their conversation about Lilly Grace.

The scene in Fresno had highlighted Lilly Grace's reliance on drugs to maintain her productivity. Jade had confided that Lilly Grace started and ended each day with a cocktail of fentanyl and methamphetamine, and every night's work began with a dose of Rohypnol. The combination was not only numbing Lilly Grace's mind but was also slowly destroying her. More troubling for Paco, it was becoming a high-risk liability he could no longer ignore. He knew that a difficult decision was looming.

The front door creaked open, and Jade stepped softly onto the porch, careful not to disturb the girls asleep inside the back of the house. She understood that their conversation from the previous night was far from over. As she approached Paco, she knew that the gravity of the situation was undeniable. Paco's focus was consumed by business – discussions about WSF expansion, meetings with the Ghost and Eduardo, and, most pressing, the issue with Lilly Grace. The reality of their predicament was clear to both, but the unspoken truth needed to be addressed.

Jade silently stepped to the small table where Paco had left the bottle of Mezcal. She took it and moved to the edge of the porch, leaning against the metal railing. Slowly, she spun the bottle in her hand, lost in thought. After a few moments, she uncorked it and took a long, deliberate swig. The liquid burned a path down her throat as she exhaled deeply, replaced the cork, and gazed at Paco.

Paco was absorbed in his thoughts, strategizing his next moves and analyzing risks. The presence of Jade, along with the tension in the air, was daunting. The situation with Lilly Grace was a thorn in their side, and while Paco seemed preoccupied with business details, Jade knew they had to confront the problem head-on.

"It's time to face it," Paco finally said, breaking the silence. "We can't keep ignoring it. Lilly Grace's situation is becoming a liability we can't afford."

Jade looked at him with contemplation, her gaze meeting his. She knew he was right. The reality of their choices was unavoidable, and someone needed to voice the truth.

"We both knew this day would come," she said slowly, taking another sip of Mezcal. "What do you suggest?"

Paco's expression was a mix of resolve and concern. "We need to decide what's best for the business. This isn't just about her anymore. It's about protecting our interests and ensuring the stability of our operations."

Jade nodded, understanding the weight of his words.

"So, what do you want to do with her?" Jade asked.

Paco took a long drag from his blunt, smoke curling in the morning air. He leaned forward in his chair, contemplating his response.

"I've never been a fan of using local motels – they're a dime a dozen for low-end pimps. But with the 7th Street Carnival coming this weekend, we've got a golden opportunity. Everyone's going to be walking over to La Clandestina. We can funnel traffic from the carnival to the club, to Riverwood Inn. We'll set up three or four rooms and press hourly. There's a lot of money to be made that weekend."

Jade frowned, her gaze shifting to the street. "What about the police? You've always said that events like this draw a lot of attention."

Paco stood, joining Jade at the railing. He took the bottle of Mezcal from her hand and took a long swig.

"Yeah, but I've got contacts who'll look the other way. We don't have to worry about cops crashing the party."

Jade's mind raced as she calculated the logistics. Four rooms, booked at an hour each for six hours – potentially a ten-thousand-dollar profit. The numbers looked promising, and the assurance about the police was reassuring. But the issue of Lilly Grace still weighed heavily on her.

"Based on last night's conversation, what's the plan for Lilly Grace?" she pressed.

Paco stiffened his back and stretched his arms. He handed the bottle back to Jade, his face set with determination.

"That's a good question, Mija. Let me think it over. Either way, this will be her last weekend with us. I'm fed up with her whining and her damn addiction – it's cutting into our profits."

Jade nodded. "I've got a couple of local girls who can step in and cover her workload. They've been around the crew, and I think they're ready to handle the real work."

Paco smiled, his expression softening. "Always thinking about the bottom line. That's why I love you, chica."

Jade returned the smile, then turned toward the door. "The Carnival starts tomorrow. I'll handle the room reservations and talk to Jose at La Clandestina to secure the best tables."

"Si, chica. Haz que suceda."

Jade handed the bottle back to Paco and went inside to make the necessary arrangements. As she closed the door behind her, a shiver of unease ran down her spine, knowing that Lilly Grace's last days with them were rapidly approaching – and that this weekend's profit might come at a far more troubling cost.

***

It was Saturday night, and Lilly Grace was deep into her shift at the Carnival party hosted at La Clandestina. The Riverwood Inn, a run-down motel on 9th Street, was where the action took place. The Inn, flanked by an underpass and near the clattering railroad tracks, shared a parking lot with the nightclub. Inside the dimly lit room, the clock showed 1:30 a.m., marking her third hour and fourth man of the late evening.

The room was shrouded in shadows, with a dark brown paisley bedspread covering a worn mattress that had seen better days. The stale odor of sex lingered in the air. The man with Lilly Grace was much older, his frame heavy and imposing as he pressed her frail body into the sagging mattress. His coarse, gray-streaked chest hair scraped against her tender stomach with every thrust. She turned her head to avoid the pungent smell of cigars and tequila, her heart racing with dread.

His moans grew more guttural and erratic. Without warning, his hand tightened around Lilly Grace's throat, cutting off her breath. Her vision dimmed as she struggled for air, her legs numb from the unrelenting pressure of his weight. Each thrust felt like a blade slicing through her insides. She squeezed her eyes shut, desperately clinging to the hope that he would soon finish.

When he finally withdrew, his grip on her neck loosened, and he stared vacantly at the ceiling, spent. Lilly Grace lay there, her legs trembling, the weight of what had just happened sinking in. He turned his gaze toward her, noting the drained color of her face and the sadness in her eyes.

"Goddamn girl."

With a sudden, brutal motion, he struck Lilly Grace beneath her left eye. She recoiled, curling her body into a fetal position, her hands instinctively rising to shield herself from further blows.

"Bitch, don't give me that look!"

He glared down at her from the foot of the bed, his anger simmering. He shook his finger at her, then hastily dressed, yanking up his pants and buckling his belt. Lilly Grace lay still, paralyzed by fear, her eyes locked on the floor. She heard the sound of running water from the bathroom but dared not move.

When he returned, his rage had only escalated. He ripped open the drawers and tossed aside the bedding, his breathing ragged and sweat glistening on his forehead.

"What'd you do with it, bitch?" he demanded.

He dropped to his knees and searched under the bed, his desperation growing with each passing second. He threw the comforter and sheets onto the floor, his movements frantic. Lilly Grace knew it was only a matter of time before he turned his anger toward her.

"Where is it?" he roared. "Fucking bitch, where's my cocaine?"

Terror gripped her as she remained silent, coiled on the bed. He seized her by the shoulders and hurled her across the room. She crashed into the dresser, sending the television crashing to the floor. As he tore through the room, searching behind the headboard, he found nothing. His focus returned to Lilly Grace.

"I know you have it," he screamed.

He paced the room, one hand on his hip, the other pressed against his forehead. Suddenly, he lunged at her and kicked her in the stomach, her small body lifting off the ground. Grabbing a fistful of her hair, he yanked her head back painfully.

Unable to remain silent any longer, Lilly Grace let out a raw, anguished scream. She struggled to free herself from his grip, but her efforts only tightened his hold. He placed one hand under her chin, lifting her tine frame into the air. With a brutal throw, he sent her crashing onto the bed. Tears streamed down her cheeks as she cried out for help, but her pleas were swallowed by his rage.

He jumped on the bed, seizing her knees and forcing her legs apart. Lilly Grace kicked weakly, but he overpowered her. His grip on her neck and knee was unyielding. Desperation made it hard for him to control her, so he struck her face with a crushing blow. The impact left a gash across her cheekbone, blood streaming down her face. The sight of her blood seemed to fuel his fury.

Her body lay still, her cries reduced to silent whispers as she faded in and out of consciousness. The pain from the punch clouded her senses, and she felt him inside her again, her mind numb to everything but the throbbing in her head.

The man continued his assault, each stroke driving further into a realm of helplessness. With a final, devasting blow to her face, Lilly Grace fell limp. The man finished, anger spent, he backed off of Lilly Grace and walked toward the bathroom.

Lilly Grace lay motionless, the man's semen trickling down her thigh, blood pooling beneath her. He returned briefly to gather his things, washing the blood from his forearm before slipping out into the night, leaving her alone in the darkness. She stared blankly at the door, dreading who might walk through next. Her heart pounded in her chest as she prayed it wouldn't be Paco – she feared him more than anything. The pain in her head was relentless, a throbbing that seemed to reverberate through her entire being. She clutched her temples, trying in vain to ease the agony.

In a desperate attempt to reach out, Lilly Grace crawled to the end table, where the phone sat beside a dim lamp. Her hands trembled as she picked up the receiver and dialed her mother's number. She slumped against the wall, trying to steady her breathing.

"Hello?" her mother's voice whispered on the other end of the line.

Lilly Grace couldn't speak; she could only listen to her mother's breaths on the other end of the line. The silence stretched.

"Hello? Is anyone there?" her mother asked.

"Lilly, is that you?" The desperation in her mother's voice made Lilly Grace tremble even more. She tried to speak again, but could only manage a few broken words through her pain and drugged daze.

"California," she whispered hoarsely.

"What?" her mother's voice cracked.

"California. Modesto."

"Where at, Lilly?" she asked again, her fear growing. "Where are you right now?"

"Motel in Modesto."

"Which one, Lilly? What is the name of the motel?"

Tears streamed down Lilly Grace's face as she looked around the ransacked room, trying to find any sign of the motel's name. The man had left the place in chaos. With a weak, bloodstained hand, she wiped her cheek and glanced out the window at the flashing neon sign below.

"Riverwood Inn."

"Riverwood Inn? Is that where you are?" her mother's voice was filled with anguish.

"Yes," Lilly Grace confirmed.

From the corner of her eye, Lilly Grace saw Jade approaching the room, her stride purposeful and her expression cold. Panic surged through Lilly Grace.

"I have to go." As she hung up, she lay down on the floor and closed her eyes, bracing for the worst.

Jade entered the room, her demeanor icy and unforgiving. She wore a black miniskirt and a white tank top that accentuated her figure. Her face, however, was set in a hard, unforgiving mask.

"What's this about you stealing coke?" Jade's voice cut through the air.

Lilly Grace, immobilized by pain and fear, could only lie still.

"What are the rules?" Jade continued. "You fuckin' junkie!"

Lilly Grace buried her face in her arms, trying to block out the onslaught.

"Paco doesn't tolerate this bullshit," Jade said.

Lilly Grace's eyes met Jades, revealing the deep cuts and bloodied face. Her body shook with silent sobs.

"What did he do to you?" Jade's voice softened, a flicker of something akin to empathy in her eyes.

Jade grabbed a clump of Lilly Grace's blood-stained hair and yanked her upright, forcing her against the wall. Lilly Grace tried weakly to pull away, but Jade's strength was overpowering. She threw Lilly Grace onto the bed, her anger simmering.

"You think any man's gonna want a girl all cut up?"

Lilly Grace huddled on the bed, her blood trickling down her cheek. Jade paced the room, contemplating the situation. A girl with an open wound was a liability, someone who couldn't earn money. And a girl who couldn't earn money was a problem for Paco.

Jade glanced out the window at the vibrant scene below, the mariachi music and laughter from the La Clandestina, scarcely making its way back to the grim reality inside the motel room. Her gaze softened momentarily as she looked back at Lilly Grace. With an unexpected tenderness, Jade walked to Lilly Grace's side, kneeling beside her. She gently brushed the blood-stained hair from Lilly Grace's face and helped her sit up against the headboard.

"Oh, honey," Jade whispered softly.

She went to the bathroom, retrieving a hand towel. After wetting it, she returned and carefully cleaned Lilly Grace's face. She then sat beside her, holding her gently in her lap, swaying slightly as she began to hum softly. Lilly Grace, exhausted and in pain, leaned into Jade, finding a rare moment of comfort.

Jade whispered, "Be still, my friend. Find peace in the sound of the silence."

Lilly Grace's eyes fluttered closed, lulled by the unexpected compassion, her body finally relaxing against Jade's soothing presence.

35

CHAPTER 35

The call came through the FBI hotline just after 2:00 in the morning. The operator quickly assessed the situation and flagged it as a high priority lead. Within minutes, the notes were forwarded through the appropriate channels. By 3:00 a.m., JB had the dispatch notes in hand. The Riverwood Inn, a notorious establishment on the South Side of Modesto, was no stranger to law enforcement, especially when it came to housing prostitutes.

After receiving the call, JB swiftly coordinated with command units. Within minutes, a plainclothes officer was dispatched to assess the location, backed by an unmarked sedan stationed discreetly with eyes on Room 23. An hour and a half since the call, and there was still no movement from the room.

At 3:30, JB pulled in Arbuckle Rentals, situated on the corner of 7th Street and Hatch Road. The site, a half mile from the Riverwood Inn, was just across the railroad tracks. Various units were already arriving, gearing up for the operation. JB donned his tactical vest and conducted a thorough gear check. On the radio, the plainclothes officer provided a walk by assessment of Room 23, reporting no activity.

At this hour, the Carnival operation nearby was closed, and the crowd at La Clandestina had mostly dispersed, leaving only a handful of cars belonging to the guests of the Riverwood Inn. The team huddled for final instructions, and JB's voice cut through the tension: "Go Time."

More than a dozen agency vehicles exited the rental lot in formation, heading north on 7th Street. JB sat in the front passenger seat of a Stanislaus County Sheriff's SUV; his mind focused as they crossed the railroad tracks onto Pecos Avenue before making a sharp right onto 9th Street. He performed a final check of his weapon, controlling his breathing, a technique ingrained during his time with Marine Special Forces. Visualizing the operation, he prepared for all possible outcomes. By the time the convoy converged on the Riverwood Inn's parking lot, JB was ready.

The L-shaped, two-story building was now surrounded by over three dozen inter-agency personnel, all poised for action. Inside Room 23, Jade and Lilly Grace lay on the bed when the door suddenly crashed inward. The force of the breach startled Jade, who instinctively leaped out of bed, reaching for a gun stashed in a bag on the floor. The first agent through the door was on her in an instant, slamming her to the ground with his knee pressed firmly into the small of her back. A second officer rushed to the rear of the room, sweeping the bathroom for threats.

JB was the third agent through the door. His flashlight beam cut through the darkness, illuminating Lilly Grace's face. The girl sat on the bed, her eyes glazed and distant, barely resembling the description provided by her mother. The once vivid image of her daughter now seemed like a distant memory, replaced by the broken figure before him.

"Lilly Grace!" JB's voice pierced through the chaos, but she only stared blankly in his direction. He couldn't tell if it was the blinding light, sheer terror, or a drug-induced stupor, or maybe a combination of all three, that rendered her immobile. Naked on the bed, she looked like a shadow of the girl she must have been, and JB's instincts warned him to proceed with caution.

"Lay face down on the bed!" JB's command was sharp, but Lilly Grace hesitated, her eyes vacant. JB didn't like to repeat himself – Afghanistan had taught him the cost of underestimating a threat. But recognizing that this girl had likely endured unimaginable horrors, he softened his tone just enough to try again. "I said, lay face down on the bed."

When she still didn't move, JB lowered his weapon, quickly closing the distance between them. He grabbed her shoulders and roughly flipped her onto her stomach, zip-tying her wrists behind her back. Lilly Grace didn't resist. Jade, on the other hand, was kicking and screaming, thrashing beneath the knee of the agent holding her down. JB watched as she was dragged from the room, her curses echoing the corridor until she was finally shoved into the back of an unmarked car.

Lilly Grace remained motionless; her face pressed against the bed. JB, recognizing she was no longer a threat, sat beside her, his voice dropping to a soothing whisper. "I know you're scared, but you need to know we're here to help. Your mother called us, and we came as fast as we could. You're safe now."

She slowly turned her head towards him, the harsh light revealing her dilated pupils and the network of open wounds marring her face. JB's breath caught as he took in the damage. Her age was supposed to be around fifteen, but the girl before him looked far older, her skin ravaged and her innocence long stripped away. Her eyes met his, and he saw the flicker of shame and fear, mixed with the raw pain of a life torn apart. Tears began to slip down her cheeks.

In that moment, compassion overrode protocol. JB gently patted her arms. "Everything's going to be okay," he said as he carefully cut the zip ties, freeing her wrists. "You're safe now."

A female officer entered, draping a blanket over Lilly Grace's frail body. She shivered, clutching the fabric as if it were a lifeline.

"Your mother – what's her name?" JB asked gently.

She sat in silence, the weight of the world on her shoulders. JB tried again. "Can you tell me your mother's name?"

A barely audible whisper escaped her lips. "Lilly Grace."

"Good, Lilly. Now, what's your mother's name?" he pressed.

But Lilly Grace had retreated into herself, her gaze distant, her mind elsewhere. JB knew better than to push. She needed medical attention more than she needed to answer questions.

Outside, the scene was chaotic – a flood of patrol cars, SUVs, and unmarked vehicles surrounded the Riverwood Inn, their lights casting eerie shadows across the rundown motel. As JB guided Lilly Grace toward the waiting ambulance, the noise and commotion of the operation seemed to close in around them.

Lilly Grace's eyes shifted to the unmarked car where Jade sat, her hands shackled, her eyes burning with rage. For a moment, the two girls locked eyes. JB felt Lilly Grace's body stiffen beside him. Before he could react, she spit in his face, her sudden fury catching him off guard.

"Get off me!" Lilly Grace screamed, pushing his chest with a surprising amount of strength. JB, momentarily stunned, quickly regained control, pinning her against the car as she writhed and cursed at him. Jade, from inside the vehicle, kicked at the windows, a wild, feral energy consuming them both.

JB restrained Lilly Grace with a fresh set of zip ties, pulling her arms behind her back and pressing her against the car. Her struggles continued as he dragged her toward the ambulance, her screams echoing through the parking lot.

The paramedics tried to calm her as they loaded her onto the gurney, but it was no use. One of the medics, a young man recently discharged from the military, pulled out a syringe and filled it with a sedative. JB and the other medic held her down as the injection was administered. Within minutes, Lilly Grace's body relaxed, her resistance fading as she drifted unconscious.

As the ambulance doors closed, JB watched it pull away, the weight of what he'd witness settling heavily on his shoulders. The next time Lilly Grace opened her eyes, she would be in the emergency department, far from the hell she'd just escaped – but still haunted by it.

36

— • —

C HAPTER 36

At 4:30 in the morning, Lilly Grace was wheeled into the Medical Center, the fluorescent lights glaring down as she clung to the sides of the gurney. The emergency bay was a scene of controlled chaos. As she was pushed down the hallway, a homeless man restrained in a chair lunged at her, screaming incoherently, his wild eyes locking onto hers. The paramedic quickly intervened, forcing the man back into his seat, but the jarring encounter left Lilly Grace trembling.

The emergency department was beyond capacity, a grim testament to the violence and tragedy that had unfolded that night. Gurney after gurney lined the walls, each carrying a body – some broken, some bleeding, all desperate for care. The air was thick with the cries and pleas of patients, their voices rising above the constant hum of machines. Nurses moved with grim determination, their faces set in expressions of exhaustion and resolve as they rushed from one room to the next, each wondering if the patient they left behind would still be alive when they returned.

Lilly Grace let her head fall back onto the gurney, the pounding in her skull intensifying with each passing moment. The confrontation at the Riverwood Inn had left her concussed, with three deep gashes marking her face – one above her right eye, another on her cheekbone, and a third splitting her lip. The drugs coursing through her system only added to her confusion, blurring the lines between reality and nightmare as the chaos of the emergency room swirled around her.

Suddenly, the harsh sound of code blue echoed through the hall. Lilly Grace turned her head just enough to see into the room where the code was called. Inside, an elderly man writhed violently on the bed, his frail body arching as alarms screamed from the monitors. A physician rushed in, immediately starting chest compressions, his movements frantic and practiced. Nurses followed, their faces masks of concentration as they worked to stabilize the patient.

Lilly Grace watched, her heart pounding in time with the chaos, as the life slipped away from the man before her eyes. The physician's efforts grew more desperate, his compressions harder, faster – but it was no use. The room fell silent as the man's body finally stilled, the life draining from him as quickly as it had once pulsed through his veins. The physician stepped back, a nursing placing a hand on his shoulder in a gesture of quiet solidarity.

"Call it," the doctor said, his voice flat with resignation. "4:25."

Lilly Grace's stomach churned as she watched the physician exit the room, his shoulders slumped with the weight of another lost life. The scene around her only grew more nightmarish as the morning wore on. Three victims from a car accident that night succumbed to their injuries, their bodies joining the growing list of the dead. Two of the shooting victims passed away, while a third was placed on a ventilator – he wouldn't survive more than three more days.

The emergency department had become a war zone, a place where life and death hung in a fragile balance, and Lilly Grace was thrust into the heart of it with no hope in sight. She was just another casualty, caught in the crossfire of a world that had long since forgotten how to care.

***

The house was cold and silent as JB walked through the front door at 5 am. It had been a long and exhausting twenty-four hours. He walked upstairs and quickly took a warm shower, the water scalding against his skin, but it did nothing to wash away the night. He kept the lights off before sliding into bed, careful not to wake Hannah. But as he lay there, eyes wide open, the events of the night replayed in his mind, refusing to let him rest.

Each time he closed his eyes, he was confronted with the moment when Lilly Grace spit in his face. He replayed it over and over, like a video stuck in a loop. He remembered following Lilly Grace's gaze toward the patrol car, seeing her body go limp in his arms as she seemed to surrender to the rescue. But then, in an instant her eyes locked with Jade's, everything changed. Her body tensed, and she lashed out with a ferocity that caught JB off guard. The sweet, innocent girl he had imagined rescuing had vanished, replaced by someone hardened by the streets, by survival.

The sudden transformation in Lilly Grace reminded JB of another shift he knew all too well – the one he'd seen in his mother's eyes when he was a child. She could be so loving, so gentle, but then, almost without warning, something inside her would snap. The woman who tucked him in at night, who kissed his forehead and told him stories, would become a stranger – a rage-filled addict, eyes wild, words cruel. JB had learned to fear those moments, to recognize the subtle signs that his mother was about to change, to brace himself for the storm that would follow.

Now, decades later, those memories came rushing back. He saw the same flicker of darkness in Lilly Grace that he had seen in his mother. It terrified him. It was the fear of losing someone you love to something you can't understand or control. The fear of seeing innocence turn into something unrecognizable.

He squeezed his eyes shut, trying to push the memories away, trying to separate the past from the present. But the connection had been made, and he knew that no matter how hard he had tried, he couldn't unsee it. The same way he couldn't stop his mother's transformation, he feared he wouldn't be able to save Lilly Grace from the darkness that had claimed her.

JB prayed for a reprieve from the memories, from the haunting resemblance between the girl he had tried to save and the mother he had once known. But as sleep continued to evade him, he wondered if this was the price he had to pay for all the things he had seen, all the lives he was unable to save.

***

It had been a couple of hours, and Lilly Grace was still abandoned in the emergency department hallway, her gurney shoved against the wall. The blood on her cheek had dried into a tight, stinging mask, and her migraine pulsed relentlessly, each throb a cruel reminder of her circumstances. As the sedative wore off, withdrawal symptoms clawed at her body, leaving her aching and chilled beneath the thin sheet that did little to shield her from the cold.

Time crawled by, marked only by the steady tick of the clock. Nurses passed by their eyes focused on the clipboard attached to her gurney, but each glance was brief, almost guilty, as they quickly moved on. Lilly Grace's voice was trapped, silenced by the trauma, the chaos, and the lingering haze of medication. She wanted to scream, to plead, but the words wouldn't come.

Finally, a nurse approached, clipboard in hand. He hesitated, a fleeting moment where his gaze lingered on her, a flicker of something – pity, perhaps, or discomfort – before he looked away. "What's your name?" he asked, his tone detached, as if by distancing himself, he could ignore the broken girl in front of him.

Lilly Grace stared blankly, her eyes searching for any sign of humanity, but her voice remained frozen, locked away by fear an exhaustion.

The nurse repeated the question, this time more firmly, as though trying to convince himself that he cared. Lilly Grace's eyes met his, pleading silently, but still, no words escaped her lips. Another nurse approached, her brows knitting together as she glanced at the gurney. "What's this? What's wrong with her?" she asked, her voice tinged with an unease she didn't want to acknowledge.

"Just another prostitute beaten by her pimp." His words were a shield, a way to dismiss the guilt gnawing at the edges of his conscience.

As they walked away, their laughter was forced, brittle, the whispered comment – "Guess she didn't satisfy her customer" – a thin veil for their discomfort. The shame hung in the air, heavy and unspoken, as Lilly Grace lay there, invisible and ignored, her dignity shattered, her body and spirit broken.

***

JB woke to the clatter of pots and pans downstairs. The morning sun filtered through the open curtains, and the bedside clock read 10:30 a.m. He was grateful for the few hours' sleep he had managed to snatch. At his age, his body needed all the recovery it could get, especially after running on fumes since Manny's death. The weight of regret and responsibility pressed heavily on his six-foot frame.

He quickly dressed and made his way to the kitchen, where Hannah was busy at the sink, scrubbing dishes and wiping down the counters. JB dropped his work bag in the dining room. The familiar tension between them palpable. The past few weeks had been marked by their absence from each other's lives – like ships passing in the night, barely a glance or a word exchanged. Hannah was recovering from surgery, and both were grappling with emotional heartbreak, but neither seemed able to bridge the gap.

"There's a plate for you in the microwave," Hannah said, her voice subdued but steady.

JB moved slowly around the kitchen; his weariness evident in each step.

"How was last night," she asked, turning to face him as he took the plate from the microwave.

JB sat at the table, his mind still reeling from the events of the night. He was eager to interrogate Jade at the County Jail and he hoped to glean some crucial information from Lilly Grace at the hospital.

"We recovered a young girl at a motel in South Modesto," JB said.

Hannah's attention sharpened, and she set the pot down, leaning on the counter. "What happened?"

"A call came in late from the girl's mother. We put together a team and went to the motel." He paused, his gaze distant. "She'd been beaten badly, and it was clear she was on several drugs. When we arrived, she was asleep in bed with another girl."

Hannah walked over to JB and placed a comforting hand on his shoulder. "Is she okay?"

"I don't know," JB said, his frustration evident. "We took her to the hospital. She's probably in detox now."

Turning towards Hannah, JB crossed his arms over his chest. "The strangest thing happened when we were getting her to the ambulance. One moment she was docile, and then the next, she turned and spat in my face."

"Really?"

"Yeah. I think the girl she was with – her madam or whatever – had some power over her. It was like she wanted to show loyalty or something when she saw her in the car. It was bizarre."

Hannah placed her hands over JB's, pressing her head into his chest. She had been planning to share her thoughts about fostering two young girls with the Pastor and the foster agency, but sensing his distress, she decided against it. The timing wasn't right.

JB squeezed her hands gently. "Last night, you mentioned wanting to talk about something. Is everything okay?"

Hannah took a step back, her eyes conflicted. "No, it's nothing important. You've got enough on your plate today. We can talk tonight when you get home. Do you think you'll make it for dinner?"

"I'm not sure," JB said, grabbing his book bag. "I'll call you later and let you know. I'm hoping we'll get some good information from the girl we arrested."

"Okay," Hannah replied softly. "I'll keep something extra for you, just in case you can't make it home tonight."

JB finished his meal and placed the plate on the counter. He kissed the top of Hannah's head, a small gesture of affection amid the growing distance between them, before heading out the door.

***

Hannah arrived at the Faith Home Adoption agency in the heart of Modesto just after noon. The building was an unremarkable office suite on a busy street, with no indication of the children who were supposed to be living there. She pulled into the parking lot, half expecting a cheerful playground scene, but saw only the mundane reality of a typical office setting. As she checked her makeup in the rearview mirror and applied some Chapstick, she felt the pang of regret that JB wasn't there with her. She hadn't mentioned the appointment to him, as their conversations had been limited and fraught with tension. Hannah wondered what Pastor Wilkins would think of her going through this alone and how it might affect their chance of becoming foster parents.

Upon entering, an executive assistant led her to a conference room where Amanda Davies awaited with a stack of papers neatly arranged before her. The two women exchanged a brief, cordial embrace.

"Can I get you a cup of coffee or water?" Amanda asked.

"No, thank you," Hannah replied.

Amanda settled into her chair and glanced up. "Is JB going to join us today?"

Hannah hesitated. "No, he's tied up with a very sensitive case and couldn't make it. Will that affect the process?"

"No, we can still proceed with the initial paperwork today. However, JB will need to be present for the site visit and will have to sign some documents," Amanda explained.

"Okay, that shouldn't be a problem," Hannah said, though a flicker of anxiety crossed her face.

As they moved through the paperwork, the conversation drifted to light topics – people from their church, favorite restaurants, and the upcoming Almond Blossom season. By the time Hannah signed the last document, they had covered nearly every safe topic for casual conversation. But Amanda's next question veered into more personal territory.

"Please forgive me if this seems intrusive, but it's important for what we're trying to accomplish," Amanda began, her tone gentle but firm. "You and your husband...Pastor and Mrs. Adams speak very highly of you both. But I'm getting a different impression from how you describe your relationship with him."

Hannah was taken aback. The comment felt like an intrusion into her private life, disrupting the friendly façade of the past forty-five minutes.

"I'm sorry, what do you mean?" Hannah asked, her voice betraying her confusion.

Amanda leaned forward slightly. "I'm not trying to be confrontational. But part of my role is to ensure that these children are placed in a positive and stable environment. From what you've shared, I'm concerned about whether you and JB are in the right place to provide that."

Hannah struggled with her response. Mrs. Davies had quickly assessed the strain in her relationship, and Hannah grappled with how much to reveal. She feared that being honest might jeopardize her chances of fostering. Her mind raced as she weighed her options, while Mrs. Davies steady gaze offered no reprieve.

"Mrs. Davies, you're right. JB and I have faced a lot lately – my surgery, infertility issues, and just the general strain of life and marriage. JB is also dealing with a significant case at work. But despite everything, we love each other deeply, and we're committed to being great foster parents."

Amanda's hands tightened on the table, and her expression softened only slightly. "If you and JB can't align on these issues, I'm concerned that it might affect our decision in the end."

"I understand your concerns," Hannah replied. "Every parent faces challenges, and we've navigated ours as best as we can. We're committed to making this work, just as we have with everything else."

Amanda reached across the table, her hand resting gently on Hannah's. A faint, reassuring smile touched her lips. "Hannah, I believe you can overcome these challenges. Let's just make sure that you and JB are fully in sync for this process. I'd hate for us to invest time only to find out later that things aren't as stable as we hoped. Can you understand that?"

Hannah nodded, her emotions a mix of relief and lingering uncertainty. As they discussed the next steps and Amanda's eagerness to meet JB, Hannah couldn't shake the worry that this might be the last meeting if JB's involvement wasn't forthcoming.

***

JB made a phone call to the hospital at 1 p.m. and learned that Lilly Grace was still in the emergency department. He wouldn't be able to speak with her for a few more hours. With that in mind, he decided to head over to the County Jail to interview Jade.

He sat in a sterile holding room, the door opening to reveal Jade for the first time in daylight and without Paco Ramirez at her side. Stripped of her makeup and revealing attire, she looked strikingly different – more like an eighteen-year-old girl than the hardened figure he had expected. Her hair was matted, and there was a vulnerability in her eyes that JB hadn't anticipated. He hoped this glimpse of her true self might work to his advantage.

"Please, have a seat," JB said, trying to keep his tone neutral.

Jade shot him a defiant glare, then glanced at the guard before taking a seat at the table. The guard began to chain her feet to the table, but JB signaled him to stop.

"Jade. Is that your real name?" JB asked.

"What's it to you?"

"You can make this as difficult as you want," JB replied. "It's up to you."

"You can't hold me here. I didn't do anything wrong."

"Really? You didn't do anything wrong? You weren't involved in running a prostitution ring with an under-aged girl?

"Man, my friend and I were sleeping when you guys' barged in. I should be suing you. You don't know what you're talking about, and you ain't got nothing on me."

JB leaned back in his chair, weighing his approach. He could claim to have already spoken with Lilly Grace and imply that the evidence pointed directly to a prostitution ring led by Paco Ramirez. He could then threaten Jade with the possibility of a harsher sentence if she didn't cooperate. Alternatively, he could be upfront about the fact that he hadn't spoken to Lilly Grace yet, but would later that day, and offer her a deal for leniency if she provided testimony against Ramirez.

The choice was critical. If he framed the conversation with misinformation, he risked damaging his credibility if Jade called his bluff. On the other hand, being honest might lead her to withhold crucial information.

He decided to play it straight. "I haven't talked with Lilly Grace yet, but I will be doing so later today. Here's the deal: If you give us information about the ring and your involvement, it could be beneficial for you during sentencing. You have a chance to lessen your sentence by cooperating now."

Jade's eyes flickered with uncertainty. JB could see the internal struggle as she weighed her options.

"If you're as innocent as you claim, helping us build a case against Ramirez should be a no-brainer," JB added, leaning forward slightly. "This is your opportunity to make things right."

Jade remained silent for a moment, her defiant posture wavering. JB could almost see her calculation as she processed his offer. It was a game-time decision, and he hoped his approach would lead her to open up.

"Okay, I'm going to be straight up honest with you," JB said. "I hope you'll return the favor. I'm going to speak with Lilly Grace later this afternoon. I'm confident she's going to point us in your direction and probably name a few others too."

"What do I care?"

"You should care because right now, you're facing at least two major felony charges for sex trafficking a minor. Each charge carries up to thirty years. Is that how you want to spend the rest of your life?"

"Eres un pendejo. I didn't do any of that shit."

Is that what you think Lilly Grace will say? How loyal do you think she is to you?"

"Like I said, I didn't do anything, so you can't charge me with nothing."

"Your files say you grew up in Santa Cruz and spent your teen years in a foster home down in Riverside County. How did you meet Paco Ramirez?"

"Who?"

"All right, Jade. I said I was going to be honest with you, and I expect the same. We met a few months back at the La Clandestina Night Club. You were with a guy named Paco Ramirez. Don't play dumb – he's the one running this whole operation."

"I don't know, man."

"Jade, as it stands, you're the main suspect for the sex trafficking of a minor. Do you really want to sit in prison for thirty years while Ramirez walks free? He'll just find someone else to replace you. Do you want to be left behind, forgotten?"

Jade slumped back in her chair, clearly rattled. Her eyes fell to the floor, and JB could see the weight of her predicament crashing down on her. She wiped at her eyes with trembling hands, trying to maintain her composure.

"I don't know, man," she whispered.

"Jade, it's alright. You were young when you met Paco. You didn't know what you were getting into. But now, you're old enough to know better. You're old enough to make a choice. Let me help you. Let me help you find the life you deserved – a life any other teenage girl would have."

Jade looked up, her face a mask of defiance and pain. "The life I never had. Like you know what kind of life I've had or what I want? Little girls don't dream of fairy tales and shit. That's not me. That's not where I came from. And you can't pretend you're doing me any favor."

Her anger broiled over, and she threw up her arms, screaming, "Guard! Guard!"

The door swung open, and the guard stepped in, eyeing JB for instructions. JB gave a small nod, signaling the end of the interview. "We're finished here."

The guard escorted Jade out, leaving JB alone with the heavy silence of the room, the weight of her choices hanging in the air.

***

The emergency department physician found Lilly Grace still on the gurney in the hallway at 3:30 p.m. He was in his early thirties, freshly out of medical school by the looks of him, dressed in blue scrubs and a red skull cap. He glanced around the bustling hallway, then called out to a nurse stationed at the Huck Station.

"Tell me what we have here. Who is this?"

"I don't know. The medics brought her in early this morning. She's been waiting here since then."

"Where are we with room availability?"

"After the shooting and the car accident, we went on divert. We're beyond full in our trauma bays, and the ER doesn't have any rooms available either."

"The chart says she was involved in a physical altercation, probably forcibly raped, and is likely on multiple substances based on the medics notes."

"Raped?"

"Yes, that's what the chart states. You're trained to conduct a medical exam, aren't you?"

"Yes, but we don't have any rooms available to perform an exam."

"Well, you'd better find one," the physician insisted, handing the nurse the patient chart. He then turned and headed down the hallway toward his next emergency.

"Me? I was trained to do one, but it was like five years ago, and I've never actually performed one."

The physician turned back briefly; his expression resigned. "I'm male, so I can't do it. And we're understaffed right now, so you're up. Figure it out."

The nurse's shoulders sagged. She glanced down the hall, then back at Lilly Grace with a deep sigh. "What's your name?"

Lilly Grace, dazed and overwhelmed by the harsh fluorescent lights, didn't respond.

"Look, kid, this isn't easy for either of us, alright? I need your help so I can do my job. Can you do that?"

The nurse, appearing to be in her mid-fifties with a stocky build, had a weary but determined look. Her raspy voice and practical demeanor suggested years of handling chaos.

"Okay, first things first. We need to find a room. Can you stand up?"

"I don't know," Lilly Grace whispered.

The nurse gently squeezed Lilly Grace's feet. "Do you feel this?"

Lilly Grace nodded affirmatively.

"Good. And this?" The nurse moved her hands up Lilly Grace's legs.

"Yes," Lilly Grace replied.

"Alright. The chart says you were in a physical altercation. Can you tell me what happened?"

"I...I don't know. Everything feels fuzzy."

"Sure, I bet it does. I'm going to take you down the hall to some back offices. We might have to do this in an office or somewhere in the hallway. Are you okay with me performing a rape assessment on you?"

"What does that mean?"

"We'll take some samples and fill out paperwork. It won't be too painful, I promise."

The nurse wheeled Lilly Grace to the back of the emergency department, stopping near a row of small, cluttered offices. The only office available was barely large enough for a desk and a chair.

"Alright, let's get you to the side of the gurney. Can you manage that?" The nurse helped Lilly Grace slide her feet over the edge. Lilly Grace's legs felt like lead, and she swayed slightly as she stood. She grasped the gurney rail for support. The nurse steadied her, guiding her into the small, chaotic office stacked with paperwork and files.

The following hours passed in a haze of invasive procedures and persistent questioning. The nurse, though clearly overburdened and tired, methodically asked Lilly Grace about her drug use, her interactions with men, and the origins of her injuries. Despite the nurses' attempts to maintain a professional demeanor, the lack of privacy and the cramped space exacerbated Lilly Grace's sense of violation.

The most humiliating part was the physical examination, conducted in the small office. The nurse, trying to make the best of a dire situation, performed a full body examination, including a pelvic and vaginal exam, an anal exam, and collected hair samples. Each touch, each movement felt like another layer of her dignity stripped away. Lilly Grace, despite having endured so much, found this to be the most egregious invasion of her personal space, further deepening her sense of violation and helplessness.

The nurses' attempts to offer some comforts were overshadowed by the stark reality of Lilly Grace's situation, leaving her to navigate a trauma far beyond the physical injuries she endured.

37

C HAPTER 37

First thing Monday morning, JB made his way through the bustling Emergency Department and checked in with the Administrative Security team on site as a precaution. He then headed up to the third floor when he briefly consulted with the attending physician to get an update on Lilly Grace's condition before entering the room. The physician explained that she was undergoing medical detox and was experiencing severe muscle aches, hallucinations, and high levels of anxiety. He advised against speaking with her due to her current state and the recovery timeline. However, JB was under pressure with Jade trying to avoid conviction and a long sentence. If he could connect Lilly Grace to Jade, Paco Ramirez, and Eric Avina, he could potentially dismantle the entire WSF.

He found Lilly Grace curled up in the fetal position, her face hidden from view. The room was an interior room with no windows to the outside. In the harsh daylight, without her makeup, she appeared every bit of the fifteen-year-old girl described by her mother. Her face was scarred from months of methamphetamine use and reliance on alcohol and stimulants. Her blonde hair was brittle and split at the ends.

JB walked around to the side of the bed to get a better look at her face. As he approached, Lilly Grace remained motionless, her gaze fixated on the wall.

"Excuse me, Lilly Grace, do you remember me?" he asked gently.

She continued to stare at the wall, showing no sign of recognition.

"I'm the man who rescued you last night at the motel. Do you remember me?"

Still no response. JB pulled up a chair and sat beside her, trying to make eye contact.

"Lilly Grace, I hope you know you're safe now. You've been through a lot, and I'm sure you're in shock." He placed his hand on the side rail of the bed, hesitating to reach out further. "My name is JB Phillips. I'm a special agent with the FBI. Your mother contacted me last night and told us where you were. She said you called her and gave her your location. Do you remember that call?"

Her gaze remained fixed on the wall, and JB began to doubt her awareness. He decided to try another approach.

"Lilly Grace, the girl you were with in the room – can you tell me who she is?"

Lilly Grace squeezed the pillow tightly to her stomach, her first visible reaction. JB saw an opportunity to delve deeper.

"Do you know that I've met her before. We met at the La Clandestina Night Club a few months ago. She was with a man named Paco Ramirez."

Lilly Grace grunted and turned her body away, facing the wall. JB seized the moment and repositioned his chair to face her directly.

"Paco Ramirez. He's a dangerous man, isn't he? I want to arrest him, but I need your help. Can you help me, Lilly Grace?"

Her eyes widened, and her body tensed. Suddenly, she screamed and began scratching at her face with her fingernails, her body convulsing in rage.

"Get out!" she shouted. "Get out of my room!"

JB jumped up, trying to restrain her hands to prevent her from drawing blood. Nurses rushed in, and together they struggled to hold Lilly Grace down as she thrashed on the bed. A physician entered, administering a sedative through her IV. Within moments, Lilly Grace's body relaxed, lying flat on the bed. JB stepped back, letting the nurses take over. He recalled a similar traumatic situation from his past – comforting a young soldier in Afghanistan, only to lose him later in combat. JB prayed that Lilly Grace's outcome would be different, knowing that overcoming such trauma required both a miracle and profound faith.

The physician approached JB at the foot of the bed. "I told you this was not the right time. She's been through so much and reliving it could be detrimental."

"I understand, doctor. But I need to ensure those responsible for this girl's suffering are held accountable. I can't do that without her cooperation."

"Her recovery will be long and difficult. It's best to give her time to heal before pressing her for more information."

"What will happen to her?"

"Where is her family," the physician asked.

"I received a message late last night from her mother. She's in Missouri, but I haven't connected with her yet."

"Most likely, she'll stay here for a few more days before being moved to a rehab facility. I can't speak to social services and how they'll handle her situation."

"How is she doing?"

"It's one of the worst cases I've seen. No fifteen-year-old girl should go through this. Her skin rashes, scabs, decaying gums, and drug levels indicate a long history of abuse. Last night was violent; the rape screen confirms multiple assaults. This has clearly been an ongoing trauma."

As the doctor spoke, JB glanced at Lilly Grace, her frail and delicate frame a stark reminder of the horrors she had endured. He resolved to ensure her safety and well-being before involving her mother, making a silent promise to himself to take care of her as best as he could.

38

— • —

C HAPTER 38

For the first time in three weeks, JB made it home for a family dinner. After the intense interview with Lilly Grace, he craved the grounding comfort of his family. The stability and peace that Hannah always provided were a balm of his frayed nerves. Hannah had her own reasons for needing JB home. Though physically recovered from her surgery, she grappled with the emotional aftermath of her infertility. She was beginning to see the idea of becoming a foster parent as a possible way to fill the void, but she was unsure how JB would react to this new desire.

As Hannah opened a bottle of Sauvignon Blanc and poured two glasses, she swirled one, savoring its fruity notes and hint of grass. JB was busy checking the steaks on the grill, his focus split between the task and conversation he knew was coming. Hannah watched Jared bounce around the dining room, setting the table with eager anticipation.

JB brought the steaks into the kitchen and set them on the stove top. Hannah handed him a glass of wine, and they completed the meal preparations together before moving to the dining room.

"So, how is the case going?" she asked, breaking the silence.

JB cut into his steak, chewing as he thought about how to respond. "It's going well. We had a breakthrough yesterday with the recovery of the girl."

"How did you get the tip, again?" Hannah's voice was gentle, probing.

"We got a call from a mother in Missouri. Her daughter had been missing for months. She got a random call form her, and she said she was in a motel in Modesto. We went in and found the girl and another teen."

Hannah glanced at Jared, noting his curiosity about the conversation. She was aware he might pick up on the nuances of their discussion.

"Is she okay?"

"She's as okay as she can be. It's going to be a long road to recovery. She's been through a lot."

"And the mother?"

"She's coming out in the next forty-eight hours. She'll have to go through family services. We don't know the full story yet."

Hannah took a long drink of her wine, steeling herself for the next part of the conversation. She had been grappling with the idea of fostering for weeks, and now was the moment to voice her feelings.

"It's been an interesting week for me, too," she began, her voice shaky but determined. "I've been talking with Barb Adams. She's been very supportive during my recovery."

Hannah took another sip of wine, feeling her anxiety rise. She looked at JB and Jared, trying to gauge their reactions before continuing.

"And I wanted to share this with you last night, but one of the things we've discussed is becoming foster parents."

JB looked up, surprised. "Foster parents? What are you talking about?"

"I've been to the foster agency and completed the paperwork. I believe it's a chance for us to make a difference," she said, noting JB's mix of confusion and amusement. "I'm serious about this, JB."

Jared's eyes lit up. "What's a foster parent?"

"It's when you take in a child who doesn't have their own home or family to live with. We'd provide them a place to stay."

"And they'd live with us?" Jared's excitement was evident.

"Yes, for a while. We'd give them a stable home."

JB stared at Hannah, processing the gravity of her proposal. "Is this because of the surgery?"

Hannah's face tightened. "No, JB. This isn't about me not being able to have a child. It's about us making a difference."

"I didn't mean to suggest that. I just don't know if now is the right time?"

Hannah's expression softened, but JB's mind was already slipping away from the present. He looked past her, feeling the weight of old memories settling on his chest like a heavy blanket.

Suddenly, he was back in old, cramped house of his childhood, standing at the edge of the worn-out kitchen, the acrid smell of alcohol in the air. His mother slumped over the dining table, eyes glazed and distant, muttered incoherently, her hand clinging to a nearly empty bottle. JB, just twelve years old, stood frozen, unsure whether to pull the bottle from her grasp or run to find his sister, who had locked herself in her room hours earlier to escape the chaos.

He remembered those nights, the helplessness, the nights his father was gone for weeks at a time, leaving JB to play the role of protector—trying, in his childlike way, to hold their fragile world together. When his father did return, there were always promises that things would change, but they never did. His mother only spiraled further into her addiction, the house growing quieter as she faded from them.

And then there was his sister. She had been so full of life once, always laughing and dragging JB into mischief. But the abuse began to chip away at her joy. The drugs, the wrong people—he saw it all pulling her under, and no matter how hard he tried, he couldn't reach her. The night he found her lifeless on the floor was burned into his memory. The pills she took were supposed to numb the pain, but instead, they had taken her completely.

He had stood over her that night, the same helplessness gnawing at him—just like he had felt when he'd stood by his mother, unable to save either of them. That failure had never left him, had followed him through his deployments and into his work with the FBI. After bringing in his nephew, he had sworn that his life, his home, would never be touched by that kind of darkness again. He couldn't bear to let anyone that close, not after everything he'd seen.

Hannah's voice cut through the fog. "JB, this is our chance to do something meaningful."

He blinked, refocusing on her, but the hesitation lingered in his voice. "I'm not saying no, but I'm also not saying yes."

"Well, that's great JB, but I need you to sign the paperwork and be present for the home visit. The girls are sisters, a seven-year-old and a five-year-old."

JB rubbed his temples. The weight of the decision pressed down on him. "Two girls? How will they fit into our family?"

"We'll make it work. Jared will adjust. We've done it before."

"But Jared—" JB stopped short, his voice tightening. He couldn't let Hannah see the cracks forming, couldn't let her know how those memories haunted him, how he was terrified of bringing that kind of pain into their home.

"JB, we've adopted before. This is no different."

"It is different," he said, his tone sharpening as he fought against the surge of emotions. "Jared was already part of our family."

"So?"

"You don't understand," JB said, his frustration boiling over.

"I do understand," Hannah started, but JB interrupted her, his words rushing out before he could stop them.

"I see the darkness every day at work. I don't want that brought into our home," he said, his voice cracking slightly under the weight of the unspoken truth. He had already lived through that darkness—his mother's addiction, his sister's death. He couldn't bear to have it touch their family.

"JB, this is a chance for us to be a a light in the darkness for these two girls," Hannah said. "We talk all the time about living our faith."

"I understand, but this is a really big commitment," JB said, trying to steady himself. "It's not like a puppy. If something goes wrong, you can't just take it back to the pound."

"You don't think I don't understand that?"

"I don't know what you're thinking right now."

"Look, let's meet the girls first. We can see how it goes. After the visit, we can decide."

JB nodded slowly, still unsure but willing to try. "Okay, but you know how unfair that is because once you meet them, it's not like you're going to say no."

Hannah's face softened, knowing JB was absolutely correct. "Thank you."

JB held up the empty wine bottle, forcing a smile despite the churning in his gut. "I think this calls for something stronger. Want a whiskey?"

Hannah chuckled softly. "I'll pass. But thank you."

They spent the rest of the evening reminiscing, their conversation shifting to lighter topics and fond memories. But as Hannah's laughter filled the room, JB couldn't shake the echoes of his past—the weight of his sister's absence, the shame of his mother's addiction, and the hollow space where his father should have been. The burden of it all seemed to loom larger with the prospect of opening their home to two vulnerable lives. For the first time in months, he found solace in Hannah's presence, but the past lingered like a shadow, never fully letting go.

39

Lilly Grace inhaled deeply as the van stopped in front of Mission Ranch. The facility, tucked away in an unassuming strip mall, didn't match her mental image of a residential treatment center. She pondered the unknowns of the coming ninety days and what they might hold for her.

"I thought you said I was going to a residential home for teenagers," Lilly Grace said.

The van driver offered a reassuring smile. "Once you go inside, you'll see that it doesn't look like what you see on the outside. It's more than just the façade."

With a nod, Lilly Grace turned her gaze to the front door. The sign read "Mission Ranch" with the slogan "Healing in Purpose," but its modest appearance did little to quell her apprehension. The sense of isolation she felt as she sat in the van was almost suffocating, akin to the deep-seated craving for her next hit of drugs.

Inside the van, the atmosphere was heavy with unspoken fears. Lilly Grace had been referred to Mission Ranch by a social worker at the hospital who had identified it as a suitable short-term facility for her needs. The recommendation was driven by concerns about her mental and behavioral state, her strained relationship with her mother, and the circumstances surrounding her departure from Missouri. The facility was to serve as an initial step, offering an assessment that would help determine whether she needed long-term restorative therapy or could return home.

The van driver's words offered a sliver of reassurance, though Lilly Grace's nerves remained fraught as she prepared to enter Mission Ranch. The upcoming ninety days would not only involve addressing her addiction but also a deeper evaluation of her family situation and past experiences. This period of time was critical for a comprehensive CPS investigation that would ultimately guide the next steps in her journey.

Lilly Grace's arrival at Mission Ranch felt like stepping into a different world – one where every detail was designed to test her resolve and challenge her perceptions. As she entered the building, the guarded atmosphere only intensified her feelings of confinement and unease.

Inside the waiting area, the Plexiglas partition and the stern demeanor of the older woman behind the desk did nothing to alleviate her anxiety. The room's muted green walls and flower decorations felt cold and impersonal, further amplifying her sense of isolation. Time seemed to drag as she waited for the driver to return, and the environment around her felt like an unwelcome reminder of her predicament.

When the drive finally led her to the conference room, Lilly Grace's apprehensions were only briefly relieved by the more personable presence of Rebecca Reeves and Pastor Jonathan Billings. Ms. Reeves' odor of cigarette smoke made Lilly Grace uneasy, but Pastor Billings' warm demeanor brought a moment of relaxation.

The tour of the facility, though enlightening, failed to ease Lilly Grace's discomfort. The complex layout resembled a labyrinth, further intensifying her feeling of disorientation. Pastor Billings' attempts to offer solace through biblical verses and comforting words were met with a mixture of skepticism and anger from Lilly Grace, who struggled with feelings of betrayal and confusion.

As Pastor Billings spoke about God's protection and the potential for good to come from her suffering, Lilly Grace grappled with her own tumultuous emotions. Her anger rooted in the painful experiences she had endured, erupted in her confrontation with the pastor. The idea of divine purpose and redemption felt distant and hollow against the backdrop of her recent trauma.

The tour continued with introductions to the staff and other residents, and Lilly Grace's exploration of her new living space brought a fleeting sense of privacy and relief. Her small bedroom, though modest, offered a private sanctuary where she could reflect on her complex feelings.

Lying on her bed and staring out at the clouds, Lilly Grace was caught between a sense of liberation from her past and the lingering questions about her future. Her thoughts wandered to Jade and the ambiguous fate of her former captors, revealing a deeper, unresolved emotional turmoil. The echoes of past trauma and the uncertain path ahead painted a vivid, poignant picture of Lilly Grace's internal struggle as she embarked on this new chapter of her life.

***

The next morning, Pastor Billings escorted Ava Harper to the conference room. The two talked about her flight from Missouri and how nice it must have been to escape the harsh Midwest winter weather. She politely listened while he talked, casually she offered an answer in response. Deep down her thoughts were on her baby girl who had run away seven months prior. On the plane flight, and now sitting in the conference room, Ava reflected on her demons. She wondered if her daughter would even want to see her after everything that had happened in the past year.

Lilly Grace entered the conference room and heaviness followed her through the door. Ava gasped, as the girl standing across the room didn't resemble the pretty teenage girl that had left Lee's Summit, Missouri. She wanted to rush over and give her a hug, but something held her back, and she stayed seated. Perhaps it was the shame and the guilt of her own past.

Lilly Grace sat opposite her mother at the other end of the ten-foot-long table. Pastor Billings walked over and shut the conference room door. He observed the two ladies and the physical and emotional distance between the two. He approached a credenza and offered the ladies a coffee or water. Neither accepted. He sat down at the table.

"Mrs. Harper, as you know, by law I am required to be present while you visit with your daughter. Please know that I am here to be a support to each of you."

"Thank you, Pastor Billings," Ava responded.

A knife couldn't cut through the awkwardness in the room. Neither lady sure of what to say. Finally, Ava broke the tension.

"Honey, how are you doing?"

"How am I doing? How the fuck do you think I'm doing?"

"You're safe now."

Lilly Grace glanced at Pastor Billings, and said, "What are we supposed to do now?" She then turned toward her mother, her eyes narrowed, and she continued, "Are we supposed to go through rehab together? Wow, I guess mother like daughter."

"Lilly -"

"No. Don't Lilly me. Don't pretend like you're going to sit there and pretend like everything is going to be okay. It's not. What the hell are you going to do? What's your plan? You want to take me home? Great, let's go home where I can watch you get high every day, and oh that's right, I can get raped by your husband. Yeah, that sounds like a good plan."

Pastor Billings quietly observed the directness of the young girl. He was grateful she was communicating, as the alternative was that she stayed quiet and shut down from all communication. He watched Ava observe her broken and defeated daughter. He did not know what had happened between these two, but he was certain there would need to be a great intervention before they could ever coexist.

"Honey, I'm going to leave him."

"Yeah, right. If you believed what I told you, then why haven't you left him yet?"

"I'm working on it."

"Your husband raped me. He raped your daughter. And you're saying that you're working on it. What the hell does that even mean?"

"I'm trying to process all of this. I'm trying to figure things out."

"Yeah, okay. Why don't you come back when you get things figured out? Until then, I really don't have anything else to say to you."

Ava glanced at Pastor Billings requesting his assistance. He felt her eyes beading down on him. But he wanted to allow the conversation to play out between the two.

"Lilly, your brothers miss you. They've been worried sick about you. I've been worried sick about you."

Lilly Grace stood up, put both of her hands on the table, and screamed at her mother, "I don't want anything to do with you. You're a fucking drug addicted whore."

She exited the room and ran down the hallway toward her bedroom. Ava was left alone in the room, broken and in tears. Pastor Billings moved from the center of the table and sat next to Ava. Her head was buried in her lap. He placed his hand on the back of her shoulder, her body trembled at his touch. The woman was broken and in dire need of help.

"Mrs. Harper, is it okay if I pray over you?"

Ava didn't respond, unable to hold back the tears.

"Dear Heavenly Father, I pray that you will fill the hearts of Ava and Lilly Grace. I pray that you will intervene in the relationship between this mother and daughter. I pray that you give each of them compassion and empathy as they work through their challenges. Lord, most of all, I pray that you offer healing, and that they have the strength Lord to rely upon you and the grace you have provided. Lord, help them forgive and release the evil held within. Holy Spirit, we welcome your presence to release these two ladies from the darkness. Thank you for a crown of beauty instead of ashes, the oil of joy instead of mourning, and a garment of praise instead of a spirit of despair. Amen."

Ava picked her head up from the table, looked at the Pastor, and said, "Pastor Billings, what do I do now? I don't know what to do?"

"Ava, when your heart is under strife, call upon the Lord through prayer, and He will answer you. He will guide you to salvation and to happier times. Now is not the time to rely upon yourself, or Lilly Grace. You must rely upon the Lord to give you peace, to give you clarity, and to help lift the despair from your heart."

"I don't even know how to pray. I don't know what to say."

"You speak to God through the beauty of your heart. It doesn't matter if it comes out jumbled or broken. If you can't think of anything to say, then scream at him. Cry out to him. But do it genuinely from the deepest parts of your heart and soul."

"I don't even know that girl sitting across from me. That's not my Lilly Grace. Where did she go?"

"Ava, you cannot rescue her from the trauma she has experienced. Only God does the rescuing. Lilly Grace is going to need to see her own path to recovery. Please forgive me for potentially overstepping my boundaries, but it sounds like you may need to seek your own path toward recovery. It may be that you are both on your own journey and until you confront your own demons, and seek the help you need, you may never have a relationship with your daughter."

"I'm trying."

"Are you trying?"

"Yes, I've been through rehab and I'm clean now. But it's just so hard being on my own. My youngest son's life is turned upside down. He doesn't even know how to cope with being separated from his older brother. Not to mention his sister running away. And now we're living in an apartment. It's just all so hard. I don't know how to do it. I'm so alone."

"You are not alone. We are never alone. God is always with us. Sometimes the hardest thing to do is to take the first step. If we're being honest with each other, I don't think you being here is going to do any good for either you or Lilly Grace. It would be best if you returned home and sought help. You show her that you are willing to make the difficult changes in your life. Remember, you are still her mother. Your actions, or lack of action, serve as an influence on your daughter. Go home now. Go get help."

Pastor Billings laid his hand on her shoulder one more time before he stood and exited the conference room. Ava Harper sat in the chair and cried for another ten minutes. Her heart reflected on everything she had heard and all that had transpired over the preceding year. Why couldn't she say no to the desire to feed her soul with drugs? Why couldn't she see that the man she had once loved was preying upon her daughter? What kind of mother allowed such a thing to happen to her daughter? These were all the thoughts that ran through her mind as she pondered her next steps.

As Pastor Billings recommended, the next day she was on an airplane and returned to Lee's Summit, Missouri. But before she left, she wrote a note for Lilly Grace and leave it with Pastor Billings.

40

C HAPTER 40

The interview with Lilly Grace left JB uncertain of her readiness to testify against Jade, Paco Ramirez, or the West Side Familia. So far, the wiretap had yielded scant evidence of any criminal activity. Meanwhile, the strain of Hannah's aspiration to foster two girls was taking its toll. JB spent his nights awake, pondering the case and contemplating evidence. Yet, there was still one move left to play that could change the game against the WSF-Dominique Velasquez. To some extent, the fate of the entire case hinged on whether a man he had only recently encountered could emerge as his most formidable ally against the WSF.

JB traveled north for an hour and a half on Highway 99 to reach Elk Grove, a Sacramento suburb. Its closeness to the state capital and the Central State FBI Office made it an ideal spot for a safe house. During the drive, JB mulled over their previous conversation. He justified Manny's death in his mind, pondered the unheeded pleas for help, and acknowledged Dominique's point—it was his fault. He vowed not to let it occur again. Doubts about Dominique's honesty lingered. Had Manny confided in him about the case? Was Dominique privy to WSF information? After turning off Elk Grove Boulevard, JB navigated through the neighborhood's eastern side and stopped at the safe house's driveway. This area, with homes developed over the last decade, was a stark contrast to the Deep South Side's streets—a community erected decades prior.

JB knocked and waited patiently for a response. After a second and third knock, a young woman eventually opened the door, her weary eyes revealing the stress she was under. Clinging tightly to her leg was her two-year-old son.

"Hi, is it Mrs. Velasquez?"

"Umm, no, we're not married. My name is Martha Hernandez."

JB surprised. "I'm JB. It's nice to meet you," he said. He bent down toward the little guy. "And who do we have here?"

She stroked the back of her sons' head. JB could tell she felt uncomfortable speaking to an agent of the FBI.

"This is Arturo."

JB smiled at the little boy and patted young Arturo on the top of the head.

"Is Dominique here?"

"Yes, he's back in the family room. Back that way. He's waiting for you."

"Thank you."

Although Dominique and Martha had been in the house for a few days, you would never know it by how clean the house appeared. It certainly didn't look like young kids were staying in it. JB rounded the kitchen corner and found Dominique sitting on the couch watching television. He looked relaxed, very different than the person JB had met earlier.

"Dominique turn the television off and let's get to work. Okay?" JB said.

Dominique turned the television off and moved over to the dining room table. Martha came through the room and offered the men something to drink. Focused on the conversation at hand, they both passed on the offer. JB placed a tape recorder on the table. Dominique looked at him with an inquisitive eye. JB sensed Dominique's hesitation: he knew the young man wondered if the two were on the same side.

"Dominique let's start from the beginning. How long have you been associated with the West Side Familia?"

"Bro, it started way back in the third grade. They put their snares in me way back then. You know, some of the boys in the hood kept comin' round tryin' to recruit us youngin's to be runners or lookouts. They'd pay us twenty bucks here and there to deliver some bag or look out while someone did something stupid. Bro, you know how it goes, everyone trusts an eight-year-old kid. You know?"

Dominique pulled a cigarette out of the box in his pocket. He didn't ask for permission, just pulled a match, and lit the tip. He pulled a long drag and turned his head as he exhaled the smoke. JB could sense he was nervous, his eyes concentrated on the tape recorder at the center of the table.

"Back then, when you were in the third grade, did you know Eric Avina or Paco Ramirez?"

"Shit man, hell yeah. Bro, they were just a little bit older than me, so they were doin' the same stupid shit I was doin'. You know how it goes."

"You say just a little bit older; you are twenty-five years old. Correct?'

"Yeah. I made it to twenty-five, can you believe that shit?"

Again, Dominique turned his head away from JB as he pulled another drag and long exhale on the cigarette. JB could sense the young man was nervous.

"And Eric Avina is twenty-eight and Paco Ramirez is twenty-seven. Is that correct?"

"Yeah, something like that. I ain't exactly best friends with 'em and sendin' 'em birthday cards and shit."

"What do you remember about Eric and Paco as they progressed through the hierarchy of the WSF?"

"Shit bro, Eric was named from on high from the beginning man. You know what I mean? His pops were a leader, and it was just a known thing that he was eventually goin' to take shit over. Although, you know, I don't think he exactly down for all that shit. You know?"

"What do you mean?"

"Bro, as long as I can remember home boy been talkin' about walkin' away. Man, he'd always been talkin' about shit about wishin' he never was born into this shit. Man, you feel me."

"When did he officially assume the leader role of the West Side Familia?"

"That happened sometime after high school, Bro. I think it was a few years after his pops was killed. I don't member. Crew was kind of crumblin' apart for a while."

"What about you? How did your role progress or change over the years?"

"Bro, I always had one foot in and one foot out. I knew shit we doin' wasn't right, but it was all I knew man. You know what I mean? I mean, I know I ain't ever goin' college and gettin' some office job and shit. So, in high school it was easier to slang that rock and drink and party with the homies man. You know how it is?"

"Did you ever get into anything to serious with the crew?"

"Naw man. My shit wasn't all that serious. A few fights here and there."

"You ended up going to County Jail for vehicle theft, unlawful possession of a firearm, and possession of methamphetamines with intent to sale. How is that not all that serious?"

"Bro, I ain't out here tryin' to kill no one and shit. Bro, I just out here's survivin' and shit. You know, got's to get mine."

JB was tempted to dig into the right and wrong of Dominique's past. It may be a concern when he testified in a court of law. He assessed the young man's character and wondered how a jury would view his history with the WSF. Instead, he opted to change focus and take the heat off Dominique's history. After all, he didn't want his only ally on the case to grow defensive and resist to turn states evidence. But, as was typical with JB, he couldn't resist one last line of questions.

"You think distributing methamphetamine and heroin to kids on the streets isn't serious or killing people?"

"Bro, you call me a killer for distributin' meth and heroin on the streets. What do you call pharmaceutical companies? Who you think's profitin' the most off the opioid crisis?" Dominique finished the cigarette and squished it the ash tray on the table. He went into his pocket and pulled a second out and lit it before he continued.

"Shit bro, you think I'm just some stupid hood rat Chicano who doesn't know what's really happenin'. Bro, shit, I ain't the one that needs to be behind bars. And I for sure ain't the one who yo ass should be investigatin'. You should be focused on those white collared bastards that makin' hand over fist. Instead of lookin' at our sorry asses barely makin' scratch."

JB knew he shouldn't have asked the question, and he kicked himself for allowing his emotion to get the better of him in this context. He knew it was time to change the focus and reengage his informant.

"All right. Calm down. That's not what this is about. Tell me about Paco Ramirez. Who is he?"

"Shit, that's an evil son of a bitch. You know, since he was a kid, he was no good."

"What's his relationship with Eric Avina?"

"Man, he's been loco like I said, since he was a kid. You know what I mean? Bro, I think someone like Eric who never really liked to get his hands dirty, you know? You feel me? He kind of needed someone like Paco around to be the bad guy. Do shit man, shit he didn't want to do. It kind of absolved him of all the shit he was doin'. Feel me bro?"

"So, they've been connected with each other since they were kids?"

"Yeah, since the elementary days those two were tied together. I think their cousins or some shit. I don't really know all that family history. Man, that's they's history."

JB knew it was time to get to the reality of what would stick in the court of law. He decided to press for current information on the WSF and members within the crew that were the ones who made the decisions.

"Tell me what you know about the business dealings of the West Side Familia. Not what you think is going on. But what you know and what you can prove in court testimony."

"Bro, my cuz, came over to my house a few weeks back. Like I said, he was all in a panic and shit. He's worried they's comin' for him. I tried to calm him down, bro, but I didn't know he was workin' for y'all. I didn't know he had some real shit to stress on. You know? I don't know how to even say this shit. Because you know I love Manny and he was a good dude, bro, but you know he didn't have the strongest fortitude. You know what I'm sayin'?"

"What is it, Dominique? What did he tell you?"

Dominique looked around the room before he refocused his attention on JB. By now, JB observed that the man across the table from his had forgotten all about the tape recorder and was ready to provide the details needed to proceed with the case.

"Bro, you know that girl that got knifed. You know that girl they found in that almond grove few months back? Yeah bro, I was the one who found her. And it was Manny who told me where she was at?"

JB suddenly felt sick to his stomach. He started to replay the events of the night of November 3rd. First, he thought of the call from Manny when he told him about the dead body and where it was located. He replayed the conversation at Marisols Taco Truck and tried to remember, word for word, everything Manny said.

"Did you ever ask him how he knew where she was at?"

JB could see the look in Dominique eyes, and he knew in that moment, that he wasn't going to like the next words out of Dominique's mouth.

"Bro, Manny came over one night all in a panic and shit. He had these video tapes man. He made my lady go to the back of the house so she couldn't see what he was about to play. Bro, at first, I thought he was just showin' me some homemade porn and shit. You know Manny, he wasn't exactly a man who was good with the ladies. You know what I mean man? Anyways, it was this chick with two guys' man. She looked young and shit. I recognized bitch from the hood. She been rollin' with the crew, you know, puttin' cano down on 'em dudes. I could tell she was drugged and shit, you know? You could just tell from her body and how she was respondin' to 'em dudes layin' it down. They must of gave her some shit man, cause chick was teetering. You know, she was comin' in and out of whatever. You could see it, bro, on the tape. Her eyes rollin' back and shit. You could see the whites of her eyes and shit. It seemed she started to come out and realize what was happenin'. You know what I'm sayin'? I felt kind of weird watching this shit with my lady in the back bedroom and all. Then, suddenly, I heard Manny's voice dude. Shit tripped me straight out. Bro, I looked at him sittin' there in the room with me. It was weird man. He had this dopey look on his face. Then, I knew he was the dude filmin' this chick getting' banged and shit."

JB was gutted to his core, mouth agape, and eyes wide open. He couldn't find the words to say what he felt. He had worked with Manny for a long time and had never once suspected that he would be involved with such a heinous crime.

Dominique continued, "Chick started screaming for help and shit. Manny started panicking with the camera. That shit started bouncin' all 'round. Then, the chick sorta seized up, you know bro? She straight hit a straight board and shit in that bed. The two dudes jumped back just starin' at the bitch. Manny dropped the fuckin' camera and started runnin' 'round the room. Man, that camera and shit was still playin'. All of it, bro. All of it was caught on that fuckin' camera. Then, the other two homies started panicking and shit. Before you know it, man, one of the dudes made a phone call."

"Could you make out on the video who they called?"

"Naw man, it was just a bunch of scared little kids tryin' to figure out what to do with this bitch."

"Did Manny tell you who was on the phone?"

"Yeah man, it was that dude ya'll caught up a while back. Manny left that camera hidin' under a pillow in the room. It got kind of kicked around a bit, but you could make out what was bein' said. About twenty minutes later GP came in the room."

JB interrupted Dominique, "GP, you mean Gustavo Perez Medina?"

"Yeah, that dude, you know. The bitch was still layin' there in her shit, you know. She seemed to be unconscious bro. GP walked up to the bitch and checked her pulse. Then, he turned 'round and started smackin' the two homies 'round. They's straight scared, you know what I mean. He was an enforcer for Eric and Paco. They been usin' this homie since they were in high school. After he knocked those two 'round he turned to the bitch. By this time, bro, he seemed crazed out of his mind. You know man? He grabbed that bitch and threw her cross the room. You couldn't see it on the video, bro, but you could hear his fist bouncin off that bitch's head man. Manny told me he beat the shit out of this little bitch. After a few minutes, in the video, you just seem 'em pacin' 'round the room and cursin' and shit. He told one of the homies to go outside and make sure no one was watchin'. He told Manny and the other homie to grab her and get her in the trunk of the car. By this time, everybody was out of the camera view and shit. Anyways, Manny told me everything that happened. He said it all started out as a good time. This bitch was havin' fun, smokin' a little dope, and earning a little bit of green. You know what I mean? Bro, they were payin' her little bitch ass a bit of money here and there to get her to do some more shit. You know, the drugs, and the alcohol was flowin'. All's that little bitch saw was a payday. Shit seemed good at the time. Then it went from fun and games to some real shit man. Manny was cryin' when he was showing me this shit. Bro, he kept saying God was goin' judge his ass for this shit and he knew he was goin' straight to hell. He kept sayin' there was nothin' he could do to regain God's favor after this shit. Man, I ain't never seen Manny like that. He was broken, man. He said he was so afraid of GP that he just went along with everythin'. After a little while he came back in the room and grabbed the camera. I guess they took chica out to that filled and GP made each of them knife that little bitch thirteen times, you know, to represent, you know? He said GP was sadistic man. Manny said he watched 'em and told 'em to do it slowly. He said if they didn't do what he wanted then they would find themselves sittin' in that field right alongside that little bitch. Bro, he told me he was goin' die one way or another. He said, there was no comin' back from this shit. And he told me I had to get this tape to you man. He made me promise to get this shit to you."

JB sat back in the chair; his arms folded over the top of his head. He took a long inhale and then he exhaled deeply. He tried to process the entire story that was just shared.

"Are these other two guys still around? Do we know where they are now?"

"Yeah man, they are still around. GP wasn't goin' to rat 'em out. And they are too afraid to say anything. Especially after what happened to Manny."

"Is any of this connected to Paco Ramirez or Eric Avina?"

"Yeah bro, if you watch the first part of the video you can hear one of the homies talkin' about how the bitch was one of Paco's whores."

"She was on Paco's payroll?"

"Bro, I don't know nothin' 'bout any of that shit. I'm tryin' to clean my own shit up. You know? I'm just telling you, bro, in the beginning of the video, that's what one of the homies says. Bro, you'll have to pick his ass up and find out what he knows."

"This is gold Dominique. This is what we need. You stay right here and don't go back to Modesto for anything. If you need something, call or text me. Okay?"

"Shit bro, I ain't leavin' this house. But I tell you what, you better take care of our asses. I don't know how all this shit works. But if they catch wind of where we're at, they'll find us. You feel me?"

"Don't worry. You're safe now. Just stay put and don't talk to anyone. Do you understand?"

The two men shook hands. JB took possession of the video and made the quick hour and half drive back to his office. He was already on the phone with Warnall on the drive. The two set up search warrants for the two men, Paco Ramirez and Eric Avina. The end was in sight.

41

—·—

CHAPTER 41

Two weeks following Lilly Grace's arrival, Pastor Billings knelt beside his desk, hands clasped tightly, seeking divine guidance through prayer. He implored God to assist him in connecting with the troubled girl, who had spoken scarcely more than a few words during their daily one-hour counseling sessions. His inquiries were often met with silence or a sharp remark likening the experience to time spent in "his prison." Despite the walls she had built, Pastor Billings held firm in his belief that beneath her defiance was a soul crying out for refuge and faith. The gnawing uncertainty troubled him – was his effort sufficient? Was he letting her down?

The knock at the door interrupted his focus, yet he persisted in his prayer, seeking the wisdom to navigate his predicament. Upon concluding, he rose, adjusted his sweater, and proceeded to the conference room, with the spark of an idea taking shape in his thoughts.

Lilly Grace was acclimating to the strict schedule of Mission Ranch. The first rule was rising at 6:30, followed by thirty minutes of silent prayer or meditation. Post-breakfast, the group engaged in therapy, then recreational activities at 10. Afternoons were reserved for academic studies tailored to different age groups, culminating in a personal counseling session with Pastor Billings. To Lilly Grace, the regimen was stifling, each moment pulling her deeper into a routine she resisted.

Pastor Billings had been grappling with how to reach out to her effectively. However, today, following his prayer, inspiration struck with a fresh strategy. Although uncertain of her reaction, he was compelled to attempt it. Following their customary short greetings, they took their seats.

Breaking the silence, Pastor Billings began, "In our first meeting, you told me that I could never understand what you've been through. Do you still believe that? That I'm incapable of understanding your unique experience?"

He sensed Lilly Grace caught the directness and the sharpness in his tone of voice. He observed her shift in the chair, a sign that she was open to his question.

To his surprise, Lilly Grace responded, "Yeah. I don't think you could possibly understand what I've been through."

"You are correct. There is no way that I can possibly understand what it's like to be a fifteen-year-old girl who was raped by her stepfather. Nor can I understand what it was like to travel cross-country alone only to find myself in a tortuous relationship with someone who I thought was my friend. Nor could I understand what it is like to sell my body for money night after night. You are right. There is no way I could possibly understand those unique circumstances."

Lilly Grace lifted herself up in the chair, her body language reflected the energy she felt. He could tell she felt validated by her assumption. Then Pastor Billings shared a revelation that he knew she was not prepared to hear.

"Lilly Grace, while I cannot understand your unique experience, it is important for you to understand that I have my own unique experience. When I was twelve years old, my mother would send me to an after schoolboys' club. It was a place where we would play sports and other games, while we waited for our parents to pick us up after work. At that time in my life, I was what many would call an introvert. I didn't like to play games because I wasn't big and athletic like the other boys. Nor was I quick witted to fire off insult after insult, as was customary. So instead, I sat quietly in the corner, and day after day, I waited alone for my mother to pick me up. One day, a counselor came and sat down beside me. He was very nice and attempted to make small talk with me while I waited for my mother. It was nice to have someone just listen to me. It was comforting knowing I wasn't alone in this world. Then one day, he asked if I wanted to go back to his office and talk while we waited for my mother. It seemed like a good idea at the time. He had a television and a couch in his office. It felt a little weird when he sat down so close to me on the couch. Our legs practically touched each other's. I knew it wasn't right, but he had been so nice to me. So, I didn't say anything. He put his arm around me and leaned in close to talk to me. He talked about being lonely and that it was okay. He shared that he was often lonely as well. With each passing moment, his body got closer and closer to mine. Then he put his hand on my knee. He started to massage the back of my neck with his other hand. He said he just wanted to comfort and relax me. It did feel good, even though I knew it was very wrong. Lilly Grace, he changed my life forever that day. He violated me in way that no person should ever be violated. He took away the innocence of my youth. I spent my teenage years hating the world and hating myself for allowing it to happen. Every night I laid in bed and wondered why I let him get so close to me on that couch. Why hadn't I said something when he put his hand on my knee and moved it up my thigh? Why did I keep coming back, day after day, week after week? I hated myself for being so weak. So no, I cannot understand your unique experience because it was a traumatic event that only you experienced. But I have my own traumatic experience that is unique to me. Maybe we have more in common than you think."

Lilly Grace's eyes filled with tears. The weight of the world, and everything that had happened in the past year, felt like it was all crushing on her shoulders. The feeling of guilt, shame, and despair, all of what he felt was exactly what Lilly Grace felt. She wiped the tears out of her eyes, and with a solemn tone, asked, "How did you get past it all?"

"It wasn't me; it was God. In my late teens, I started going to a neighborhood church. I was fortunate enough to make a connection with my church leader. There was something I found, going to church, where I realized we're all broken people. We're just broken in different ways. The trauma you experienced, and the trauma I experienced, can isolate us and keep us entangled in dangerous emotions and a continuous series of vivid flashbacks, locking us in that trauma. God understands how lonely this cycle can be. After all, he sacrificed his son for us. Jesus, placed on that cross, so that he could let us know that he endured all that pain and misery for us. He suffered more than any one of us. God sees you, and he's given you his word so you can see him too. Psalm 56:8 says, 'You keep track of all my sorrows. You have collected all my tears in your bottle. You have recorded each one in your book.'"

"How can you tell me God is so loving, so willing to accept my tears and bottle them up? If he was so great, so powerful, why would he allow all of this to happen to me?

"Great question. Are you familiar with Adam and Eve?"

"Yes."

"And you're familiar with the story of Eve eating the apple in the garden, correct?"

"Yes."

"Why did God allow her to eat that apple?"

"I don't know, she was hungry?"

"No. The garden was fruitful beyond comprehension. When God created Adam and Eve, he gave them what we call free will. That means, he gave them the opportunity to choose whether they wanted to sin. In fact, he knew they would sin. And when sin entered our world, evil came along with it. But the most important thing to God, is the ability for every person to act of their own free will. It's more important to him than even the evilest."

"Okay. So, God gave us a free will to make our own choices, why did he do that? Wouldn't it have been better, if he was so mighty and so powerful, to not allow sin or evil in our world in the first place?"

"A minute ago, I spoke of Jesus on the cross, now think of that as the evilest thing done to man in the history of the world. The death and resurrection of Jesus Christ, it was done to wash away our sins. It was done, in fact, it was planned by God, to demonstrate his righteousness. It was done to demonstrate his power and authority over this world. Our free will, from the beginning, created the sin and evil of this world. The savior murdered on that cross, washed away our sins. Through all of this, it shows the power and authority of our God."

"It doesn't seem fair that we have to go through all of this pain and suffering."

"It doesn't make sense to you right now, but you are asking all the right questions. One day, you'll discover that neither you, nor I, can help you move away from the feelings that you feel. That can only be accomplished through your surrendering to God."

"I don't even know if I believe in God, how am I ever going to surrender to something I don't believe in?"

"Lilly Grace, this will be a prayer of my every day. That you will come to faith. That you will grow to release control of your healing journey, and that you will ultimately, surrender the journey to God. It may seem like a far leap today, but it is my prayer that by the end of your ninety days you'll see just how weak you are and the great strength of God."

Lilly Grace's eyes started to lose their light. Pastor Billings sensed that her moment of reflection would soon end. He knew patience would be his greatest ally in Lilly Grace's transformation. And his senses were correct, as in a matter of seconds, she sat back in the chair and the light in her eyes was gone.

"Whatever, I don't care about this God and I for damn sure don't trust someone that allowed me to go through all of this. He can be your God but he ain't mine." Lilly Grace stood up from her chair, "Is our time up for today?"

"Yes, Lilly Grace, you may return to your room."

Pastor Billings hoped that their fleeting moment was enough to sustain their next engagement. And he hoped his prayers would soften her heart.

42

— · —

C HAPTER 42

JB nervously rummaged through his closet, searching for the perfect combination of dress pants and a shirt for the adoption agency's home visit. He tried khakis and a dress shirt first, but the image of Derek Widman and his boy Yates immediately flashed in his mind, making him uncomfortable. After several more attempts, he finally settled on a pair of Levi's, a polo shirt, and a half-zip sweater. It wasn't too formal, but it wasn't too casual either. In this whirlwind of uncertainty, the one thing he could control was how he looked. With everything else spinning out of control, at least he could look and feel like himself.

Downstairs, Hannah was meticulously cleaning every nook and cranny of the living room and kitchen. She had yelled for Jared to go outside and pick up the dog poop, and to tidy up the patio. It was all hands-on deck for the adoption agency.

JB walked downstairs, immediately spotting Hannah as she wiped down the kitchen counters. He wrapped his arms around her, pulling her into a hug. Gently, he tucked a loose strand of hair behind her ear, kissing her forehead. "You're amazing," he whispered, holding her shoulders. "No matter what the agency thinks, you're perfect for these two girls." Seeing Hannah so excited – so alive – made JB feel a surge of excitement too. He hadn't seen this side of her in years, and it warmed his heart.

The three of them convened in the living room, taking a moment to admire how they had managed to pull the house together in such a short amount of time. "I don't think I've ever seen the house this clean," earning a playful elbow to the ribs from Hannah.

Then, a car pulled up in the driveway. JB's stomach tightened as he watched Amanda Davies step out, followed by another woman and Pastor Wilkins.

"Geez, they brought the big guns for this visit," JB muttered, a nervous chuckle escaping his lips.

Hannah greeted them at the door, her voice warm but with an underlying edge of nerves. As they entered the foyer, JB couldn't help but notice their eyes scanning the house – their home – taking in every detail. The cleanliness of the yard, the arrangement of the furniture in the living room. He suddenly felt exposed, as if they were under investigation.

"Hello, Hannah, it's so great to see you again," said Mrs. Davies, her smile warm but her eyes sharp.

"You too. Thank you for coming. Can I get you something to drink? A glass of lemonade or tea?"

"Oh, no thank you, not yet at least. Allow me to introduce my colleague, Heather Dubreau, our site visit coordinator. Heather helps facilitate ongoing site visits with families, manages the child-to-foster-parent relationships, and will generally be your go-to person if your family is selected as a foster family."

Hannah only heard one part of that statement: if your family is selected.

Immediately, doubts flooded her mind. Why wouldn't they be selected? The pressure she already felt intensified tenfold.

"And of course, you know Pastor Wilkins," Mrs. Davies continued.

"Yes, good morning, Pastor Wilkins," Hannah replied, her voice steady despite the rising tide of anxiety.

JB stepped forward, extending his hand to the pastor, then politely greeted the two women. Hannah introduced Jared, who, dressed in khakis and a polo shirt at his mother's insistence, looked like he was making his best impression of Yates Widman.

"Do you mind if we sit down and go over a few things before we get started?" Mrs. Davies asked,

"Not at all. Let's go to the living room where we'll be more comfortable," Hannah responded, guiding the group from the foyer to the living room. Once they were settled, Mrs. Davies prepared a few pamphlets, her manner efficient. Then, the questioning began.

"So, since we've had the opportunity to visit with Hannah, why don't you tell us about yourself, JB?" Mrs. Davies asked, her pen poised above her notebook.

"Not much to tell on my end. I'm a Marine, and now I work for the Federal Bureau of Investigation."

"What do you do for the FBI, if you don't mind my asking?" Mrs. Davies inquired, her tone neutral, but JB could sense the underlying curiosity.

He was keenly aware that he was under the microscope. "As I'm sure Hannah has shared with you, I work on the gang task force unit. We cover cartel activity and child trafficking."

As Mrs. Davies scribbled notes, JB felt the watching eyes of Pastor Wilkins, who was no more than a vague acquaintance. Heather Dubreau, meanwhile, was glancing around the room, taking in every detail.

"So, what does that mean – cartel activity and child trafficking? Like, what do you do?" Mrs. Davies pressed.

"Essentially, I analyze the financial operations of cartel units, collaborate with inter-agency partners for intelligence and information sharing, and spend a significant amount of time online reviewing child predator activity," JB replied, keeping his tone even.

"So, how dangerous would you say your job is as a special agent?" Mrs. Davies asked.

JB caught Hannah's downward glance and gave his standard response. "I'm really a desk junky, Mrs. Davies. The most dangerous part of my job is getting carpal tunnel from being at the keyboard all day."

He felt a pang of guilt for the half-truth, especially with Pastor Wilkins sitting across from him. But if Mrs. Davies and Ms. Dubreau knew the full extent of his work, they might have serious reservations about approving Hannah as a foster parent.

"How do you feel about serving as a foster parent, especially given what you do for a living?" Mrs. Davies continued, her eyes searching.

Hannah shot him her perfect southern smile – his cue to get this answer right.

"What I do for a living doesn't factor into how I feel about our family serving as foster parents. We believe it's our responsibility to give back and help those in our community who need it most. We're blessed to be considered as candidates for foster parenting. We understand you have many families to choose from, and we just hope we can put our best foot forward for these two girls."

Hannah was amazed at his ability to bend the truth, especially with Pastor Wilkins watching, but she was grateful. In some ways, it made her love him even more.

"And, as I'm sure Hannah shared, Jared is our adoptive son. We took him in when he was five years old, so we're familiar with this process. We're looking forward to giving these two young girls a chance at life, just like we did with Jared. It would be our honor."

"Well, thank you, JB." Mrs. Davies said, though there was a glint of something more in her eyes. "I must admit, I'm a little surprised by your enthusiasm. The last time I spoke with Hannah, she mentioned that you weren't fully on board and that might be a challenge. Has something changed since then?"

JB admired Mrs. Davies' tenacity – she would make an excellent interrogator with the FBI. Realizing he might have laid it on a bit thick, he dialed it back.

"Yes, I'm sure Hannah shared that. I did have reservations, but Hannah and I had the opportunity to sit down and discuss this at length. We've talked about where we see our family going in the future. As much as we could be a blessing to these girls, they could be an equal blessing to us."

Mrs. Davies nodded, seemingly satisfied. She glanced at Pastor Wilkins and Ms. Dubreau before closing her notebook. "Why don't we take a tour of the house?"

"That sounds like a great idea," Hannah said.

The next thirty minutes were spent casually walking and talking, moving from one room to the next. Family photos, vacation stories, and glimpses into their life were shared, offering insights into their family without feeling intrusive. Eventually, JB found himself alone in the backyard with Pastor Wilkins.

"JB, do you mind if we sit down and have conversation?" Pastor Wilkins asked.

JB hesitated but knew he couldn't refuse. The pastor's stature in the community demanded respect. "Sure, what's on your mind?"

"Since Hannah's surgery, I've spent a great deal of time with her, talking about her life, your home life, your work, and frankly, helping her process the outcome of the surgery and the reality of infertility. I don't mean to be direct, but she's shared that you haven't been the most empathetic through all this. Normally, I wouldn't get so involved in a couple's business, but since you're considering fostering these two girls, I feel compelled to be more intrusive. Do you understand?"

JB leaned back slightly, feeling the weight of the pastor's words. He was accustomed to tough conversations, but this was different. He was being scrutinized in a way that felt deeply personal, and he wasn't sure how to navigate it.

"Pastor, I appreciate everything you've done for Hannah. We've gone through a lot in the past few months. It's been challenging, to say the least. But we're getting through it the best we can."

"That's good to hear, JB. I wasn't going to bring this up in front of Mrs. Davies, but I have to ask – when did you have this change of heart about fostering? Because Hannah painted a very different picture of your feelings."

JB paused, considering his words carefully. "As I told Mrs. Davies, Hannah and I have had many conversations about this opportunity. I'd be lying if I said I was on board from the beginning. I wasn't. But I'm willing to go through the process and find my way. One thing I've learned is that I can' say not to something I don't fully understand. It's in my DNA to investigate, identify facts, and make a judgement based on those results."

Pastor Wilkins nodded, but his eyes remained focused on JB. "Given what you see in your day-to-day life, how do you think you'll respond when these girls have serious problems? Are you okay with them bringing those issues into your home? Are you okay with Jared being exposed to any issues they might bring?"

JB felt his patience thinning. He understood the pastor's concerns, but this felt like an overreach. It was time to reassert himself.

"Pastor, Jared has been through enough in his life already. He's not oblivious to the problems kids face, and we've worked hard to raise him to be understanding and empathetic. If these girls have problems, and they likely do, we'll deal with them together as a family. But I have no intention of shielding Jared from the realities of the world. I'm not going to put a wall around our home. That's not how we're raising him, and it's not how we'll approach this situation. We'll provide these girls with the stability they need and show them the same love and care we've shown Jared."

There was a long pause as the pastor studied JB, weighing his words. "JB, I know you're a man of action. I respect that. But these girls will need more than just stability. They'll need a father figure who can open his heart to them, even when it's difficult. Can you do that?"

JB met the pastor's gaze head-on. "I can."

The pastor held his stare for a moment longer, then nodded slowly. "Alright, JB. I'll trust your judgement. But remember, this isn't just about doing what's right. It's about what's right for these girls, for Hannah, and for Jared."

JB's response was measured, but inside he felt a rush of emotions. "I understand. And I won't let them down."

As they made their way back to the house, JB was filled with a sense of unease. He had succeeded in the pastor's test, yet he was aware that the true test still lay ahead. He could only hope that he was prepared for what was to come.

43

— • —

C HAPTER 43

The first light of dawn had yet to break over the eastern slope of the Sierra Nevada Mountains as JB walked through the heavy doors of the Stanislaus County Sheriff's Office. Inside, an energy charged the air, a murmur of voices and hurried footsteps echoing down the sterile corridors as word spread of the imminent raid on the WSF. The targets: Paco Ramirez, Eric Avina, and three others implicated in the brutal murder of a fifteen-year-old girl found discarded in a vacant almond grove.

JB made his way into the Tactical Operation Command Center, where the tension was almost tangible. Inside, Warnall, the Stanislaus County Sheriff, stood over a projector, his face illuminated by the blue light of the screen. Gathered around the table were the Chief of Police for the Modesto PD, the Criminal Incident Response Group Leader, the Modesto Gang Unit lead, and the head of the DEA. On the overhead screen, a map flickered, highlighting the two primary targets, with detailed aerial views of their homes and the surrounding neighborhood.

Warnall's voice was steady but firm as he finalized the unit leads and meticulously outlined the sequence and timing of the operation. The room was filled with the rustling of gear checks and the quiet murmurs of last-minute strategies. JB felt the weight of the moment settle in his chest as the clock on the wall ticked closer to 6:00 a.m. In one hour, they would move. There was no room for error.

***

Eric Avina lay in bed, the darkness of early morning still heavy in the room, when his burner phone vibrated on the nightstand. His hand fumbled, knocking it to the floor with a dull thud. He considered ignoring it, but then his personal phone buzzed again a minute later, his curiosity piqued when he recognized Anita's number. And at this hour, it must have been urgent.

He quickly grabbed the phone, his fingers brushing against the cold surface before finally redialing the missed number. He heard Anita's voice, sharp and panicked.

"Eric, they're coming for you right now. You've got to get out of there."

He blinked, trying to shake off the haze of sleep. "What are you talkin' about?"

Her urgency cut through his grogginess. He sat up, rubbing his eyes to clear his vision.

"The cops are on their way. They're coming to your house now. You have to go."

"How do you know? Is this legit?"

"Yes, I got a text a few minutes ago. They were in a briefing, about to roll out. It's you and Paco they're after."

Adrenaline shot through him as he leaped from the bed. He moved swiftly through the house, careful not to turn on any lights. At the front window, he peered outside. The street was quiet, too quiet. He scanned the parked cars, searching for anything out of place.

"Okay, okay. How much time do I have?"

"Not much. They might already be on their way."

"Got it. I'll call you later."

He hung up, the phone slipping from his hand as he rushed back to the bedroom. His mind raced as he threw on a pair of jeans, a shirt, and shoes. From the closet, he grabbed two bags – one packed with clothes, the other with cash, a handgun, and forged travel documents.

As he zipped up the second bag, he paused, mentally mapping his first move. But then, a faint noise outside the bedroom window snapped him back to the present. He froze, heart pounding, before sliding along the wall to peek outside. The backyard was cloaked in shadow, nothing visibly amiss, but the creeping dread in his gut told him otherwise.

His time was running out.

***

Two units crept down the back-alley of 1629 Spokane Avenue, their engines low, while three more pulled up silently in front of the house. DEA Special Agent Walter Stephen approached from the rear, moving like a shadow through the backyard. His sights locked on the house as Special Agent Bryan Salazar slipped past him, advancing toward the house.

Special Agent Salazar peered through the bedroom window, spotting the target, Paco Ramirez, asleep in bed. In another room, two young girls lay curled up, oblivious to the impending danger.

As the first light of dawn colored the horizon, a faint darkness still lingered, casting long shadows across the Ramirez home. Agent Salazar maintained his vigil at the window, eyes fixed on Paco. The signal was given, and the units converged. Simultaneously, three agents breached the rear entrance, while four others smashed through the front door. The quiet of the morning shattered as they stormed the house.

Paco awoke with a start, the sound of boots pounding through his home jolting him upright. He reached for the firearm stashed in the bedside drawer. Special Agent Salazar, hearing the commotion, relayed that the suspect was armed but lost visual as Paco moved out of sight.

Inside, the agents swept through the narrow hallways, systematically clearing each room. They burst into the bedroom where Tiffany and Veronica were huddled together on the bed, terror etched on their faces. The lead agent barked orders, and the girls, trembling, obeyed, lying face down on the floor. Their hands were swiftly bound behind their backs.

Meanwhile, across the hall, Paco crouched low against the wall, gun in hand, waiting. DEA Special Agent Thomas Shelter kicked open the bedroom door, and in an instant, the first shot rang out. Paco's bullet whizzed past Shelter's head, missing by inches. Shelter pivoted, returning fire, but Paco's second shot found its mark, striking Shelter's left shoulder. The impact sent him staggering back, his vision blurring as pain shot through his body. A third shot hit Shelter dead center in the chest, knocking him off balance.

As Shelter crumpled against the wall, Special Agent Tony Cardena charged through the doorway, his weapon ready. In a split second, he unleashed a barrage of six rounds, each one hitting Paco Ramirez squarely in the chest. The force of the bullets drove Paco to the floor, his lifeless body slumping against the wall.

Cardena kicked the gun from Paco's hand, ensuring the threat was neutralized. Meanwhile, a team rushed to Agent Shelter's side, the sight of blood staining the floor adding urgency to their movements. They quickly assessed his injuries – the round that struck his chest had been stopped by his steel protective vest, but the bullet that tore through his shoulder had ricocheted off bone and was dangerously close to his heart. Blood poured from the wound, and Shelter's pulse weakened with each passing moment.

As the team worked frantically to stabilize him, they called for immediate medical evacuation. Shelter was rushed to the medical center, but despite their efforts, he succumbed to his injuries three hours later.

***

JB stood beside a Stanislaus County Sheriff's SUV, his breath visible in the crisp morning air. As he waited for the command team to get into position, his thoughts drifted to his first encounter with Eric Avina, a young man who, under different circumstances, might have led a very different life. Intelligent, charismatic, and with a natural magnetism, Avina had qualities JB couldn't help but admire. He understood why young men were drawn to him, why they saw him as a leader. But now, as the clocked inched toward 7:00, JB's mind was focused on the task ahead. He prayed that God would intervene, that this wouldn't end in bloodshed.

At precisely 6:59, JB checked his watch. With the turn of the hour, he gave the order. The front and rear doors of the house were breached simultaneously, the silence of the morning shattered by the explosive bangs of flash grenades. The agents moved with precision, flowing through the house like a well-rehearsed dance, each call of "clear" echoing through the rooms as they advanced.

JB followed the team inside, the adrenaline pulsing through his veins. Room after room was secured, until they reached the back bedroom. There, in the center of the room, stood Eric Avina, his eyes wide but resigned. As the door burst open, he let the bags in his hands fall to the floor. The agents, guns trained on him, ordered him to the ground.

Without a word, Avina dropped to his knees, his expression unreadable. One agent circled behind him, while another cleared the closet. With his hands tied behind his back, Avina was pushed face down onto the hardwood floor.

JB entered the room, a wave of relief washing over him. The tension in the air dissipated as the realization set in – there would be no gunfight today. He approached Avina, knelt beside him, and placed a hand on his shoulder, a rare gesture of compassion for a man on the other side of the law.

JB whispered, his voice a mix of regret and resolve. "I told you I was going to get you, didn't I?"

Eric looked up at him, his eyes hard, but there was a hint of something else – acceptance, maybe even peace. "This life owes me nothing," he replied, his voice firm and steady. He then lowered his head back to the floor, his body surrendering to the inevitable.

In seventeen minutes, two of Modesto's most dangerous men had been taken down. One had chosen to go out fighting, driven by the violence that had shaped him. The other had opted for a different path, one that, in its own way, required a different kind of strength.

44

— • —

C HAPTER 44

It was late February, and the valley floor was awash with the delicate white blossoms of almond trees, an early spring casting a soft beauty over the landscape. Lilly Grace sat on a weathered bench in the backyard of Mission Ranch, the warmth of the sun a welcome reprieve to the coldness that had gripped her life for the past year. Pastor Billings had mentioned that JB wanted to visit her to discuss the WSF case. As she sat, her mind wandered through the past three weeks at the rehab facility, the counseling sessions with Pastor Billings, and the fragile hope of reuniting with her mother.

JB entered the small courtyard, his eyes instinctively drawn to the imposing nine-foot cement wall that surrounded the facility. It was a reminder of the boundaries these girls were trying to break, not just physically, but emotionally. He wondered how many had tried to escape, how many had succeeded, and how many had failed. His gaze shifted to a swing set and sandbox on the far side of the courtyard, the presence of little girls a bittersweet reminder to the realities these young girls faced.

He noticed Lilly Grace on the bench, her fingers fidgeting, picking at her skin – signs of someone in the throes of withdrawal. Beneath the hardened exterior, he could see a glimmer of the young girl she once was, a faint resemblance to the innocence that had been stolen from her. It was an improvement on the last time he had seen her at the hospital. JB offered a small wave as he approached the bench, hoping to put her at ease.

"Hi, Lilly Grace. Do you remember me?" he asked.

"Vaguely," she replied, her eyes narrowing as she tried to recall. "But I don't remember anything we talked about."

"That's okay," JB said with a reassuring smile. "My name is JB Phillips, and I'm a special agent with the Federal Bureau of Investigation."

Her eyes widened slightly, a flicker of fear crossing her face. "Am I in trouble?"

"No, not at all," JB quickly reassured her. "This isn't about you directly. It's about the people you've been associated with over the past few months."

JB reached into his briefcase and pulled out a file, the seriousness of the moment not lost on Lilly Grace. Her fidgeting increased, anxiety building as she anticipated what was to come.

"I need your help," JB said, holding up a photograph of Paco Ramirez. He watched as Lilly Grace eyes locked onto the image, her body recoiling slightly as she recognized the face. "Lilly Grace, do you recognize this man?"

"Yes," she whispered. "That's Paco Ramirez."

JB continued to probe gently. "What was your relationship with Paco Ramirez?"

"Am I going to be in trouble?"

"No, Lilly Grace," JB reassured her. "This is about the people in these photos. What was your relationship with Paco Ramirez?"

"He was..." She faltered, her eyes dropping to her feet, her body curling inward as if to protect herself from the memories. "I was so afraid of that man."

"Did he make you do things you didn't want to do?" JB asked, though he regretted the question the moment it left his lips.

"What do you think?" she shot back; her voice laced with bitterness.

JB winced inwardly, cursing himself for the clumsy question. "I'm sorry. Can you tell me how he made you do those things?"

"He said he would ruin my life. I didn't know what to do."

JB nodded; his heart heavy with the weight of her words. "When did you first meet Paco Ramirez?"

"I met him when I came out here from Missouri."

"Did he contact you in Missouri and get you to come to California?" JB asked, leaning forward slightly.

"No," Lilly Grace said, shaking her head. "It wasn't him."

"Who was it then?" JB pressed, already knowing the answer but hoping Lilly Grace would lead him to Jade.

"I met a girl online," she said quietly. "She was the one who got me to come out to California."

JB carefully placed Paco's photo back in the briefcase and pulled out another. This time, it was a mug shot of Jade. As soon as Lilly Grace saw the image, her demeanor changed. The fear melted away, replaced by a tender look in her eyes. She leaned in closer, her gaze fixed on the photo, the connection between her and Jade clear.

"Do you know who this person is, Lilly Grace?" JB asked, holding up the photograph.

"Yes. That's Jade."

"And is this the girl you met online?"

"Yes."

"How did the two of you meet?"

"It was after...after the abuse of my stepfather," Lilly Grace's voice faltered. "I went online, trying to talk to other kids who'd been through the same thing. Jade sent me a message one day. We just started talking from there."

JB nodded, careful not to interrupt the fragile flow of her words. "What was Jade's relationship to Paco Ramirez?"

"I think they were dating. At least, that's how it seemed. I don't really know what they were."

JB leaned in slightly, his tone gentle but probing. "What was her role in making you do the things you did?"

Lilly Grace's gaze dropped, her fingers resuming their nervous fidgeting. "I don't know."

JB had spent years reading people, and it was clear Lilly Grace was holding something back. The connection she had with Jade was evident, and he suspected she was reluctant to implicate her. He hesitated, debating whether to push further. "You don't know, or you don't want to say?"

Lilly Grace tensed, her eyes darting to the far end of the courtyard.

"Lilly Grace, you're not in trouble. I'm just trying to understand how this group operated. Any details you can share will help us build this case."

"Are they going to go to prison?"

"If we can build an effective case, secure eyewitness testimony, and present it in court, then yes, they will go to prison for what they've done. Not just to you, but to many others as well. So, what was Jade's role in all of this?"

"She didn't make me do anything," Lilly Grace insisted, her tone defensive. "She was a friend...she got caught up in all this stuff too."

JB recognized the lie for what it was – an attempt to shield Jade from responsibility. He would have to tread carefully, knowing he couldn't push too hard without jeopardizing the fragile trust he was building. He pulled out photos of Tiffany and Veronica next.

"Do you know these girls?" he asked.

Lilly Grace nodded. "They worked with me...they were with Paco too. We were all teenagers he recruited for...for that work."

JB could see the strain in her eyes, the effort it took to admit even that much. He placed the photos of Tiffany and Veronica back in the briefcase and pulled out another – this time, a photo of Eric Avina. He watched Lilly Grace closely, noting the absence of recognition in her expression.

"Do you know this man?" JB asked.

Lilly Grace shook her head. "No. I don't know him."

Her response confirmed JB's suspicion that Eric Avina wasn't directly connected to her. There were a few more questions he needed to ask, but they were delicate – questions that could either solidify or fracture the trust they were slowly building.

"Lilly Grace, how many times did you contact your mother while you were here in California?"

"A few times, why?"

"What made you decide to call her that night in the motel?"

"I don't know," she said.

"You don't know? Did you call before or after you were beaten by that man?"

"After. Why?"

"And who beat you?"

"I don't know," she whispered. "I don't know what that man was."

"Was Paco Ramirez at the motel that night?"

"He was around. He was always around. Every waking moment of every day, that son of a bitch was around."

"Where was Jade when the man beat you?"

"I don't know."

"Do you mean you don't know, or you don't want to say?"

"I mean I don't know!" Lilly Grace's voice trembled with frustration." I was in the room with some strange man, and he was high. He got mad at me for stealing his drugs."

"Did you steal them?"

"What? No. He just...he just got all pissed and started raging out. The next thing I knew, he was throwing me around the room."

"When did Jade come into the room?"

"It was after. I don't remember how long after, but it was after the man left."

"Did she try to help you?"

"I don't know."

JB noted how often Lilly Grace used the phrase 'I don't know' whenever Jade's name came up. It was a pattern he would need to explore further, but not now. He needed to speak with the other two girls – Veronica and Tiffany – and gather their perspectives on Jade's role within the WSF. He was certain one of them would be willing to testify rather than face jail time.

"Lilly Grace, you've been through a lot," JB said, his voice soft. "It's my hope that you'll continue to receive help here at Mission Ranch. Pastor Billings will keep providing counseling, and we'll keep talking as we build this case against Paco Ramirez and the WSF.

JB stood up to leave, but as he reached the doorway, he turned back to her. "One more thing – did you ever hear Paco Ramirez talk about Gustavo Perez Medina?"

Lilly Grace shook her head, her brow furrowing in thought. "No, I don't recall ever hearing that name."

"Okay," JB said, as he turned to leave. Then at the last moment, he turned back around toward Lilly Grace. "One last thing, you won't have to worry about Paco Ramirez anymore. He was killed."

JB watched the thoughts flow through Lilly Grace's expressions. He offered a small wave as he left the courtyard, leaving Lilly Grace to grapple with the ghosts of her past.

***

Before leaving Mission Ranch, JB decided to pay a visit to Pastor Billing's office. He knew that the Pastor might be called as an expert witness at some point, though client privilege would likely prevent him from sharing any specifics about Lilly Grace or her counseling sessions. JB knocked on the door, and Pastor Billings waved him inside.

"How did it go with Lilly Grace, Agent Phillips?" the Pastor asked.

"It went fine," JB replied, settling into a chair. "She's looking a lot better than the last time I saw her in the hospital."

"Yes," Pastor Billings nodded, a hint of a smile on his lips. "She's been through quite an ordeal, but she's coming along."

JB leaned forward, his voice lowering slightly. "Pastor Billings, has Lilly Grace spoken about Jade and their relationship?"

"Agent Phillips, you know I cannot divulge what Lilly Grace and I've been discussing."

"I understand," JB said, choosing his words carefully. "But it seems like she's holding back when it comes to Jade specifically."

Pastor Billings sighed, leaning back in his chair. "As you can imagine, with what she's been through, there are all kinds of emotions running through her mind. It'll take time for her to fully process, if she ever can."

JB paused, considering his next question. "Is she of sound mind?"

Pastor Billings' eyes narrowed slightly. "What do you mean?"

"I mean, will we be able to use her testimony in court?"

"That depends on her and how she manages the recovery process," the Pastor replied, his voice firm. "I cannot speak to whether she'll be able to testify or not."

JB realized he had reached the limits of what Pastor Billings was willing to discuss. It was clear the Pastor was committed to protecting Lilly Grace's confidentiality and emotional well-being, and JB respected that boundary. He decided to leave it alone for now and come back another day if needed.

"Thank you for your time, Pastor Billings," JB said, standing up.

"Of course, Agent Phillips," the Pastor replied, standing as well. "Take care."

As JB left the office, he couldn't shake the feeling that there was more to uncover about Lilly Grace's relationship with Jade, but he knew he would have to be patient. For now, he would focus on gathering more evidence and speaking with the other girls involved.

45

— • —

CHAPTER 45

Two weeks later, on a Saturday afternoon, JB and Hannah turned off the narrow highway onto a long, dusty driveway. The group home, nestled three miles outside of town, was bordered by a railroad track and an aqueduct, both serving as natural boundaries. The buildings had a rustic charm, but the grounds were unkempt, giving the place a desolate feel. In the distance, a group of small children played on a worn playset. The home housed kids ranging from three years old up to eighteen, with nearly forty-five children living there at any given time, including Abigail and Sariah Furtado.

As they parked in a dirt lot near the main residence, Hannah glanced out the car window. She spotted Abigail pushing Sariah on the swing set. The girls seemed distant; their movements mechanical, devoid of the joy that should accompany childhood. A pang of sorrow tugged at Hannah's heart as she watched them, feeling the weight of their young lives already marred by hardship.

JB stepped out of the car, stretching his legs and rotating his torso to ease the stiffness from the drive. He placed his hands on the hood of the minivan, looking at Hannah. "Are you ready for this?" he asked.

"Yes," Hannah replied, though her arms wrapped around her chest betrayed her nervousness. "I couldn't think of a better Easter present." She glanced back at the girls, feeling a mix of excitement and anxiety.

JB opened the door, and Hannah stepped out of the minivan. "Do you see them, JB?" she asked softly. "They look so lonely over there."

"Are you sure that's them?" JB questioned, peering in the direction of the swings.

"Yes," Hannah nodded. "I couldn't forget their faces. I just don't know what to say to them."

JB placed a reassuring arm around Hannah as they both observed the girls from a distance. Just then, Mrs. Davies, and the group home's director emerged from the front door with a warm smile, striding toward them.

"Hello there!" Mrs. Davies greeted, her voice cheerful.

"Hello, Mrs. Davies," Hannah replied, her own smile tentative.

They exchanged pleasantries in front of the van, both JB and Hannah fidgeting nervously as they waited for the chance to meet the girls.

"How does this work, Mrs. Davies?" Hannah asked, trying to mask her apprehension.

"Well," Mrs. Davies began, glancing toward the swing set, "they've been out there for a little while. I imagine they're just as anxious and nervous as you two are. Why don't we walk over, and you can introduce yourself."

JB felt a wave of awkwardness wash over him. The idea of meeting two girls who might one day live in his home felt surreal, and he couldn't shake the nagging doubt that this might be a mistake. Still, he followed as they walked toward the playground, where Abigal and Sariah continued to swing, their faces downcast.

As they approached, Mrs. Davies explained that the girls were likely to be very shy and hesitant to engage. She emphasized that it had been a tough year for them, with multiple moves between foster homes and their mother's frequent stints in jail. The group home, she added, had been running at full capacity for the past six months, making it difficult for the children to receive the one-on-one attention they desperately needed.

Sariah remained seated on the swing, staring down at the ground as Hannah walked up. JB hung back a few feet, letting Hannah and Mrs. Davies take the lead. Abigail, noticing their approach, crossed her arms defensively and took a few steps back.

"Abigail, Sariah, I want you to meet a very nice couple," Mrs. Davies said gently. "Let me introduce you to Hannah and JB."

Hannah knelt on one knee, extending her hand toward Sariah, who didn't acknowledge the gesture. Undeterred, Hannah turned her attention to Abigail. "Hello there, you must be Abigail. My name is Hannah Phillips. It's nice to meet you."

Abigail stared at Hannah's outstretched hand, her expression unreadable. When she didn't respond, Hannah let her hand drop to her knee. "I've heard so many great things about you two girls," she said softly. "I've been looking forward to meeting you today."

Her words were met with silence. Hannah glanced up at Mrs. Davies, hoping for some guidance, but the older woman simply offered an encouraging smile. The tension hung heavy in the air, and Hannah's heart sank as she wondered if the girls wanted anything to do with her or JB. Maybe they were content here at the group home, or maybe they didn't want to leave.

"Abigail," Mrs. Davies promoted gently, "do you want to tell Mrs. Phillips about your art class?"

Abigail stood still, kicking at the dirt with her shoes. Hannah found a small comfort in the fact that Abigail enjoyed art, but JB noticed the emptiness in the eyes of both girls. Watching Abigail scuff the dirt triggered a memory he hadn't visited in years.

It was 2008, during his second tour in Afghanistan. JB was stationed in a small village near Tikrit, working on a mission to help rebuild homes after a series of devastating bombings. The assignment involved collaborating with local men to restore their community and recruit Afghan soldiers to resist Al Qaeda's influence. One afternoon, while repairing a well on the outskirts of the village, JB spotted a young girl playing in the dirt about twenty yards away. Something about Abigail reminded him of that girl – the dark hair, perhaps, or the way both girls seemed distrustful of his presence.

In Tikrit, the girl had been drawing pictures in the dirt, her focus entirely on the ground beneath her feet. JB watched her for a while, but she never looked his way. Eventually, he decided to approach her. As he drew near, the girl turned her body away from him, her silence and avoidance a clear message. JB tried to greet her, but she ignored him, her small frame hunched over as if to protect herself.

He remembered the suckers he kept in his rucksack, a small gesture that often helped bridge the gap between him and the local children. JB jogged back to the well, dug through his bag, and pulled out a brightly colored sucker. Returning to the girl, he extended the treat toward her, hoping to break through her shell. After a few tense seconds, she turned slightly, revealing the right side of her face, heavily scarred from what appeared to be a third-degree burn that stretched from her forehead down to her jawline. The sight shocked JB, and he couldn't suppress a small gasp.

Despite the scar, he knew a certain beauty in the girl – a quiet resilience that tugged at his heart. There was an innocence in her posture, a deep loneliness that mirrored the emptiness he now saw in Abigail and Sariah. Tentatively, the girl accepted the sucker. JB asked her name, and though there was a language barrier, she murmured something in response. She handed him a stick she had been using to draw in the dirt, a small gesture of trust.

JB took the stick and began to draw a simple stick figure in the dirt, causing the girl to chuckle softly. She took the stick back, erasing his drawing, and then handed it to him again. JB drew a man with a happy face, complete with a top hat – the only picture he knew how to draw well. The girl laughed again, the sound a small but precious victory.

But just as they began to share this fragile connection, a woman's voice shattered the moment. She ran toward them, scooped up the girl, and hurried back to the village, casting wary glances over her shoulder. Out of everything that happened during his time in Afghanistan, that brief encounter with the girl remained etched in his memory. It was a moment he would hold onto more vividly than any other – a moment that echoed now, years later, as he watched Abigail and Sariah.

JB didn't know exactly why, but he felt a deep conviction that these girls needed Hannah. They needed the chance to live a life free from fear, to know what it felt like to be loved and to feel safe when they laid their heads down at night. And in that moment, JB realized that they also needed him. They needed a father figure they could trust, someone who wouldn't turn his back on them. With that clarity, JB knew there was no way he would walk away from these girls.

46

— ◆ —

C HAPTER 46

JB sat in his cubicle on Monday morning, his thoughts drifting back to the girls and the visit. As he mechanically cataloged data from the wiretap on Eric Avina's phone, something unusual caught his attention. A recorded call from the morning of the raid, timestamped at 6:49 – just minutes before the first agent breached Avina's home. JB's heart raced as he cross-referenced the call with the FBI Telephone Application Database. The call had originated from within the Stanislaus County Sheriff's Office. The number belonged to Anita Lopez, a clerk at the sheriff's office.

JB scribbled the information onto a notepad and bolted down the hallway to Warnall's office. As expected, Warnall was on the phone, deeply engrossed in a conversation with DC. He motioned for JB to sit, but JB ignored the command, pacing back and forth, tapping his watch and circling his finger, trying to signal the urgency of the situation. Warnall glanced up, annoyed, signaling that the person on the other end wouldn't stop talking.

Frustrated, JB marched behind the desk and abruptly pressed down on the receiver, cutting off the call. Warnall stared at him in shock.

"What the hell are you doing?" Warnall snapped.

JB handed him the notepad, pointing to the number, the timestamp, and name of Anita Lopez.

"What the hell is this?" Warnall asked, confused.

"That's a rat inside our ranks," JB replied, his voice tense.

Warnall frowned. "I don't understand. What are you talking about?"

JB moved to the opposite side of the desk and sat down, leaning forward with his head in his hands before running his fingers through his hair. He took a deep breath before delivering the next bombshell.

"Anita Lopez is a clerk at the Stanislaus County Sheriff's Office. That's her personal cell number. She called Erica Avina eleven minutes before we broke down his door."

"What?"

"Yes. I've already listened to the call. She tried to warn him we were coming. And she mentioned a 'friend' who tipped her off."

Warnall's expression hardened as the implications sank in. "So, we have at least two people connected to this raid – either on Avina's payroll or close enough to give him a heads' up?"

"Exactly. With Ramirez gone and Avina on his way to prison, I thought we'd hit a dead end with the WSF and the Deep South Side. But this – this could be our way to expose a deeper connection to the cartels."

Warnall leaned back, considering. "That's assuming she knows more than just what Avina was up to. For all we know, she was just someone he kept on the side."

"We won't know until we pick her up," JB said, determination in his voice.

"I'll ger a warrant for her arrest. Let's go get her."

JB grabbed the yellow notepad from Warnall's hands, a surge of adrenaline coursing through him. On his way out of the office, he pumped the notepad in the air, a silent victory. While waiting for the arrest warrant, he returned to his cubicle and began sifting through the Stanislaus County Sheriff's Office employee records. He needed to review every individual who might have known about the investigation and the raid on Ramirez and Avina. It was an exhaustive list, but JB was determined to uncover every connection.

***

It was 4:30 p.m., and Anita Lopez was at her desk, gathering her things as she prepared to leave for her son's soccer practice. Her mind was preoccupied with the routine of her day, unaware that a contingent of FBI agents, led by JB, had just entered the large room filled with a dozen cubicles. One agent moved along the north side of the room, while two others circled the south. JB and Agent Houser made a direct line for Anita's cubicle. As the agents advanced, one by one, the clerks began to stand in their cubicles, their eyes following the unusual procession. Anita, still engrossed in packing her bag, had no idea that her world was about to be turned upside down.

"Anita Lopez," JB's voice cut through the murmurs, "we have a warrant for your arrest."

Anita, still bent over, finally stood upright, startled to find JB and the other agents encircling her cubicle. The color drained from her face, and her legs wobbled as if the floor had been pulled out from under her.

"What?" disbelief clouding Anita's voice.

"Please, turn around," JB instructed calmly.

Anita slowly turned her back to JB, placing her hands on top of the cubicle wall. Her movements were mechanical, her mind struggling to process what was happening. Around her, a dozen or so clerks had gathered, watching in stunned silence. Her supervisor, sensing the gravity of the situation, started toward her cubicle, but Agent Houser quickly intercepted him, a stern look silencing any protest. The supervisor stepped back, joining the rest of the staff as they watched their colleague's world unravel.

"What is the charge?" Anita asked.

JB's tone was steady as he listed the charges. "Aiding a criminal syndicate, human smuggling, drug trafficking, and money laundering. You have the right to remain silent. Anything you say can and will be used against you in a court of law. You have the right to attorney and to have an attorney present during questioning. Do you understand your rights?"

Anita nodded weakly, the weight of the words sinking in. As a clerk with the Stanislaus County Sheriff's Office, and a loose associate of the WSF, she was well aware of her rights. But now, those rights were no longer abstract; they were her reality. JB moved to cuff her hands, but he noticed the tremor in her legs. He wondered if she could even make it out of the room.

"Wait, wait," Anita suddenly pleaded. "What about my son? I have to pick him up from practice."

These were the moments that gnawed at JB's conscience, even after everything he'd endured in his military career and his time with the FBI. There would be a little boy waiting for his mother, unaware that she might not return for a very long time. JB could see the realization dawn on Anita, her eyes wide with the terrifying implications for her sons.

"Ma'am, if he's really at practice, we can have an officer pick him up and take him home or to a relative," JB offered, trying to inject some humanity into the procedure.

The words seemed to hit Anita all at once. She swayed, and JB moved to catch her, but it was too late – her legs buckled, and she crumpled to the floor, sobbing and screaming.

"What about my sons? What's going to happen to my boys?" she cried.

JB gently lifted her to her feet, Anita leaning against the cubicle wall as she wept. Agent Houser stepped in, taking her other arm. Together, they escorted a broken Anita Lopez out of the Stanislaus County Sheriff's Office, leaving behind a room full of stunned silence and a mother's anguished cries echoing in the hallways.

***

Anita Lopez sat in a hilding cell at the Stanislaus County Courthouse, her feet chained to the floor and her hands cuffed behind her back. The room was stark, with only a single table and two chairs, the air heavy with the weight of what was to come. A two-way mirror occupied one wall, behind which SAC Warnall and the Sheriff of Stanislaus County silently observed. JB entered the room, his expression unreadable.

"Anita, my name is Special Agent JB Phillips. This must all be a shock to your system," he began, his tone calm but firm.

Anita remained motionless, her head bowed, eyes fixed on the floor. JB walked behind her and gently released the handcuffs. She brought her hands to her front, rubbing her sore wrists.

"There, that should be a little more comfortable," JB said.

Anita whispered, "Thank you."

"First, let me say that we had an officer pick up your son. He's at home with a relative now."

Anita looked up at JB with a blank stare, as if the words barely registered. JB recognized the signs – she was in shock, her mind struggling to grasp the reality of her situation. He knew she was likely calculating the years she might spend in prison, already seeing the future unraveling before her.

"Anita, honestly, this doesn't look very good for you," JB continued.

Anita lifted her head, meeting his gaze. Her eyes were filled with sadness and desperation as she placed her hands on the table, stretching them out toward him.

"I don't know what you're talking about. I didn't do anything wrong. I didn't do anything," she pleaded, her voice trembling.

"Anita, stop. Please, just stop," JB said, his tone softening slightly. "I understand you're in shock, but I've got it all. We have you on a recorded call to Eric Avina, eleven minutes before we raided his house. You warned him, saying, 'They are coming for you.' Do you remember making that call?"

"I don't know what you're talking about," Anita repeated, shaking her head in denial.

"Who gave you the information about the raid?" JB pressed.

"You're not listening to me. I don't know what you're saying."

"Anita, what's your boy's name? Daniel, right? The one our officer picked up at practice today?" JB asked, hoping to ground her in the reality of her situation.

"Yes, his name is Daniel," Anita whispered, her voice cracking. "His name is Daniel. My other boy is Jose."

"Okay, Anita. Think of Daniel and Jose. Think about how much time you want with them as they grow up. You don't want this to be the reason you miss all those years. Do you really want to lose the chance to hug your sons again until they're in their thirties?" JB's words measured, each one designed to break through her defenses.

"What are you saying? I don't understand what's happening," Anita cried, her voice filled with confusion and fear.

"Anita, who gave you the information about the raid? It's a simple question," JB repeated, learning forward slightly.

Anita's body trembled, her breath coming in ragged gasps as tears streamed down her face. She was on the brink of breaking, her resolve crumbling under the weight of what was at stake.

"Anita, do you want this person to be the reason you don't see your kids grow up? Is this person worth losing everything?" JB asked.

"No. No," Anita sobbed, her resistance finally shattering.

"Who gave you the information, Anita?" JB urged gently. "I need to know."

"Anthony Bernal," she whispered, barely audible. "It was Anthony Bernal."

JB glanced at the two-way mirror, where he knew the Stanislaus County Sheriff's Office was already making calls. Anthony Bernal, a Special Investigator with the Community Service Agency, was about to find himself in the same situation as Anita.

"Thank you, Anita. You did the right thing by telling us. If you continue to cooperate, you'll have a much better chance of seeing your sons again," JB reassured her.

He knocked on the door, signaling the court officer to enter. The officer handcuffed Anita's hands behind her back, unshackled her legs from the table, and stood her up.

"What about me? When will I get to see my sons?"

"We'll be in touch, Anita." JB said, his voice steady but noncommittal.

As the officer escorted Anita down the hallway back to her holding cell, JB knew that their next conversation would be crucial – essential to whether she would see her sons again before they graduated high school.

47

— • —

CHAPTER 47

It was late afternoon, the sun sinking behind the cement wall of the Mission Ranch facility. Lilly Grace sat outside, wrapped in a blanket, her gaze fixed on the almond blossoms scattered across the ground. The beauty seemed distant.

Pastor Billings approached, cradling a steaming cup of tea. He settled beside her.

"Lilly Grace, I'm glad to find you here. Can we talk for a minute?"

She nodded, her eyes still on the petals.

"I truly admire your strength through these challenging times. Our conversations over the past eight weeks have been meaningful, and I'm hopeful for the progress we can make in your final month here. I know it's not easy, talking with me or with Special Agent Phillips. But you're showing incredible bravery. I appreciate you sharing so openly."

A slight smirk touched Lilly Grace's lips, her head tilting slightly. Pastor Billings knew he was walking a fine line, but he needed to see how she'd react to a more personal probe.

"You've made significant strides here and are opening up more in your counseling sessions. I want to challenge you to deepen this work. What do you need from me to support you in going further into your experiences?"

"I'm here every day. I have no choice but to be here. It's like a prison."

"No, it's not a prison." Pastor Billings sipped his tea, leaned in closer, and continued. "Last week, you spoke with Special Agent Phillips. Since then, you've been quiet about your feelings. Is there something specific you'd like to discuss?"

"What's the point?" Lilly Grace said as she pulled her blanket tighter.

"I noticed something about your conversation with him, particularly when he mentioned Jade. Can you tell me more about her?"

"Why does it matter?"

"Jade is in County Jail now. You know that, right?"

Her eyes widened slightly at Jade's name. Pastor Billings pressed on gently. "Are you curious why she's there?"

"Are you saying that there are groups that use girls to manipulate others? Jade was part of such a group, wasn't she? A 'bottom bitch' for Paco Ramirez. Is that the term?"

Lilly Grace's gaze hardened. "So what? What does that have to do with me?"

"Special Agent Phillips mentioned a story about a night in Santa Cruz. It was the night you were introduced to prostitution. Do you want to talk about it?"

"No, I don't want to talk about that night."

Pastor Billings studied her. "I know it's painful. You're not responsible for what others did to you. You understand that, don't you?"

"It is what it is."

"What was it about Jade that drew you to her? You met online, right? What were those early conversations like?"

"Why does it matter now? She's in jail, I'm here, and it's over."

"It may seem over for Jade and Paco Ramirez, but for you, it's just beginning. Are you sad about Jade's situation?"

"Sad? All this counseling talk won't fix anything. Life's hard, and it's harder for some. I got a bad deal and have to deal with it. Talking with you won't change that. I'll finish my time here and be out. End of story."

Pastor Billings tried to pivot. "What about when you leave? Have you thought about where you'll go? Your mother? Your brothers?"

Lilly Grace looked away. "I'll figure it out. Maybe stay with a friend. I don't know."

"Your mother has been in touch with me. She's worried about you."

"If she was so worried, why didn't she protect me?"

"Maybe she couldn't."

"You mean, maybe she didn't care," Lilly Grace said as she stood, wrapping the blanket around her tightly. "I don't want to talk anymore. I'm done here."

"If not with her, where will you go? It's important to plan your exit strategy. You'll need a safe place and continued counseling."

Pastor Billings watched her retreat, knowing the journey ahead was far from over. In thirty days, he might have to let her go, ready or not.

48

—•—

CHAPTER 48

It was the first day of May, and the air was filled with the scent of freshly cut grass and blooming flowers. Hannah busied herself inside the house, making sure every corner was spotless, every cushion perfectly fluffed. The anticipation had kept her awake the night before, but now, as she watched JB and Jared making the final adjustments to the new wooden playground set in the backyard, she felt a mix of hope and anxiety swirling in her chest.

JB had insisted on the playground. "They need a place to feel safe, to just be kids," he had said, and Hannah couldn't have agreed more. But now, as the agency van pulled into the driveway, the reality of their decision hit her like a wave. What if the girls didn't feel at home? What if they didn't like it here?

She wiped her hands on her apron, trying to steady herself. This was more than just a home visit – it was a test, a chance to prove that they could provide the love and stability Sariah and Abigail needed. Hannah knew it was premature to set up the playground before the girls were officially theirs, but she couldn't help herself. She wanted them to know that they were already a part of this family, if only temporarily.

JB caught her eye through the kitchen window and gave her a reassuring smile. He was just as nervous as she was, though he hid it well. She could see it in the way he double-checked each bolt on the playground, making sure everything was perfect.

The van door opened, and Hannah took a deep breath. This was it – the moment they had been waiting for. She walked to the front door, her heart pounding, ready to welcome Sariah and Abigail into their home, into their lives.

Mrs. Davies and Pastor Wilkins walked to the front porch, with hands on Sariah and Abigail's shoulders. Hannah yelled for JB and Jared to come inside. She noticed each of the girl's shyness. Their shoulders slumped forward, chins down, and sadness in their eyes.

They reminded Hannah of wounded dogs with tails between their legs. Hannah opened the door and knelt to greet the girls.

"Hi, my name is Hannah Phillips. Do you remember me from our visit a month ago?"

The girls each nodded their heads up and down. Hannah pointed to JB and Jared. "And this is my husband JB, whom you met, and our son, Jared. He's close to your age Abigail."

Jared was swaying back and forth, moving from one leg to another. Hannah could sense his excitement.

"Why don't we go inside, and we can sit down in the living room?" Mrs. Davies said.

"Of course, of course," Hannah said.

Hannah got up from her knees and everyone walked into the house. Pastor Wilkins waited for JB. He put his hand to the small of his back and the two men walked into the house together. Hannah knew Pastor Wilkins wanted to have a long conversation with JB.

"Girls, do you see what I see?" Mrs. Davies said. "I think there is a play structure in the back yard. Do you want to go check it out with Jared while we have a conversation with Mr. and Mrs. Phillips?"

The girls slowly walked toward the rear of the house. Jared joined them with glee and anticipation. Mrs. Davies watched them open the screen door and go out toward the playground. Jared and Abigail both started to climb the structure. Sariah, the younger sister, stood near the screen door and watched. Hannah kept a keen eye on Mrs. Davies, watching her telling eyes glance around the house. Mrs. Davies sat down, then Pastor Wilkins joined her on the couch. Hannah and JB sat in each of the love chairs in the living room.

"So, tell me what you are thinking right now? What's going through your heads about the potential of what could happen over the next six months to a year with these girls?" Mrs. Davies said.

"Mrs. Davies, as you know, we've come a long way over the past couple of months on this topic. I don't think JB was too on board with this idea when we first met."

"No. I don't think he was too eager. How are you now JB?"

"I'm fine with that. In fact, I'm better than fine with it. I um, I would be very disappointed now if we weren't selected to be their foster parents."

"JB, do you mind sharing with us how you came to change your mind on this over the past couple of months? I'm very intrigued," Pastor Wilkins said.

"Pastor Wilkins, I don't know how to explain it. When I saw those two girls playing in that yard, I saw their loneliness, I just knew that it was something we needed to do. Even though they have been through hell and back, at such a young age, I can see a love between the two that makes me hopeful that we can really help them. I don't know how yet, but I just know Hannah would be perfect for those two."

"Yes, I agree Hannah would be perfect for the two. But what about you? What do you think you can bring to these two girls?"

"Pastor, I honestly don't know. I didn't know what we could bring to Jared when we decided to adopt him all those years ago. I wasn't a father back then. In fact, I was the furthest thing from it. I was on deployments all the time and there wasn't much I could offer. It was all Hannah who took that young man in and raised him to be the great kid you see today. He too saw some evil things early in his life. I guess, what I can bring is just trying to show a love between Hannah and I that as an example of what they can have when they grow up."

"Do you think it will be any different with the fact that these are girls you are fostering, and not a boy?" Mrs. Davies asked.

"It's not about a boy or a girl Mrs. Davies, it's about helping another human being out. I suppose that's one thing I've witnessed during my military life, we're all in this world together and we're all dealing with all the same BS. It doesn't matter what part of the world you're living in. I've seen poor kids who were homeless in all four corners of this world. I just want to do what I can do, when I can do it, to help others out. If we can help these two young girls out, even if it's for a short period, then that'll be our blessing in this world."

Hannah sat back in her chair, surprised by the moment, as JB rattled off response after response to Pastor Wilkins and Mrs. Davies. There was a sweetness and caring in his eyes when he talked about these girls. It was a look she hadn't seen in him for many years. It was a look that was so familiar, yet so distant.

Mrs. Davies and Hannah toured the house with Abigail and Sariah. Hannah showed them the bedroom they would share with each other. It was a pink wooden bunk bed, with a pink standup dresser. There was a desk under the window overlooking the back-yard. Other than the furniture, it was a blank room. Hannah made sure to tell the girls they could add anything they wanted to make it feel like home.

Pastor Wilkins asked if it was okay if he and Jared took a walk down the street. Jared didn't realize it, but this was arranged by his parents as a way for Pastor Wilkins to have a conversation with him. Pastor Wilkins towered over him as the two walked down the sidewalk toward the school playground across the street.

"Jared, this is a big change for you son. How are you feeling about it all?"

"Do you have to interview me like you did my mom and dad?"

"Oh no son, I don't interview you. I thought the two of us could talk a little bit and make sure your thoughts and impressions are represented in all of this. How are you feeling about it?"

"I'm good with it. I think it's great. And Abigail seems like a lot of fun. I don't know about Sariah. She's quiet."

"Yes, she is quiet. I'm glad that you and Abigail had a fun time playing in the backyard. That is good. So, how have your mom and dad been doing lately? The last time I talked to them everything seemed stressful."

"Yeah, it's been a rough few months. I don't really know what my dad does for a living, but he's been pretty stressed out. And then everything with my mom, with her surgery and all, it's been rough on her too."

"Yeah, she's been through the ringer with cancer. That'll do it to anybody. How about you? How have you been managing since all this has been going on?"

"Me? I'm fine. I'm always fine. I mean, I just play baseball and go to the park or something if they're fighting. It's no big deal really."

"Do they fight a lot?"

"Pastor, this is starting to feel an awful lot like an interview."

Pastor Wilkins laughed, and replied, "Well I'm sorry Jared. I guess it kind of is an interview of sorts. And you're doing a great job of being honest."

"Well, if you're asking me about my parents fighting, I don't know sir. It doesn't seem like such a big deal for me. But then again, if you've seen what I've seen, their fights aren't really fights. I'm just grateful that I got to live with them. And I'm pretty sure that Abigail and Sariah would be grateful too."

"Yes, I think you are right about that Jared. Say, do you mind if we cut this interview short and head back to the house?"

"Sounds good to me."

Pastor Wilkins gave Jared a gentle tap on the back. He admired his honesty and directness and knew he was right about Abigale and Sariah.

$$49$$

— ◦ —

CHAPTER 49

It was Tuesday, May 3rd, discharge day at Mission Ranch for Lilly Grace. She anticipated her first steps outside the confined wall with a mix of hope and uncertainty. Sitting on her familiar bench in the backyard, she pondered what awaited her beyond the facility. With no home to return to and no relatives willing to take her in after the turmoil of the past few months, her future seemed bleak and solitary.

The patio door groaned as it opened, revealing Lilly Grace's mother. Lilly Grace hadn't seen her since her departure. Her mother's face briefly registered hesitation before she moved into the bright June sunlight, where the shade tree provided little respite from the warmth. For Lilly Grace, the bench had been a rare haven during her ninety-day stay—a place of comfort and a memory to hold dear.

As her mother approached the park bench, Lilly Grace remained stoic. When they were close enough, her mother, Ava, covered her face with her hands and began to weep. She hurried to Lilly Grace, sitting beside her, enveloping her in a tight embrace, and gently stroking her hair. It was the first reunion since Lilly Grace's arrival at the hospital over three months ago.

Pastor Billings watched from the back door, a gentle smile on his face. After a moment, he turned and quietly retreated inside the building.

"Oh, girl, I missed you so much," Ava said.

Lilly Grace noticed something different about her mother. The dark circles under her eyes had diminished, and her hair had a renewed polish and shine. Despite her desire to embrace her mother, Lilly Grace struggled with a well of anger that she wasn't ready to release. Ava sat back, her hands resting gently on Lilly Grace's shoulders, her gaze fixed intently on her daughter.

Ava's voice was a mix of longing and regret. "Look at you! Look at my girl. It's been such a long time. Do you remember that night at the hospital?"

"What night?" Lilly Grace asked, her confusion evident. "When?"

"After you were rescued," Ava's eyes searched Lilly Grace's face for recognition. "Do you remember seeing me there?"

"No, I don't remember anything from the hospital. It was all a blur."

Ava's tone was apologetic. "After you called me, I caught the next flight to see you. The FBI agent – Phillips, I think? – he told me you'd likely be moving from the hospital to a rehab facility. So, I went back home."

Lilly Grace's eyes narrowed; her voice was edged with hurt. "You mean you left me here all alone?"

"No, not at all," Ava quickly assured her. "I met with the social worker before you were discharged. She agreed this facility was the best place for you."

"Why didn't you stay with me?" Lilly Grace's voice cracked. "Why did you leave me here?"

"Baby, I was a wreck. So much has happened over the last ninety days," Ava said, her voice filled with anguish.

"Yeah, a lot has happened. Do you know how hard it's been for me here?" Lilly Grace's eyes were filled with tears.

"Yes, I know. You're incredibly strong for everything you've endured here," Ava said softly.

"What would you know about it?" Lilly Grace's question was sharp, filled with unresolved pain.

Lilly Grace was overwhelmed by the chaos of the past nine months. The trauma had left her deeply scarred, and she wondered if those wounds would ever heal. She struggled to imagine ever trusting her mother again after everything that had happened over the past year. The woman sitting across from her seemed transformed – new haircut, new wardrobe, and a new demeanor. She was a different person from the mother Lilly Grace remembered before she left Missouri. Meanwhile, Lilly Grace felt like the same broken girl, with her world unchanged.

"Honey," Ava began, her voice filled with remorse, "when you left, I was frantic. All I could do was pray that you would be found safe. After you disappeared, I realized I needed answers for my own life too. When you called, and they found you, and I started talking to Pastor Billings, I knew I needed help as well. I couldn't' heal or break free from my own struggles on my own. I went through rehab and have been clean. I can't claim to have everything figured out, but I know that our future will be very different from our past."

"Our future? What does that even mean?"

"When we go back to Missouri," Ava explained softly, her eyes pleading, "I know I wasn't there for you these past years. So much happened, and I know it's my fault. I can't change the past, and I'll have to live with that. But when we get back to Missouri, I want to get you connected to a restorative therapy program designed for girls who've been through what you have."

"For girls like me? What does that even mean?" Lilly Grace's voice was edged with bitterness. "I don't care about your changes. I have to live with what happened for the rest of my life. The things I've seen can never be unseen. The things I've done can never be undone. I don't believe there's a God who would save someone like me after all I've been through."

"Lilly Grace, that is absolutely not true," Ava said urgently, her voice breaking.

"You might be able to forgive yourself, but I'll never forgive myself. And I certainly can't forgive you," Lilly Grace shot back, her eyes filled with unshed tears.

"Oh, honey," Ava whispered, her heart breaking.

Ava reached out, pulling her daughter into a tight embrace. Lilly Grace remained rigid, her face a mask of emptiness. As Ava held her, she cried for the evil that had torn their lives apart and clung desperately to the hope that it wasn't too late to mend their fractured family.

***

Two hours later, Ava and Lilly Grace left Mission Ranch and made their way to the DoubleTree Hotel in downtown Modesto. For the first time in ninety days, Lilly Grace inhaled the fresh air outside the wall of the place that had felt like a prison. The sensation was both liberating and unsettling.

In the hotel room, Lilly Grace took a long, hot shower, letting the water wash away the remnants of her confinement. She dressed in the new clothes her mother had bought for the journey home. From the sixth floor, she stood by the window, gazing out at the streets of downtown Modesto. Her eyes locked on a familiar sight in the distance, just one block south of the hotel – the Amtrak Greyhound Bus Depot. The sight churned her stomach, a visceral reminder of where it had all begun, where she had first met Jade and Paco Ramirez.

A surge of nausea overwhelmed her as memories came rushing back, the burden of all that had transpired since she disembarked from the bus bearing down on her. She yearned to scream, to vent the torment accumulating within, yet she restrained herself, unwilling to wake her mother who was asleep on the bed.

In an attempt to ground herself, Lilly Grace reached into her bag and pulled out a letter from her mother, the one she had left with Pastor Billings. She unfolded it slowly, her hands trembling slightly, unsure if she was ready to confront the words written on those pages.

As I write these words, my heart is heavy with regret and sorrow. There are no words that can express my pain for not being able to protect you from the evils of this world. It pains me to see you hurt and to know that I couldn't shield you from harm. I want you to know that my love for you knows no bounds, and I would do anything to take away your pain. As your mother, it breaks my heart to see you suffer, and I carry the weight of my inability to keep you safe. Please know that I have done everything in my power to get my life back on track. I've gone through rehab and haven't had a drink of alcohol or drugs. I've left your stepfather and have started a new life. I wish I could shield you from every hurt and danger and I'm sorry that I didn't uphold my end as your mother. I hope you can find it in your heart to forgive me for how I've raised you. Know that I have always acted out of love for you, and my greatest wish is for your happiness and well-being. As you navigate through your recovery, remember that you are not alone. Lean on those who love you, seek support when you need it, and know that you are stronger than you realize. I will always be here for you, my precious daughter, ready to offer my love, support, and guidance whenever you need it. You are my greatest blessing, and I will continue to cherish and protect you to the best of my ability.

Love, your mother!

Lilly Grace folded the letter with trembling hands, her emotions a tangled mess. Without a second glance, she stuffed it back into her bag. She stood for a moment, watching her mother asleep on the bed, her expression peaceful, unaware of the storm raging inside Lilly Grace.

The room felt suffocating. Needing to escape, she quietly slipped out of the hotel room, closing the door behind her with a soft click. The hallway felt strangely quiet as she walked away, the weight of everything left unsaid pressing heavily on her shoulders.

***

She found herself standing at the corner of Ninth and K Steet, the fading sun casting long shadows over the city. The heat of the day lingered, making it hard to breathe. Was it the oppressive warmth or the gnawing need for another hit to number the pain? Lilly Grace wandered aimlessly, observing the people around her. Couples strolled toward the movie theatre, while others headed to downtown restaurants. Yet, behind the façade of normalcy, a deeper darkness awaited the setting sun. Lilly Grace felt drawn toward it.

As the hour ticked by and the sun dipped below the western mountains, the swelting heat gave way to a cooler evening breeze. Lilly Grace found herself in a dimly lit parking garage at Ninth and Eleventh Street. In the far corner, a group of four men huddled together, smoking and drinking beer.

She approached them with a casual air. "Got an extra smoke?" she asked.

One of the men eyed her with a mixture of curiosity and caution, while the other glanced around, checking for any unwanted attention. After a moment, he handed her the blunt he was smoking. "You can take a hit."

Lilly Grace inhaled deeply, savoring the effect, then exhaled slowly. She handed the blunt back. "Got anything stronger?"

"What do you have in mind?" he asked.

"Anything that'll help me forget the past," she replied.

"Hell, girl, memories have a way of sticking around whether we like it or not. No drug's going to make them go away for good," he said.

"Who said anything about permanent? I just need something to get me through the night."

The men closed in, their energy shifting. Lilly Grace could see the desire in their eyes, a look she had become familiar with during her time with Jade. The man who handed her the blunt asked, "How do we know you're not a cop?"

Lilly Grace lifted her shirt, revealing her breast just below her bra line. She turned around, showing them that she wasn't wearing a wire. One of the men gestured toward her pants, indicating that he wanted to see more. Reluctantly, Lilly Grace unbuttoned her jeans and slowly lowered them to her thighs, giving them a clear view of her panty line. One of the men even licked his lips, his gaze lingering.

"I'm not a cop," she said, her voice steady. "I'm just looking for a hookup. You know?"

"That'll cost you," one of them replied.

"Doesn't' it always?"

"You've done this before, haven't you? You don't look as innocent as you seem."

"Looks can be deceiving. So, do you have anything or not?" Lilly Grace pressed.

"We're gonna need to take a ride," one the men said.

"Then what are we waiting for?"

The men led Lilly Grace to their car, parked a few slots away in the dimly lit parking garage. As they drove out, two of the men crowded into the back seat with her. Almost immediately, they began to push themselves on her. Lilly Grace lay back against the seat, her hands outstretched as one man pulled her shirt over her head. Another man unbuttoned her jeans and pulled them down to her ankles. Lilly Grace, her body numb and disconnected, help them remove the jeans completely.

When they stopped at a red light, Lilly Grace was fully exposed in the back seat. She glanced out the window and saw the Greyhound Bus Depot across the street, a stark reminder of the dark path she had been forced to walk. The sight of the depot brought a rush of painful memories and a sense of overwhelming despair.

"Go the other way," she said, her voice trembling. "I don't want to go that way. Go south." She tried to negotiate, "Just give me something to help the time go by. I'll do whatever you want."

The man in the passenger seat opened a bottle of pills and handed a few to Lilly Grace, along with a bottle of beer. Without question, she swallowed the pills and chased them with the beer, hoping to numb the pain that seemed to engulf her.

As the car continued south on Ninth Street, the familiar route reminded her of the time she had spent with Paco, heading from downtown to the Deep South Side. One of the men in the back seat climbed on top of her, using spit to ease the process. The pills began to take effect, dulling her senses. Lilly Grace shifted her body, trying to guide the man, but the sensation was distant and muted. He held her tightly, thrusting awkwardly.

A second man, sitting in the rear passenger seat, prepared for his turn. Lilly Grace moved on top of him, sliding back and forth. Black spots began to cloud her vision as the numbness spread through her body. She could no longer feel her limbs; the only sensation was the pressure of the man's hands around her waist, pushing and pulling. Her head bobbed with each movement, and as her consciousness started to fade, she turned her head one last time. The final image that registered in her mind was the lion's head staring at her as the car veered off the road.

***

JB's phone rang at 1:30 in the morning, jolting him awake. The urgent instructions to head to the 7th Street Bridge were clear. As he navigated off Highway 99 onto Tuolumne Boulevard, the sight of flashing lights and a large crowd on the north side of the bridge confirmed the gravity of the situation. The bridge, spanning the Tuolumne River and marking the boundary between South Modesto and Ceres, was now a scene of grim activity.

Parking on a dirt access road, JB made his way towards the bridge, the floodlights of the Stanislaus County Sheriff's Office casting stark shadows. The area was cordoned off, and the murmur of the crowd was a low, anxious hum.

As he approached the base of the bridge, the scene came into sharper focus. His stomach churned when he saw the lifeless body lying near the lion statue at the bridge's entrance. The figure, pale and unmoving, was unmistakable – Lilly Grace. The sight of her naked body, crumpled and cold, struck him with a force he was unprepared for.

JB's steps quickened as he approached the medical examiner, who was crouched beside the body, meticulously examining the scene.

"What happened?" JB's voice was tight, struggling to maintain its steadiness.

The medical examiner looked up, his face a mask of solemnity. "It appears to be a drug overdose," he said, his tone heavy with the weight of the news.

JB's heart pounded in his chest. The cold reality of Lilly Grace's death was setting in, mingling with the fear of what this would mean for the ongoing investigation. He stood there, staring at the tragic scene, trying to process the enormity of it all.

"Was she raped?" JB asked, a knot forming in his stomach realizing the absurdity of the question and already knowing the answer.

"I'll need to conduct a full examination at the lab, but it looks like forced sodomy postmortem. It seems she may have been having sex when she overdosed. The perpetrators likely continued after she lost consciousness and then disposed of her body."

As JB stood beside Lilly Grace's lifeless form, the weight of the scene pressed heavily upon him. His thoughts drifted back to the girl found in the almond grove—the first haunting image that had etched itself into his memory. That girl, left abandoned in the dirt, had been a grim prelude to the tragedies he had encountered since. The almond blossoms that symbolized renewal and beauty of the Central Valley, had become twisted symbols of lost innocence.

He recalled his conversations with Lilly Grace, each one a fragile thread in a complex tapestry of pain and hope. Her stories, her defiant resilience, and the flicker of vulnerability she had occasionally allowed him to see, all came rushing back. He remembered her struggle to open up, the moments of raw honesty that cut through the veneer of her defenses. Each conversation had been a dance around the heart of her trauma, a delicate balance of trust and tension.

The depth of the investigation loomed large in his mind. The countless hours spent chasing leads, piecing together fragmented testimonies, and confronting the grim realities of the child trafficking world had drained him, both physically and emotionally. The endless paperwork and the never-ending fight against a shadowy, relentless network seemed to stretch into infinity. He had poured every ounce of himself into this case, determined to make a difference.

Now, standing over Lilly Grace, a gnawing thought plagued him: could he have done more? Could he have saved her from falling back into the life that had claimed her? The feeling of inadequacy was suffocating, a relentless echo of "what ifs" that haunted his every thought. He grappled with the reality that despite his best efforts, he had been unable to shield her from the horrors that had reentered her life.

But amidst the turmoil, a stark realization began to crystallize. We all make choices, JB thought, and we all have to live with those choices. Some people face the consequences of their decisions much earlier in life than others. Lilly Grace had been forced to confront the harsh realities of her existence far too soon, and her choices had led her down a path fraught with peril.

As the chill of the early morning settled around him, JB understood that while he could not change the past, he could honor Lilly Grace's memory by continuing to fight for those who still had a chance. The burden of his choices, the weight of his failures and successes, was a part of the journey he had chosen. The struggle to make a difference, to save others from similar fates, was a responsibility he would carry with him, every day.

In the quiet of that moment, as the world around him began to stir with the dawn, JB vowed to remain steadfast. He would face the difficult choices ahead with the resolve to do better, to be better, and to ensure that Lilly Grace's story would not be one of futility but a catalyst for change.

50

— · —

C HAPTER 50

It was early Wednesday morning when Avina was jolted awake by the sound of a guard's footsteps approaching his cell. Since arriving at County Jail, he had managed only a few hours of restless sleep each night. The guard knocked on the steel door.

Eric, groggy and alert, walked cautiously toward the door, wondering where the guard might be taking him at this ungodly hour.

"Hands," the guard instructed.

Eric extended his wrists through the slot in the door, and the guard secured them with zip ties. Without a word, the guard then shackled Eric's feet together.

"Where you takin' me?" Eric asked, his voice tinged with apprehension.

The guard remained silent, placing a firm hand on Eric's shoulder as he guided him down the corridor. They descended a flight of stairs, and Eric struggled to maintain his balance with each step. On the main floor, the guard led him through a set of electronic doors and down a long hallway toward a conference room. Once inside, the guard seated Eric at a table and shackled his feet to a steel beam beneath it. The cold metal and the oppressive silence of the room heightened Eric's anxiety as he awaited further instructions.

"What am I doin' here, man? What's up?" Eric demanded.

The guard ignored him, turning on his heel and leaving the room with a clang of the door closing behind him. Eric, shackled to the table, waited impatiently for fifteen minutes until JB entered.

"It's you again," Eric exhaled deeply. JB approached and released the zip ties from around Eric's wrists, allowing his arms to move freely. "What do you want now?"

"A lot has happened in the four days you've been locked up," JB began, taking a seat at the table and laying a file before him.

"Oh yeah? And I bet you're here to tell me if I help you, you'll help me. Is that about, right?"

JB glanced at Eric, then at the file. "That's not exactly what I had in mind."

"Well, I'm not going anywhere, so you might as well tell me what you got in mind."

JB paused, focusing his eyes on the man in front of him. "You've been careful over the past few months. I'll give you that. Our surveillance didn't catch much. But we know you authorized the hit on that little girl. We've got Gustavo Medina and his crew for that one."

"Man, you ain't got shit on me. And GP, he's a real one – he ain't tellin' you shit."

JB paced around the room. "I'll give you credit; when you took out Manny, I wasn't sure we'd build a case against you and Ramirez. Did you know Manny liked to film things?"

Eric shot a confused look toward JB. "I don't know what the hell you're talking about."

"Manny left behind a video from the night that girl was killed. Did you know that?"

"I know I'm not in that video. So, what's it to me?"

JB with a knowing stare, continued. "No, you're not in the video. But Hector Valdez is."

"You think I'm worried about anything Hector Valdez might say."

"Well, according to Manny, Hector called you in a panic that night, and you told him to handle it."

"It doesn't matter what Manny might have said, 'cause he ain't around to say nothing no more."

"No, but Hector Valdez is, and so is Gustavo Medina Perez. Also, Angel Jose Torres and Antonio Hernandez Vargas, who were in the room that night, and are willing to talk."

Eric pushed back into his seat with an air of arrogance. "All I hear is circumstantial evidence. It's all he said, she said. Good luck making any of that stick in court. See, Mr. FBI, I'm not just some low-level gang banger. You can't scare me into confessing with your stories. You've got the wrong guy. I'll see my day in court, and when I do, I'll be walking free."

JB stood up, placed the file folder on the table, and began to pace the room. The conversation was unfolding exactly as he had anticipated. He knew Eric Avina was not a man easily intimidated. He also knew that without careful handling, the names he had mentioned might not make it to trial. If Avina had a competent lawyer, some of this evidence could be dismissed as circumstantial. But JB had one more card to play, and now was the time to lay it down.

He circled back to the table, stood next to Eric, and slid the file folder toward him. "Take a look at that file."

Eric opened the manila folder, revealing the mugshot of Anita Lopez, dated three days earlier. JB watched as Eric struggled to mask any sign of recognition. He had to give it to him – he was doing a better job than JB had expected.

"Tell me about Anita Lopez."

Eric wiped the sweat from his upper lip and tried to steady his breathing. His temples glistened with perspiration.

"What'd you pick her up for?"

"You were meticulous in avoiding mistakes these past few months," JB said. "I was genuinely impressed by how you managed your operations without a trace on the wiretap. The issue is, Anita called you before we raided your place. The first call was made to your burner phone, which we didn't have tapped. When you didn't answer, she called your cell phone number. And guess what? We recorded the entire call."

Eric's face drained of color as the gravity of the situation hit him. The thought of Anita Lopez – a clerk of the Stanislaus County Sheriff's Office – being involved was a significant blow. JB could see Eric scrambling for a rebuttal, but he knew it was futile. It was checkmate.

"Our analysts have done their homework on Anita Lopez," JB continued. "We matched her history with yours. Let me guess, her little boy – Daniel, isn't it? I'd wager anything that you're the father. Am I right?"

JB smirked, relishing the moment as he watched Eric's reaction. The truth was out, and the weight of it was undeniable.

"Fucking pendejo," Eric spat out, his frustration evident.

"So, I was right," JB said calmly.

"You don't know what the hell you're talking about."

"I know more than you give me credit for, Eric. Let's be real for a minute. You might be able to deal with Perez, Torres, or Vargas – maybe you get to one or two of them. And sure, some of that might be seen as circumstantial in court. But Anita Lopez? That's not circumstantial. We've got her dead to rights, and we're planning to hit her with the maximum sentence."

"God damn you, son of a bitch."

"Eric, you're facing charges for first-degree murder with special circumstances, conspiracy to commit murder, conspiracy to commit kidnapping, drug trafficking, firearms violations, and gang enhancements. You're looking at life in prison."

"As I said before, this life owes me nothing – naked I came into this world and naked I will leave."

"Yes, such is your life. But that's not life for Anita Lopez or her son, Daniel. Did you know that someone charged with aiding and abetting can face the same penalties as the principal perpetrator? She's looking at thirty years to life. Think about what that means for Daniel. What kind of future will he have with his mother locked up?"

"What are you tryin' to say?"

"I'm not saying she doesn't deserve to go to prison for what she did. But how you handle this could impact the length of her sentence."

"What, you want me to turn state's evidence and start rattin' out my homies?"

"Eric, I've met a lot of good and bad people. You don't strike me as someone completely devoid of conscience. Your associate, Paco Ramirez, he got what was coming to him. But you, I still believe there's good in you. I think you're capable of doing the right thing."

"I don't know what you're talkin' about."

"Eric, be smart. We've heard chatter about something big happening in the Central Valley with cartels. Anita's already started to talk. Help me, help yourself, and help Anita. Give me the names of the guys you were working with."

Avina sat in the chair, visibly processing the weight of the situation. JB sensed the man was weighing his options, contemplating the implications of his decision. The fate of Anita and her son Daniel rested heavily on his shoulders.

"Look, how do I know if I give you any information it'll actually make a difference for her?" Avina asked, a hint of desperation in his voice.

"Eric, I'm not playing games here. I'm being as honest as I can be. You're going to pay for your crimes, as you should. But once you're gone, another group will take your place, and they're probably already lined up. I'm after the big players, the ones running the show. Do you understand?"

"You know how this works. I might know a few guys, but the real leaders, that's above my pay grade homes."

"Eric, I'm not naïve. You don't get involved with people you don't know. Here's the deal, we can talk now, or you can wait and hope for a deal later. But if you wait, I won't be here to make one. It's now or never. Do you understand? It's now or never for Anita.

Do you want her to be around for Daniel's graduation? Because if you don't start talking, she won't even see him grow up. And he might end up here with you before he turns twenty-one. Do you get what I'm saying?"

Eric slammed his fist on the table, cursing under his breath before letting out a guttural scream. He realized he had no real choice but to cooperate with JB Phillips. He was responsible for dragging Anita into this criminal world. If it wasn't for him, she would never have been involved. The weight of that responsibility was too heavy to bear.

JB and Eric spent the next three hours detailing connections to Eduardo Hernandez, the NF links to Pelican Bay, and the cartels in Mexico. By the end of the day, an arrest warrant was issued for Hernandez, an accomplice known as the Ghost, and a network of leaders spanning seven counties from the California-Mexico border up through the Sacramento Valley.

By the week's end, nearly thirty individuals, including Eduardo Hernandez, were arrested. Thanks to Eric Avina's information, the operation led to the recovery of approximately 88 firearms, 215 kilograms of methamphetamine, 14.3 kilograms of fentanyl, 23 kilograms of cocaine, 7.2 kilograms of heroin, 309 kilograms of marijuana, and $650,000 in cash. It was one of the largest seizures in California's history.

$$51$$

CHAPTER 51

Every day for the past six months, JB had made the thirty-minute commute to his office in Modesto. The drive was a constant reminder of the darkness he had encountered. As he passed the vacant lot on Highway 99 just before the Tuolumne River, he couldn't help but think of the spot where the young girls battered and bloodied body had been found. A quarter mile up the freeway, he crossed the river and glanced at the 7th Street Bridge, the site of Lilly Grace's recovery.

The West Side Familia case had been a career-defining moment for both Special Agent Warnall and Special Agent JB Phillips. It was the type of high-profile case that could lead to significant career advancements. JB knew for certain he didn't want to become a desk jockey like his friend Warnall. Yet he also understood he didn't want to spend his days immersed in the darkness of child trafficking cases. After much deliberation, and consulting with Hannah, they both agreed on a new direction for his career.

On the way to Warnall's Office, JB decided to take a last-minute detour through the Deep South Side. He traveled along 7th street and passed the California Truck Stop, just before Pecos Avenue, a known location for prostitutes and pimps. It was a reminder of the futile effort to control the oldest occupation known to man. A quarter mile down the road, he pulled over into the dirt landing on the side of the road. From his vantage point, he was able to see across the railroad tracks at the La Clandestina Night Club and the Driftwood Inn. It was only eight months prior, when he had pulled into the parking lot and rushed through the door to find a fifteen-year-old girl, naked and alone. The memory of her eyes staring vacantly at him, her body battered and bruised. It was a memory like so many others that would haunt him for the rest of his days.

JB cut through the neighborhood streets of the Deep South Side, driving along El Paso Avenue. He passed the location where they found Hector Valdez holed up in a rotted out recreational vehicle in the back of a multi-site residence. He continued and passed the home of Eric Avina. He turned right on Crows Landing Road and drove past Mariscos Taco Truck. Just passed Mariscos was the vacant lot where he had discovered the body of the young girl in the vacant lot. He pulled his car down the short service road, just off Crows Landing Road. He got out and walked a few hundred yards through the dirt lot. The space seemed smaller in broad daylight. He knelt, as he had nearly a year ago, and grabbed a handful of dirt. He allowed the grain of the dirt to sift through the palm of his hands. The wind blew the dust north toward the Tuolumne River.

A farmer had recently tilled over the solid ground leaving no remnants of a life lost. He thought of the majestic sound of the dogs howling at night. Now, the valley was quiet except for the sound of cars travelling down Crows Landing Road and the Freeway. JB stared at the sky, wondering about the girls' mother and whether her other children would share a similar fate. It was a thought that he closed as soon as it came to his mind. He listened to the cars pass through the South Side. It was time to move on.

JB returned to his Toyota Tacoma, taking one last glance at the vacant lot. He turned left onto Crows Landing Road where he travelled over Highway 99. He drove a mile, looking right and left, at the low budget auto car lots, auto-wrecker yards, and old aluminum recycling facility. He wondered if the area was destined to despair and desolation. He wondered if the area would ever return to what it once was. It didn't matter because his decision was made and there was no turning back now.

On the approach to the 7th Street Bridge, JB noticed the two lion statues standing guard. Their stone facades smeared and scarred from decades of abuse. A grocery cart full of trash bags and luggage sat next to one of the lions. A dog lay at its wheels, as if on guard. He briefly caught sight of a woman curled up in a ball on the bench just behind the lion. Her head was buried in her thighs. He thought of stopping for a moment, to see if all was okay. But then he continued in anticipation of the memory a few hundred yards away at the other end of the bridge. He chose not to stop this time, instead driving slowly past the remaining two lions at the north end of the bridge. To his left was the dirt access road where Lilly Grace's body was found. If the legend was true, about the Lions standing guard, how could they not have saved this girl? He lay awake many nights, wondering how he could have saved her from her own self-destruction. He wondered about Manny and how he didn't respond to his cry for help. He also knew they we are beholden to our decisions and the wrath that follows.

JB pulled into the office parking lot, and after walking in, he took notice of his colleagues. He walked through the hallways for the last time. As usual, Warnall's head was buried in the computer when JB entered the office. Warnall motioned for him to sit down. JB glanced through a few of the files on Warnall's desk, not because he was interested in the various cases, but rather to annoy his friend. He put them back in different order just to see if he would notice. Finally, Warnall closed his laptop and slid back in his chair.

"So, you're actually going to go through with it?" Warnall asked.

"I don't think there is really any other decision to make. It's simple when you really think about it."

"It's a life changing decision."

"Yes, but we're ready and couldn't be more excited to see what life brings."

"So, when does the decision become final?"

"We find out at the end of this week."

Warnall got up and went to a cabinet in his office. He pulled out two whiskey glasses and a bottle of Blanton's Gold Edition.

"I know it's not Basil Hayden, but I hope it'll do."

Warnall poured a glass and handed it to JB. He poured a second glass and lifted it up to cheer.

"This must be a special occasion if you're breaking out the good stuff."

"It certainly is my friend. Stephanie and I couldn't be more excited for you and Hannah. Here is to Abigail and Sariah Phillips."

The two men cheers their glasses and took long sips of the Blanton's. JB stood and gave his friend a hug. The two men held the embrace. Warnall took a couple of steps back and leaned against the cabinet in his office.

"So, when did you guys know you wanted to adopt them?"

"Hannah knew she wanted to adopt them the moment she saw their photos for the first time."

"Yeah, I doubt you ever had a say on this one."

"No. I don't think I really did. But you know what, they've been the biggest blessings in our lives. They've brought us together in ways that I never thought possible."

"Yeah, girls have a way of doing that."

They both took another sip of their whiskey. JB sat his glass on the end of Warnall's desk. It wasn't just time to say goodbye to a boss. It was time to say goodbye to a friend. It was time to say goodbye to a brother.

"Thank you for providing the recommendation."

"It's my pleasure. You go give them hell at Counterterrorism."

"I'm going to do my best.".

"And, if you ever come across the Ghost, you be sure to let me know."

"He is the one person left who has not paid for his sins. I'm going to find him and I'm going to serve him justice."

"I have no doubt that you will."

The two men finished their glasses, the rich, smoky aroma of bourbon lingering in the air. They embraced one last time, a gesture that spoke of years of camaraderie and mutual respect. As JB turned toward the office doorway, he cast a final glance back. His smile widened when he saw Warnall meticulously arranging the files on his desk, returning them to their proper order.

"You're going to miss me," JB teased, a lighthearted note in his voice as he made his way down the hallway.

Warnall looked up, a grin tugging at the corners of his mouth. "You bet I will," he replied, his tone filled with genuine fondness.

JB smiled as he walked away, the warmth of their shared moments and the anticipation of new beginnings filling him with a quiet sense of excitement. He was confident that their paths would cross again and looked forward to the future with optimism and eagerness.

Author's Note

Jacob McDougal

Thank you for reading Whispers Among the Blossoms! If you enjoyed it, I'd love if you would consider writing me a review. Reviews help readers find books they love.

Whispers Among the Blossoms was born out of a personal experience that changed my life. My daughter was nearly abducted at a county fair, and that moment opened my eyes to the horrific reality of child trafficking. This story is more than just a novel—it's a reflection of the whispers we often ignore, the harsh truths about the most vulnerable among us. Every day, countless children vanish into the shadows, and yet, so many cases go unaddressed. It's my hope that this book sheds light on a problem that is all too often overlooked.

Child trafficking is not a distant issue – it's happening in our neighborhoods, towns, and cities. Every year, an estimated **4.8 million people** are trapped in forced sexual exploitation worldwide, with a significant percentage being children. In the United States alone, the National Center for Missing & Exploited Children receives tens of thousands of reports of child sex trafficking. This is not just a statistic; it represents lives torn apart and futures stolen.

My passion for raising awareness of this atrocity runs deep, and I hope this book can be a small voice in a much larger conversation.

Beyond trafficking, this book also reflects another part of my personal journey—my passion for marriage and family. My wife and I faced a five-year battle with infertility, a trial that tested our faith and our bond. I know firsthand the emotional toll that infertility takes on a marriage, and I also know the healing power of faith, love, and perseverance.

Through that struggle, we found our purpose in ministering to other couples, helping them navigate the storms of infertility and stay rooted in their faith.

Whether through the fight against child trafficking or supporting marriages through infertility, I believe in the power of hope and faith to bring healing and change. I hope *Whispers Among the Blossoms* inspires action, stirs compassion, and reminds us all to listen to the whispers that too often go unheard.

Thank you for reading.

—Jacob

About Jacob McDougal

Jacob McDougal is a storyteller at heart, driven by his passion for weaving tales that dive deep into the human condition. *Whispers Among the Blossoms*, his debut novel, takes readers on a gripping journey through the dark world of child trafficking, exposing the depths of depravity while offering a glimpse of hope through the power of redemption.

When he's not writing novels, McDougal shares his reflections on life's trials, triumphs, and the dreams that shape us in his blog, *A Boy from Blocker*. His stories are born from the red clay of Southeastern Oklahoma, where he first discovered his love for creativity and expression.

In addition to writing, McDougal is a Senior Director at OSU Medicine and is pursuing his Master of Health Care Administration. He lives in Edmond, Oklahoma, with his wife and three children, continuing to create stories that stir the soul.

www.ingramcontent.com/pod-product-compliance
Lightning Source LLC
Chambersburg PA
CBHW022108310726
48972CB00007B/1932